D0174838

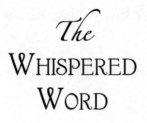

The
WHISPERED
WORD

Also by Ellery Adams

The Secret, Book & Scone Society

The WHISPERED WORD

ELLERY ADAMS

KENSINGTON BOOKS
www.kensingtonbooks.com

KENSINGTON BOOKS are published by

Kensington Publishing Corp.
119 West 40th Street
New York, NY 10018

Library of Congress Card Catalogue Number: 2018944171

Kensington and the K logo Reg. U.S. Pat. & TM Off.

ISBN-13: 978-1-4967-1240-0
ISBN-10: 1-4967-1240-4
First Kensington Hardcover Edition: December 2018

eISBN-13: 978-1-4967-1242-4
eISBN-10: 1-4967-1242-0
Kensington Electronic Edition: December 2018

10 9 8 7 6 5 4 3 2 1

Printed in the United States of America

To you, reader, because you understand that every book is a journey waiting to be taken. A magic carpet ride.

Come along, then. Climb aboard.

A library of books is the fairest garden in the world, and to walk there is an ecstasy.
                              —The Arabian Nights

Chapter 1

Hide until everybody goes home. Hide until every-
body forgets about you. Hide until everybody dies.
                                    —Yoko Ono

"That girl's got one foot in the grave."

Nora Pennington, proprietress of the only bookshop in Miracle Springs, North Carolina, glanced from her friend to the empty chair where she expected to find the pale-faced slip of a girl who'd hidden in the stacks until past closing time.

The girl wasn't there.

Recalling the hospital ID bracelet encircling the girl's bony wrist, Nora turned her attention back to her friend. "June, did she say anything to you? Or to Hester or Estella?"

June grunted. "Oh, sure. She told the three of us her whole story. Yes, ma'am. She donated a kidney to the love of her life and the surgery took place without a hitch, but when the sweethearts woke up, Miss Skinny-As-A-Broom-Handle found out that Mister Right was Mister Seriously Wrong. According to a news report, he was an escaped serial killer. No, that wasn't it." June frowned. "He ran a cult. Yeah, one of those brainwashing cults with a male leader and lots of female disciples. When our girl found out, she bolted from the hospital when the nurses weren't watching, snatched a housedress from a clothesline, and hopped a train to Miracle Springs."

Behind June, a woman issued a throaty chuckle.

"June Dixon, I believe you could write fiction if you were so inclined," said Estella Sadler in an exaggerated Southern drawl. She languidly rose from her chair and jerked a thumb toward the back of the bookstore. "Since you're perfectly capable of evicting your bubble-wrap refugee, Nora, I'm calling it a night. I don't *need* beauty sleep, but I'll take it all the same. Sweet dreams, ladies."

After Estella sauntered out, Nora turned to Hester Winthrop, the fourth member of the Secret, Book, and Scone Society. "Bubble-wrap refugee?"

"You'll see," Hester said, picking up her handbag. "I need to get going too. The bread won't knead itself at five in the morning and I have to bake extra loaves for our Secret Kindness bags."

June shook her head. "I don't know many people who can wake up when the stars are still shining and buzz around all day like a bee on crack. But you do it. With your freckles and energy, you remind me of Pippi Longstocking."

Hester shook her head. "Estella's the redhead, not me."

"Estella's not that kind of book character," June said. "She's far more catlike. Who *does* she remind me of?" She looked thoughtful and then slapped her hands together. "Shere Khan. The tiger from *The Jungle Book*. That's Estella's literary double."

"And what book character are you?" Nora asked. Though she wanted to check on the strange girl, she was too intrigued by the conversation to move.

June put her hand over her heart. "When I worked at the nursing home, one of my favorite patients called me a Black Mary Poppins. I'm older, darker, and my hair is way curlier than Mary's, but that's what she called me."

Seeing the shock on Hester's face, June burst into laughter. "Honey, it was meant as a compliment. That lady knew how much I tried to put a little magic into the residents' lives."

Hester gestured in the direction of Nora's small stockroom. "I don't think there's been any magic in her life lately. What will you do about her, Nora? She seems . . . fragile."

Nora frowned. She'd moved to Miracle Springs in search of peace and privacy. She hadn't wanted a single responsibility beyond her tiny house and her bookstore. She hadn't wanted pets or close friends. She hadn't wanted a lover. She refused to join a place of worship or participate in charity events. She didn't sponsor children's athletic teams, enter bake-offs, or take sides in local politics. She didn't seek anyone's company.

Despite this, people sought hers.

They came looking for her. People with different backgrounds, different skin colors, and different accents. People from all over the globe brought her their stories. They all carried a burden they couldn't put down, no matter how much they wanted to be free from its weight. These weary souls came to her, the bookseller known to the locals as "the beautiful, burned woman," or "the bibliotherapist with the scars," in search of relief.

Sometimes, these people liked Nora. Sometimes, they didn't. But they all felt at home in Miracle Books. It was almost impossible not to. Walking through the bookshop was like falling in love for the very first time.

New customers would enter the store and hesitate, fearing the only offerings would be New Age titles and crystals. This was a reasonable concern in a town built upon the premise of healing, but Miracle Books had something for everyone. They just didn't always know how to find it.

Nora had never bathed in the famed mineral baths of Miracle Springs, so she couldn't tell her customers that the waters possessed restorative powers.

She believed books had the power to heal. She believed that carefully chosen words and well-crafted phrases could gift readers with the ability to let a painful past go—to turn the page and start a fresh chapter in their lives.

Because she believed that every story had something to offer, Nora's store was stuffed with books of every format and genre. The latest best-selling novels, in their glossy dust jackets, shared shelf space with dog-eared paperbacks. Other shelves held rare first editions, coveted signed editions, and antique leather-bound books. There were books in all conditions. Books for all ages. Books to satisfy every need. Every wish.

There was much to see in the warren of shelves and the cornucopia of books for sale, so Nora let her customers wander undisturbed. In fact, she encouraged them to become lost in the labyrinth of colorful spines, to pull down books and read blurbs, to touch one of the many shelf enhancers.

Nora had dubbed these knickknacks "shelf enhancers" before Miracle Books was up and running. Back when she was still assembling her initial inventory, she'd been rummaging through a box of books at the flea market when she'd come across a pair of bronze owl bookends. They weren't in perfect shape. There was minor flaking to the bronze, undoubtedly due to age. Nora liked the owls despite their flaws. Their gaze was stern and their sharp talons curled protectively over a stack of thick tomes.

"If you buy the set of Nancy Drews, I'll give you a discount on the owls," the vendor had said to Nora while overtly studying her burn scars.

Nora wasn't used to negotiating, but she knew she had to buy every book at the lowest price if she wanted her business to succeed. She turned the bookends over in her hands and thought of how much more interesting her future store would be if her shelves were enhanced by unique, vintage items. And then, she'd looked the vendor straight in the eye and started haggling.

The shelf enhancers were impulse buys for locals and visitors alike. As Nora moved deeper into the stacks, heading for the stockroom, she noticed some of her recent additions. She walked by a wooden mortar filled with crushed lavender, a marble and brass letter holder, a picture frame in pink Lucite, a Victorian child's porcelain tea set, and an art nouveau trumpet vase. Those were just the treasures in the Contemporary Romance section.

Nora rounded the corner of a bookcase crammed with pulp fiction novels and heard the loud clang of brass bells smacking wood. The bells, which had once been attached to a horse harness, now hung from a strip of leather behind Nora's front door.

The clanging sound meant that her friends had left Miracle Books.

Nora was alone with her books and the strange girl.

She found the girl curled among layers of bubble wrap and packing paper. She looked like an undernourished Goldilocks who'd passed out after partying too hard.

Nora studied the stranger in the dim light of the stockroom's single bulb. Though her slim figure and pallid skin made her seem childlike, Nora guessed that she was closer to twenty than ten.

"What am I supposed to do with you?" she murmured under her breath.

Despite Nora's intention to live an uncomplicated life in Miracle Springs, she'd recently become friends with three remarkable women. Together, they'd formed the Secret, Book, and Scone Society. In the middle of their investigation into the murder of a visiting businessman, Estella, June, and Hester had all shared their deepest secrets with Nora. And eventually, she'd entrusted them with hers—the terrible truth behind the jellyfish burn scar swimming up her right arm and the pod of bubbly octopi scars floating up her shoulder and neck to caress her cheek with their puckered tentacles.

I've already risked enough, Nora thought, staring down at the sleeping girl.

Though the investigation was over, the abrupt closure of the community bank had left Miracle Springs reeling. Dozens of people had lost their jobs. Others had been jailed. The town needed to recover. So did Nora.

Recovery meant peace and calm. Strange girls sleeping in her storeroom did not make Nora feel peaceful or calm.

She was torn.

Part of her wanted to shake the girl awake and tell her to move on.

This is a bookstore, not a hotel, she could hear herself saying.

But another part remembered how the girl had caressed the book spines when she thought no one was watching. There had been such tenderness in that touch. Such longing.

There'd been pain too.

At that moment, Nora had seen herself in the girl. Had seen her own need for stories, for escape, reflected in the girl's hungry eyes and desperate fingers.

It was this tenuous connection that had Nora striding to one of the shop's reading nooks, grabbing the throw blanket from the back of the fainting couch, and returning to the stockroom to drape the length of soft cotton over the slumbering girl.

I wish I could sleep that soundly, Nora thought.

She changed her mind almost before this thought was completed. The girl's hospital bracelet and ill-fitting clothing hinted at sleep that was anything but sound. Her sleep was probably deep because she was bone weary. It was the dreamless slumber of someone who'd been running and running until their legs couldn't carry them another step.

Nora lingered long enough to wonder why a person would run away from a hospital. But she didn't want to know the answer to that question. She didn't want to get involved. She'd give the girl food and shelter. That was all.

After writing a brief note to the sleeping stranger, Nora locked the girl in the bookstore and went home.

* * *

The next morning, Nora woke early. She hadn't slept well and her first cohesive thoughts focused on brewing and drinking plenty of strong, dark coffee.

She'd showered, run a brush through her brown hair, dressed in her typical uniform of jeans and a T-shirt, and was well into her second cup of coffee when she remembered her stockroom Goldilocks.

"Damn it," she muttered and hurriedly made a plate of food for the girl.

She walked the short distance from her tiny house, a modified railway car the townsfolk had dubbed the Caboose Cottage, and unlocked the back door to Miracle Books. Nora loved that her bookstore had once been a train station and that her home had once been a train car. The aura of adventure embedded in every board and bolt was almost tangible.

"It's me! Nora!" she called out. She didn't want to scare the girl, especially if she was still asleep.

However, the stockroom was empty.

Nora stood in the doorway and tried to understand what she was seeing. Or more accurately, what she wasn't seeing. The room had been completely altered. Every cardboard box had been flattened and lined up along one wall. There wasn't a shred of bubble wrap or packing paper in sight.

Moving through the store to the ticket agent's booth, Nora glanced around for signs of life. Had the girl used one of the hundred coffee mugs hanging from the pegboard to make herself a cup of coffee or tea? It didn't look like it.

"I have fresh bread. It's toasted and buttered," Nora said, her voice echoing through the stacks. "Hester baked it. You met her last night. She's the one with the freckles and the frizzy blond hair." Nora continued toward the checkout counter. "I also have blackberries. I picked them yesterday. And farmer's cheese. I could make you a cappuccino or a latte. Or just a plain coffee. Whatever you feel like."

By this time, Nora had reached the register. She put the plate of food on the counter and stopped to listen. The girl was here. She could feel her presence. Why was she hiding?

Nora threaded her way to the front of the store and stopped short behind the display window. Something was wrong. The display hadn't looked like this last night.

"What the—?"

Digging out the skeleton key that unlocked the front door, Nora rushed outside to view the window from the sidewalk.

What she saw was magical.

She was facing a scene created entirely of packing materials. The central figure was a woman sculpted out of clear packing tape. The female sculpture held a string fastened to a balloon bouquet made of bubble wrap. Both woman and balloons were surrounded by hundreds of origami birds fashioned from white paper. The birds swayed and spun, coaxed into subtle movement by the air exiting a nearby duct.

For a moment, Nora felt as if she were in motion. She felt as weightless as the paper birds. Like she could float. She almost glanced down, half expecting her feet to be hovering above the sidewalk.

This time, when she looked back at the window, she saw the books. Books with blue covers, and only blue covers, dangled from the ceiling. White string was wedged in their gutters, forcing the books to spread open, and creating an illusion of wings. Nora found herself moving around in an effort to read all the titles.

The girl—for she must be the creator of this masterpiece—had selected books from a variety of genres. There was *The Cat in the Hat*, *Go Set a Watchman*, *Wonder*, *All the Light We Cannot See*, *The Great Gatsby*, *Eragon*, *The Mystery at the Moss-Covered Mansion*, *A Brief History of Time*, and a dozen more. On the bottom of the window, a series of cardboard letters spelled out the phrase, MY BLUE HEAVEN.

Nora reentered the store and found the girl standing next to the plate of food. She hadn't touched it, but was leaning so close to it that her hunger was almost palpable.

"It's beautiful." Nora gestured at the window behind her. "Did you spend all night making that?"

The girl took a long time to reply. When she finally spoke, her voice was a faint whisper, like a breeze winding through reeds. "A few hours."

"I think you've earned your breakfast," Nora said, indicating the plate. "Come on. I'll make you a coffee while you eat."

Though the girl said nothing, she picked up the plate and followed Nora to the circle of chairs near the ticket agent's booth.

Nora tapped the chalkboard menu affixed to the wall next to the ticket window and asked, "What would you like?"

The girl stepped up to the menu. Her lips moved as she murmured every word aloud.

The Ernest Hemingway—Dark Roast
Louisa May Alcott—Light Roast
Dante Alighieri—Decaf
The Wilkie Collins—Cappuccino
Jack London—Latte
Agatha ChrisTEA—Earl Grey

Nora turned away, giving the girl time to make a decision. She occupied herself by searching for the perfect coffee cup for her guest.

The majority of Nora's mugs, which were purchased at yard sales or flea markets, bore book-related sayings or humorous phrases. Glancing at her collection, she decided that none of it was a good fit for this girl. She wished she had one of her handmade pottery mugs from home, especially since the girl seemed to have an affinity for blue. Nora could serve her in one of the mugs she used for children, but her Cookie Monster, Batman, Snoopy, or Harry Potter mugs didn't feel right either.

Nora selected a white mug with a donut covered in pink icing and rainbow sprinkles. The picture of the donut was flanked by the words *I* and *care*.

For the first time ever, Nora wished she owned an innocuous kitten or puppy mug.

"Anything tempt you?" she asked the girl.

"A Wilkie Collins, please. I loved his *Woman in White*."

Nora was impressed. She didn't run across many twenty-somethings familiar with Collins or his work.

"Me too," she said, moving behind the espresso machine. "Even more than *The Moonstone*, actually."

She hadn't asked the girl if she wanted sugar or special milk because she didn't make a habit of giving her customers too many choices. If they wanted sugar, they could stir it in themselves. If they wanted soy, almond, or coconut milk, they were out of luck. Nora didn't stock those items. She was neither a Starbucks nor a grocery store. Her espresso machine was a refurbished model that ran on a wing and a prayer. Since she expected it to die without warning, Nora was always a little relieved when her customers ordered a cup of black coffee or herbal tea.

"What's your name?" Nora asked over the hiss and sputter of the machine. She glanced at the girl while frothing the milk.

There was no answer, so Nora finished preparing the drink. When she was done, she set down the donut mug next to the dish of food.

The girl kept her eyes fixed on the counter. "It's . . . Abilene. Abilene . . . Tyler."

Given the pauses, Nora couldn't help but wonder if the girl had just dreamed up that name. If so, it didn't matter to Nora. She'd call the girl whatever she wanted to be called.

"That's a pretty name." Nora gave the girl a friendly smile. "I

don't like it when people watch me eat, so I'll leave you to your
meal. Sit here and enjoy your food. I'm going to head to the front
and take care of my opening chores. I don't need to mess with the
window display, thanks to you. In fact, I won't want to change
that for weeks. It's really amazing."

Abilene returned Nora's smile with a small, shy smile of her
own. "Thank you."

Later, Nora was behind the checkout counter, circling yard-
sale ads in the paper, when Abilene silently appeared. "Thank
you for the breakfast. The bread and berries were really good.
And thank you for letting me stay here last night. I'll show myself out."

She turned toward the front door.

Nora knew the girl couldn't show herself out. The door was
locked and the heavy brass skeleton key was inside the cash
register. As she watched Abilene and tried to decide what to do
about the young woman so clearly in need of help, something
occurred that prevented Abilene from leaving Miracle Books.

She was close to the front door when the rubber strap on her
left flip-flop snapped and she lost her balance. Pitching forward, she collided with a floor spinner crammed with paperbacks. The display was made of acrylic, and Nora gasped in
dismay as it gave way in a series of violent cracks. With the
cracking sound came another noise. A cry of pain.

By the time Nora dropped to her knees beside the girl, Abilene was cradling her right hand. She tried to hide the blood
seeping from between her fingers and the tear tracks wetting
her cheeks, but failed on both accounts.

"Don't move," Nora ordered and ran to get a dish towel
from the back.

When she returned to Abilene, the girl refused to let her look
at her hand.

"I'm fine," she stubbornly insisted.

Nora scowled. "The hell you are. You're bleeding all over my floor. Come on. I need to see how bad it is."

Averting her gaze, Abilene offered Nora her injured hand.

Nora gently pried off the fingers covering the wound, and blood immediately welled from a cut across Abilene's palm. It was deep enough to require sutures. This wasn't a shallow wound that would heal on its own. It had to be closed by a professional.

"You need stitches," Nora said, balling up the towel and pressing it against Abilene's palm.

The girl drew back so abruptly that she nearly knocked Nora over. "No."

Nora glanced at the girl's wrist, but the hospital bracelet was gone.

She didn't think she stood any chance of getting Abilene to an urgent care facility or a doctor's office. She probably wanted to avoid all health care facilities. Why else would she have shown up last night in a dress that was far too big for her, Dollar Store shoes, and the look of someone who hadn't eaten or rested well in weeks?

"Listen to me, Abilene." Nora spoke very gently. "I have a friend who can patch you up. I'm going to call him. He won't tell anyone about you and you're going to stay with me today. No arguments. You're going to rest and eat. No one will ask you questions. If they do, you don't have to answer them. Okay?"

Abilene shook her head and Nora feared the girl would bolt the second her back was turned. She'd have to find another way to coerce her into staying put, which wouldn't be easy. Abilene was as agitated as a caged bird.

Why? Nora silently wondered as she held the girl's hand. *What happened to you?*

"This isn't a debate." Nora adopted the firm, no-nonsense tone she'd employed during her previous life as a librarian. Pretending that Abilene was an unruly high school student, she said, "You broke my spinner and you've made a mess. This has to be cleaned up before I open at ten. The way I see it, you have two choices. You can make a dash for the back exit and pass out in some field a few miles away. Your left foot will be torn to shreds because you have only one shoe, which clearly doesn't fit. And what happens to your foot doesn't matter because your hand will eventually get infected. You'll run a fever. You're obviously too weak to handle that and you *will* pass out. Whoever finds you *will* call for an ambulance. Or the police. Is that what you want?"

Abilene refused to answer.

"Your other option is to let my friend patch you up. You can get a little strength back, change into clothes that actually fit, and do a few light chores to earn your keep." Nora cocked her head. "Do you like books?"

Judging by the window display, the girl definitely did. But Nora wanted to see if the question would elicit a response.

Abilene's head whipped around. She faced Nora without flinching and her eyes were lit with twin sparks.

"I love them," she said in a voice that was almost loud. There was passion in her reply. Anger too.

Nora was relieved by this show of emotion. The girl had a layer of steel beneath that translucent skin. She'd probably drawn on this strength to have made it to this point. Wherever it was she'd run from, the running had taken its toll. She still had fight in her though. That was good.

"I love books too," Nora whispered to the girl. "They saved my life." She traced the burn scar on her cheek, holding Abilene's gaze the whole time. "Which is why you should believe me when I tell you that this is a safe place for you. Here, among the books. And with me, a woman who was rescued by them."

Abilene glanced around the shop. The glint left her eyes. It was replaced by a look of longing. Doubt flickered across her face. Or was it fear?

Nora wondered just how long Abilene had been on the run. Why was she afraid? Was Nora inviting more danger into her world? She'd already risked life and limb for a complete stranger that summer. And yet here she was, offering shelter to a young woman who acted like she was being hunted. Was she? And if so, who was the hunter?

This maelstrom of thoughts was interrupted by a buzzing noise outside the bookstore. Nora told Abilene to press the dish towel against the wound on her right palm and walked over to peer out the front door. What she saw made her breath catch in surprise.

A crowd had gathered on the sidewalk. Men, women, and children were all staring at the bookstore's display window. The collection of locals and visitors were pointing, smiling, and snapping pictures of Abilene's creation with their cell phones.

Nora looked at her watch. It was nine thirty, which meant the trolley from Miracle Springs Lodge had arrived early and delivered Nora's favorite kind of customers: the wealthy kind.

"There's a group of people out on the sidewalk, admiring your work," Nora told Abilene. "Apparently, I'm not the only one who thinks you can make magic."

The compliment brought a rush of color to Abilene's cheeks and she glowed with delight. The reaction was so powerful that Nora sensed her guest was unaccustomed to praise.

"So? Should we see to that hand?" Nora asked.

After a brief hesitation, Abilene reached out with her index finger and held it over Nora's pinkie knuckle—over the empty space where the rest of her finger should have been.

"When did the books save you? After the fire?" she asked in a timid whisper.

Nora snatched her hand away. "We all have a story. We all have secrets. But we don't have to share them."

Someone knocked on the front door and Abilene gave a start.

Since she didn't recognize the man, Nora walked over to the door and pointed at the sign indicating the business hours. He'd have to wait until she opened at ten, because she had to clean up the broken spinner and figure out what to do with Abilene.

She muttered a line of poetry to herself. " 'How did it get so late so soon?' "

" 'It's night before it's afternoon,' " Abilene said, quoting the next line in the poem.

When Nora gaped at her in surprise, Abilene responded with a shy smile. "I like Dr. Seuss. That's why I chose *The Cat in the Hat* for the display."

"You're obviously a reader." Nora waved her arm, indicating the shelves behind them. "This is where you belong."

Abilene slowly got to her feet. Facing Nora, she took a deep and steadying breath. "I'd like to stay. For a little while. With you. And the books. All of these wonderful, wonderful books."

Chapter 2

He feels himself buried in those two infinities, the
ocean and the sky, at one and the same time: the one
is a tomb; the other is a shroud.

—Victor Hugo

Jedediah Craig accepted a mug of black coffee with a frown. Normally, the text on a black mug covered with white paw prints—THE ONLY VICIOUS THING ABOUT MY DOG IS ITS GAS— would have elicited a grin from the handsome paramedic. Not today.

"What's her story?" Jed asked, and then held up his hand. "Forget I asked. You don't know her story and I don't think she's going to give it to you. She's not in very good shape, Nora. And she's obviously hiding something. She's too banged up *not* to be keeping secrets."

"I don't need medical training to see that," Nora replied irritably. She was instantly contrite. It wasn't Jed's fault that Abilene had decided to pick Miracle Books as her stowaway spot. "I'm sorry. I really appreciate your taking care of her, but I can handle things from this point. I think. At the very least, I can get some food in her and give her a place to rest. Beyond that . . ." She shrugged.

Jed gestured at his medical kit. "You might have to change

her bandage tonight. I left supplies in your kitchen. She wouldn't tell me what her pain level is. She wouldn't even take a sip of water. She just stared out the window and went away someplace in her mind. I've seen patients do that. It's a coping mechanism."

"Maybe she froze because you're a man," Nora said, feeling guilty that she'd left Abilene alone with Jed so she could clean up the broken spinner rack. "Was she afraid of you?"

Jed considered this for a moment. "Not afraid. Uneasy. She couldn't wait for me to leave." He took another sip of his coffee and handed the mug back to Nora. "Thanks for that. You brew a mean bean."

Nora walked him to the front door. On the opposite side, customers were lined up, eagerly waiting to gain entrance to the bookstore.

"Are you having a major sale or has another national network plugged the badass bookstore bibliotherapist from Miracle Springs?"

Though Nora was relieved by the reappearance of Jed's humor, she was too distracted to think of a witty response. "I guess they're here for the bubble wrap" was the best she could manage.

When Jed looked confused, she directed his attention to the display window.

He whistled. "I had no idea you could do that with packing tape. That's amazing."

"Abilene created this scene last night. I thought she was in the storeroom, sleeping. I guess she was trying to thank me for letting her crash here."

Jed stared at the transparent tape figure for several seconds before turning to Nora. "Be careful, okay? You don't know a thing about this woman. Yes, she created something beautiful. Yes, she's wounded and fragile. But she's not a child and there are probably many sides to her. Sides she hasn't shown you yet."

"I certainly hope so," Nora said. Smiling at Jed, she thanked him again for his help. She then opened the door to let him exit and to invite a crowd of customers to enter.

Over the next few days, Nora learned very little about Abilene other than she was extremely tidy, was perfectly comfortable with silence, wore a size two, and could recite entire passages from her favorite novels, all of which Nora would categorize as classics. She was also completely and utterly mystified by technology.

"I have this weird feeling that she's never owned a computer or cell phone," Nora told Hester on the phone one afternoon. "She knows her way around the kitchen though. Last night, I was too tired to cook. It had been another crazy day at work, and I'd resigned myself to the idea of wolfing down a sandwich and a clump of grapes and going to bed early with Finn's *The Woman in the Window.* I'd barely walked into my house when Abilene announced that she'd make supper for us if I'd trust her to do it."

"Trust her? That's a weird choice of words," Hester said. "It's not like you stock cases of Dom Pérignon or white truffles in your kitchen."

"I thought it was odd too, but Abilene *is* odd. I don't mean that in a bad way. She's just different. She sure can cook though. Which is what I wanted to talk to you about."

Hester released a low groan. "I already don't like where this is headed."

Nora had been rehearsing her speech in her head and now presented her plan to Hester. "I'm not used to sharing my life, and while I can handle having Abilene crash on the couch for a few nights, I can't hire her to work in the bookstore. She isn't cut out for customer service. She hides whenever a customer enters. Not only that, but having her around all the time is throwing me off balance. You, on the other hand, could use her. She could take over some of the prep work or the less complicated baking. At the Gingerbread House, she can stay in the back. She'd be out of sight, which would make her more comfortable."

Hester didn't answer right away, and Nora didn't press her. She stayed quiet, giving her friend the chance to weigh her options.

"Neither of us are used to sharing our lives," Hester said. "We have the Secret, Book, and Scone Society. That's enough for me. I'm not looking to widen my social circle. And to be honest, something about this girl makes me nervous."

"Me too," Nora agreed. "I think she reminds us of ourselves—of the parts of ourselves we'd like to forget. The scared, weak, foolish parts."

Hester sighed. "You're probably right, which means I can't turn my back on her. I just hope she can handle the Gingerbread House. It's a cute name, but there's nothing cute about the hard work that goes into every roll, cake, and scone. I'm not sure Abilene's up to it. How's her hand?"

"Of all her wounds, whatever they are, the one on her hand will probably heal the cleanest," Nora said.

The women of the Secret, Book, and Scone Society met that Saturday night to assemble the first of their Secret Kindness tote bags.

"My contributions are loaves of honey wheat, marbled rye, cinnamon raisin, and rosemary focaccia bread as well as buttermilk biscuits and cheddar rolls," said Hester. "Who's getting the inaugural round of bags?"

June upended a canvas sack and pairs of colorful, scented socks tumbled out onto the coffee table. "We should pick six people from the bank. After all, those folks had no clue they'd all be losing their jobs because their coworker was a thieving, lying son of a bitch."

Estella scooped up a pair of socks and held them to her nose. "I love the purple ones. They're as soft as a puppy's ears and smell like fresh lavender. We should give these to that lady who was so sweet to you, Nora. I can't remember her name, but you said her hairstyle made her look like a blond pineapple. *Not* a client of mine. As the premier beautician in this town, I don't style hair into fruit shapes."

Nora felt a rush of shame over her choice of words. The woman with the bouffant hairstyle had been kind to her. Now, she was unemployed. "Her name's Melodie, and she didn't have much to spare before she lost her income stream. Money was too tight for her to treat herself to more than one new book per month. I gave her a manga book to see if she'd enjoy the genre. She loved it. So yes, let's drop a bag on Melodie's doorstep. I'll give her a Sailor Moon adventure and I bet she'd love that loaf of cinnamon bread, Hester." Nora pointed at the mound of socks. "The fuchsia socks? What's their scent?"

"Pink grapefruit."

"Perfect," Nora said, and Hester put the socks next to the loaf of cinnamon raisin bread.

Estella picked up a pair of gray socks. "Are these for a man?"

June nodded. "I assumed we'd be spreading kindness to both genders, so I learned to knit heavier socks—the kind guys wear with work boots or what-have-you. They're unscented." She studied Estella. "Do you have something for the men? I'm not sure they'll understand if they find a Magnolia Day Spa sampler kit complete with candles and a face mask on their doormat."

Estella rolled her eyes. "When will you give me credit for having beauty *and* brains? Of course I have something for the guys. It's pretty cool too. Check it out."

Reaching into a paper grocery bag, Estella pulled out a cigar box and opened the lid. She'd artistically arranged a bar of soap, a tube of shaving cream, disposable razors, shaving cream, washcloth, and a roll of breath mints inside the box.

"Nice," June said. "So that's it. I guess we're ready to assemble bags and make our first delivery."

Hester shot Nora a questioning glance. "What about the books?"

Nora retrieved the stack of gift-wrapped books she'd set behind the checkout counter and carried them back to the circle of chairs. "I don't view books about hope as gender specific, so these could go in any bag. For this round, I selected *A Prayer for Owen Meany*, *A Country Doctor's Notebook*, *Odes to Common Things*, *Kite Runner*, and *All the Light We Cannot See*. I believe the right book will end up in the right hands. Also, I'd like to add Amanda Frye to our list of recipients."

Estella, who'd been in the middle of piling spa samplers and cigar boxes on the coffee table, stopped what she was doing. "Seriously? You don't even like her."

Nora thought back to the last time Amanda, a notoriously difficult customer, had shopped at Miracle Books. Nora knew more about Amanda's personal life than she cared to because Amanda was one of those people who overshared. Minutes after meeting her, Nora learned that Amanda was a widow whose husband had died while still in his prime. He'd made no financial arrangements for her, and her bitterness over his lack of foresight practically eked out of her every pore. As for her only son, he lived in Chicago and never called. Never.

"With all the sacrifices I made for those men, you'd think they'd have treated me better," was one of Amanda's oft-repeated lines.

Amanda Frye typically spent over an hour in Miracle Books. She'd read Nora's books and replace them on the shelf when she was done. She was manically particular about the condition of the books she actually purchased. From the outset, she argued with Nora that a new book wasn't worth its full purchase price unless it was in pristine condition. And she'd yet to find a book in pristine condition.

"I think you should knock a dollar off. Someone folded this corner," she'd say, showing Nora the offending page.

Nora, who suspected Amanda of having done the folding in hopes of a discount, would refuse. "That hardback was released two weeks ago," she'd explain. "I can't reduce the price for such a minor flaw."

"Minor? It belongs in the used books section in this condition," Amanda would grumble.

Later, after reading the books she bought, Amanda would expect Nora to buy them back at a reasonable price. She was never satisfied with what Nora offered.

One day, a few weeks before the unexpected closure of the Madison County Community Bank, Nora had lost patience with Amanda Frye.

Amanda had approached the checkout counter and, without bothering to say hello, had unceremoniously dumped a pile of used paperbacks on top of the newspaper Nora was reading. After launching into a litany of complaints on how she hated the summer because the heat and humidity made her glasses turn foggy, her clothes stick to her skin, and her feet swell, she dropped a paper bag on the counter next to the paperbacks.

"I figure you don't need to ring me up," she'd said to Nora. "I'm swapping twelve used books for another twelve used books."

Nora's last customer had just left with a pair of teenage girls who'd tried to take a picture of her "Hamburger Helper face" before their mother noticed and shooed them out of the store. The mother had dumped the armload of books she'd planned on purchasing on a nearby chair before making her hasty exit. Between the loss of the sale and the rudeness of the teen girls, Nora was in no mood for Amanda Frye.

"This is a bookstore, not a lending library," Nora had told Amanda as she pulled her newspaper out from under the bag of books and gave it an angry rustle. "This is my living. I work very hard, six days a week, to earn a meager profit. I won't be retiring in ten years to a charming villa in Tuscany like the one in *Where Angels Fear to Tread*. I won't end up begging on the street corner because I gave away my inventory either. I'll gladly look at your paperbacks and offer you a fair price for them. You can accept or reject my offer, but I am not, *nor will I ever be*, open to negotiation."

Amanda had not responded well to Nora's speech. Mumbling that she'd never been so insulted in all her days, she scooped up her books and left the store. Nora hadn't seen her since.

"No, I'm not her biggest fan," she said to Estella now. "And though none of us have been living high on the hog, I get the impression that Amanda had nothing to spare. Whatever little she had is probably gone. Like so many, I'm sure she lost everything when the bank went under. She trusted that institution to keep her money safe. When the bank went belly-up, our terrified neighbors waited in line for hours to take out money that was no longer there. Amanda was one of those people in line. I saw her when I rode by on my bike."

Estella raised both hands. "You don't have to tell me. I have a list of clients who can't afford my services anymore because they lost their life savings. It makes me sick."

Hester opened empty grocery bags and placed a book at the bottom of each bag. "Speaking of sick, have you seen Abilene? She looks better. Less gaunt."

"That's good. But does she talk to you?" June asked as she dropped a pair of socks into a bag. "Nora hasn't gotten a thing out of her."

Nora shrugged. "I haven't pushed too hard either. If she isn't ready to talk, she'll just lie to get me to stop asking questions."

"You're probably right." Estella shooed June away from the bags. "The socks have to go in *after* the spa baskets. Come on.

You're in management now. Don't you know how to organize things?"

"I have *people* to do this kind of stuff for me. My peeps at the thermal pools take care of all the menial tasks." June flounced into a chair and struck a regal pose. "Wanna give me a foot rub when you're done?"

Estella pretended to be insulted. "Nora, give me your heaviest book. I want to throw it at June's head."

The women finished assembling the bags, talking and kidding around as they worked. Though their friendship was still new, it was a welcome change from the lonely existence they'd chosen for themselves. Previously, they'd been secretive, distrustful people. Such people often found themselves alone.

We shared our secrets, Nora thought, gazing at her friends. *Our stories are now knit together like a pair of June's socks.*

Hester folded the top of each paper bag multiple times, punched a hole through the folds, and wove an aubergine-colored ribbon through the hole.

"This is our signature color," she said, referring to the bookmarks Nora had given to the members of the Secret, Book, and Scone Society. The bookmarks were made of aubergine satin ribbon and had a tiny brass key affixed to the bottom. The key opened a secret compartment concealed inside the coffee table positioned in the middle of their circle of chairs. The table's hidden nook was currently empty, but Nora had invited her friends to use the space whenever the need arose.

"Should we write a message on the bags?" Nora asked, observing Hester's ribbon handiwork with approval. "Nothing trite. These people don't need motivational poster quotes."

"Lord, that brings back bad memories." Estella grimaced. "My high school guidance counselor had an office filled with those stupid posters. She had a HANG IN THERE with a kitten dangling from a ledge and SOME BUNNY CARES with a baby rabbit staring out at you with giant, creepy eyes. Do people really think baby animals and cheesy expressions help when your life is in the toilet?"

Hester shook her head. "If you're a little kid? Maybe. None of these people are kids, though. Let's just write, *From a friend*."

The other women agreed and took turns penning the message. When the bags were ready, they loaded them into June's Bronco and headed out for their first stop.

"It's not totally dark yet," Estella said as June pulled out of the parking lot behind Miracle Books. "Should we wait?"

"It'll be dark by the time we get to Amanda Frye's house," June said. "There's a pig roast at the fire station, so traffic will be backed up from here to the county line."

However, the road was clear. June reached Amanda's rural address in fifteen minutes. After slowing to a stop by a mailbox pitted with rust holes, she stared down the length of the narrow gravel driveway.

"I think that pig roast is next week," Nora said, following June's gaze. "But we're here now, so let's drop off the bag. We don't have to ring the doorbell and run away like teenagers pulling a prank. We'll just leave it on the stoop."

"I don't know." June was doubtful. "We're out in the country. All kinds of critters could gobble up Hester's bread before Amanda has the chance to find it. Raccoons, possums, foxes. The animals aren't shy in these parts. I work with a guy who lives near here. He said that the deer in these parts are hungry enough to eat right out of a person's hand."

"That's sad." Hester glanced at the shadowy woods surrounding Amanda's property. "Nature should be allowed to be wild. Animals shouldn't have to live off our leftovers because we've destroyed their habitat. You have the right idea, Nora. Your tiny house has a humble footprint. I wish I could be like that, but I can't part with my vintage kitchen collectibles. Stuff isn't supposed to make you happy, but my stuff does."

Estella, who was sitting in the back seat with Hester, smiled and said, "My beauty products make me happy. I love all the colors, and glitter, and what my pretty things can do to transform a girl's mood. So let's not feel guilty over our things. Didn't some famous writer say that rolling in the muck isn't the best way to get clean?"

Nora turned around to face Estella. "You never cease to surprise me. That's from *Brave New World*. The line—"

Something caught Nora's eye. There was an object floating in the pond off to the side of Amanda's house. The pond was far too small for a boat. And no one would enter the algae-covered water to cool off. Still, the shape looked eerily human. If the human in question was partially submerged, that is.

"What's wrong?" June asked Nora. "It feels like there's a spider crawling up the back of my neck and I don't even know why."

The space where the rest of Nora's pinkie finger once was tingled. This sensation had happened before, and recently too. In that instance, the tingling had foretold a death. A terrible death.

"Out of the car!" she commanded.

To their credit, her friends didn't hesitate.

They exited the car to a chorus of wild barking coming from the neighbor's backyard. There were three dogs. Big black-and-brown dogs. Too big for the tiny fenced area they'd been given. They sounded agitated. Frenzied. Their barks rising in pitch until they were almost baying. Nora was glad of the fence.

"I think someone's fallen in!" she yelled. After pointing at the pond, she broke into a run.

Hester, who was younger and faster than the rest of the women, reached the pond's edge first.

"Ohhh!" She cried out in horror and immediately backpedaled.

When Nora took in the full scene, she understood why Hester had felt compelled to retreat.

There was a body in the pond.

Judging by the floral-print dress, it was a woman's body. She was floating facedown, her hair forming a murky cloud around her head. Her limbs were partially hidden by electric-green pond scum. Insects hovered over her. Buzzing flies. A billow of persistent gnats. Ravenous mosquitoes.

Some of the bugs gravitated toward the living women.

"I'm not getting any bars," June said. Her voice was low and hoarse. "We'll have to use Amanda's landline to call for help."

Hester shook her head violently. Her face was ashen. "*No!* We have to pull her out! What if she just fell in? What if she's drowning right now and we're just standing here, letting her die?"

Estella, who'd maintained a distance from the pond, swatted at a fly before reaching out for Hester. "Honey, that poor woman isn't dying. She's already moved on. All we can do now is see that she's treated with dignity. Let's get away from this disgusting pond. No one in their right mind should be within inches of that petri dish. Maybe Amanda *wasn't* in her right mind."

Wordlessly, Hester turned her back on the dead woman, the bugs, and the stagnant water.

June offered to call the authorities. Nora thought Hester might volunteer, seeing as she and Deputy Andrews were practically dating, but as soon as Hester entered the house, she dropped into a chair in Amanda's living room and stared at the floor.

Nora disliked being in Amanda's home without her permission. She knew there was no other choice and that no one was home, but it still felt wrong. Her friends were clearly uncomfortable too. After finishing her call, June paced back and forth near the front door, while Estella took up a sentry position by the living room window. From this vantage point, she could watch for the sheriff's department cruisers.

Nora felt a pull from the opposite side of the room. From the bookcases. She wandered over to them and silently examined Amanda's collection.

Amanda's books were neatly arranged in a series of wooden packing crates that had been nailed together by an unskilled hand. Despite the crudeness of the shelving, Nora approached the books with reverence. They were all hardbacks and the dust jacket of each book was meticulously covered in a protective layer of plastic. Some of the books were contemporary fiction while others were old, leather-bound volumes.

After glancing around the rest of the room, which consisted of the sagging recliner Hester occupied, an equally droopy couch, and a television set that was state-of-the-art two decades ago, it was clear that Amanda's books were her greatest treasures.

Without touching anything, Nora moved through the living room into the kitchen. The room was small and dated, but pin-neat. Which is why the book and pill bottle on the counter looked completely out of place.

She felt a hand on her shoulder and flinched in surprise.

"Sorry, I didn't mean to spook you," June whispered. "Help will be here in a few minutes. They're wrapping up a call where the Trail crosses the highway."

June was referring to the Appalachian Trail, which curved around Miracle Springs for several miles and was another natural revenue stream for the town. Each day, dozens of hikers patronized the local businesses. Unlike other nearby towns, the merchants of Miracle Springs welcomed hikers into their shops. Some had even created storage areas for their packs or offered hikers the use of their hoses or spigots.

On occasion, conflict arose between individual hikers or between hikers and townies. These conflicts usually involved petty theft, trespassing, or violence brought on by too much alcohol, and were swiftly dealt with by the Miracle Springs Sheriff's Department.

"I'm glad they're close," said Nora. "I hate leaving her out in that water."

"You think that's Amanda out there?" June asked.

As Nora nodded, June's gaze landed on the pill bottle. The crimson-colored plastic was hard to miss, and June was drawn to the meds like Nora was drawn to the books.

Because the bottle had fallen on its side, June had to tilt her head to read the label without touching the bottle. "Methadone. That's for pain relief."

"Amanda complained about pain to anyone who'd listen," Nora said. "She said she had back, hip, neck, and knee pain. When she first started visiting Miracle Books, I asked after her symptoms so I could give her book recommendations on treating pain with diet or holistic remedies, but she wasn't interested in those kinds of books."

June shrugged. "Maybe she wasn't looking for a substitute for her painkillers. It sounds like she went to Miracle Books to escape her problems and didn't want reality interfering once she'd settled down with a book."

"You're probably right," Nora said and moved closer to June. She pointed at the book on the counter and muttered, "This, however, isn't right."

"What do you mean?" June asked.

Nora was formulating her answer when the wail of sirens severed the tranquility of the country twilight. Next door, the dogs commenced another round of frantic barking.

She and June returned to the living room to find Hester standing near the front door. She looked scared.

"Should we even be in here?" she asked. "Will we get in trouble?"

Estella took Hester's hand. "We had to call for help from this phone, remember? If it'd make you feel better, we could go outside and put ourselves at the mercy of those thirsty mosquitos. They seem to like to my jasmine perfume."

Hester practically pushed Estella through the doorway.

June and Nora followed. By the time the sheriff's cruisers pulled to a stop, all four women were lined up in front of Amanda's stoop. They stood with their hands clasped, like naughty children awaiting a reprimand.

The new sheriff, whom they'd all seen around town but had yet to meet, was the first to approach them. Originally from Raleigh, Grant McCabe was serving as the interim sheriff until the next election.

The sheriff was of average height and build and walked with a brisk, confident stride. When he drew up to the members of the Secret, Book, and Scone Society, he immediately doffed his hat to reveal a receding hairline and a pair of dark brown eyes. His gaze was both patient and intelligent.

Deputy Andrews, who was in his late thirties but had the slim figure and smooth complexion of a man ten years younger, stood next to his boss. He tried to give off an air of professional detachment, but he kept shooting quick glances of concern at Hester. A second deputy waited by the cars.

"Good evening, ladies," said the new sheriff. "I'm Sheriff Grant McCabe. I understand you reported the finding of a body. Could you take me to the lady?"

Estella pointed at the pond. "She's floating in the middle of that scummy water. You can't miss her. I'm sure you don't want us back over there. We might trample a clue or something."

"Thank you for your consideration, ma'am." The sheriff replaced his hat and touched the brim in deference. "Most people aren't as savvy." After issuing orders to his deputies in low murmurs, he turned back to the women. "Would you ladies mind waiting in your car while we take a look at the pond?"

"Not at all," Estella said coquettishly.

Nora knew Estella was just being her usual self, but she didn't think now was the time to start flirting with the new sheriff. Apparently, neither did June.

"Let's get away from these bugs," she said. "And those dogs! Lord have mercy! Why don't their owners get them inside?"

The four friends returned to June's Bronco. They waited in relative silence for a good twenty minutes before Deputy Andrews appeared.

June rolled down her window.

"The sheriff would like to take your statements in town," he said and made to leave.

"Hold on," Hester called from the back seat. "Is it Amanda? Is it her body?"

Andrews hesitated. "We'll need a positive ID before we can say for sure. But my guess is that it'll end up being Mrs. Frye. I mean, she left a note." He looked at Hester and dipped his chin. "See you at the station."

The women watched him walk away. His phrase about the note sat in the car like an extra passenger.

Finally, June spoke the word that everyone was thinking. "Suicide?"

Estella dismissed this with a flick of her wrist. "Who'd kill themselves in that god-awful pond? There are less nasty ways to do the deed than that."

June frowned at her in the rearview mirror. "Nora and I found an empty bottle of painkillers in the kitchen. I doubt that poor woman wanted to end up in that water. But somehow, she did."

Everyone fell silent again.

June turned the car on and released a heavy sigh.

Nora fastened her seat belt and gazed out the window. The same shadows she'd seen earlier had spread around the woods behind Amanda's house, creating an undergrowth of soupy darkness. Soon, the dark would rise into the leafy canopy. From there, it would stain the entire sky like a bottle of spilled ink.

"What did you mean back there, Nora?" June asked quietly

as she put her car in gear. "In the kitchen, you said that something wasn't right. What did you mean?"

Nora turned away from the dark woods and looked at her friend. "The book. Amanda wouldn't have done that to her book. I don't care if it was her last day on earth. That woman would never break a book's spine."

Chapter 3

Always read something that will make you look
good if you die in the middle of it.
                                                    —P. J. O'Rourke

"I don't get it," Estella said. "What book?"

Nora told Estella and Hester about the empty bottle of pain
pills and the book sitting on Amanda's kitchen counter.

"The book is a hardcover," Nora went on. "There's a certain
way to break in a hardcover before reading it for the first time.
Basically, you set it down on its spine and open one cover at a
time while holding the pages together with one hand. After
that, you allow a few pages near the front to open. Then, a few
pages toward the back. You repeat this process, slowly and gently. It allows tight or unforgiving bindings to be broken in
without damage."

Hester said. "I don't open my books that way. Does anyone?"

Nora shrugged, even though Hester was sitting behind her
and might not catch the movement. "Collectors do. So do particular readers who don't want their book pages falling out because the bindings have been ruined. I guess Amanda was both
a collector and a particular reader. The book in her kitchen was
covered with the same protective plastic as the books in her living room. I didn't have much time to study them, but I think
her books are worth something."

"Except the one in the kitchen," June said. "That thing looked like it had been stepped on. It was spread-eagled on the counter and the pages were mashed and crumpled. I don't know if you noticed, Nora, but there was a pinkish stain on the counter. I only saw it when I got right up on the pill bottle, but it reminded me of the stain left from cutting a fresh tomato."

Closing her eyes for a moment, Nora envisioned the view through Amanda's kitchen window. There'd been several nightshirts or housedresses, Nora couldn't tell which, pinned to a clothesline in the backyard. Closer to the house was a cracked concrete birdbath that probably hadn't held water in years. There had also been a small garden. A raised bed featuring some wilted plants. Nora remembered seeing supports for bean and tomato plants. She also remembered the aluminum pie tins Amanda had placed around the perimeter of the garden to ward off pests. The tins, which dangled from wooden stakes of various heights, turned and twisted in the air currents, catching glints of sunlight until there was no light left to catch.

"The rest of the room was very clean," Nora said. "She even had laundry drying outside. The only untidy place was near that book in the kitchen."

Estella released an exasperated sigh. "I don't see why a mashed book raises doubts about her suicide. It sounds to me like Amanda had nothing left to live for except books. I'm sorry to say this in your hearing, Nora, but books aren't enough. The woman in that pond had no money, no family, and was suffering from chronic pain. She probably swallowed the pills and decided to read while waiting for them to kick in. When they did, she dropped the book and leaned on it with all her weight before stumbling outside."

"She *stumbled* all the way to the pond?" June asked wryly. "It's not exactly close to the house. That'd be quite a feat for someone on the brink of death."

"I'm just saying that she did this to herself, as sad as that is," Estella said. "Who'd want to kill Amanda, other than the people she regularly irritated? What would happen if we all went around killing those who annoyed us?" Since no one replied, Estella pressed her point. "Okay. Let's say that Amanda's books are her most valuable possessions. Did it look like any of the books were missing, Nora?"

"I noticed an empty space in the cases in the living room, but the missing book was the one we saw in Amanda's kitchen."

June shot her a quick glance as she paused at a four-way stop. "How do you know that it came from the living room?"

"It was the second book of a trilogy by Philip Pullman," Nora said. "There was a space between the first and third books on Amanda's shelf. *The Subtle Knife* is the second book in the His Dark Materials series."

Silence followed Nora's explanation. Each woman seemed to be lost in her own thoughts until June pulled into the lot shared by the sheriff's department and the DMV.

As June looked for a spot, Hester said, "That title sounds like a murder weapon. I read Pullman's *The Golden Compass*. I loved that book, but I haven't tried any of his other books."

"*The Golden Compass* was originally called *Northern Lights*," Nora said. "The third book is *The Amber Spyglass*. There's actually a fourth book in the series now, but Amanda only collected the original trilogy. She seemed to like trilogies. She had several of them."

"In that case, I hope she's with the Father, the Son, and the Holy Ghost," said Estella with unusual solemnity. "Anyway, I was just trying to say that the only thing of value in Amanda's house was left untouched. Her books. Which is why I think it's safe to assume that she made the decision to end her own life. It's horrible, but there's nothing mysterious about it."

With Estella's words ringing in their ears, the women filed

into the sheriff's department and took turns giving their statements to a female deputy.

Like Sheriff McCabe, the deputy was a new hire and a welcome sight to the members of the Secret, Book, and Scone Society. The former sheriff had made it perfectly clear that he believed a woman's place was in the home. Therefore, it was a marked improvement to see not one, but two women sporting the brown and khaki uniforms and wearing utility belts weighed down with gear as if they'd been born with them encircling their waists.

By the time the four friends left the sheriff's department, it was truly dark. There was no light left in the sky. Not even starlight. Clouds covered the moon, and the shadows from Amanda's woods seemed to have fallen over the entire town.

"I know we're not in the same mood we were in when we left to deliver our kindness totes, but the people we chose still need what we have to give," June said.

Nora smiled at her friend. "Then let's do what we set out to do."

On the way to the first stop, Hester decided to ring the doorbell.

Estella looked at her as if she'd lost her mind. "I thought you were just going to leave the bag and go. What if they release the hounds or reach for their shotgun?"

"I'll take my chances," Hester said. "I want to be sure they get the bread. We have raccoons in town too. I think I have a whole family living in my garbage cans."

At the first house, the doorbell chime caused a chain reaction. On the other side of the door, a little dog started yipping and the porch lights came on before Hester had a chance to jump back into the Bronco.

"Hurry!" Estella cried.

The second Hester was back in the truck, June pressed her

foot to the gas pedal and the Bronco peeled out, leaving rubber tire marks on the asphalt. The four friends chortled with relief.

The rest of the stops were uneventful. There were no dogs and the other recipients responded to the doorbell at a much slower pace.

"They're probably loading their shotguns," Hester said, examining a fresh constellation of bug bites on her arm.

By the time June returned to the parking lot behind Miracle Books, they all felt better for having delivered their anonymous gifts.

Despite this, Nora didn't ask her friends in for decaf coffee or tea. She didn't want company. She wanted to be alone in her tiny house.

Of course, she couldn't be alone. She had a guest.

Abilene was a very quiet person, but her physical presence intruded on Nora's space. Especially her headspace. Abilene hadn't been with Nora for a week, and Nora was already looking forward to the day the young woman moved on. Or at least, moved in with someone else.

When Nora entered the tiny living room of Caboose Cottage, she saw its tiny cast-iron woodstove, the coffee table with built-in storage, and the sliding bookshelves that concealed her television. She didn't see Abilene. The house was silent and still.

In the kitchen, Nora found a note from Abilene saying she'd gone out for a walk. Next to the note were two pastries under a tent made of toothpicks and plastic wrap. Nora pulled off the wrap and stared down in delight at a pair of book-shaped puff pastries. One book was topped with a sprinkling of cinnamon. The other was dusted with confectioner's sugar. Nora wondered if Hester had made the pastries and forgotten to mention them to Nora.

Recently, the two women had decided that Nora should add a special pastry to the Miracle Books menu. Hester would bake the item and Nora would split half the profits with her. However, these weren't the pastries Hester had baked as a test run. Those were much smaller and had included lines of text made of chocolate sauce or jam.

Nora raised one of the book pastries to her nose. She smelled apples. The pastry was heavy, and she realized that Hester had injected the pastry with a fruit filling. Unable to resist the aromas of butter, apples, and cinnamon, Nora took a bite. And another.

She moaned in delight. It was like eating a hand pie, but the golden-brown dough was lighter, flakier, and butterier than any piecrust Nora had ever tasted.

She was just wiping her mouth with a paper towel when Abilene appeared, holding the flashlight Nora kept in the cupboard below the kitchen sink.

"Did you like it?" she asked, her expression eager and a little anxious.

Nora nodded. "It was delicious."

"The other one's filled with chocolate," Abilene said, smiling with pleasure. "Hester let me experiment when I finished my other work. She said that, if you approved, I could bake a dozen of each flavor and deliver them to the bookstore before you open. She also said that she'd send the smaller book pastries with the writing on top."

After what Nora had witnessed earlier that evening, discussing pastries with Abilene was a welcome relief. "I'd love to add these to my menu," she said. "My regular customers will be so pleased. They've always hinted that it would be nice if I offered an accompaniment for their coffee or tea. Now, they'll have something truly unique. I might even gain new customers after people post photos of these edible books on social media. What do you think?"

Averting her eyes, Abilene mumbled, "I don't know much about social media."

"But you're of the tech generation," Nora teased. "And you're the only twentysomething I've met who isn't constantly checking their smartphone. Do you own one?"

Abilene shook her head.

For some reason, Nora found this unusually curious. Also, she'd used the term twentysomething to see if Abilene would state her exact age. To Nora, she looked closer to seventeen than twenty anything, but Abilene hadn't taken the bait. "Have you ever used a cell phone?"

Shaking her head again, Abilene picked up the piece of plastic wrap from the counter and twisted it around her first three fingers. She was clearly agitated.

"It's refreshing to know that a person can survive without one," Nora said airily. She didn't want to spoil the mood Abilene had created with her surprise pastries. "Hester's my youngest friend, but she doesn't walk around with her eyes glued to her phone. Nor does she take it out during meals. So many people do that these days. They sit together, but spend the whole time focused on their phones. Why do they bother meeting if they're just going to ignore each other?"

When Abilene shrugged, Nora could see that this topic wouldn't bring her any closer to her guest. "Hester learned to bake by reading cookbooks. Did she tell you that?"

"Yes," Abilene said.

Nora was struck by Abilene's formality. She didn't make noises of assent or say *yeah*, or *sure*. It was always *yes*.

"Is that how you learned to bake too?" Nora pressed. "Or did someone teach you?"

Another shrug. "A bit of both."

Seeing that it was futile to pry, Nora gestured at the remaining pastry. "I'll save that for tomorrow. By then, I hope I've come up with a clever name. If you have an idea, let me know."

* * *

The next morning, Nora woke to a second note from Abilene. This one read, *When I was making these, I thought of them as* book pockets. *I don't know if that works, but I thought I'd tell you. I'll deliver the trays after nine.*

Nora liked the name very much.

As she waited for her coffee to brew, she studied the note. Abilene's cursive looked like an example from a handwriting workbook. She was so different from other young women her age. She'd never used a smartphone, she was a skilled cook, she loved to read, and she wrote in perfect cursive. She also spoke with the formality of one completely unfamiliar with slang.

Was she raised by technophobes? Nora mused while sipping coffee out on the small covered deck of Caboose Cottage. *Did she escape from a cult? Was she someone's prisoner? Is that why she's so pale? And what about all her bruises? And her malnourishment?*

The hospital bracelet Nora had seen on Abilene's wrist was long gone. Gone with the bracelet was the information printed on it. Information like Abilene's full name.

Examining the note left by her mysterious houseguest reminded Nora of another note. One written by Amanda Frye.

"I know a certain deputy who drops by a certain bakery for breakfast," she said to Hester later that morning. "Did Andrews mention Amanda's note?"

Nora had Hester on speaker so she could update the chalkboard menu at Miracle Books.

"Actually, Jasper just left." There was a slight pause. "It feels so weird to use his first name. It shouldn't, but it does."

Nora was happy to hear the giddiness in her friend's voice. Hester had very little experience dating, but Jasper Andrews was a good man and Nora trusted him to treat Hester well.

"Jasper." Nora tried the name out. "I like it, but I'll keep calling him Deputy Andrews. So did he say anything about the note?"

"He told me exactly what it said." Hester sounded sad. "*I have nothing left to live for.* That's all she wrote."

Nora rolled the stick of chalk between her thumb and index finger. A powdery film turned her skin ghost white. She looked out the ticket agent's window at the bookshelves and thought about what Amanda had written. Could a person's existence be reduced to a single line? Amanda Frye, who always had so much to say, had reduced her entire vocabulary into a sentence of seven sorrowful words. The note's brevity made Nora feel mournful.

"I expected more detail," Nora said. Though she couldn't shake the feeling that something was off about Amanda's death, she pushed the thought aside. She didn't know Amanda intimately. She'd been a customer. That's all. Seeing her twice a month hardly made Nora an expert on the woman.

But the book . . . a nagging voice in Nora's head whispered.

"Where was the note found?" Nora asked Hester.

"It was in the kitchen. Inside the front cover of the book," Hester said. "That's all Jasper told me—other than Mrs. Frye's son is on a flight from Chicago. He's coming to identify her body. Didn't you say that she complained about her son? That he never visited or contacted her?"

Her son's lack of communication had been one of Amanda's constant gripes. "Yes. She said she made every sacrifice a mother could make for his benefit and that he repaid her by moving away as soon as he graduated from high school. He never returned. Not for holidays. Not for illnesses. Not for any reason." Nora had heard the complaints about Amanda's son so often that she could repeat them verbatim. "She also said that he made really good money, but even though he knew she didn't have a dollar to spare, he never gave her a cent. She was angry at him, she was disappointed in him, but she obviously missed him being in her life too."

"It sounds like Amanda was really lonely," Hester said. "But like Estella said last night, her struggles are over. Wherever she is now, I hope she has company. If there's a heaven, it has to be a place where no one is lonely. And you can eat whatever you want and read books all day."

"Speaking of heaven, let's talk about those book pockets," Nora said.

Hester informed Nora that Abilene would be swinging by in a few minutes to deliver the inaugural batch.

"It would make Abilene happy if they sell," Hester said. "She puts her heart into her work. I can see it. I've never hired an assistant because no one bakes to my standards. Except Abilene. Having her here first thing every morning is turning out to be a good thing for both of us."

"I'm glad. I wish I could say the same," Nora said. "I like Abilene, but if she stays in Miracle Springs much longer, she'll have to find another couch to crash on. My tiny house is just too tiny for us both."

"I have the solution to your problem," Estella announced that afternoon. Following a last-minute cancelation, she'd decided to walk over to Miracle Books for a cappuccino and a chat.

"Buy a book pocket too," Nora said. "Abilene made them and I'd like to be able to tell her that we sold out of her first batch. I have a few chocolate ones left. The apples are all gone."

Estella touched her flat belly and appeared to engage in a brief internal debate. "Oh, fine," she said, taking out her money. "Twist my arm. Can you warm it up? I like everything a little toasty."

Nora popped the pastry into the microwave and made the cappuccino. After serving Estella, Nora asked her to explain what problem she'd found a solution for.

"You know that expression about guests," said Estella as she got comfortable in a reading chair. "They're like fish. After three days, they start to stink."

Nora frowned. "Abilene barely makes a peep. She cooks me dinner and she invented the pastry you're devouring. She's a nice person. The real problem is me. I don't want a roommate. If I'd wanted a roommate, I'd have a cat. A fat, lazy cat to keep my feet warm in the winter."

"That's what men are for, honey."

Nora spread her hands. "What's your solution?"

Estella took a folded sheet of paper out of her handbag and passed it to Nora. "A new business is opening in town, and I think it has the power to grant all of your wishes."

Unable to comprehend Estella's words or her ridiculous brow wiggling, Nora examined the glossy flyer.

NEED CASH FAST?
YOUR CLUTTER IS ANOTHER'S TREASURE!
LET US SELL IT FOR YOU!

VIRTUAL GENIE

WE TURN WISHES INTO REALITY!
QUICK PAYMENT!
LOW SELLER'S FEE!

COME TO OUR APPRAISAL FAIR
WEDNESDAY, 10AM–6PM
EXCHANGE COLLECTIBLES FOR CASH!

Nora glanced from the flyer to Estella. "I don't see how this helps me."

Estella's mouth split into her cat-got-the-cream grin. "I got this from the new owner. He was outside his shop, overseeing the placement of his new sign. It's tasteful, by the way. Just a brass lamp, like the one from Aladdin, with a plume of purplish smoke embellished with sparkling lights. The owner is also quite lovely to look at. He has dark hair, dark eyes, and gorgeous hands. I could just imagine those long fingers—"

"He's good-looking. I get it," Nora said, interrupting Estella before she could get too graphic. "You still haven't said how the arrival of this Virtual Genie solves my problems. I certainly don't have collectibles to sell other than the ones I intend to sell in my own shop."

"If you'd let me finish, I'd explain that Mr. Kingsley—he's the proprietor—plans to rent out the studio above the store. Because it's in need of lots of TLC and he doesn't plan on investing in it, he's looking to rent it out cheaply."

Nora had to admit that this was intriguing news, but before she could get too excited, she realized that the idea was unlikely to see fruition. "Abilene would have to provide personal information. She can't even rent a post office box without completing paperwork and having a picture ID of some kind."

Estella gazed into her mug. "That's true. Abilene will have to decide if she'd prefer to keep running or trust us to help her stay in Miracle Springs. If she decides to move on, the least we can do is get her some sneakers. That outfit she was wearing the night we met her—the housedress and the flip-flops—weren't even close to her size. Do you think she stole that stuff?"

"Maybe. Or else they were given to her by another woman who was willing to help without asking questions."

"Or Abilene asked one too many and had to run after getting the clothes," Estella said. "But she can't live the rest of her life in fear. Eventually, she has to face her demons. Better to do that while she has other people around than facing them out there"—she pointed toward the front of the store—"all alone."

Nora recalled Jed's warning. "For those of us in the Secret, Book, and Scone Society, the demons we needed to face were in here." She touched her temple. "And in here." She moved her hand to her heart. "What if Abilene's are made of flesh and blood?"

Estella stood up and put her empty mug on the ticket agent counter. "Some of us have been cut on the inside. Clawed at by a person we were foolish enough to trust. Or to love." She gently rested her fingertips on Nora's scarred forearm. "I bet these healed faster than your internal scars. Some wounds never close."

Nora waved her free arm, encompassing the whole bookstore in the gesture. "Which is why we need places like this. Places where we can connect with other people. Places where we can sit quietly, read, and drink a cup of coffee while the rain falls. Small sanctuaries disguised as bookstores."

Shouldering her purse, Estella pointed at the flyer. "Show that to Abilene and give her a choice. She can become like us—strong, scarred, wise, and wonderful—or she can keep running from her secret. You and I both know that it'll come out eventually. Secrets always find a way of surfacing."

Nora wondered if Estella had been thinking of Amanda when she'd made that remark. Nora had, and the image of the body in the pond haunted her for the rest of the day.

That night, Nora took the empty book-pocket tray home to Abilene.

"People loved them," she told her. "You should be proud."

Abilene's face glowed. Even though Nora had already washed the tray, Abilene washed it again.

"I learned to cook out of necessity," she said as she dried the tray with the dish towel, rubbing it until the steel shone like glass. "My parents were missionaries. When I was very young, they went on a mission trip and never came back. I was sent to live with my mother's second cousin. He was a very demanding man who didn't like children."

This was the most Abilene had ever shared, and Nora waited

a long moment before responding. She wanted to say the right thing, to keep the conversation going.

"You don't ever have to see him again," she assured Abilene. "Not ever. You're not a little girl anymore. He has no power over you. You're in charge of your fate."

Abilene shook her head, silently conveying the message that Nora didn't understand the situation. This was true. Nora didn't understand. But she knew enough to recognize that Abilene was afraid of this man. Her fear was a tangible thing. It made Abilene's eyes go dark. It made her fingers turn fidgety and her shoulders droop.

"Do you want to stay in Miracle Springs?" Nora softly asked. "Do you want to keep working at the bakery?"

Meeting Nora's gaze, Abilene said, "Yes."

"Okay, then." Nora put her hand over Abilene's. With a light, gentle touch, she uncurled Abilene's clenched fist. "Okay," she repeated.

Abilene glanced down at Nora's scarred hand. After a long pause, she turned her own hand over, offering Nora her bandaged palm—her own scarred skin.

Both women looked down at their imperfect hands, which were stacked like two pieces of warm bread.

"Okay," Abilene said and smiled.

The next morning, Nora walked across the park in the center of town, keeping to shaded areas beneath the trees. Though she liked the sunshine, she'd forgotten her hat and didn't want to expose her burn scars to direct sunlight.

The square was crowded with tourists, which didn't surprise Nora. School would be starting soon and there was an end-of-summer feel to the day. The sun was still hot. The air was still damp and sticky. But there had been a subtle shift—a sense that the season had lost much of its vigor.

The countdown to September had an uncanny effect on visitors to Miracle Springs. They tried to squeeze in as many activities as possible during their stay. They scheduled spa treatments, went on hikes, bathed in the hot springs multiple times, dined at local eateries, and they shopped, shopped, and shopped. Based on previous summers, Nora had learned to stock extra shelf enhancers for this time of year.

As she walked, she wondered how a new business catering to locals could survive in a tourist town.

I bet the owner is a vulture in disguise, she thought. *He's here to pick the bones of the people who lost their jobs and must now sell their possessions if they want to put food on the table.*

Nora slowed her pace as she approached her destination. Standing under the shade of the awning belonging to a neighboring business, she studied the Virtual Genie sign. As Estella had said, the sign looked like an antique Middle Eastern lamp. It was covered with several coats of shiny bronze paint and the purplish-blue smoke plume was pierced with dozens of tiny electric lights.

Glancing from the sign to the storefront, Nora saw a dark-haired man of medium build exit through the doorway. He held the door open for a large, bearded man with a stern face who exited Virtual Genie as if escaping a gas station restroom.

"Again, I'm sorry for your loss, Mr. Frye," said the dark-haired man.

The name immediately caught Nora's attention and she watched the bearded man with interest. She assumed she was witnessing an interaction between Amanda Frye's son and Mr. Kingsley, the owner of Virtual Genie. Estella had described him as being dark-haired and handsome. This man fit that bill.

"Everyone says that when a person dies," said Mr. Frye. "But can I tell you something that might surprise you?"

Mr. Kingsley spread his hands in invitation. "Please do. What fun would life be without surprises?"

Mr. Frye hesitated a moment before continuing in a hostile

tone. "I'm *not* sorry. My mother is dead, but it wasn't a loss for me." He held out a finger to forestall the other man from interrupting, even though it was clear by Mr. Kingsley's expression that he was too shocked to respond. "I'm sure that sounds cold to you, but you don't know the whole story. You don't know the half of it."

"I'm—" Mr. Kingsley began.

"Here it is in a nutshell," Mr. Frye went on. His voice was cold and sharp, like an icicle. "My dad and I were really close," he said. "I loved that man and he loved me."

Mr. Kingsley managed a tight smile. "That's good."

"Oh, it *was* good. Everything was good," snarled the bearded man. "Until my mom killed him."

Chapter 4

Great books help you understand, and they help you to feel understood.

—John Green

Having issued this shocking statement, Amanda Frye's son walked away without so much as a good-bye. He stepped out into the street, blatantly putting himself in the path of an oncoming car.

Nora tensed and waited for a horn blare or the shriek of brakes. But Frye simply held out his arm like he was a traffic cop and sauntered to the opposite side of the street as if he owned the town.

He then squeezed his oversized frame into the driver's seat of a yellow Mazda Miata. He barely fit in the small convertible and looked like a cartoon figure as he pulled into traffic, cutting off a driver and forcing him to swerve into the other lane. The driver honked in indignation and Frye responded by flipping him the bird. Watching this scene, Nora was reminded of Bluto, the villain from the Popeye comic books. She found the comparison between Frye and the famous bully amusing.

"A lovely smile for a lovely morning," said a voice. Nora turned to find Mr. Kingsley standing next to her.

"Not for him, apparently." She pointed at the Mazda seconds before it rounded the block and disappeared from view.

Mr. Kingsley quietly surveyed the passersby for a moment. "People have different ways of processing grief. Anger is a typical response. And a natural one as well." Looking at Nora, he continued. "But let's not dwell on unpleasant thoughts. I'm Griffin Kingsley, proprietor of Virtual Genie."

Nora rarely warmed to others straightaway, but Griffin's bright brown eyes and direct gaze drew her in. He looked at her like she wasn't scarred. He looked at her like people had looked at her before she was burned. His directness made Nora feel good.

"I'm Nora Pennington. I own Miracle Books."

Griffin's smile widened. "Ah, the bookstore in the train depot! I've been looking forward to visiting—I love books—but I've been working like a madman preparing for our appraisal fair. I—" He lowered his head and touched his fingers to the bridge of his nose in a self-effacing gesture. "Forgive me. Won't you come in and have something cool to drink? Tamara, my business partner, makes the most wonderful iced chai tea. It's the perfect remedy for the humidity."

Nora accepted his invitation and followed him inside Virtual Genie. When the door closed behind her, she felt like she'd left her small town in the North Carolina mountains out on the sidewalk and had entered another world.

She stood in a large, open space that might have been transported from a medieval sheik's palace. There were gilded birdcages, opulent divans, carved desks and chairs, brass light fixtures, and a dozen exotic plants in pots embellished with mosaic tiles. The hardwood floors were completely covered by Persian rugs and the walls had been draped with multiple layers of colorful silks. Over the silks, Griffin had hung poster-sized quotes from *The Arabian Nights*. Each quote, printed in a stylized font with lots of graceful curls, was encased in a gilt frame.

Griffin clearly enjoyed witnessing Nora's reaction. His eyes danced as he led her to a pair of chairs covered in crimson velvet.

"It's hard to believe this was once a candle shop," Nora said in amazement. "The transformation is magical."

Griffin waited for Nora to be seated before sitting in the chair opposite her. "People often have a hard time naming their favorite book. I don't have that problem."

Nora laughed. "I think I know which one made a serious impression on you. And why not? What wonderful stories. When did you first read it?"

"My mother read it to me when I was very young," Griffin said. "She had a beautiful voice. I imagine part of the reason Scheherazade was such a skilled storyteller was that she was also gifted with a melodious voice." He pointed at the framed quotes. "Did you know that *The Arabian Nights* is not the book's original title? *Arabian Nights* comes from the later version. The English edition. The original title is *One Thousand and One Nights*."

"You should prepare yourself. People might ask if those quotes are from *Aladdin*. Or they might wonder why you don't have a blue genie coming out of the lamp outside."

Griffin raised a finger and made an imaginary check in the air. "There's a woman in her eighties, a grandmother to twelve, who's seen the Disney movie at least twenty times. She asked me both of those questions."

"Are you talking about that sweet lady from Atlanta? The one who took care of her daughter's kids all day so she could go back to school?" asked a woman who'd suddenly appeared from an opening in the silk. Nora saw a doorway concealed behind the fabric.

Griffin got to his feet. "I had the good fortune of running into Ms. Pennington on the sidewalk. She owns Miracle Books. Ms. Pennington, this is my associate, Tamara Beacham."

Nora told Tamara to call her by her first name and shook the other woman's outstretched hand. Tamara's handshake was so brief that it bordered on rudeness.

My scars aren't contagious, Nora felt like saying, but suppressed the comment.

After smiling nervously at Nora, Tamara offered to make iced chai tea and ducked back through the opening in the silk.

"No wonder I didn't see her come in," Nora said.

Griffin followed her gaze. "Like the setting of a well-written story, a business should invoke a certain mood. We've attempted to create an aura of luxury and escapism. It's an artifice, yes, but an artifice built with the intention of putting our customers at ease. When people come to us looking to sell their possessions, they're often facing hardship. A relative has passed away, leaving unexpected debts. Or they've suddenly lost a job." He paused, reflected for a moment, and then continued. "We also have clients looking to downsize or declutter. These people can experience anxiety in letting go of their possessions. Our business appears to focus on material goods, but it's truly about helping people through challenging transitions."

Griffin went on to ask about Miracle Books, and since the shop was Nora's favorite subject, she was able to exchange innocuous small talk until Tamara reemerged from the back room carrying a silver serving tray. She placed the tray on the table between Griffin and Nora and touched the gold box in the center of it.

"Please help yourself to Belgian chocolate," she said. "And if you don't care for the drink, I'd be glad to make you something else."

Nora, who considered the thought of iced chai rather distasteful, changed her mind after one sip.

"It's the fresh cinnamon and cardamom," Griffin said, reading Nora's expression of surprise. "We've turned Hells Angels bikers and French-press coffee snobs into fans of this tea. People have emailed Tamara in hopes of obtaining her recipe, but she never gives it to them. It's a trade secret."

Though Nora liked Griffin, and she didn't want to ruin her

chance of relocating Abilene, she couldn't stop from asking the question that had been on her mind since she'd first heard of Virtual Genie. "Does your business follow financial fallouts? Like the dissolution of the Madison County Community Bank? Or the bankruptcy of The Meadows, the town's biggest real estate development?"

Griffin's reaction to such a blunt question was a slight tensing of his shoulders. That was all. "We did read about the unfortunate events in this community, and yes, those events influenced our decision to open in Miracle Springs over another town. But it wasn't ambulance chasing alone that led us here. I visited a lifetime ago with my parents and had very fond memories of our trip. Even as a boy, I felt the town's peaceful vibe. I hated to know that a scandal had disrupted that peace, so here we are. This is a business, and I want make a profit, but I also want to help restore balance to a place that gifted me with good memories."

Nora was unaccustomed to such transparency. She decided it was only fair to repay Griffin's honesty with honesty. "I stopped by because I was curious about Virtual Genie, but my main reason for being here is to inquire about the room for rent."

Griffin looked aggrieved.

"It's not an attractive space, I'm afraid. Not for a lady," he added. "I assume we'll rent it to a man who can easily ignore the peeling paint or rust stains. With the appraisal fair coming up, finding a tenant is low on my list."

"There are women who can't afford attractive spaces," Nora said flatly. "And peeled paint can be fixed. Will you show me the apartment?"

Griffin set his cup of tea aside and laced his fingers.

As if she'd heard a silent call, Tamara emerged from the other room and smiled at Nora.

"I'll show it to you," she said. "Griffin has so much to do right now."

Nora thanked Griffin for his hospitality and followed Tamara through the opening in the curtains.

The difference between Virtual Genie's public and work areas was marked. While the main room was a show of exotic opulence, the back room was utterly spartan.

Nora saw folding tables and chairs, racks of steel shelving, and a photography nook. With the hard cement floors and unadorned walls, the workroom was a stark contrast to the vibrancy of the public space.

Tamara led Nora through a doorway and into a vestibule lined with cardboard boxes of various sizes and shapes. Ahead of them was the rear exit. On the opposite wall, there was a narrow, dimly lit staircase.

"I should tell you that I'm not looking at this for myself, but for a young woman in need," Nora said as she and Tamara ascended the stairs. "Abilene works part-time at the Gingerbread House, our local bakery. I don't know what you're charging for rent, but my friend is on a very tight budget. She's at the bakery right now, which is why I'm looking at the apartment for her."

"The space is in rough shape, but I heard what you said to Griffin." Tamara took out a key ring and unlocked the dead bolt. "And you're right. Some people aren't in a position to afford anything other than rough, regardless of their gender."

Tamara opened the door and flicked on the lights, illuminating a dingy room with a galley kitchen, and a living/sleeping area with a futon. A moth-eaten curtain separated the main room from a bathroom. Nora peeked in at the sink and shower stall, both of which were stained with rust, mold, and lime deposits. The linoleum was cracked and curling and there were thick layers of dust coating the blinds. In the main room, the pine flooring was scarred with scratches and dents and the kitchen cabinets were just as rough. The two appliances, an oven and a refrigerator, were old enough to qualify as vintage.

"We just don't have the time or the capital to make improvements," Tamara said, a note of apology in her tone.

Nora considered how to use the apartment's dilapidated state to Abilene's advantage. "Would you let my friend make improvements if she became your tenant? Paint the walls and jettison the blinds and futon, for example?"

"Of course," Tamara answered.

When Nora suggested they return to the main floor to discuss terms, Tamara was even more surprised. "Won't your friend want to see the apartment first?"

"She's entrusted this task to me," Nora said. "If the rent is doable, I'll take the paperwork back to her to fill out. If you want to meet Abilene in person, I should warn you that she's extremely shy. She keeps to herself."

"That's probably a good thing. The studio isn't a great space for entertaining. Also, your friend will have to access the apartment through the back door, which means coming and going using the alley access. I like the idea of a quiet, shy, baker living above our business. I'm sure Griffin will feel the same. We store the items we sell in the back room until they can be shipped, so a trustworthy tenant is a must."

The two women returned to the ground floor and sat at Tamara's desk. She gave Nora what she vowed was their rock-bottom rent rate and promised to email her a standard lease agreement.

Nora thanked Tamara for her time and left Virtual Genie. As she crossed the park toward Miracle Books, she thought about what Tamara had said about having a trustworthy tenant.

Damn it, she thought. *They're going to run a background check on Abilene. When they do, what will they learn?*

*   *   *

She found Deputy Andrews waiting for her at the bookstore.

"Good morning, Deputy," Nora said, noting the speckles of confectioners' sugar on his uniform shirt. She guessed that the lawman had just come from the Gingerbread House, which meant he probably hadn't dropped by the bookstore to pick up another Orson Scott Card novel.

Andrews returned Nora's greeting before gesturing at the display window. "Hester told me that the woman who designed this just started working for her. I haven't met her yet."

"Her name's Abilene. And you might not meet her for a while. She's extremely shy." Unlocking the front door, Nora waited for the clanging of the sleigh bells to subside before she asked the deputy if he'd stopped by to browse.

He cast a longing glance toward the Science Fiction section. "I wish I could, but duty calls. I'm here to ask you a question about Mrs. Frye's books."

After dumping her keys and handbag on the checkout counter, Nora gave the deputy her full attention. "The collection in her living room?"

"Yep. Do you have any idea how much they're worth?" When Nora didn't answer right away, Andrews added, "I know you weren't in her house long, but you're a bookseller, Ms. Pennington, so I'm sure you checked out her books. I just want to know if you looked at them long enough to be able to estimate their value."

"I can't give you a dollar amount," Nora said. "Not without examining each book and searching online for its current market value." When she saw the deputy's face fall, she added, "However, Amanda's collection is valuable. Why are you asking? Why are her books important?"

Andrews shot a glance at the surrounding shelves, his expression inscrutable. "The sheriff is just being thorough. Mrs.

Frye left her books to a former neighbor. Someone from another state, and her son isn't too happy about it."

"I don't blame him. From what I saw, those books were the only things of value in that house," Nora said. "Then again, Amanda was pretty vocal about her relationship with her son. From what she said, it wasn't a good one."

"Definitely not," agreed Andrews.

The memory of Amanda's body in the scum-covered pond arose in Nora's mind and she was suddenly angry. She was angry that Amanda had died such a terrible death and she realized that she was looking for someone to blame. The son who'd abandoned her? The husband who'd left her without any money? Or the bibliotherapist who'd failed to establish a relationship with a customer so clearly in need of healing?

"I can't believe her possessions have been divvied up already," Nora said, unable to keep ire from creeping into her voice. "For Christ's sake, doesn't there have to be a minimal amount of investigating before the vultures swoop in? Or an official cause of death given?"

Andrews shifted his utility belt higher on his waist. "We're not taking short cuts, Ms. Pennington. Mrs. Frye's son found a copy of her will after he identified her body. The bank owns her house and her car and there's no savings to speak of. In fact, there's nothing for the vultures to swoop in and take."

"I overheard an exchange between Frye and the owner of Virtual Genie. That new business?" Nora waited for Andrews to indicate that he'd heard about Virtual Genie before continuing. "I caught only the tail end of their conversation, but Amanda's son made a pretty startling remark."

She repeated the bearded giant's line about his mother killing his father.

"Mr. Frye told us the same thing, but he didn't mean it literally," Andrews explained. "He blames his mama for driving his daddy to an early grave. He said that she never stopped nagging him and never stopped telling him how much she'd sacrificed for the men in her life. Mr. Frye told us that he and his daddy heard this every day of their lives. He went on and on about how his mama was a bitter, sullen woman who was never happy. Not for one day."

Nora's curiosity about the bearded man deepened. "I guess that's why he cut her out of his life. Because he blamed his mother for the loss of his father."

Andrews shrugged in a way that suggested he wasn't going to share any more information.

"I wonder if Mr. Frye went to Virtual Genie because he suspects his mother's book collection is worth something," Nora mused aloud. "Virtual Genie is having an appraisal fair this week. If an embittered son learns that a former neighbor is getting the only thing of value his mother owned, he might contest the will."

A cloud passed over Andrews's face. "I guess it wouldn't hurt to mention the fair to the sheriff. Thanks."

The sound of the sleigh bells made Nora glance at her watch in alarm. It was after ten and she'd yet to brew a pot of coffee. A pair of women in their midthirties who were so similar looking that they had to be related entered Miracle Books. Nora smiled at them in greeting.

Already turning toward the back of the store, she tossed out a final remark to Deputy Andrews. "If you need someone to take a closer look at Amanda's books, you know where to find me."

Andrews nodded, tipped his hat at the visitors, and left the bookshop.

Nora hustled to the ticket agent's office and set a pot of regular coffee to brew. She also retrieved the bakery box of pastries Abilene had left for her by the back door and arranged them under the protective glass domes of a pair of vintage cake plates. As she was completing her other opening tasks, such as switching on reading lamps and fluffing pillows, she heard a woman crying.

This wasn't an unusual sound in a town called Miracle Springs—a place people traveled to from all over the globe in search of healing. People suffered from many kinds of injuries, but Nora found that some pain was simply too deep for the minerals or the heat of the warm water to reach. This pain was deeper than bone. It lived in the depths of the soul. The pain was a dark seed that sprouted in the dead of night. It was fed by too many drinks. Or bumping into a former lover. Or losing a job. Or by being worn down by life's hardships.

Nora listened as the woman cried, and felt compelled to respond. She didn't always feel this way, but today, with Amanda haunting her thoughts, she did.

Carrying a tray with cups of hot tea and apple book pockets to where the sisters were sitting in a corner by the Illness and Grief section, Nora put down the tray. "I don't mean to intrude, but I find a hot drink and a little sugar improves even the crappiest situation."

Taking a beverage napkin from the tray, she offered it to the sister with the red-rimmed eyes and the tear tracks on her cheeks.

The woman accepted and managed a wobbly smile of gratitude.

"Has it helped at all?" Nora asked gently, keeping her gaze on the woman. "Being in Miracle Springs?"

The woman moved her shoulders in the ghost of a shrug that Nora took to mean that she hadn't gotten all that she'd wanted from her visit.

Nora waved her hand at the books surrounding their chairs. Books on illness, addiction, grief, and divorce. "There's rarely a direct path to healing," she said. "It's just as winding and confusing as the rest of life."

This elicited a bigger smile from the woman. "I wish my therapist had told me that from the get-go. She made me believe that all I had to do was put forth the effort and I'd feel better.

But I don't feel better. I'm as miserable as I was yesterday. And the day before that."

"Maybe I can help." Nora explained how she used bibliotherapy with certain customers.

The woman, whose name was Irene, was clearly dubious. Despite her misgivings, she told Nora how she'd been dumped by her partner of eleven years.

"He didn't leave me for another woman," Irene said. "That would have hurt, but in a weird way, it would have made our breakup easier. How things ended is almost worse than another person coming between us. Max just fell out of love with me. That's what he claims, at least. He woke up one morning, looked at me over the rim of his coffee cup, and decided that he couldn't spend another day with someone he didn't love. That was it. *I* was perfectly content, so this was a serious punch in the gut. I loved him. I *still* love him. I don't know why things changed!"

Irene began to cry again. Her sister, who introduced herself as Iris, pressed the teacup into Irene's hand and begged her to drink.

"Max has moved on," Iris continued on her sister's behalf. "He lives in a different area of the city and is dating again. I keep telling my sister that he's not a bad guy. He didn't mean for this to happen and had enough integrity to be honest with her. And for the record, I think he's pretty unhappy. His smiling pics on Facebook mean nothing. He's just as lost and lonely as my sister. He's just lost in wine bars with a different woman every weekend."

Irene seemed to shrink following this remark.

"You're going to be okay," Nora told Irene. "There's something missing in Max, not you. He ended your relationship so he could go out and search for it. Unfortunately, he took part of you with him when he left. Don't be ashamed of your pain. You feel it because you loved him. But you need to heal that hole in your heart enough to move forward with your own life. I think I can help you do that. Will you give my method a shot? You'll have to read a handful of books."

"Yes," Irene whispered.

Leaving the sisters to their tea and pastries, Nora moved among the bookshelves, collecting titles. She made a stack of books at the checkout counter. When the sisters were ready, she totaled and bagged a graphic novel called *Heart in a Box*, Greg Behrendt's *It's Called a Breakup Because It's Broken*, *Bridget Jones's Diary*, Nora Ephron's *Heartburn*, and *Porn for Women* by Cambridge Women's Pornography Cooperative.

Irene raised her brows at this last title. Nora caught the look and grinned. "It's not what you think. The images are PG-rated. There's a photo of a hot guy vacuuming, for example. In fact, there are several photos of hot guys cleaning."

Iris craned her neck to catch a glimpse of the cover. "Do you have another copy?"

While Nora fetched the last copy and made a note to order a replacement, Iris selected a shelf enhancer for her sister as a gift. She had Nora ring up a vintage picture frame made of sterling silver and tortoiseshell. Immediately after paying for it, she presented the frame to Irene.

"I want you to keep this empty until you read all those books," Iris said. "When you're done, we'll go out and celebrate. And take a picture to put in here."

The sisters embraced, thanked Nora, and left.

Their visit had started Nora's day on a positive note. Irene had allowed Nora to minister to her, which made Nora feel useful and fulfilled. And Nora believed that Irene would recover from her heartbreak. She was lucky to have a loving and supportive friend in her sister.

As Nora scanned the books on her shelves, she thought about the friends she'd known throughout her life. These people had come and gone. She couldn't always count on them, but she could count on books. Books didn't desert her, move away, or break her trust. They'd always been her lifeline. Whenever life threatened to drag her under, the sheer power of the written word could pull her out of the roughest seas. Was there ever such a worthy or reliable friend as a book?

The sleigh bells banged against the front door again. After calling out a greeting to her latest customer, Nora went into the ticket agent's office to pour herself a cup of coffee.

And then, deciding that she'd earned a treat, Nora slid an apple book-pocket on a plate and sat down to savor every bite.

"I've never lived alone," Abilene told Nora over supper that night.

"All women should learn to live independently," Nora said matter-of-factly. "You can take care of yourself. You're smart, creative, and a very accomplished cook. Are you scared of being on your own?"

Abilene poked at her fried catfish, but didn't answer.

"If you don't want to be found, then you don't have to be," Nora went on. "Completing a lease application won't shine a spotlight on you. Your references will be strictly local. Hester, June, and me. You don't need a phone and you can have your bills sent to a post office box." She waited. When Abilene didn't speak, Nora touched her hand. "Is something going to show up on a background check? You can tell me without going into detail. It's okay if you've made a mistake. I made a terrible mistake, and I'll regret it as long as I live."

This, at least, got Abilene to look at her.

"We're not saints." Nora went on. "We're not angels. We're just people. We screw up. The best we can do afterward is ask for forgiveness, learn from what happened, and try to move on."

Abilene released a long, slow exhalation. "I hit a nurse. I did it so I could get out of the hospital. I hit her harder than I should have. With a metal tray." She put her palm down on the lease agreement. "What I did was wrong. But I can't apologize. I can't make it right. If I do, *he'll* find me. He'll find me and take me home."

She pushed back her chair and jumped up so abruptly that she knocked over her empty water glass. She scooped up the glass and carried it to the sink. She stood there, motionless, her body tensing, as if expecting a blow.

"I can't go back there. I should leave tomorrow." Abilene directed her voice downward into the sink. She spoke quickly. Her words sounded like running water.

Nora got to her feet and said, "No."

Shocked, Abilene turned to face her. Nora beckoned her outside. Leaning over the deck railing, she pointed down the steep slope toward the railroad tracks.

"Every day, a train pulls in to the Miracle Springs station. Every day, a new crowd of hopefuls spills onto the platform. The people of this crowd hope and pray that the water, the yoga, the massages, the therapy, the kale smoothies, or the fresh mountain air will heal them. It may be the beauty of this place that restores the soul. It may be its tranquility. I don't know. But many of those people leave Miracle Springs feeling restored. Despite the peace strangers have found here, a local woman drowned in a pond on her property. A woman who'd lived here for many years. The theory is that she committed suicide—that she took a bunch of painkillers and left a note."

Abilene blanched, but Nora ignored her reaction and went on.

"Do you want to end up floating in a backyard pond? Because even in this haven, a woman grew so lonely that she didn't want to live anymore. What do you think will happen to you if you strike out on your own?" Nora asked. "Yes, you could run tomorrow. Or you could stay here with a group of women who'll stand by you."

Hugging herself, Abilene watched the haphazard flight of a lightning bug until it disappeared behind a copse of trees.

"What would I have to do?" she whispered. "To be able to stay?"

"You'll have to be brave," said Nora. "Brave enough to share your story."

"Share my secrets, you mean."

Nora gazed up at the stars. "Your story. Your secrets. Aren't they one and the same?"

Chapter 5

*There are perhaps no days of our childhood we lived
so fully as those we spent with a favorite book.*
—Marcel Proust

Abilene typically left for the bakery before Nora was even out
of bed.

When Nora woke the next morning, she wasn't sure if Abilene had left for work. Or just left.

When she showed up at Miracle Books with a fresh batch of
book pockets and an expression of resolve, Nora was surprised
by how happy she was to see her.

That evening, while Nora set the table for supper, Abilene
announced that she'd be moving into the apartment over Virtual Genie the following day.

Nora was stunned. "What about the lease application? And
is there a security deposit?"

"I don't need to fill out any paperwork, and Mr. Kingsley
didn't asked for a deposit. He and I came to an understanding,"
Abilene said. She was heating baked beans in a saucepan and refused to meet Nora's gaze.

Nora put her hands on her hips and stared at Abilene. "*An
understanding?* That sounds like a line from a Victorian novel—
one of those novels featuring a penniless girl who offers her body
in exchange for a favor from the aristocratic gentleman."

Abilene's cheeks flushed and she backed away from the stove. She turned a pair of angry, glittering eyes on Nora. "It's not like that at all! *I'm* not like that!"

She ran out of the tiny house and into the August evening.

Two minutes later, the oven timer beeped and Nora opened the door to find two perfectly cooked pork chops. She left the hot tray on the cooktop and went outside to call Abilene.

The moment she stepped onto the deck, she sensed an emptiness. There were night noises. The insects sawed and small animals rustled in the undergrowth in the woods bordering the train tracks. But there was a lack of human presence.

Abilene was gone.

Nora called her name anyway. Twice. When no one responded, she went back inside and waited at the table.

After an hour passed, she wrapped up the pork chops and beans, put them in the fridge, and ate a bowl of cereal for supper. She sat on the sofa in her cozy little living room and tried to read. But the words wouldn't stick. They slipped out of Nora's head and by the time she gave up on the book, night had fallen around Caboose Cottage.

Downtown Miracle Springs would be hopping, Nora knew. The streetlamps would be aglow, eateries would be serving patrons, and music would fill side streets and alleyways. She could almost hear the instrumental melodies from the vegan restaurant, the bluegrass from Pink Lady Grill, and the classic rock from the bar on the edge of town.

Abilene wouldn't go to any of these places, so Nora waited up for her. She turned on a television show that failed to capture her attention and drifted off in the middle of it. When she woke hours later, an infomercial for a skincare line was playing.

Nora looked at her watch. It was after midnight.

Grabbing her phone and a flashlight, she left her house and started walking.

She had no destination in mind, but hoped inspiration would

strike as she headed into town. Without thinking about it, she stopped to look at the window of Miracle Books when something furry rubbed against her calf, making her jump in surprise.

The furry thing was a cat. Offended by her cry, it issued an angry meow before bounding down the sidewalk to rejoin what could only be described as a herd of cats. In the center of the herd, gently scooting cats out of her way with the toe of her sneaker, was June.

June's face was concealed by a black hoodie and baseball hat. Her café au lait skin, which looked more like espresso in the darkness, seemed to meld with the night shadows. Despite this, Nora knew the hooded figure was June. She'd heard about the nocturnal cat parade phenomenon. Estella had told her how June had become somewhat of a legend in Miracle Springs. June and her feline followers. Nora hadn't truly believed Estella's story until now.

"Nora?" June called out. "Is that you?"

"Yes," Nora replied as quietly as she could. She watched the horde of approaching felines and was slightly discomfited by all the glowing yellow eyes. They were like fairy lights—the kind that lured a person into a bog and left them there to die.

The two friends met in the middle of the street and June took off her hat. "I didn't think you were a member of the Miracle Springs Insomniacs Club."

"I haven't slept through the night since I was in my twenties, but that's not why I'm here with you and your cats."

June shooed away a large striped tomcat. "I never signed up for this pied-piper crap. I've done everything I can to avoid smelling like catnip potpourri, but it doesn't matter. These damn cats haven't gotten a crumb of food from me, but they act like it's only a matter of time before I turn into the lady who lived in the house before me. I keep telling them that I refuse to feed them roast chickens every Sunday, but they don't listen."

Six or seven cats sat at June's feet and gazed up at her with looks of unadulterated adoration. The rest of the felines, too restless to stop moving, began to disperse. They disappeared under bushes and behind trashcans as if they'd never been there.

June told the rest to beat it, but they just sat there and purred. "Why are you out here?" she asked Nora.

"I'm looking for Abilene."

Nora explained what had happened that evening.

"She probably crashed at Hester's place," June said. "Swing by the bakery tomorrow and Abilene will be there. I wouldn't worry too much about it."

Nora had her doubts. "What if she's not at Hester's?"

"Then she and her secret are moving on and there isn't a damned thing we can do about it." June's tone was grim. "I hope she didn't make that choice, because you and I both know that her secret will weigh her down. It'll sink her. And without people like us to pull her out of the water, that girl is going to drown."

When Hester finally responded to Nora's repeated thumping on the bakery's back door the next morning, the first thing she did was assure her that Abilene was all right.

"She's not working for me today. She borrowed some supplies and went off to clean her apartment. She won't be back today." A timer beeped from somewhere in the kitchen and Hester beckoned Nora to follow her inside the Gingerbread House.

Nora watched Hester remove a pair of oversized muffin trays from the oven. The scent of warm blueberries and cinnamon crumble wafted into the air.

"How do you know she won't be back?"

"She said she'll be working for Mr. Kingsley every day as part of their lease agreement. After she cleans the apartment and moves in, which should take two minutes considering she has one garbage bag's worth of possessions, she'll start work at Virtual Genie." Hester glanced at the muffin tray. "I'm glad she found a place, but I hope she comes back here tomorrow. I like having her around."

Hester dropped one of the hot blueberry muffins into a bag and handed it to Nora. She told her to come back in an hour to collect the day's book pockets and then turned to slide another batch of muffins into the oven.

Instead of riding home, Nora pedaled to Water Street.

Jedediah Craig's Chevy Blazer was parked in front of a dove-gray cottage. The front windows were cracked and Nora could hear music playing from inside the house. She hesitated on the sidewalk, wondering how Jed would react to her dropping by.

Jed had never invited her to his place. In fact, he'd made it clear that his home was in no shape to receive visitors, as his rooms were still crowded with unpacked boxes. He'd recently moved to Miracle Springs from somewhere on the coast and claimed that he worked too much to bother organizing his living space.

What am I doing here? Suddenly deciding that this was a mistake, Nora began to turn around.

Jed's front door opened and he stepped onto the porch, coffee cup in hand, and looked right at her. He smiled warmly, leaned against his porch post, and called, "Are you stalking me?"

"I was just riding by, getting my daily dose of vitamin D, when I got this powerful feeling that someone in the vicinity had just finished brewing coffee. Was that you?" Nora gestured down the sidewalk. "Or should I keep going?"

"It depends what you have inside that white bag," Jed said. "Is that from the Gingerbread House?"

Nora picked up the bag and gave it a little shake. "In these parts, we like to barter. I have a fresh-from-the-oven blueberry streusel muffin to offer. What do you have?"

"Coffee. And anything else your heart desires," Jed said with a playful smile.

Nora parked her bike alongside Jed's truck. "If people see my bike here, they're going to talk."

Jed pretended to be dismayed. "Mabel Pickett is sure to notice. I believe she has me lined up as husband number four."

Nora laughed. Mrs. Pickett was in her eighties and, according to her book-buying history, was more interested in crocheting, historical fiction, and investing in the stock market than acquiring another husband.

"Tell me when you need to leave for work. I don't want to make you late," she said as she entered Jed's home.

Jed led her straight to the kitchen and pulled out a chair at a table overlooking the backyard. Nora surveyed the unadorned room while Jed poured coffee.

"My mugs aren't as interesting as yours," he said, joining Nora at the table.

"For every mug that ended up on the pegboard in Miracle Books, I rejected hundreds of others." Nora picked up the plain white mug Jed had given her. It felt too light in her hand. "A local potter sells his wares at the flea market. You should check him out. I bet you'd like his style."

Jed looked aggrieved. "I'm sure I would, but my budget is pretty tight these days."

Detecting she'd hit on a sensitive subject, Nora asked after Jed's dog. His Rhodesian ridgeback was still at the coast, living with his mother, and Nora knew that the dog suffered from anxiety.

"He's doing better since Mom made changes to his diet. I miss that big, slobbery bugger. Henry, that is. My mom doesn't slobber." Jed's expression turned wistful. "Me and Henry Higgins have been through so much together."

Strike two, Nora thought. Her conversational skills were totally lacking this morning.

Jed filled in the silence with a question of his own. "How's Abilene's hand?"

"It seems to be healing okay. You'll have to track her down at the bakery or at her new apartment above Virtual Genie when it's time to remove the sutures. She isn't staying with me anymore."

Jed cocked his head. "Is that a good thing? Her moving out?"

"You've been to Caboose Cottage. I don't have room for extra things, let alone an extra person." Nora sipped her coffee before adding, "So, yes, it's a good thing."

They chatted for a few more minutes, but the sidewalk flirtation had fizzled from the moment Nora had entered the house, so she told Jed that she needed to pick up her book pockets and get to the shop. He didn't entreat her to stay, and she was surprised by the strength of her disappointment.

As she made her way to the front door, Nora shot a quick glance into the living room. There were no stacks of boxes. There was no mess. There wasn't a stick of furniture to be seen. The entire space was empty.

Nora couldn't understand why Jed had lied to her, but she suspected it had something to do with the tight budget he'd mentioned. She knew that he regularly sent money home to his mother and felt that he owed his mother a great deal.

Judging by his living room and his ill-equipped kitchen, Jed was sending everything he could spare to his mom. Maybe even more than he could spare.

As Nora rode away from Jed's house, she thought of how he'd sat vigil by her hospital bed for countless hours. It hadn't been that long since the sensitive and sexy paramedic had made it clear that he had feelings for her.

Does he regret telling me how much he cares for me? Nora wondered. *And what do I feel? I haven't had the headspace to think about Jed since I found Abilene hiding in my bookstore.*

Stopping for a red light, Nora caught sight of her reflection in the window of a parked car. She saw a woman with full lips and a graceful jawline. Her hair was unbound and fell from under her baseball cap in a shiny, brown curtain. The cap's brim cast a shadow over the burn scar on her right cheek, and her pale blue cotton blouse hid the scars on her arm. For just a second, Nora saw her old self. The pre-burned self.

The abrupt blast of a car horn made her jump. She whipped her head around, fully prepared to glower at the impatient driver.

"I didn't mean to scare you!" shouted one of Nora's customers from behind the wheel of her vintage Mustang convertible. "I just wanted to tell you I'll be seeing you at the store later. Word has it that you're serving a sweet new treat just for us book people."

"Looking forward to it!" Nora smiled and waved as the woman carefully drove around her.

She studied her reflection at the next red light but this time, because she'd rounded the corner, the sun hit her at a different angle. Its morning beams highlighted the burn scars on her cheek and neck. Nora grinned at her image. She wouldn't trade this version of herself for her younger, unburned self. Even if a genie came along and granted her a single wish, she wouldn't choose to go back in time.

The subject of genies kept popping up for Nora. Yesterday, a frazzled-looking mother came into Miracle Books with three children in tow. Two of her kids, who appeared close in age, began to argue over which Bailey School Kids to read next. The girl wanted *Genies Don't Ride Bicycles*. The boy wanted *Aliens Don't Wear Braces*.

"You got to pick last time," the girl whined. "It's my turn."

The mother, who told the siblings to stop arguing or they'd get nothing, rummaged around in her purse until she'd located her phone. As soon as she showed something on the screen to her children, the boy fell into a defeated silence and the girl carried *Genies Don't Ride Bicycles* to the checkout counter.

"It's nice of you to share books with your sister," Nora later told the boy. He was waiting by the front door while the rest of his family examined the wares on the bookmark spinner. "I thought you might like to try this." She proffered a copy of Jon Scieszka's *Knight of the Kitchen Table*. "It's part of a series called The Time Warp Trio. There are a bunch of gross scenes that I think are hilarious."

Accepting the book, the boy gazed at the cover with interest. "I don't have any money, but I can tell my mom about it."

"Oh, you can have this one for free," Nora said. "It's a used copy and I probably paid a quarter for it. If you tell me your favorite part the next time you come in, that's worth twenty-five cents to me. Deal?"

The boy agreed and ran over to his family to show off his good fortune. Nora hid in the stacks until they left because she didn't want the boy's mother to feel like she was being treated like a charity case and return the book. Luckily for the boy, she didn't search too hard for Nora, and all of her children departed with smiles on their faces.

The memory of this scene elevated Nora's sour mood, but not by much. Between her lack of sleep, her concern for Abilene, and the unsettling visit to Jed's house, she felt like calling it a day. And it was barely noon.

The genie theme came up again when Nora was reading the paper during her lunch break. Several customers were wandering throughout the store, but after calling out a friendly greeting from the ticket agent's booth, Nora let them browse undisturbed.

The paper's front page was riddled with the usual doom and gloom. International unrest, political upheaval at home, a nosedive for the stock market, and a teaser for a juicy celebrity scandal. Nora skimmed the headlines and moved on. In the middle of the paper, her attention was caught by an ad for Virtual Genie's appraisal fair. It was taking place right now.

Nora stared at the brass lamp in the ad and realized that she very much wanted to see what this fair was all about. Specifically, she wanted to know what role Abilene was playing in the event.

Over the past few days, foot traffic in Miracle Books had been slow between five and six, which was when many of the locals shopped for, or began preparing, their supper. As for the tourists, five o'clock meant happy hour at the lodge. Nora could see a brief but profitable rush after six o'clock because many tourists came downtown to dine or shop after a round of cocktails.

Since she hadn't had a customer since quarter to five, Nora locked the cash register, propped a note on the checkout counter, and left the shop.

Crossing through the park, she noticed that every parking spot in the vicinity had been taken. When Nora drew closer to Virtual Genie, she saw why.

A line of people stretched from their front door to the hardware store, which was two blocks away. Each person was carrying a collectible in their arms, which they shifted around or briefly rested on the ground until the line moved again.

The people waiting for their appraisal appeared tired and anxious, but those exiting Virtual Genie looked totally transformed. Their faces were radiant with hope and they walked with a renewed vigor.

Nora wondered exactly what promises Griffin Kingsley had made to these people.

She headed to the front of the line, politely responding to the friendly greetings of her fellow townsfolk. As she walked, she took note of the treasures in people's arms. She saw a pewter teapot, a guitar, a Shirley Temple doll, an antique coffee grinder, a toy train set loaded into a Red Ryder wagon, a Tiffany-style lamp, and a wedding-ring quilt. Her experience in purchasing vintage items for the bookstore had taught her to develop an eye for such things, and she guessed that one-third of the items she'd seen were worth a few hundred dollars at most.

And that's before *the genie takes his commission*, she thought.

When she reached the front of the line, she told a man with a wheeled suitcase that she hadn't come to participate in the appraisal fair. He nodded in acceptance and opened the door for her.

Inside, Nora was immediately enveloped by an aura of peace. She guessed it was a combination of the cool air, the lux décor, and the soothing string music, but there was more to it than that. There was a sense of deep calm in this space—of being able to truly take one's time. That was a rare gift these days, and Nora could see that the ability to simply sit and relax for a moment was greatly cherished by all those who entered.

Nora recognized most of the people contentedly settled on chairs or divans. They were all sipping iced chai tea or selecting pieces of Belgian chocolate from the gold box in the center of a silver tray.

Both Virtual Genie partners were busy. Tamara was seated behind her desk, showing a client an image of a Lladró figurine on her computer. Griffin, who stood next to his client, was giving instructions on filling out the consignor agreement.

Nora strode up to Griffin, but waited for him to glance her way before speaking. "I'm sorry to interrupt," Nora said. "I'm just looking for Abilene."

Griffin didn't seem the least bit bothered by the intrusion. "Our clock and watch expert is in the other room. Do you remember the way, Ms. Pennington?"

"I do, thank you. And I won't be long," she added, though she wasn't sure why.

After flashing her a courteous smile, Griffin returned his attention to his client. "Just leave everything in our hands, Mr. Bailey. That's why we're here. I look forward to seeing you again on Saturday."

Mr. Bailey shook hands with Griffin, leaving his silver candlesticks behind. Nora could see that Virtual Genie was acquiring a bevy of new clients. Judging by the number of items cluttering the tables and shelves in the back room, the event had been a smashing success.

Abilene was seated at one of the worktables. She was peering at a watch face through a jeweler's loupe and didn't hear Nora's approach.

"Hi," Nora said softly.

Abilene dropped the loupe and hurried to cover the watch with her hand. It was such a furtive gesture that Nora's curiosity, which was already aroused, now deepened into something else. Something akin to suspicion.

Indicating a nearby folding chair, Nora asked, "May I?"

Abilene responded with an indifferent shrug, but Nora knew indifference could be a version of anger. She pointed at the watch.

"Will it bring a good price?"

Removing her hand from the timepiece, Abilene's demeanor suddenly changed. Her eyes became animated and her face shone. "Yes. Between six and eight hundred dollars. This is an Omega ladies' watch," she explained. "It's fourteen karat gold with diamonds around the face. The diamonds have excellent color and clarity and the watch is in very good condition— other than a little oxidation to the face and minor scratching on the clasp."

"Wow. You're incredible," Nora said and meant it. "You can cook like a trained chef, you're extremely well-read, *and* you can appraise jewelry."

Abilene blushed. "I'm better with clocks, but I can handle jewelry evaluations too."

"I don't know how you learned these things, but I'm guessing you had to. They were all necessary."

The light vanished from Abilene's face. The spark fled from her eyes and she stared down at the watch with a mournful expression. Regretting her words, Nora attempted to repair the damage. "It looks like you enjoy this work. Just like you enjoy working at the bakery. So are you glad you decided to stay?"

Abilene picked up a pen and made a note on a legal pad. "Why are you here?"

"Because I've been worried about you," Nora said softly. Though she wanted to put a hand on Abilene's arm, the young woman was sending out a clear vibe that physical contact wouldn't be welcomed. "I'd also like to apologize for my behavior. I didn't mean to chase you off last night. I was a jerk and I'm sorry."

Abilene gave Nora a small smile. "It's okay. And you don't need to worry about me anymore." She turned back to her notepad. "I'm fine."

Knowing that the words were meant as a dismissal, Nora made to leave.

"I'd like to be your friend," she said, pausing at the doorway. "I'm out of practice, so I'll probably make more mistakes like the one I made last night. But if you'd like a cup of coffee tomorrow morning or supper later tonight, I could cook for you for a change. Just show up when you're ready. You're always welcome."

Abilene murmured her thanks and Nora returned to Virtual Genie's main room. When she saw Jedediah Craig talking with Tamara, she nearly tripped over the corner of a Persian rug. How had she missed him outside?

There was no use in pretending that she hadn't seen him, so she walked right up to him and raised her hands in surrender.

"I guess my stalker status is now official."

Though Jed smiled, his eyes remained guarded. "A stalker who travels with magical treats in her bike basket." He turned his smile on Tamara. "Nora brought me the world's best blueberry muffin this morning. If you haven't been to the Gingerbread House yet, you need to go. Like, tomorrow. As soon as it opens. After meeting with half the town today, you'll need at least two muffins. Maybe three."

"I think I met more than half the town," Tamara said with a hint of boastfulness. "But no one has a toy as wonderful as yours."

Nora glanced down at the object on Tamara's desk. "That doesn't look like one of the antique soldiers you played with when you were a kid."

"No, but like those soldiers, my mom gave me this mechanical bank."

Jed sounded remorseful. Again, Nora wondered what kind of money issues he was dealing with.

"I've seen banks like this before, but they've always been way beyond my price point," Nora said. "Does it work?"

"To perfection," Tamara answered for Jed. "Would you like to see it in action?"

Intrigued, Nora nodded.

Tamara put a coin in the top of a cast-iron tree trunk and depressed a metal lever. An iron buffalo reared his head, butting the bottom of the young boy clinging to the tree trunk. As the buffalo's head moved, a startled raccoon popped out of the top of the tree, coming face-to-face with an equally startled boy.

It was a charming old toy.

"Do you have to part with it?" Nora whispered to Jed.

"Mr. Craig might not mind when he sees what one of these recently sold for online," Tamara was quick to say. "And yours is in better condition, Mr. Craig."

Sensing Jed needed privacy to conclude his business, Nora wished him luck and headed outside.

Back at Miracle Books, Nora tidied up and then plunked down on her stool behind the checkout counter. She'd just opened to her place in her current read, *The Sun Is Also a Star*, when a group of women poured into the shop.

Seeing Nora, a lady with purple hair exclaimed, "We're on a girls' trip! Five *girls* in their sixties who've left our husbands at home. We're eating too much, drinking too much, and spending too much money, so stand back!"

And spend they did. The purple-haired woman bought a pile of books and shelf enhancers, including a black lacquer desk set, a lion doorstop, and a brass hand mirror with a floral handle.

"Could you ship these to me, hon?" she asked Nora and put a fifty-dollar bill on the counter. "This should cover the postage and the hassle."

After closing the shop, Nora decided to hunt for a shipping box. She was on her way to the storeroom when she remembered that Abilene had cut out pieces from Nora's stock of cardboard boxes to make her window display. As for the rest, Abilene had taken them to the recycling dumpster the following day.

Because the dumpster had been emptied recently, the flattened boxes were scattered across the bottom. Nora stared down at them and scowled. She was going to have to climb inside and retrieve the right box.

"I should have charged more for shipping," she grumbled and jumped down into the dumpster.

After choosing a box and tossing it onto the ground, Nora was on the verge of heaving herself back over the dumpster's side when she spied a piece of cloth peeking out from beneath a flattened box. Curious, Nora tugged at the cloth. It got snagged on a box corner, but after Nora shook it roughly, it came free.

When she held it up to the light cast by the streetlamp, she recognized it at once. It was the housedress Abilene had been wearing the night she'd hidden in Miracle Books.

"Why are you in this dumpster?" Nora asked the dress.

The longer she stared at it, the more unsettled she became. There was something off about Abilene putting the dress in the recycling bin—something beyond the fact that it wasn't made of cardboard or plastic. Had Abilene deliberately dropped the dress into the wrong dumpster?

A breeze swept down into the metal receptacle. It filled the skirt of the dirty floral print dress and Nora was reminded of the enormous mushrooms that sprung up in the woods after a rainstorm.

The space where Nora's pinkie finger used to be tingled. Ignoring the sensation, she tried to concentrate on another tingle. A mental one. Nora felt the dress was familiar, like she'd seen it somewhere before.

"How could it be familiar? No one I know has ever worn a dress like this." Her voice bounced off the metal walls. When it came back to her, it sounded foreign. Strange.

Far off in the distance, Nora heard the lonely whistle of a train.

She looked back at the dress as if it were a living thing. "I think I know where you came from."

Chapter 6

Beware the man of one book.

—Latin Proverb

When the ringing of Nora's phone jarred her awake, she was overcome by a feeling of déjà vu. It wasn't a good feeling. It was a feeling of dread. Nora realized that she was reliving the post-dawn phone call of a few weeks ago. The one where June had called to tell Nora that Estella had been taken into custody for murder.

This time, the edges of Nora's window shade were filled with a buttery light as she fumbled for the phone. The ringing stopped before her eyes had a chance to focus on the caller's name. Rolling onto her side, she turned on the lamp and squinted at the phone screen.

Jed had left her a text message.

I'VE HAD A LOT ON MY MIND LATELY, BUT ALL I WANT TO THINK ABOUT IS YOU. I HAVE A QUESTION TO ASK, BUT YOU HAVE TO GO OUT TO YOUR DECK TO HEAR IT.

Nora's heart gave a leap. Was Jed outside right now?

Shoving her covers aside, Nora ducked into the bathroom to

make herself presentable. She quickly brushed her hair and teeth before pulling a thin sweatshirt over her BOOK LOVERS NEVER GO TO BED ALONE tank top.

Jed wasn't waiting on the deck, but he'd obviously been there. And what he'd left behind took Nora's breath away.

She noticed the flowers first. Chains of wildflowers looped around the deck railing and a carpet of multicolored petals had been strewn over the floorboards. A white cloth covered Nora's small café table and Jed had set a place for one. The setting included flatware, a glass of orange juice, and a dinner plate covered by an overturned bowl. When Nora picked up the bowl, her breakfast was revealed.

She gasped in delight.

Jed had made an edible bouquet using fresh fruit, cheese, and bread. He'd fashioned pieces of pineapple, mango, and cantaloupe into a dahlia. Strawberry and watermelon slices formed a red carnation with kiwi leaves. A hard-boiled egg daisy was positioned below a piece of toast shaped like a butterfly. The golden-brown toast wings were sprinkled with cinnamon and a light drizzle of honey.

Glancing around, Nora wondered if Jed was close by.

If he is, I should show him how much I love his surprise, she thought and did something she'd never done before: She used her phone to photograph the artistic meal. The presentation was so lovely that Nora hated to eat it, but the fruit looked fresh and juicy and she was hungry. Besides, Jed wouldn't want her to preserve the meal in glass. He'd want her to enjoy it.

She opened the napkin curled around her flatware and went to spread it over her lap. That's when she saw a message written in its paper folds.

Will you be my date for the Fruits of Labor Festival?

Nora let out a tinkling laugh. The sound was like little bubbles bursting in the morning air.

The napkin reminded her of the notes kids passed in grade school. They were always so direct. Do you like me? Will you be my boyfriend? Will you sit with me on the bus? If Jed's note had included a box to check, Nora would have happily checked the *yes* box. Instead, she sent a text to Jed saying he would learn her answer soon. She didn't want to accept over the phone. That wasn't creative enough. She wanted to give him a magical reply worthy of his breakfast gesture.

"Magical and fruity," she joked aloud. Smiling at her own corniness, she speared a strawberry slice with her fork.

No one had done anything like this for Nora before. No one had ever put forth this much effort to impress her. To make her heart leap with delight.

Because she was focused on Jed's surprise, Nora momentarily forgot about the dress she'd found in the recycling dumpster. Even as she plated the daily delivery of book pockets, her thoughts were on Jed. Abilene had been pushed to the back of her mind.

Nora carried her cheerfulness into work and her secretive smile and sparkling eyes proved to be good for business. Though she'd always been an excellent listener, Nora had never been adept at small talk. Today, however, she was unusually chatty. She asked after people's health, family members, and pets. She encouraged patrons to linger over cups of coffee and pastries. When they eventually left the shop, each and every customer carried a Miracle Books shopping bag loaded with books.

Nora had just finished ringing up a sale when Amanda Frye's son approached the checkout counter. He was even more physically imposing up close. When Nora had seen him speaking with Griffin Kingsley in front of Virtual Genie, she didn't fully appreciate his size. Again, she thought of Popeye's Bluto. The main difference between the two men was their clothing. Bluto wore a shirt and pants while Frye's massive torso was stuffed into a suit jacket. The jacket looked expensive, but it didn't fit Frye's wide chest or thick arms well. If he twisted too far in one direction, Nora was sure the jacket would rip apart with the violence of Bruce Banner turning into the Incredible Hulk.

Frye's face was marked by dissatisfaction. Deep ruts traversed his forehead and even deeper frown lines bracketed his mouth. His lack of crow's-feet proved how seldom he smiled, but the grooves between his brows were evidence of consistent anger. Nora didn't know if she could reach past so much anger and disappointment, but she'd try.

She greeted him with a friendly smile. "Good morning."

Frye, who was just about to set a plastic bag on the counter, abruptly froze. The bag dangled in the air and he gazed at Nora's face with the unapologetic stare of a small child. Children could be excused for such behavior, as their curiosity was free of judgment. Frye was no child though, and there was no excuse for his openmouthed gawking or the way his lips curled in disgust.

"Why not take a picture? It'll last longer." Nora turned, giving him a clearer view of her scars.

"What the hell happened to you, lady?" Frye asked. He had yet to blink.

Nora stared back at him. "I used to be a circus performer. A sword swallower, actually. For my finale, I'd always set my blades on fire. The crowd would get *so* quiet, waiting for me to swallow the fiery metal." Her mouth curved into a maniacal grin. "Anyway, during my last performance, I was a bit heavy-handed with the fuel. When I flicked my Bic, *whoosh*! My circus career and chance of marrying well both went up in flames."

Frye's mouth widened another half inch. Nora stared at his maw and thought of how much she'd like to plug that round O with a golf ball when another customer entered the shop, causing the sleigh bells to bang against the door.

The noise roused Frye from his stupor. He shut his mouth and managed to place the bag on the counter. Eying Nora with suspicion, he asked, "Is that story true?"

Ignoring the question, Nora pointed at the bag. "Is there something you'd like to show me, or should we keep talking about my face?"

Thankfully, Frye took the hint. "Can you tell me what this book is worth? Just a ballpark. I don't need anything in writing."

In other words, you don't want to pay for a professional appraisal, Nora thought. But she was dying to look at whatever was inside the bag, so Nora told Amanda's son that she'd do her best to help.

Frye glanced at the couple who'd just entered the shop. "Do you have a more private place?"

Nora wasn't going to make things easy for him. Not after he'd been so rude. Besides, she wanted to watch his expression when she mentioned Virtual Genie.

Primly folding her arms across her chest, she said, "Perhaps you'd be better off at Virtual Genie. They're in the appraisal business. I'm just a bookseller."

Frye's face darkened. "And hand over twenty percent of the profits after agreeing to a laundry list of bogus fees? How many people actually read the fine print in that swindler's contract? Well, *this guy* does. I haven't climbed the corporate ladder by skimming over the fine print. *That's* where the real money is made or lost."

Jed and his mechanical bank appeared in Nora's mind. She thought of all the people who'd stood in line, anxiously waiting to learn if their treasures might ease their financial burdens. If only a little. These people were Nora's neighbors, and all they were looking for was a chance to keep the wolf from the door. Were Griffin and Tamara helping, or were they as bad as the scammers who'd tricked the townsfolk in the first place? The people from the bank and the real estate development firm who'd swindled the locals into buying into a dream that was really nothing but a nightmare.

The Secret, Book, and Scone Society would have to find out

for themselves, but in the meantime, Nora told Frye to follow her to the ticket agent's office.

As they walked, Nora introduced herself.

"I'm Kenneth," Frye replied. He glanced at Nora's scarred hand and quickly stuffed his own into the front pocket of his jeans.

Nora found it interesting that he'd omitted his surname. Miracle Springs was a small town, and Kenneth's mother was a reader, so he must realize that Nora and Amanda knew each other. Was his evasiveness deliberate?

The answer became clear as soon as he removed the book from the bag.

Nora immediately recognized it as one of Amanda's. Nora remembered exactly where it had been shelved, and she could also picture the other books in the series.

"If this is yours, you have excellent reading taste," she said to Kenneth Frye. "There's a reason some books are called classics."

Kenneth didn't show the slightest hint of guilt over stealing a book his mother had bequeathed to someone else. He simply gazed down at the plastic-covered copy of J. R. R. Tolkien's *The Two Towers* with a dismissal. "I'm a businessman. I don't waste my time on books. I read the *Wall Street Journal*."

Nora could understand why Amanda had left her collection to someone other than her son. Perhaps her former neighbor was a fellow book lover. Perhaps Amanda knew that her son would sell her collection within seconds of getting his massive hands on it.

"May I?" Nora gestured at the book.

"Knock yourself out," said Kenneth.

Nora examined the dust jacket first. It was in very fine condition. Though she'd seen and held many versions of this title, she found this edition a bit unsettling because of the staring red eye ringed by red runes on the front. Floating in the center of this stark white background was the infamous gold ring, the source of Middle-earth's trouble.

Nora carefully opened the book and searched for the copyright information. She noted that this was a first edition in its eleventh impression, printed in 1965. Next, she looked for an inscription. Finding none, she examined the page edges and other parts of the book for condition issues. Other than a few very minor marks, it was in what book collectors would deem fine condition.

"To give you an idea of its value, I need to check prices on my laptop. Would you like a coffee while you wait?"

Kenneth cast a dubious glance at her espresso machine. "No offense, but I'm from Chicago. We have really good coffee shops. Is yours strong? Because this guy needs strong."

After carefully sliding Amanda's book back inside the bag, Nora moved to her pegboard to select a mug for Kenneth's drink. She was tempted to remind "this guy" that he was from Miracle Springs and that people in these parts were perfectly capable of making a cup of coffee, but she refrained. "If you'd like to pay for an extra shot, I'd be glad to give you one."

Kenneth wrestled his wallet free from the back pocket of his pants and slapped down a few bills on the ledge where Nora placed completed drink orders. Without consulting the chalkboard menu, he said, "I'll take a latte with whole milk. Two shots. Not too foamy. I don't like foam on my mustache."

The foam reference reminded Nora of Kenneth's mother, a woman who'd been found floating in her foamy green pond. Nora thought of how lovingly Amanda had wrapped her books in plastic and displayed them in her living room. She probably gazed at them every night. Her books were her shield against loneliness. They were her companions. Her family.

It gave Nora a small measure of satisfaction to serve Kenneth his latte in a mustard-colored mug featuring a colorful chicken and the text, I DON'T GIVE A CLUCK. She suspected he wouldn't even notice the design, and she was right. He was too fixated on what was inside his mug to pay attention to the outside.

"Not bad," he said after a tentative sip.

Nora took his money and turned to her laptop. After calling up the website of a renowned international bookseller, she typed the Tolkien title and the publication year in the site's search box. She found two books that were a near-perfect match to Amanda's book.

Frye tried to look over her shoulder, but Nora closed the laptop before he could see anything. "Your copy of *The Two Towers* is worth around five hundred dollars. However, if you had the other books in the trilogy, *The Fellowship of the Ring* and *The Return of the King*, the set would be worth even more." Watching Kenneth carefully, she asked, "Do you own the other two books?"

"I might," Kenneth said cagily. "If I did, where would I sell them? Who'd get me the most money?"

Nora shook her head. "I couldn't say. As you can see, I deal in new, used, and a few collectible books. My most expensive books cost much less than the one you carried in, so I'm not the person to advise you on selling your, um, collection? Or it is just a handful of titles?"

Instead of answering her questions, Kenneth put his empty mug on the coffee table and gave Nora a wave. "I've got it from here. Thanks for your help. It's nice to meet a decent person in this crap town."

Kenneth Frye scooped up his book and barreled into another customer on his way out.

As soon as he was gone, Nora sent a group text to the members of the Secret, Book, and Scone Society. It said, **Emergency meeting tonight. We need to stop a book thief.**

Nora could hear her friends before she saw them. They entered through the back door and appeared by the circle of chairs. They were all carrying covered dishes and had bags dangling from the crooks of their elbows.

"We should eat while this is still hot," June said, setting a casserole dish down on a pot holder in the center of the coffee table.

Nora sniffed the air. "What's that amazing smell?"

June whipped the lid off her casserole dish. "Get ready for your daily serving of dairy, ladies. And then some. This is my famous mac and cheese recipe. I'll share two of the three secret ingredients. Muenster cheese and eggs."

"Eggs? In mac and cheese?" Estella sounded alarmed.

"Go on. Put a big scoop of cheesy heaven on your plate." June handed Estella a serving spoon. "You'll thank me after one bite."

Nora's contribution to the meal, a salad of mixed greens tossed with homemade vinaigrette dressing, was already on the table. Estella placed a platter of tomatoes roasted with basil and thyme next to the salad bowl.

"How beautiful," Hester said. "Did you grow the tomatoes?"

Estella snorted and spread her fingers in the air. "Do these hands look like they dig in dirt? No, the truth is that I had a client give me fresh produce as a tip today. I'd rather have cash, but I'm glad to still have her as a client. I think I jumped the gun when I hired part-time help after the bank and builder's scandal. I'm starting to realize that lots of my new bookings were one-hit wonders—local reporters or curiosity seekers. When our town stopped being a major news story, my extra clients vanished. If that isn't bad enough, my list of regular clients is shrinking fast."

"The town needs a bona fide real estate developer to buy The Meadows," June said. "If those contracts to the electricians and plumbers and lumber houses were honored, so many folks could get back on their feet."

Hester laid a paper napkin on her lap. "Like Roy Macklemore, for example. He used to drop by the bakery every morning, but I haven't seen him for a few weeks. He stopped by yesterday to do maintenance on my air-conditioning unit before heading over to Virtual Genie to get his grandmother's cameo pin appraised. He looked totally heartbroken about it too. It's his only heirloom, but he's going to be a dad in November. He needs money for when the baby comes."

Nora served herself a scoop of mac and cheese, unintentionally leaving cheese strings hanging like tightropes from the edge of her plate to the edge of the casserole dish. June severed the cheese strings with her fork.

"I'm glad you mentioned Virtual Genie. We need to look into that place." Nora repeated what Kenneth Frye had said about the laundry list of fees.

Estella stopped eating. "Kenneth Frye? As in, Amanda Frye's son?" At Nora's nod, she grew more excited. "He's from Chicago, right? Word on the street is that he's *very* successful. What's he like?"

"He's a jackass," Nora said. "A rude, oversized, bearded jackass."

"I like a man with a beard," Estella murmured.

Nora gave Estella a sharp look. "You don't want to use your sex-kitten powers on this guy. He has no class."

This extinguished the glint in Estella's eyes. "I should have guessed by the way he treated his mother."

"I don't know what happened between mother and son, but Kenneth clearly held her responsible for his father's death." Nora repeated what she'd heard Kenneth say to Griffin Kingsley about his mother killing his father. She also told them what Deputy Andrews had shared about the Frye family's dynamics.

June pulled a face. "Sounds like Little Boy Frye passed judgment as only an aging bachelor can. What the hell would he know about the give-and-take a marriage requires? About the sacrifices? He wouldn't. He just picked a villain and a victim and decided to see black and white when we live in a world with a hundred shades of gray."

"Not fifty?" Estella asked, nudging June with the toe of her shoe.

Smiling, June flicked Estella with her napkin. "Thanks, hon. I was getting all riled up, but why should I let Kenneth Frye ruin my amazing mac and cheese?"

"You might want to hold on to that riled feeling," Nora said. "It seems that Kenneth intends to continue mistreating his mother, even after her death, by stealing the books she left to someone else."

Nora snuck in another bite of food before telling her friends about *The Two Towers*.

When she was done, Hester performed a time-out gesture. "Don't you think we're condemning a total stranger without proof? Seriously, we know nothing about him, but we're already assuming that he's a terrible son and that he broke into his mother's house to swipe a book and learn its value." She spread her hands. "Does that sound like the behavior of a successful businessman? Why would he risk his career for a book?"

Estella glanced at Nora. "That's a good point."

"Selling those books might not have anything to do with money," June said. "It might be about the anger Kenneth feels toward his mama—anger that he didn't have the chance to express to her before she died."

Hester got up, walked into the ticket agent's booth, and returned to the seating area with a gorgeous tart. Pear slices peeked through a thin, flaky crust, and Nora, who thought she might be too full for dessert, knew she'd find room for a slice.

"Brown-butter-roasted pear tart in a shortbread crust." Hester began cutting the dessert into even slices. "Let's say you're right, June. How can we prove the book is missing in the first place?"

"Easy," Nora said, eagerly accepting a plate from Hester. "We go to Amanda's house. We can combine it with another round of Secret Kindness bag deliveries. It sounds like Roy Macklemore could use a lift."

"I'm game," said June. "But don't you rush my dessert. I plan to savor every bite. Hester, Hester, Hester. Your baking is good for my soul, but it is *not* good for my hips."

Estella waved off her comment. "What are you worried about? You'll walk that off with your cats four or five hours from now." A mischievous gleam surfaced in her eyes. "It's too bad that you can't find a way to harness that kitty energy. You'd be a rich woman."

"Who says my aim in life is to be rich?" June retorted. "You know what I'd like? I'd like my socks to cover the world's cold, tired feet. That's what I'd like. I love to take care of folks. It's what I was born to do."

Nora opened five shopping bags and lined them up on the floor. "Okay, then. Let's decide where we're going tonight. We'll get to the world later, June. For now, we have plenty of tired feet in our own backyard."

The Secret, Book, and Scone Society members were much calmer during their second round of deliveries than they'd been for the first. Few people were quick to respond to a ringing doorbell after dark, which gave Hester plenty of time to return to June's car without having to run. June learned that she didn't have to peel away so violently that she scored the asphalt with tire marks. She crept forward slowly, keeping her headlights off until the targeted house was out of sight.

After the five Secret Kindness bags were delivered without incident, June drove to Amanda's house.

Unlike the other homes on the street, her house sat in a pool of darkness. There wasn't even a porch light or electric bug zapper to keep the night at bay.

June hesitated at the top of the gravel driveway.

"Are you sure about this, Nora?" she asked in a quiet voice.

"I'll just be a minute." Nora tried not to stare at the surrounding woods. For some reason, the trees felt closer. And taller. They seemed to loom over the open spaces of Amanda's yard, reclaiming it whenever there were no humans to witness their movement. "No one else has to get out of the car."

June made the turn and eased down the driveway, the gravel crunching beneath her tires. She came to a stop at an angle in front of the house, her headlights illuminating the sagging stoop and collection of massive cobwebs.

"You'd better duck when you go up those stairs," Estella whispered. Nora didn't even have to look at her to know that she was shrinking into her seat in revulsion. Estella was not a fan of spiders.

Nora grabbed her flashlight and exited the car, shutting the passenger door behind her. She listened for the neighbor's dogs and said a silent prayer of thanks when no frenzied barks pierced the quiet of the night.

Wary of the cobwebs, Nora pressed her flashlight beam against the glass of the front window. It took a few seconds for her eyes to adjust to the various objects in the dark room, but she was able to train her light on the books lined up along the bottom row of crates. What she saw confirmed her theory. *The Fellowship of the Ring* and *The Return of the King* were leaning, shoulder-to-shoulder, when they should have been standing up straight. They couldn't remain upright, because the book that had filled the gap between them was missing. It had been removed by Kenneth Frye.

Nora passed her light over the rest of the books, searching for a sign that Frye had pilfered other volumes. She couldn't be sure, because the crate closest to the hall was too cloaked in shadow, but she thought she saw a second pair of leaning books.

"Bastard," she grumbled and returned to the car.

Hester didn't need audible confirmation from Nora to know what she'd seen. Nora's anger spread through the car like a thundercloud.

"Are you going to report him?" she asked.

"I'll call Andrews in the morning," Nora said. "I don't want anything to happen to those books. Amanda left them to someone else—probably a fellow reader—and I owe it to her to see that her books reach that person."

June glanced over at her. "There's no guarantee you could have helped Amanda, even if she'd opened up to you. I know you feel partially responsible, but I don't think she was ever going to confide in you. You said it yourself. She came to Miracle Books in search of escape. Why would she want to drag her hard, ugly reality into her beautiful, warm, cozy escape place?"

"I would have liked to try to combine the two," Nora said, smiling at her friend. "The unique and magical nature of books is their ability to grant us temporary escape from our reality while also providing ways to cope with that reality when we're forced to return to it."

"I think book people do that too," Estella said. "Isn't that the real reason people go to book groups? Sure, they want to talk about the book. But they're looking for so much more than that. They want to be a part of a community of like-minded people—of people who will accept them as they are. Book people will do that for each other."

June grunted as a way of acknowledging Estella before directing a warning finger at Nora. "The cops need to bust Amanda's boy now, before he jets back to Chicago with a suitcase stuffed with books. Once the Fruits of Labor Festival starts, the lawmen and law ladies will be too busy breaking up fistfights and tossing people in the drunk tank to give you the time of day."

"Don't worry. I'll call as soon as I've had my first cup of coffee," Nora promised.

Estella tapped June's shoulder. "Can you back out of this driveway now? I feel like a million eyes are watching us."

"That's because every spider has eight," June said, putting the car in reverse. She knew Estella had an aversion to bugs and enjoyed teasing her about them.

Estella glared at June's headrest. "At times, I really do not like you, June Dixon."

After Nora said good night to her friends, she popped back inside Miracle Books to clean up the ticket agent's booth. While she tidied, she tried to think about how she'd reply to Jed's question. She needed to send her response in the morning or he might come to the conclusion that she didn't want to go to the festival with him.

And though she wasn't sure if pursuing a relationship with Jedediah Craig was a good idea, she was going to do it anyway. Whenever she ran into him or heard his voice, common sense and logic fled and other parts of her took over. Parts that wanted to laugh too loud. Parts that wanted to get lost in a long kiss in the rain. Parts that remembered the pleasure of a suppertime conversation. Of movie nights and weekend hikes.

She wanted all of these things. She wanted new experiences too. And she wanted to have them with Jed.

As she tried to come up with a creative and memorable way to say yes to Jed, she spied Estella's tomato platter next to the espresso machine. Nora decided to wash it and leave it under the checkout register until Estella could pick it up.

Nora turned on the tap water and picked up the platter. The white porcelain was marked by a pinkish stain. The same stain June had seen on Amanda's counter.

Instantly, Nora was transported back to that day. She could see every detail of Amanda's kitchen as if she weren't standing at her sink in Miracle Books, but at Amanda's sink. She also remembered the view through the window. She saw the garden, the overgrown grass, and the housedresses hanging from the clothesline.

At the time, Nora hadn't known if they were nightgowns or housedresses, but she now knew that they were housedresses. She was sure of this fact because she'd seen another dress just like those hanging from Amanda Frye's clothesline. Only this dress had been hanging off the malnourished frame of a mysterious young woman.

Nora stared at the steam rising from the sink, She felt hypnotized. Unable to move. She stood in a state of total confusion as a name echoed over and over inside her head.

Abilene. Abilene. Abilene.

Chapter 7

*A book is the only place in which you can examine a
fragile thought without breaking it.*
——Edward P. Morgan

Nora had aspired to a more creative response to Jed's beautiful breakfast, but with her mind divided between Amanda's
books and Abilene's dress, she had to make do. So she rode to
the grocery store at six thirty, filled her bike basket with fresh
fruit, and pedaled to Jed's house.

Tiptoeing up to his front porch with the bags of fruit in
hand, Nora fashioned the letter Y out of bananas and the letter
E from limes. She made a curvy S using oranges. Nora had deliberately chosen those three fruits because she could use them
to create end-of-summer mocktails. Having recently fallen off
the wagon after years of sobriety, Nora distrusted her relationship with alcohol. For now, she decided it was best not to have
it at all.

After finishing her produce-themed reply without being
spotted by Jed or his neighbors, she headed to the Gingerbread
House.

"You're too early," Hester protested when she answered
Nora's knock on the back door. "The book pockets are still in
the oven."

"That's okay," Nora said. "Can I come in and wait?"

Hester studied Nora for a moment before stepping aside. "Sure. Have you had coffee?"

"No, but I'd kill for a cup," Nora said. "I was at the grocery store at half past six this morning."

Hester raised a brow. "If you skipped coffee, it must have been an emergency."

"It was for a good cause, which I'll tell you about in a minute. But first—"

"Coffee," said Hester with a smile.

Hester served Nora a mug covered with pastel macaron designs. Nora poured half-and-half into her coffee and watched the white curlicues blend into the dark brown liquid.

Abilene, who'd been arranging cinnamon twists in the display cases in the front room, came into the kitchen and froze when she saw Nora.

Nora raised her cup in greeting. "Good morning."

"Good morning," Abilene replied and began kneading a ball of dough resting on the flour-dusted worktable.

In the warm light of the bakery's kitchen, Abilene looked markedly different from the pale, skinny, and frightened girl who'd cowered in the stacks of Miracle Books not too long ago. In a week's time, her sickly look had vanished. Her cheeks were rosier. Her hair was shinier. And though she was still painfully thin, she wasn't gaunt. After seven days in Miracle Springs, she was blooming like a late summer flower.

If Nora was startled by how quickly Abilene had adapted to her new life, she was even more shocked by how the rest of the women in the Secret, Book, and Scone Society had accepted her into the fold.

Hester reemerged from the walk-in carrying a pound of butter and a carton of eggs. Catching sight of Nora's expression, she asked, "So tell me what's going on. Is this about last night?"

When Nora didn't answer right away, Hester put the food on her butcher block and retied her cherry-print apron. She then repeatedly smoothed the apron, despite its lack of wrinkles. This behavior was a sign of anxiety.

Though Nora disliked being the source of that anxiety, she had to proceed. "Can Abilene take a quick break? I need to ask her something."

Hester was clearly confused but gave her assent with a nod.

As for Abilene, she kept her eyes on the dough. "We can talk while I work," she said.

"No, we can't." Nora's tone was gentle but firm. "I want us to look at each other while we talk."

A timer began beeping and Hester moved swiftly to the oven to turn it off. Grabbing an oven mitt, she pulled out a tray of book pockets and moved the tray to a cooling rack.

Like the air escaping from the oven, tension was slowly filling the room with heat. It was a prickly, uncomfortable kind of heat, and spots the color of ripe raspberries appeared on Hester's cheeks.

Abilene wiped her flour-covered hands on a dish towel and shot a glance at the exit. For a moment, it looked like she might make a run for it. But she pulled her gaze back to Nora and perched on the stool across from her.

"What I have to ask you is very simple," Nora said, staring fixedly at Abilene. "Did you know Amanda Frye?"

Abilene's expression was completely inscrutable. It was as if she'd gone to another place inside her mind.

"No," she said.

Nora decided to rephrase her question. "Okay. Have you met Amanda Frye? Have you ever been to her house?"

"I don't know why you're asking me these things."

Hester opened her mouth to protest, but Nora raised a hand to stop her. She sensed deceit in Abilene. Deceit by omission. She could feel its presence. It was like an animal. A low, slinking rodent. A creature that lived in the shadows, surviving off scraps.

"Answer the question, please." Nora's eyes never left Abilene's. Keeping her tone conversational, she went on. "It's just one question. Have you ever been to Amanda Frye's house?"

Abilene turned to Hester. "I don't understand—"

"Don't do that," Nora interrupted. She was losing patience. "Don't try to deflect. Don't you realize that your unwillingness to answer this question makes me wonder what else you're hiding? Considering Amanda died recently, it's alarming that you can't give a straight answer when asked if you've ever been to her house."

Folding her arms across her chest and glaring like a defiant child, Abilene spat out the words, "I've never been to her house. May I go back to work now?"

Hester couldn't contain herself any longer. "Okay, Nora, she gave you an answer. Are you going to tell me what this is about? If the work is going to come to a dead stop in my bakery, I have a right to know why."

Looking at her friend, Nora was suddenly overcome with doubt. What if Abilene was telling the truth? What if the dress she'd hidden in the dumpster hadn't belonged to Amanda Frye?

But Nora's instincts were screaming that Abilene was putting on an act. She'd probably become accustomed to acting, to putting on different faces as a means of self-preservation. But Nora suspected there was more to it than that.

"I wish I could explain everything, but I can't." she said to Hester. "Only Abilene can tell us where she got the dress she was wearing the night we found her in Miracle Books."

The defiance in Abilene's eyes winked out. In its stead, Nora saw fear. Quick as a lightning flash, Abilene looked away, hiding the fear. But it was too late. Nora had seen it.

So had Hester. She rushed to put an arm around Abilene. "It's okay," she whispered. "You're safe. It's okay."

Abilene didn't respond. She stared down at her lap and pulled herself inward as if trying to make herself smaller.

The weighted silence in the kitchen was abruptly disturbed by the beeping of the second oven's timer.

"That's the rest of your book pockets." Hester cast an accusatory glance at Nora. "I'll let them cool for a minute before boxing them. After that, you should probably go."

Having been given her marching orders, Nora waited outside until Hester handed over the box of warm pastries. "I have no idea what's gotten into you, Nora, or why you're doing this to Abilene. We're supposed to be helping her, not harassing her. We've stood where she's standing, remember? In that isolated, scary, horrible place? The cliff's edge?

Nora was about to share her theory about the dress when a loud crash came from inside the kitchen.

"Sorry!" Abilene called out. And then, "Nothing's broken!"

Hester was already turning toward her protégé, so Nora let her go.

As soon as she entered the bookstore, she dropped the pastries in the ticket agent's booth and called Deputy Andrews.

"I've had two visitors asking about Amanda Frye's books in two days," she said when Andrews got on the line. "Don't you think that's a little odd? And yes, you were one of the two."

There was a pause as Andrews processed what Nora had said. "Who was the second?"

"Kenneth Frye. He wanted me to appraise a book he'd stolen from his mother's house."

"Stolen? That's—"

Nora didn't let him finish. "Would you take me to Amanda's? I can prove the theft. I still have a good hour before I have to open the shop."

"Why do I feel like I'm being manipulated, Ms. Pennington?" Andrews asked without ire.

Nora shoved Abilene's dress into her handbag and said, "You're not. I promise that I'm trying to help. I don't even need to handle Amanda's books. If you open to the copyright page, I can compare two of the books in her home with the book Mr. Frye showed me. That way, I can confirm that the book he had is from Amanda's collection."

Andrews made a contemplative noise. "All right, Ms. Pennington. I have my own reasons for revisiting the premises, so you might as well tag along. I'll be in front of Miracle Books in five minutes."

Andrews was a man of his word. Nora had time to arrange the book pockets on a platter, cover them in plastic wrap, and print out a description of *The Two Towers* Kenneth Frye had shown her, by the time the young deputy pulled up to the curb.

"Every able-bodied law enforcement officer in the county is gearing up for this weekend's festival except for me. I'm going to look at books." Deputy Andrews smiled at Nora as she slipped into the passenger seat.

"Trust me. You didn't draw the short stick. Time spent in the company of books is time well spent. Besides, I think Amanda's collection is worth a closer look." Nora told him the estimated worth of her *Fellowship of the Ring* trilogy.

Andrews whistled. "Didn't she have, like, a hundred books in her collection?"

"Whatever the number, they don't belong to her son."

"He's contesting the will," Andrews said with a frown. "He let us know that he hired a lawyer and told us to stay out of his mother's house. But the house doesn't belong to him and the sheriff hasn't closed Mrs. Frye's case, which is why we're going in."

Andrews drove through town. As the shopping and business district fell away and the sun-dappled woods, rolling hills, and verdant fields of the countryside spread out all around, Nora thought of how Tolkien's hobbits would have loved this part of North Carolina. His dwarves and elves would have felt at home too. Most of this region was still pristine land—land unblemished by interstates, strip malls, and cookie-cutter housing developments. It was this untainted beauty that drew the hikers, artists, tourists, and those searching for healing, to Miracle Springs.

Recalling another series in Amanda Frye's collection, Nora reflected on Philip Pullman's characters. They wouldn't care for Miracle Springs and would likely try to escape a town supporting a local government and multiple places of worship, just as Lyra Silvertongue had escaped in *The Golden Compass*.

From the recesses of her memory, Nora recalled Pullman's description of Lyra. She was thin with dirty-blond hair and pale blue eyes.

Like Abilene.

Nora hugged her handbag and glanced at Andrews. "Is the sheriff viewing Amanda's death as a suicide? I know it was written up in the paper as an accidental death, but I assume tests have been run since that piece was printed. I saw the bottle of painkillers in Amanda's kitchen. Did Amanda swallow those pills before wandering outside to drown in that horrible pond? Because that seems pretty far-fetched to me."

Andrews set his jaw. "I can't discuss that with you, Ms. Pennington."

Since Nora wanted to maintain a positive relationship with the young deputy, she didn't press him.

At Amanda's house, Nora stood to the side as Andrews unlocked the door. She felt a twinge of doubt. The feeling wasn't unlike the doubt she'd experienced interrogating Abilene at the bakery. What if Kenneth had already returned *The Two Towers*? If he had, Nora would lose her credibility with Andrews. She'd also lose her chance to learn more about the woman they knew as Abilene Tyler.

Andrews held the door open for Nora. She entered the living room and spotted the space between the Tolkien books. She sighed in relief and Andrews stared at her in confusion.

"I was doubting myself," she explained. "It's a little messed up to be relieved when you confirm another person's crime, but the gap between books proves that I'm not crazy."

Taking the printout out of her bag, she handed it to Andrews before squatting next to the other Tolkien novels.

"Please don't touch anything," he warned.

Pointing at the other two books in the series, she said, "If you could compare the copyright information on the printout to what's on the copyright pages of each of these volumes, I think we'll be able to conclude that Kenneth has the missing book from this series in his possession."

Andrews gestured toward the driveway. "I'll just grab my kit from the car."

Nora stood up. "Um, is it okay if I use the bathroom? I had a really big cup of coffee this morning . . ."

"Sure, sure," Andrews said and hurried outside

Nora hustled back to Amanda's bedroom. She used a tissue to open the pocket door of Amanda's closet and reached for a dress, triggering a burst of fresh scent from a sachet with a frayed purple ribbon. Nora, who'd never been fond of the smell of lavender, wrinkled her nose and retreated from the closet, dress in hand. She carried it over to the window to examine the label.

After replacing the dress exactly where she'd found it, Nora looked at three more dresses. Amanda wore a size fourteen and had a preference for cotton blends. She also liked pastel floral patterns. All her housedresses were made by the same brand, a company called Casual Her.

Nora heard Andrews moving around in the living room, so she slid the closet door shut and tiptoed into the bathroom. She ran the sink water for several seconds while pulling out the dress she'd stuffed into her handbag. Like the others in Amanda's closet, it was a size fourteen and had been made by Casual Her.

Nora stared at the dress. Though she had no idea what to make of it, she felt suddenly repelled by it. She didn't want to touch it.

She stood in Amanda's bathroom, furious with Abilene for lying to her, and gazed at the dead woman's angel soap dish until she'd calmed down enough to rejoin Andrews.

When she reentered the living room, he showed her the copyright page of *The Return of the King*. "Is this from the same series as the book Mr. Frye asked you to appraise?"

After inspecting the page, Nora said, "Yes."

Andrews tried to suppress his excitement, but failed. Though he kept his voice under control, his eyes were shining. "Is anything else missing?"

Nora scanned the other end of the shelves, recalling the dark space she thought she'd seen the night before. And there it was—a shadowy void following Catherine Cookson's *The Mallen Girl*. She pointed it out to Andrews. "There might be another book missing. If I remember this series correctly, it's called *The Mallen Litter*."

Andrews photographed the section of bookshelf using his phone. "Mr. Frye didn't mention this book?"

"No. Only the Tolkien," Nora said. "And he wasn't about to share details about other books in this collection. He clammed up the second he realized that I wasn't going to tell him exactly how to sell 'his' books online, or how to find a cheap but reputable dealer to do it for him."

Andrews looked pensive as he scanned the shelves. "Is the other book Mr. Frye may have taken worth as much as the Tolkien? This *Mallen Litter* book?"

"Not to a collector," Nora said. "Ms. Cookson is a wonderful writer and has millions of fans, but even a first edition Cookson novel in its original dust jacket isn't as rare as a first edition Tolkien in its original dust jacket."

"Then why would Mr. Frye steal it?" Andrews asked.

Nora shrugged. "Because he doesn't know his Cookson from his Tolkien?"

"Is that the literary equivalent of his ass from his elbow?"

"That would be deeply insulting to both Ms. Cookson and Mr. Tolkien," Nora replied.

"Well, Frye *is* an ass. He wasted no time making enemies in town," Andrews said, putting his professional demeanor aside for the moment. "Mr. Kingsley came into the station to see if he could file a complaint about him. Apparently, Mr. Frye's been telling anyone who'll listen that Mr. Kingsley is a crook. When one of our new deputies asked Mr. Frye for details, he was so rude to her that she stormed out of the room. He used words that no lady should ever have to hear. She told us that she was worried she'd shoot the guy if she spent another second with him."

Nora could easily imagine Kenneth Frye using extremely coarse language. "What happened next?"

"Mr. Frye left, but the sheriff wasn't going to stand for anyone speaking to one of his deputies like that, so he drove out to Mr. Frye's hotel to have a few words with him. Ginny Pugh runs the front desk and is dating Deputy Fuentes, and she told Fuentes that Mr. Frye didn't enjoy his visit from Sheriff McCabe. Their conversation took place in Mr. Frye's hotel room, but Frye yelled loud enough to shake a candy bar loose from the lobby vending machine."

Andrews removed his gloves and turned off the light in the living room. It was time to go.

"The sheriff never raised his voice." He continued the story as he locked the front door. "That's not his way. And I know he'll be interested to hear that Mr. Frye's been helping himself to his mother's books without waiting for an official ruling on her will. Thanks for letting me know about this, Ms. Pennington."

"Just doing my civic duty, Deputy." Nora smiled at Andrews before getting in his car. She could feel the pull of the pond from across the yard and didn't want to look in its direction.

On the ride back to town, Andrews and Nora were lost in their own thoughts. Nora fixed her gaze out of the window and wondered what, if anything, her discovery about Amanda's dress proved. The questions she had about Abilene and about Amanda's death had only increased. The major difference was that the two disparate subjects now seemed to be connected.

Nora had muted her phone during her time with Deputy Andrews, so she hadn't known that Jed had texted her twice in the last fifteen minutes. She waited until she was inside Miracle Books to check her phone. Jed's messages made her grin, but neither his witty humor nor his flirtatious tone could distract her from her obsessive thoughts. She had to share what she'd learned with the only people she trusted, because this secret was too convoluted for her to handle on her own.

"I'm sorry, ladies. I could *not* meet in the bookstore again," Estella said as she slid into a booth at the Pink Lady Grill. "There are times when a woman wants to be seen. Especially when she's just done her hair and nails. I mean, look at me. I can't waste this artistry on just you three."

Nora did as she was told and looked. Estella was beautifully coiffed, as always. Tonight, however, her red hair was even glossier, her nails were a bright shade of apple red, and her makeup was so skillfully applied that she could pass for a woman a decade younger.

"Why are you so dolled up? Are you hanging out at the lodge this evening, in hopes of hooking up with a rich tourist?" June was clearly poking fun at Estella, but when Estella averted her gaze, June's smile turned into a frown. "Good Lord! Didn't you learn your lesson after your last conquest tried to choke the life out of you?"

"He tried, but he failed. I'm sure you remember. Anyway, I have *needs*," Estella said. "I need attention from men." She splayed her hands and examined her nails. "Okay, I don't *need* it, but I *like* it. What I don't like is you judging me." She turned to Nora. "I'm not in a Jack's-strawberry-milkshake kind of mood tonight. I want something sexy, like a martini. I love to pull the olives off the tip of the cocktail stirrer, nice and slow, when I know a man is watching. Drives them wild. You should try it with your cute deputy sometime, Hester."

Hester blushed and suddenly became very focused on her menu.

"Well, I'm having a milkshake," June declared. "You can have your olives and your men, Estella. And I'm not judging. I just worry about you." She glanced toward the kitchen. "Oh, here comes Jack."

Jack Nakamura was a Japanese-American transplant from Alabama who cooked traditional Southern comfort food as if his family had been making biscuits, fried chicken, grits, and ham steak for generations. The Pink Lady's name and color scheme were a tribute to Jack's late mother. After breast cancer claimed her life, Jack became a passionate advocate for breast cancer prevention. Letters and photographs from women who'd battled breast cancer were displayed throughout the diner, and a percentage of Jack's profits were donated to area women in need of early-detection screenings.

That summer, Jack had added a memory garden to the diner's grounds. Though not large, it was a peaceful place where people could remember the women they'd loved and lost to cancer. Jack invited friends or family members to write the name of their loved one on a rock and add it to the river of stones he'd created in the center of the garden. He'd also placed a small bell that sang with every breath of air. Under the bell was a plaque inscribed with a Bashō haiku:

> *The temple bell stops—*
> *but the sound keeps coming*
> *out of the flowers.*

Jack was a kind, quiet man who often stopped by Miracle Books on his day off. His reading interests focused on health and wellness, cooking, gardening, and poetry.

Tonight, however, he seemed mostly interested in Estella.

"I'm going to be your server and your chef this evening," he informed them, his gaze lingering on Estella. "May I tell you about the specials?"

Estella flicked a wave of hair over her shoulder, exposing the pale, smooth skin of her neck. "We'd be delighted to hear *all* about them."

Jack described the soup-of-the-day and the catch-of-the-day in great detail. Estella moaned appreciatively during his recitation and then proceeded to order a Cobb salad. "I have to watch my figure," she explained in an apologetic tone to Jack.

"You're wonderful just as you are," Jack said before heading into the kitchen.

June pointed at the swinging doors. "That, my friends, is what every person should aspire to hear from their partner. It's the ultimate compliment."

Estella flicked her wrist. "He only said that because he doesn't know me." She shifted her gaze to Nora. "Are you ready to tell us why you called this auspicious meeting? Your texts were like a teaser to a juicy novel, but I have a feeling we're not here to talk about books."

Nora produced Amanda's housedress, which was folded inside a plastic baggie, and set it on the table. "Do you recognize this dress?"

"Of course we do," Hester snapped. "What is up with you and this witch hunt?"

"Hester." Nora kept her voice soft. "When you look at Abilene, you see a young woman in need of rescue. I get it. You were once a young woman like that. You were mistreated and misjudged. And no one came along to rescue you. You had to be your own heroine." Seeing the anger flare in Hester's eyes, Nora spoke even faster. "I need you to stop seeing yourself in Abilene. She isn't you. She's a stranger. And she might be dangerous."

June held out a finger. "Come on, now. Abilene and danger-ous aren't PB and J. They do *not* go together."

"Where is this coming from? Is this because she tossed that muumuu in the wrong dumpster?" Estella asked Nora. "Remind me to keep you away from my recycling. I don't always remember to rinse my milk cartons."

Nora was about to tell Estella to shut up when a waitress appeared with their drink orders.

She distributed the drinks and then cheerfully informed them that their food would be out shortly.

"I believe this dress belonged to Amanda Frye," Nora said after taking a sip of sparkling water to calm herself. She then went on to tell her friends how she and Andrews had visited Amanda's house.

When she finished her story, Hester pointed at the dress and shrugged. "How many women own this same brand? Abilene could have gotten that dress anywhere."

"Maybe," Nora conceded. "She was also wearing flip-flops the night we met. They were a size nine—way too big on her. I know the size because I climbed back into the recycling bin and found them in the same spot Abilene hid the dress." She paused to take another drink. "Guess who else wore a size nine?"

"Lord Almighty, please don't say Amanda Frye," June whispered.

Hester slapped the table, her face contorting with anger. "Stop it! For shit's sake, Nora, just stop! Who cares how Abilene got the dress or the shoes? Why can't you leave her alone? Can't you see that she needs kindness? Can't you see that she needs help?" Shaking her head, Hester looked at Nora with doleful eyes. "I thought that you were all about trying to heal people, but I guess I was wrong."

Estella, who had the misfortune of sitting next to Hester, put a hand on her shoulder. Hester swatted her hand away.

"Let me out!" she cried and gave Estella a fierce shove.

Hester had the powerful arms of a baker, and Estella had to jump out of the booth or risk being pushed out.

"Hester! Don't go running off!" June called out.

Ignoring her, Hester ran past a couple ambling toward the exit. Veering abruptly to avoid her, they barreled into Jack. Or, more specifically, into the tray balanced on Jack's shoulder.

The tray tilted and a trio of white platters crashed against the floor, fracturing into pieces. Food skittered across the polished tiles. A woman shrieked in surprise.

"What the hell was that?" Estella asked, staring at the mess.

"Our dinner," June grumbled.

Nora gazed out the window. "No. That was our friend, coming undone."

Chapter 8

The mysterious magnet is either there, buried some-
where deep behind the sternum, or it is not.
—Elizabeth Gilbert

"You two stay here," June said. "I'm going after her. I'll call you later if I can."

June picked her way over the broken china and exited the diner.

Nora watched her go. "Right now, all I want is a giant glass of wine, which is how I know I have an alcohol problem."

"That's not an alcohol problem. There are just times when strawberry milkshakes just don't cut it. This is one of those times," Estella said. "Do you realize that we now have two things to investigate? We need to learn the story behind Abilene's dress and we also need to find out if Virtual Genie is committing highway robbery. Half the town is hocking stuff with them, and though Kenneth Frye is a total jackass, even jackasses tell the truth once in a while."

"Jed took an antique bank to the Virtual Genie appraisal fair. I don't know if he committed to selling it, but I think he's having financial problems."

Estella wagged a finger. "Don't ask him about it. Nothing will kill passion quicker than money talk. Leave that alone for now. You two haven't even worked up a decent sweat yet, so you hardly need to compare bank account balances. I can't imagine anything that would make his noodle go limp faster than—"

"I get the picture," Nora interrupted. "I don't have anything to sell, which makes it hard to find out if Virtual Genie is doing things by the book. The pieces I buy for Miracle Books are wonderful, but they're not expensive. What about you?"

Estella shook her head. "I invest every penny back into my business. It's my greatest asset. Besides my looks. And we both know which will stand the test of time."

Their conversation was curtailed by the arrival of a waitress. After presenting each of them with a complimentary order of spicy chicken dumplings, she promised that their meals would be out shortly.

"I've never had these before." Estella gave the dumplings a wary look. "I don't normally go for spicy things. Outside the bedroom, that is."

Nora noticed the artistic sprinkle of sesame seeds and the garnish of scallion sprigs over the soy-ginger chili sauce before spearing a dumpling with her fork and popping it into her mouth. She loved spicy food.

"Delicious." She motioned for Estella to try hers.

A few minutes later, Jack delivered their entrées. His white chef's coat was a painter's palette of fresh stains, and he was clearly distressed by the empty places at their table. "I'm sorry about the delay. Did your friends leave?"

"It's not your fault," Estella said with a kind smile. "Hester acted like she was in the running of the bulls, which is why you're wearing our food. Red is a very nice shade for you, by the way."

"June went after Hester," Nora added, seeing the look of confusion on Jack's face. "They won't be back. We'll pay for their meals."

Jack wouldn't hear of it. Not only did he refuse payment, but he also surprised Nora and Estella by asking if he could have a word in private when they were finished eating.

The women readily agreed, and when Jack had seen to the rest of his customers, he signaled for Nora and Estella to follow him outside to the garden.

"You're both savvy businesswomen, so I thought you could advise me," Jack began. "I was thinking of selling an item through Virtual Genie, but I've heard rumors about them. I don't usually pay attention to rumors, but I'm going to donate the money from the sale of this item to a person who needs medical treatment. I want to get every dollar of this item's worth. No one on my staff has any experience with Virtual Genie. Have either of you?"

"Yes," Nora said. She shared her favorable impression of Griffin Kingsley as well as Kenneth Frye's conviction that the Virtual Genie contract was padded with unnecessary fees.

When she was done, Jack laced his hands together and gazed at the river of memorial stones.

After a moment of silent contemplation, he turned back to Nora and Estella. "I'm going to take my item to them. They should have a chance to prove themselves."

"But if Mr. Frye *is* correct, something should be done about it," Estella said with feeling. "We can't let anyone else take advantage of our neighbors. Which is why I'd like to come with you, Jack."

Jack's face shone like a lighthouse beacon. "You would?"

"Yes. Many of my clients are selling things through Virtual Genie. *Someone* should be looking out for them." Estella pulled up the calendar app on her phone. "I have a full day tomorrow, what with the festival and all, but could we find an hour to run over to Virtual Genie?"

Jack nodded. "Yes, yes. We could."

After the pair had settled on a time, Estella asked, "What are you selling?"

"A cloisonné box," Jack said. "It's old. From the Meiji period."

Seeing the blank looks on the women's faces, he elaborated. "The box was made by a Japanese artist named Kyoto in the second half of the nineteenth century. It's decorated with a phoenix and enameled peony flowers. A woman I never met sent it to me after my mother passed away. My mother's name was Peony."

"How lovely," said Estella. "The peony is my favorite flower."

Jack beamed at her. "Would you like to see the box? I have it under the register."

Estella said that she would, but Nora demurred. She wasn't quite ready to leave the peaceful garden, so she said goodnight to Estella and Jack and watched them reenter the diner.

Nora sat down on the bench facing the river of stones. A breeze pushed the clapper of the little brass bell and a chorus of clear, high notes floated into the air. As Nora watched the light fade over the garden and listened to the haunting call of the bell, she had a strong and sudden longing to be in another's company. And she knew just whose company she wanted.

She took out her phone and dialed Jed's number.

"Want to come over?" she asked without preamble.

"Yes," he answered with equal directness.

Nora left the lonely river to the dying light.

At home, she knew what would happen when Jed appeared. She felt electric with anticipation. It was much like the sensation of prickly heat she'd felt in Hester's kitchen when the tension had risen and swelled like bread dough, but this tension was different. Its hunger wasn't fed by suspicion or anger. It was fed by desire.

Nora moved around her house, throwing open windows, inviting the nighttime scents and sounds to gather inside. The only light she lit was a battery-powered lantern. She knew that if she stood in front of it, the light would shine through her thin sundress, outlining the curves of her body.

Because she'd left her front door ajar, Nora could hear the tread of Jed's work boots as he mounted the deck stairs. The moment he entered her house, Nora's skin erupted in goose-flesh and her heart began to pound like a drum.

When Jed saw her, he didn't smile or speak. He just stood on the threshold and stared. His gaze slowly traveled down the length of her body. His gaze lingered on every part of her. It was like a caress. A prelude to his touch.

Just when Nora didn't think she could wait a second longer, his eyes met hers. What she saw in his eyes was an acceptance of her silent invitation. Jed had understood that her phone call, her open windows, her lack of words, and her bare feet were inviting him to do one thing. She wanted him to touch her.

Without speaking, he closed the space between them, took her in her arms, and kissed her. His mouth was hungry. His hands were hungry. They slid over her shoulders and under the straps of her dress. His fingertips moved down her back, hurrying to find purchase on the curve of her hips. He used her hips as leverage to press the length of her body against his. She didn't resist. He tugged on her hair, forcing her neck to arch, and when he kissed her throat, she moaned and melted into him.

Jed's hands were strong and callused. The stubble covering his chin and cheeks was rough. She liked how he felt. All of him. This was exactly what she'd wanted. This feverish, fearless release.

She was unaware that her dress had pooled to the floor until Jed picked her up, wrapped her naked legs around his waist, and carried her to the bedroom.

Later, as they lay tangled together in her dark room, Nora spoke for the first time since Jed had walked into her house.

"Any chance you brought that fruit I left on your porch? I could make us a reenergizing smoothie," she joked.

He laughed. "I barely stopped for red lights. I was burning for you. I've been burning for you since the day we met." He suddenly cupped Nora's cheek in his palm. "Shitty analogy. I'm sorry."

"You can use fire metaphors with me. I can take it." She gave him an elbow to the ribs to restore the playful mood. "You've tested me out. I don't break."

"No, you don't. And I find your toughness very sexy." The smile had returned to his voice. "That, and many other parts of you. But I'd rather explain myself by showing instead of telling." Using his hands and his mouth, he demonstrated his appreciation of Nora's parts so thoroughly, that it was quite some time before either of them spoke again.

It was Jed who eventually whispered into the silence. "Does this mean that you're ready to tell me your story? When you were in the hospital, you asked if I wanted to hear it. I did then. I still do."

Nora, who'd been on the cusp of sleep, said, "I'm close to drifting off, which is your fault for wearing me out, so I'll give you the abbreviated version."

"I'll take whatever you want to give," Jed said in a soft voice. "I'll just close my eyes and listen."

Nora liked that he'd offered to close his eyes. The darkness and the feeling of Jed's warm body touching hers allowed the words to flow from the deep well in which she stored them. "I used to be a librarian. And I used to be married. I thought I had a good life until I discovered that my husband was having an affair. A serious affair. It was New Year's Eve when I learned about his double life. I also learned that his mistress was pregnant."

"Wow," Jed whispered.

"The discovery ripped me apart," Nora said. "People use

that expression without really knowing what it means, but *I* know what being ripped apart feels like. There was a tearing in my heart. A partial death. In one night, I no longer recognized my life. And before the night ended, I lost far more than my marriage. I lost my job, my house, and my friends. My reflection in the mirror would never be the same either. That was my fault, not my bastard husband's."

Nora paused before telling Jed the terrible truth about how she got her scars.

"When my husband didn't come home that New Year's Eve, I looked on his computer and found things that cut me so deeply that I felt like I'd been stabbed a thousand times," she eventually continued. "I wanted the intensity of the pain to stop, so I drank. And drank. When I'd had way too much, I drove to the other woman's house to confront my husband."

Nora stared upward where the moonlight streaming through the window had painted a glowing opal in the center of the dark ceiling. Jed sensed her hesitation and laid his hand on her arm. It was a comforting, reassuring touch, and it gave Nora the courage to finish her story.

"I screamed at the two of them, but I knew it was useless. I was no longer wanted. Blinded by fury and hurt, I got back in my car. My emotions made me crazy and I hit another car on the highway. The car caught fire and I had to pull a mother and her toddler out of the burning wreckage. The mom was okay, but the boy suffered some burns to his lower legs. He healed beautifully. The very young heal so beautifully . . ."

There was more Nora could say. She could explain how her guilt had burrowed deep into her bones, where it would always stay with her. She could tell Jed that the end result of that night was that she lost the will to live—that she spent weeks in the burn unit praying for death. But she didn't tell him these things.

She listened to Jed's rhythmic breathing and was glad the first part of their night hadn't included words. It was one thing for Hester, Estella, and June to accept Nora after hearing her secret, because they had secrets of their own. But Jed? Whatever dark thing he was hiding could hardly be comparable to hers.

She prepared herself for his withdrawal. He might not leave right now, but he'd surely want to escape her with the dawn.

Jed covered Nora's hand in a protective gesture. "I don't know the details of your marriage and I don't need to know them. Your idiot husband's loss is my gain. I also don't know what you looked like before. I don't need to know that either. To me, you're the most beautiful woman on this earth. And I'm not feeding you a line, Nora. I've told you before. I don't see your scars. I just see you. Do you know why?"

Nora felt his eyes on her in the dark. She moved closer to him. Their faces were an inch apart. Their exhalations mingled. He slid his arm around her waist and she slid hers around his. With their knees and the tips of their toes touching, they were like one body instead of two.

"Why?" she whispered.

"Because my mom's beautiful. And she's a burn victim," he said. "She'd smack me for saying *victim*, but there's a reason I chose that word. A victim is injured due to an accident, an event, or someone else's action. In my mom's case, that someone else was me. *I* caused the fire that burned her. It was an accident, but what does that matter? If there's another person in Miracle Springs that gets what it's like to have guilt chewing away at you, it's me. I've seen June and her cats walking in the middle of the night, because I don't sleep well either. One memory keeps me up. I caused a fire. I created a victim. Two, actually. Mom and Henry Higgins. That's why I asked you for books on canine anxiety when we first met. He can't sleep, and neither can I."

Nora moved her hand through Jed's hair and shushed him. "Tonight, you'll sleep. You're going to let these heavy thoughts float away like balloons. Let them go. See them drift into a clear, blue sky."

Jed released a weighted sigh. Nora continued to rub his head, slowing her passes through his hair each time. "The balloons are rising higher and higher," she whispered. "There are so many colors. Purple, red, green, yellow, orange, blue. In the sunlight, they glow like Christmas lights. They're like gumballs rising into space. They're getting smaller and smaller. There's no sound. It's completely silent. There's only sunlight. Brilliant sunlight and the big, wide, sky."

Jed was asleep before she finished speaking, and Nora hoped that he would wander in a lovely dream until morning. She didn't anticipate a restful night for herself. It had been years since she'd shared a bed with a man, and there was a huge difference between rolling around in the sheets with someone and sleeping through the night next to someone.

Nora was accustomed to flopping on her belly, stretching one leg over the edge of her bed, and curling an arm under her pillow. None of these actions were possible with Jed slumbering away in what was normally her side of the bed.

Still, it had been a long day. Nora's emotions had been through the wringer and her body had had quite a workout, so she managed to grab a few hours of sleep before the sensation of being cold pulled her toward consciousness. Searching for the edge of the top sheet, which she expected to find within reach, she encountered her naked hip. It took a second for her to remember why she wasn't wearing pajamas and that she wasn't alone.

Her skin was cool to the touch and the sheet didn't warm her fast enough, so she turned around and backed into Jed until their bodies resembled a set of quotation marks.

When she woke for the second time, Jed was gone and she was on her belly with her right foot and calf dangling off her side of the bed. The light in the room was bright. Too bright.

Nora lunged for the clock in a panic. She then grabbed a T-shirt and shorts from her hamper and hurriedly put them on.

Jed was in her kitchen. He was dressed and his hair was damp. He smiled at Nora.

"You showered?" she asked, her tone slightly accusatory.

"Guilty as charged," he said. "I made coffee too. Tell me how you like it and I'll fix you a cup. I won't expect you to be civil before coffee. No one should have to be."

This earned Jed a small smile. Nora said that she liked a teaspoon of raw sugar and a splash of half-and-half.

"I brewed this pot with an extra scoop of grounds," he said, handing her a mug. "In case you needed the extra get-up-and-go. *I* don't. I slept like the dead. I haven't slept like that in ages and I have you to thank for that bit of magic, as well as all the other magic tricks you showed me last night. After I thank you up close and personal, I'll leave you to get on with your day." He put his mug down, crossed the room, and kissed Nora softly on her coffee-laced lips. "Hm, there's nothing like the taste of coffee to start the day off on the right foot."

Nora, who felt self-conscious because she hadn't brushed her teeth or her hair and was wearing dirty clothes, retreated a step. "To be continued? At the festival tonight?"

Jed grinned. "I can't wait."

Nora watched him walk to the door. He opened it, paused, and turned back to face her. "You're beautiful. Every bit of you. Your scars, your messy hair, your painful past, your wrinkled T-shirt, your bare feet, your fiery eyes, your perfect mouth— all of you. You are *so* damn beautiful."

With a final wave, Jed left.

Nora stood in the kitchen, cradling her coffee mug. No one had ever spoken to her like that. No one had ever looked at her like that or touched her the way Jed had last night. It was unnerving, frightening, and exhilarating. She wanted to throw up. She wanted to break into song. She wanted to hide.

*   *   *

That afternoon, June poked her head around the corner of the mystery section shelves and said hello, causing Nora to startle.

"Who put the twinkle in your star?" June asked.

"What do you mean?" Nora fixed her gaze on the back cover of a Louise Penny mystery.

June put a hand on her hip. "You can't fool me. I've been watching you from my favorite purple chair for the past fifteen minutes and I can tell there's something up with you. I actually think I heard you hum."

"I'm not important right now. Hester is." Nora gestured at the purple chair and June resumed her seat.

After giving Nora an assessing stare, she shrugged and reached behind her to fluff the throw pillow imprinted with the text, WARM TEA, GOOD BOOKS, SOFT PILLOWS, GOOD COMPANY.

"When Hester let me inside her house last night, I thought everything would turn out okay. It didn't," June said, settling deeper into the chair cushion. "She thinks we're jumping to conclusions about Abilene without a lick of proof. I can see her side of things, Nora. We have some oddball coincidences, but no proof."

"None of us believe in coincidence." Nora sat in the crimson velvet chair next to June. "I don't pretend to understand any of this, but there's a reason Abilene won't tell us how she came by that dress. There's a reason Deputy Andrews wouldn't discuss the cause behind Amanda's death. I asked him point-blank if she swallowed those pills from the bottle you and I saw on her kitchen counter, but he refused to answer. Lastly, there's a reason Kenneth Frye hired an attorney to contest his mother's will. He wants her book collection. And I think he wanted it before he understood its worth. Everything seems to come back to Amanda."

June held up a finger. "Abilene is only connected *if* she was wearing Amanda's dress, but how could we ever be sure of such a thing?"

"I'm going to ask for help," Nora said.

"Like Jack asked for Estella's help last night?" June chuckled. "I know you were there too, but Estella isn't one to share a man's attention."

Nora leaned closer to June. "Did she call you?"

"No, I bumped into them as they were leaving Virtual Genie. I didn't have to work at the pools today, so I did some errands around town. If I had something to sell, I could have investigated Virtual Genie myself, but I put everything I have into my house or a savings account for my son. He's never made a withdrawal, but this mama keeps hoping."

The laughter immediately left June's eyes and Nora responded with a sympathetic nod. She couldn't think of anything else to do. What comfort could she, a childless woman, offer a mother who'd trade everything she owned for a single word from her child?

Though June had been estranged from Tyson for well over a decade, she never stopped trying to reconnect with him. She wrote him letters and mailed him birthday and Christmas gifts. More often than not, these packages came back unopened, but June vowed to continue sending them.

Though June had recently been promoted to a managerial position at the thermal pools run by the lodge, her income was still modest. Nora hadn't realized that her friend had set up a bank account for her son, and it saddened her to think that June might be denying herself small material pleasures in order to put money aside for a grown man who'd made it quite clear that he never wanted to see or speak to his mother again. Tyson blamed June for ruining his chance at a college education and for forever altering his destiny. He blamed her, refused to forgive her, and ultimately, denied her very existence.

"So what happened with Jack and Estella?" Nora gently changed the subject.

"Other than the fact that Jack has clearly fallen under Estella's wicked spell, you mean? God help him." June put her hands together as if in prayer and glanced at the ceiling. She then resumed her narrative. "Since Jack had to hurry back to the Pink Lady to prep for the dinner rush, Estella was able to tell me about their visit before she was due to meet her next client. Here's what happened: Jack gave his box to Griffin Kingsley to sell and Estella gave *me* a copy of the consignment agreement to go over with a fine-tooth comb."

June produced a pink sheet of paper and set it on the coffee table and the two women bent over the document and began to read.

Nora skipped the blank lines asking for the consignor's personal information and moved down to the middle of the page. The terms of the contract were neither lengthy nor difficult to understand. The consignor agreed to a sixty/forty split. Sixty percent of the selling price would go to the consignor and forty percent would go to Virtual Genie. In addition, Virtual Genie would deduct priority-rate shipping and insurance costs for each item. Items would be auctioned online for a period of one week. If unsold, they'd be relisted at a slightly lower price. If, after four relistings, the item remained unsold, the consignor would be contacted to reclaim the item or have Virtual Genie lower the price even more.

"This seems reasonable to me," Nora said when she'd finished reading. "The only additional fees I saw, other than the shipping costs, are here." She pointed at the bottom of the page. "If a consignor cancels an ongoing auction, they have to pay an early termination fee of five percent of the item's list price. That might seem harsh, but I suppose it makes Virtual Genie look bad when an ongoing auction item is canceled, especially if the item already has bids."

June grunted. "So far, this seems legit. There's more on the back."

The flip side contained a paragraph of legalese stating that Virtual Genie did not guarantee the safety of the consignor's items. The company carried only fire and liability insurance and the fine print on the reverse made it quite clear that they were not responsible for the loss of an item due to theft, flood, or a natural disaster.

"While not reassuring, it's also not surprising," Nora said. "Imagine the insurance premiums if Virtual Genie had to provide coverage for every treasure they agreed to sell until it was shipped out."

"After reading this, I think we can confirm that Virtual Genie is playing fair, Kenneth Frye's a jackass, Abilene remains a total mystery, and your twinkle can only be the result of one thing."

Nora was spared from having to respond because a customer stepped up to the ticket agent's booth with the intention of ordering a beverage.

After taking her drink order, Nora asked the woman, "Would you like to try a book pocket to accompany your Dante Alighieri?"

"No, thank you," the woman answered. "Unless they happen to be gluten-free."

Suddenly realizing that she'd never ridden to the Gingerbread House to collect pastries that morning, Nora told the woman that she didn't carry any gluten-free treats.

"That's okay," the woman said. "I had a huge lunch at the lodge. Not that my full tummy stops me from wanting all of your gorgeous cookbooks. I'm a self-professed cookbook hoarder. I don't cook. I just like looking at photos of food."

"You're into food porn," Nora said.

The woman frowned. "I'm not a fan of that term. Porn objectifies people—mostly women—while food is nourishing. It doesn't seem right to combine the two terms."

No one had ever commented on the phrase before, but Nora found herself agreeing with the woman. "Do you like food fetish better?" she teased, sensing that her customer wished to linger over the topic a little while longer.

The woman laughed. "You remind me of my ex's mom. She enjoyed coming up with alternative names for my addiction. She also had a great sense of humor. In fact, I got along better with her than I did with her son. Guess that's why he's my ex." She accepted her decaf coffee with one hand and raised a warning finger at Nora with her other. "Never date a guy who's looking for his mom in younger form. It's a giant red flag. And somehow, I missed it."

"I won't," Nora said before quickly turning away. Is that why Jed was attracted to her? Because she reminded him of his mother? Because she and his mother had both been burned?

Out by the circle of chairs, June and the woman customer had fallen into conversation. Their voices—the woman's flute-like soprano and June's honeyed alto—rolled into the ticket agent's booth like the comforting current of a woodland stream. Nora thought of pouring a cup of coffee and joining them, but when her gaze fell on the mug hanging closest to her on the peg board, which was embellished with the text, GO AWAY! I'M ON A DATE WITH MY BOOK BOYFRIEND, she sat down inside the booth instead.

She sat there, thinking about questions that had no answers, until her coffee went cold.

Chapter 9

Are we not like two volumes of one book?
                    —Marceline Desbordes-Valmore

The Fruits of Labor Festival was one of the town's most antic-ipated events. It was wildly popular with both the locals and the hundreds of tourists who flocked to Miracle Springs to ex-perience an event with real Southern flair.

Once upon a time, the festival had been a harvest celebration. Farmers had carted their end-of-summer bounty to the center of town in hopes of winning a prize in Perfect Potato, Amazing Apple, Terrific Tomato, Super Squash, or the Watermelon Weigh-Off category. There'd been livestock awards and bake-offs. There'd been cake, pie, and preserved-food competitions. In fact, many local ladies still prided themselves on their ability to pickle anything under the sun.

The Fruits of Labor Festival had evolved since its county fair origins. Though farmers attended the event, their livestock was no longer welcome, as the festival was now completely vege-tarian.

To Nora, the highlight of the weekend was the abundance of food trucks. Vendors from all over traveled to Miracle Springs to delight the inhabitants with their unique eats, and Nora remembered how tight her jeans were after last year's event. Still, she didn't plan on holding back just because she was on a date.

Nora waited for Jed in front of Miracle Books. As soon as he saw her, he quickened his step. When he reached her, he immediately took her hand. They crossed the street and entered the park, their gait matching the lively fiddle music coming from the bandstand.

As they joined the ticket line, Jed glanced at the throngs of people moving among the food trucks. Looking at Nora, he said, "Since you're the veteran festivalgoer, why don't you tell me how this works?"

Nora pointed at the ticket stand. "The punch card gives you the best deal on food. You can try an item from ten trucks. After most people have stuffed themselves on the savory goodies, they take a time-out. They browse the craft stalls or play carnival games. There's dancing on the lawn next to the bandstand too. Anyway," she hurried on, hoping Jed wouldn't want to dance, "everyone circles back to the food trucks for dessert."

"I like this plan," Jed said with approval. He cast another glance at the long row of food trucks. "How to choose?"

Nora followed his gaze. "In case you didn't know, this is a vegetarian festival."

"Well, that's a deal breaker. I'm out of here." Jed pretended to step out of the line. He then spun on his heel and turned back to Nora. "Wait. Is any of this super-healthy food deep-fried?"

Nora laughed. "Lots."

"In that case, I'm staying. You could deep-fry a boot heel and I'd eat it."

At the ticket stand, Jed purchased two punch cards. He was also given a sheet of paper that served as the festival schedule, map, and vendor list. He passed the sheet to Nora and told her to pick their first destination.

"I hope you like chickpeas," she said and led the way to a food truck called The Falafel Fix. When it was her turn, she ordered a falafel sample and handed the vendor her punch card. When it was Jed's turn, he told Nora that he'd always wanted to order baba ghanoush.

"It just sounds cool," he explained to both Nora and the young woman taking orders.

She flashed him a coy grin. "It's Arabic, you know. Some say the translation is 'pampered daddy.' Are you a pampered daddy?"

Jed examined his fingers. "I don't know. It's been *ages* since my last mani-pedi."

The woman laughed and ducked her head inside the truck to convey the order to the cook.

"It's your pick next," Nora said after they'd devoured their first round of food.

Jed pointed at a yellow food truck. "Mac and cheese pie. I need something unhealthy to balance out that eggplant. I should get huge bonus points just for eating eggplant. It has the consistency of a wet sponge. I'm not totally convinced that it's actually food."

"Bonus points? Maybe for eating a handful of ghost peppers. But eggplant?" Nora shook her head in mock disgust. "You modern men. John Wayne wouldn't know what to make of you."

Without warning, Jed steered them away from the Perfect Pie truck to the Keep Calm and Curry On truck.

"What's the spiciest thing you've got?" he asked the man at the window.

The man gave Jed the once-over and said, "We can make anything as spicy as you like, but our paneer wrap has jalapeños and curry. We usually serve it mild, but you can ask to dial up the heat if you want."

"Oh, I want. Dial my heat up *all the way*, my good sir."

Nora couldn't stop grinning as she ordered a vegetable samosa. She also requested a small container of raita in case Jed needed to quench the fire he was about to ignite in his mouth.

He ate his wrap in three bites, declared that he barely felt any heat, and was already looking down the row of food trucks for his next sample when tiny dewdrops of sweat sprouted across his forehead.

"Delayed reaction?" Nora asked, trying not to laugh.

Jed nodded and wiped his forehead with a napkin. Turning away from Nora, he pressed the napkin to his tongue. When he faced her again, his cheeks were flushed. "I should have gotten something to drink."

Nora handed him the container of raita. "Eat this yogurt sauce. It'll help neutralize the spices."

Jed accepted the container with a grateful groan. Tilting his head back, he let the sauce coat his tongue. He swallowed, waited a moment, and smiled at her. "You're a genius."

"Not at all," she said. "I used to live really close to a restaurant that served authentic Indian food. I ate there once a week."

Nora immediately focused on the map in her hands, shocked that she'd mentioned her former life. She never spoke of it. Not to anyone outside the Secret, Book, and Scone Society.

"Do you ever miss it?" Jed asked. "The place you used to live."

Nora shook her head and pointed at the All Fried Up food truck near the end of the row. "Let's go there. Maybe they'll have those fried boot heels you were looking for."

Ten minutes later, Jed and Nora sat down at a picnic table with samples of Cajun-fried mushrooms, fried pickles with buffalo ranch dipping sauce, and bottled water.

"Is there an antacid food truck?" Jed joked. He'd finished his food and was watching Nora dip a fried pickle in the spicy ranch. The smile faded from his face and his eyes turned solemn. "Look, I'll never bring up what you shared with me last night. Your past belongs to you. As far as my story goes, I only told you part of it. It was really late, but not telling you the rest would feel like a cop-out. Whenever you want to hear it, just ask."

Nora gazed at the crowd milling around a wood-fired pizza truck. The night was buzzing with noise, aromas, and energy. "Let's not talk about heavy stuff tonight. Let's just have fun." After a pause, she added, "I've never been good at fun. I'm good at work. But I'm trying to change."

Jed grinned. "I can help." He swiped the map from Nora and ran his finger down the list of vendors. "Okay. This is it. Finish your pickles, book lady, because we're heading to a libation station."

Suppressing a bolt of panic, Nora asked, "Which one?"

Jed refused to answer, and when Nora tried to reclaim the map, he held it out of reach.

"You'll have to take this back by force," he teased.

"Don't tempt me," she said, smiling to cover her nervousness.

Suddenly, a shadow fell across their table. "Is there a problem here, folks?"

It was Deputy Andrews. He was in uniform and stood with his thumbs hooked under his utility belt and a grin tickled the corners of his mouth.

"Would you like a front-row seat to an assault and battery?" Nora asked, patting the bench next to her.

Andrews shook his head. "A tempting offer, but I'm on my way to judge the Little Miss Honeybee pageant. I tell you, these little girls have to answer some seriously tough questions about sustainable crops, organic food production, and the effect of bees on the food chain."

"Asking tough questions is better than having them parade around in pretty dresses, waving and smiling those fake smiles," Nora said. "This way, they get to show off their brains."

"They still parade around in dresses. The winners of the Little Miss and the Miss Honeybee competitions will lead the antique car parade tomorrow. Every girl in town is dying to sit in the back of that vintage Corvette. Shoot, *I'm* dying to sit in that car."

Jed and Andrews started talking cars, and Nora excused herself to search for more bottled water. All the salty foods she'd eaten had made her thirsty.

She was in line when Andrews reappeared at her side. "Did you see the paper this morning?"

Nora had been too busy to read anything that day and told Andrews as much.

"You gals are in it," Andrews said, glancing around to be sure that he couldn't be overheard.

"For what?" Nora asked, checking to see what Jed was doing. He was standing next to the trash can, talking to a coworker. The other paramedic was in uniform. Both men were laughing and seemed totally relaxed.

"Your secret tote bags." Andrews lowered his voice to a whisper. "Ms. Washington told half the town about hers. She's working at the grocery store now," he added, referring to one of the former Madison County Community Bank tellers. She calls you her Night Angels, and that's what the paper's calling you now too. Guess you four should start wearing costumes."

Nora sighed. The last thing she and her friends were interested in was publicity. "Please don't tell anyone," she begged. "The whole point of our efforts is to deliver *anonymous* gifts to our neighbors."

"Your secret is safe with me. Hester already made me promise not to tell a soul. Not even the sheriff. She said she'd never bake for me again if I snitched." He shook his head. "I couldn't face that. I love everything that woman makes."

Hearing Hester's name, Nora felt a constriction in her chest. What would happen to their Secret Kindness bags if Hester stopped contributing breads, biscuits, and rolls? A second, much more disturbing thought followed this. What would become of the Secret, Book, and Scone Society if Hester stopped attending their meetings? It wouldn't be the same. Nora didn't think the rest of them could handle such a loss. Their friendship was too new. And because of its newness, it was also fragile.

"Are you all right, Ms. Pennington?"

Nora was torn. She could confide in Andrews. He was a good man. He'd recognize the significance of Abilene showing up at Miracle Books that first night wearing a hospital wristband as well as a dress that might have belonged to Amanda Frye. Confiding in Andrews meant going behind Abilene's back, however. For some reason, betraying Abilene felt like a betrayal of Hester. Nora wouldn't do that to her friend.

Since Jed was now heading their way, Nora changed the subject. "Ms. Washington reminds me of someone else with a wagging tongue. You told me that Kenneth Frye has been doing his best to slander Virtual Genie, but I looked at their contract and his complaints are unfounded."

"I know. Remember how the sheriff paid Mr. Frye a visit at his hotel?" Andrews waited for Nora's nod before continuing. "When he was done reading Frye the riot act, he went to Virtual Genie and looked them over from top to bottom. Mr. Kingsley and Ms. Beacham were helpful and hospitable. The terms and fees are spelled out clear as day in their contract. Sheriff McCabe was so impressed that he's going to use Virtual Genie's services himself. That should help restore their reputation. The sheriff has more influence than some smack-talking outsider."

"That's true," Nora agreed. "Then again, Griffin and Tamara are outsiders too. A person has to live in Miracle Springs for at least a decade to be considered a local."

Jed reached them in time to hear Nora's remark. Looking at her, he asked, "Does that make you an outsider? Because it seems like you belong here as much as anybody."

Nora shrugged. "I guess I'm still being vetted."

"You've got that wrong, Ms. Pennington," Andrews said. "You and your bookstore are part of this town's soul. I've heard folks say as much." He touched the brim of his hat. "I'd best be going. Enjoy your evening."

Jed watched Andrews leave. "I like that guy. The sheriff's a good egg too. I guess Miracle Springs needed an outsider. It's always good to switch things up. Take something that's been around for ages and make it new. Like cinnamon apple pie moonshine, for example."

The comparison was so random that Nora shot Jed a surprised glance. "What?"

Jed's reply was lost when a voice boomed from the nearest loudspeaker. An announcer warned that the Little Miss Honeybee pageant would be starting in five minutes.

Nora didn't ask Jed to repeat his answer. They passed under an archway festooned with artificial fruits and the words SHOP LOCAL, SHOP BLUE RIDGE, and continued onward until they reached a very popular booth. Nora examined the illuminated sign hanging over the main table. It was shaped like a mason jar surrounding neon-blue letters that spelled Blowing Rock Distillery.

"Ever had moonshine before?" Jed asked.

"After hearing people say that it tastes like turpentine, no," Nora said. When disappointment flooded Jed's face, she amended her answer. "Still, there must be a reason why it's so hip these days. Distilleries and craft cocktails featuring moonshine keep popping up. Either 'shine doesn't taste like turpentine, or all these people are lining up because they're dying for a swift burn to the esophagus."

Jed laughed. "I tried it once. It was my buddy's homemade concoction and, man, it was nasty stuff! It smelled like corn but tasted like the inside of a teenage boy's gym locker. It must have been a thousand proof. After three shots, I started seeing dead relatives."

A group of older ladies dressed to the nines in skirt suits, pantyhose, and heels came tottering back from the booth's counter, giggling with every step.

"Jedediah Craig!" one of them shouted in an exaggerated drawl. "You might be giving us a ride in your emergency bus later on. We've had *lots* of *special* cherries."

"Would you do us a favor, darlin'?" another lady added. "Drive us around without those awful sirens. I don't think I can tolerate any more noise. Just strap me onto a bed and hold me tight when the driver makes a sharp turn. Or any turn, for that matter."

This comment elicited a renewed fit of giggles from the ladies, and they wobbled off toward the food trucks.

"Cherries, eh?" Jed murmured in amusement. "More like cherry bombs."

By the time she and Jed had reached the front of the line, Nora couldn't decide what to do. She didn't think that sampling a single Blowing Rock product would be a problem, but she knew she had to be careful. It had been a tumultuous week, and she didn't want an array of powerful emotions riding on a wave of hard liquor to take control.

"Here's a menu, ma'am." A young man wearing denim overalls and cowboy boots offered Nora a laminated list of available samples. "If you need a recommendation, just holler."

"I do," she said before he could move to the next person. "What's your least potent sample?"

Though he looked like a young Clint Eastwood, he seemed to lack Eastwood's quick wit. Flipping his sandy hair off his brow, the boy mumbled, "Um . . ."

Nora pointed at the menu. "Which one won't burn on the way down?"

"Oh!" His face brightened in understanding. "You want more sweet than heat."

"Exactly," Nora said.

Young Eastwood told her to try the moonshine cherries or peaches. If she liked those, she could sample a shot of strawberry or lemon-drop moonshine. But if she was only going to try one thing at their booth, he suggested that she select the distillery's most popular product, the cinnamon apple pie moonshine.

"It's amazin'," he said. "Most folks go right home, get on

their computers, and order a case after tryin' a sample. We have a helluva time keepin' it in stock." Reddening slightly, he added, "Excuse my language, ma'am."

"I bet you'll hear worse than that before the night is over," Jed said. "Not from me—my mom wouldn't tolerate a foul mouth—but from the people who are sampling from all the twenty-one-and-over booths without eating something first."

Jed's reference to his mother reminded Nora of the customer she'd had that afternoon—the one who warned her not to get involved with a man searching for a surrogate mother figure. It was because of this, no doubt, that Nora stepped up to the distillery booth's counter, looked at the array of colorful mason jars, and said, "I'd like moonshine cherries and the cinnamon apple pie moonshine."

"The game is on," Jed said and ordered a sample of white lightning as well as summer orange moonshine.

The pair moved to the tasting area. A dozen high-top tables were covered with vinyl cloths, and the table they chose was sticky with spots of dried liquor.

Nora speared her cherry with a toothpick and held it aloft. "As Lord Byron once said, 'What's drinking? A mere pause from thinking!'"

Jed saluted her with his tiny sample cup, which appeared to hold a thimbleful of liquor, and downed its contents.

Nora popped the moonshine-soaked cherry into her mouth and studied Jed. He closed one eye and grimaced. He looked like an angry pirate.

To keep the cherry from going down her throat whole, she pushed it toward her cheek with her tongue and bit down. She'd expected something sweet. Something akin to a maraschino cherry, but with a little bite. The bite on this cherry was big. Very big. Nora winced, chewed again, and quickly swallowed.

Jed blew raspberries with his lips and murmured, "That was false advertising. The menu described summer orange as tasting like an orange candy. I figured it would be like Fanta on the front end and an amaretto-in-your-coffee kind of warmth on the back end." He held up his hands. "I didn't taste *any* candy. It was all atomic orange from the get-go. My mouth still doesn't know what hit it."

Nora pointed at his second sample cup and arched her brows. "You're going to lose all trace of sweet with the pure moonshine. Are you sure you want to go there?"

Jed shrugged. "My mouth is partially numb already. What's the harm in another shot?"

How many times have people asked that question before doing something really stupid? Nora thought and picked up her cup.

She sniffed the contents and was surprised by the pleasant apple aroma. She could also detect a subtle hint of cinnamon and, if she wasn't going crazy, a faint buttery scent. It was like walking into a room where someone had just taken an apple pie from the oven.

How bad can it be when it smells this good?

She was about to drink when Jed held up his hand to stop her. "Another toast," he said. "I like your toasts."

Nora tried to think of a second literary toast, but all she could come up with was a quote from F. Scott Fitzgerald. It didn't exactly inspire joviality, but she said it anyway. "'Here's to alcohol, the rose colored glasses of life.'"

They touched rims and Nora knocked back her drink. She tasted apple, cinnamon, and buttery piecrust. But for only a second. The enjoyable tastes were overshadowed by heat. Too much heat. It felt like she'd swallowed a shooting star. Through watering eyes, she could see that Jed was having a similar reaction to his sample.

They both started chortling with laughter.

"I feel like I just emasculated myself," Jed said after regaining his composure. "I think I should try that again."

Nora gestured at the line. "Go right ahead. I'm done with

my moonshine-tasting experience, so I'll just hang out on that bench by the hard cider booth until you're armed with your second round."

She sat on the bench, feeling the apple pie moonshine continue to spread warmth through her upper body. There were no lights shining on her area, which allowed her to watch people from the shadows. It was nice to simply sit, undetected, and look at people. She enjoyed seeing their clothes, their gestures, their expressions—everything. It was a unique kind of voyeurism, but a harmless one.

She was watching a gaggle of teenage girls walk toward the food truck row when she heard a man shouting from somewhere behind her bench. If the voice hadn't sounded familiar, she wouldn't have bothered to turn around. Listening to an eruption of hostility and anger, Nora knew that the voice belonged to Kenneth Frye. She couldn't see the person he was yelling at, however, because a thick tree trunk blocked her line of sight.

"I already told you—the deal's off! You have nothing to offer me. You failed to do what you promised and we're done!" He jabbed his pointer finger toward the unfortunate recipient of his wrath. The movement made him sway unsteadily, but he managed to stay on his feet. "And just so you know—when I find whatever it is that you've been pretending *not* to be looking for—I'm keeping it. It's mine. Now piss off!"

A beer bottle sailed through the air and crashed somewhere in the darkness.

Nora stiffened. A sober Kenneth Frye was bad enough. She couldn't imagine having to face a drunk Kenneth Frye. Alcohol and rage were dangerous bedfellows. No one knew that more acutely than Nora.

Still, she wanted to know who Frye had been yelling at. To do this, she needed to move so that the tree was no longer obstructing her view.

Before she could stand up, a voice said, "I hope this seat isn't taken."

Nora glanced up to find Jed gazing down at her. Even in the relative darkness, his eyes sparkled. "This sample will never be as good as the time I could have spent with you, but I'm determined to restore my manly rep. Are you ready for my poker face?"

Jed downed the shot. Other than a telltale clenching of his jaw, he gave no sign that the moonshine had set his mouth or throat on fire.

"Your macho-ness is restored," Nora said. "You're almost on par with Ernest Hemingway."

"Don't mock me," Jed scolded solemnly. "That guy was a stud. He ran with bulls, hunted big game, drove an ambulance in the Great War, *and* survived a plane crash."

Nora was impressed. "You're a Hemingway fan?"

"I wrote a paper about him in high school. I picked Hemingway because he wrote the shortest book on the reading list. *The Old Man and the Sea*. I hated the book, but I liked the author. The guy was good at so many things"

"Except relationships," Nora said and turned to see if Frye was still there.

He wasn't.

Nora stared into the shadows, hoping the other person would step into the light. After a moment, it was clear that no one was there.

Jed, who hadn't noticed Nora's lapse of attention, kept talking about Hemingway. "I remember him saying that writing was a lonely life. I thought that was strange because he'd been married so many times. So many women wanted to be with him, but he wasn't happy with any of them for long." He paused, and when he spoke again, his voice carried a hint of sadness. "Do you think some people are meant to be alone?"

The question brought Amanda Frye to the forefront of Nora's

mind. She pictured Amanda's humble house with its aged appliances and sagging furniture. She saw the row of dresses in her closet. Her outdated but tidy kitchen. Her wonderful books. And then, though she tried not to, Nora saw Amanda suspended in a pool of green muck. She remembered how the flies had gathered around the dead woman's bloated body.

"Sorry." Jed waved his hands as if erasing his previous question. "No heavy stuff. Tonight's about fun. You pick the next event." He passed the map to Nora.

She chose to visit the local beekeeper's booth. Though she and Jed tasted several varieties of honey and were treated to a lively cooking demonstration, the festival's spell had somehow been broken. And Nora had no idea how to rekindle the magic.

After Jed had seen her home, Nora stood on her deck and stared at the high, distant stars.

"Leave it to Hemingway to put a damper on the first date I've had in years," she complained to the pinpricks of light.

As expected, they had no solace for her.

Chapter 10

*He could feel how fast he was falling, and he knew
what was waiting for him down there.*
—George R. R. Martin

Even though it was a Saturday, Nora set her alarm for six thirty
because she wanted to hike through the woods before hitting the
flea market.

As usual, she brewed coffee while getting dressed and drank
a cup before heading outside. She also grabbed her trusty walking stick. It would be many weeks before the snakes would
slither into their burrows or hollow logs for the winter, and
Nora didn't want to step on a copperhead or timber rattler.

Nora's walking stick was one of her favorite possessions. It
was also one of the few items she'd purchased from the flea
market that she hadn't immediately repriced to sell in Miracle
Books.

Her walking stick was special because of its literary theme.
The artist who'd carved the stick was not only well-read, but
also incredibly skilled. He'd created a vertical scene showing a
fox running through a field of flowers and butterflies. The fox
ran from the bottom of the stick to the top, where he was forever captured in the act of leaping over a bubbly stream.

When people took a close look at Nora's walking stick, they

tended to see the fox, the flowers, and the trees. What they usually failed to spot were the words etched into the tree trunks. The words spelled *Now here is my secret*, a quote, albeit an incomplete one, from *The Little Prince*.

Nora shared the quote in its entirety to anyone expressing curiosity about her stick. The line was simply too important not to share.

" 'And now here is my secret,' " she'd say, " 'a very simple secret: it is only with the heart that one can see rightly; what is essential is invisible to the eye.' "

Her walking stick became a topic of conversation only if she paused to enjoy the scenic view from one of the lookouts along the Appalachian Trail and another hiker climbed up on the cluster of massive boulders. Hikers were a friendly lot and many tended to travel with sticks of their own. Although Nora wasn't big on talking during a hike, she liked to hear the stories behind other people's sticks. These exchanges were usually brief and interesting, which was how Nora thought all conversations should be.

She didn't plan on stopping at the lookout today, however. She had too much to do before opening the shop. By the time she crossed the railroad tracks and entered the woods, it was just shy of seven o'clock.

The forest was filled with nature's white noise. Nora liked these sounds. She found their predictability comforting. As she moved, she was surrounded by the drone of insects, squirrel chatter, and leaf rustle. There had been little rainfall in August and the leaves were starting to dry out and separate from their branches. They drifted down from the treetops like brown and gold confetti and, every so often, Nora would reach out and catch one.

Nora made noise too. She snapped twigs underfoot and excited the nagging of squirrels. The squirrels, who lined up on the limbs and stared down at Nora, reminded her of a group of old ladies who'd booked their wash-and-set appointments together so they could gossip for an hour or two. Estella was fond of these women, despite the fact that they whispered about her behind her back.

When Nora had asked Estella how she could possibly enjoy the company of such women, she'd said, "It's just what their type does. They're not malicious, but bored. I'm glad I'm not related to any of them, though. The things they say about their family members are the worst. Sometimes, having your only relative incarcerated is a good thing. Daddy only knows what I want him to know."

Estella's comment reminded Nora of all she hadn't shared with Deputy Andrews last night. She didn't regret her choice, but omitting what she'd omitted meant she'd have to investigate Abilene on her own.

Nora walked on until she came to a fork in the trail. As she always did at this spot, she checked her watch. She could continue hiking and spend less time at the flea market, or take the loop that wound behind the Tree House Cabins and back into town. If she took the loop, she'd have plenty of time to shop for shelf enhancers and still open Miracle Books by ten.

She decided to take the shorter route and made it all the way to the edge of the Tree House Cabins property when she realized that she hadn't run into anyone on the trail. This was surprising, especially since the lodge offered daily sunrise hikes, complete with a mountaintop yoga or meditation session.

After taking a downhill path from the main trail and stepping into a clearing near the first section of tree house cabins, Nora quickly understood why her hike had been solitary.

Something had happened in one of the smaller cabins, which were grouped together in the center of the property. Through the trees, Nora saw three patrol cars with flashing light bars, and a parked ambulance. Though its lights were also flashing, its siren was silent. The presence of emergency vehicles inspired dread, but the absence of a siren made it worse. It was as if the lights were repeatedly casting a message into the trees that said, *too late, too late, too late.*

Nora had no choice but to walk toward the scene. There was only one path through the rental property. One path and a narrow dirt road. Eventually, the two converged, which put Nora two cabins away from where the vehicles were parked.

As she proceeded, she saw Sheriff McCabe descend the last two stairs of a tree house cabin and duck under a length of yellow crime-scene tape secured to a pair of tree trunks. Nora didn't have a line of sight to the ground below the cabin yet, but the moment she did, her pace slowed so dramatically that the sheriff immediately spotted her.

Sheriff McCabe raised his arm, signaling for Nora to stop. She complied, too shocked to do anything else. Her gaze was drawn to the body on the ground below the cabin. She nearly tripped over a root as her mind took in the impossible angles of the dead man's right leg and neck. He didn't look real. He looked like a crash-test dummy jettisoned from a car.

"Ms. Pennington?" The sheriff came right up to her, effectively blocking her view of the body. He folded his arms across his chest and gave her a disapproving stare. "Why are you here?"

Nora pointed behind her shoulder, hoping one of the deputies had told the new sheriff about the walking path. "I was hiking. This is how I go home." She gestured toward the body. Though she'd caught only a brief glimpse, she thought she recognized the large bearded man. "Is that Kenneth Frye?"

The sheriff's look of disapproval morphed into a deep frown. "Do you know him?"

"I don't know him, but we've met," Nora said. "He came to my bookstore looking for a free appraisal."

Something changed in the sheriff's face. "Deputy Andrews told me about that meeting. Have you seen Mr. Frye since then?"

Nora had to force herself to concentrate on the sheriff's question. She was still trying to absorb the fact that the bent body on the ground was Kenneth Frye. Questions were tripping over each other in her head and it was hard to focus on just one.

"Ms. Pennington?" Sheriff McCabe prodded.

"I saw him last night," she said, finally gaining command of her thoughts. "At the festival. He was standing behind the hard cider booth—way back behind it. And he was yelling at someone. He sounded drunk and he seemed unsteady on his feet. I couldn't see the other person because a tree blocked my view. I wish I'd looked when I had the chance."

Her remorse wasn't feigned. If she could identify the recipient of Frye's wrath, she might be able to help the sheriff understand why his body was splayed like a discarded doll at the base of a tree house cabin.

"Could this cabin have been rented by the person he was arguing with?" Nora asked, her glance moving upward to the cabin, which was built on a platform thirty feet off the ground.

The sheriff shook his head. "Kenneth Frye rented it."

This caught Nora off guard. Andrews had told her about the sheriff's visit to Frye's hotel, and none of the locals referred to the Tree House Cabins as a hotel. Of all the places to stay around Miracle Springs, the most famous properties were the lodge and the Tree House Cabins. There were a few quaint B and Bs and chain hotels too, but there was only one place where people could stay in a log cabin perched in the tree canopy.

Kenneth had rented a single-occupancy cabin. These were the least expensive cabins on the property because they had the smallest square footage, but all the cabins included a balcony furnished with two chairs and a side table.

Nora pointed at the balcony of Frye's cabin. "Did he fall from there?"

"Looks like it," Sheriff McCabe said and turned around to respond to a question from one of his deputies. When he turned, Nora saw Andrews jog down the cabin's wooden stairs. The sheriff raised his arm and hailed Andrews over.

"Ms. Pennington." Andrews touched his hat in greeting. He looked a little peaked and Nora wondered if he'd been first on the scene.

"Would you show Ms. Pennington an image of the book we found in Mr. Frye's cabin?" the sheriff asked his deputy.

Andrews produced his phone and scrolled through dozens of photos before passing the device to Nora. Taking the phone, she immediately recognized the image.

"It's the other missing book. Catherine Cookson's *The Mallen Litter*." She pointed at the cabin. "Is the Tolkien novel up there too? *The Two Towers*?"

Andrews nodded.

"Why?" Nora murmured to herself. To the sheriff and Andrews, she said, "I didn't catch most of what Frye said last night. There was too much competing noise. But it sounded like he was firing someone. He said that the deal was off and that the other person hadn't kept their promise. The last thing I heard didn't make much sense."

"Tell us anyway," the sheriff said.

Nora didn't blame McCabe for his impatience. Behind him, Kenneth Frye's broken body silently demanded attention. Kenneth Frye. He'd come to Miracle Springs because his mother had suddenly died. Now, he was dead too. His death was also sudden. And unexpected. McCabe, the interim sheriff who'd been hired to rebuild the department following a scandal, had to investigate two suspicious deaths within days of accepting the job.

"Frye told the other person that if he found what he or she had been looking for, he was going to keep it," Nora said. "I don't think Frye had any idea what *it* was."

"Could it be another book?" Andrews asked the sheriff.

Nora fixed her gaze on McCabe. "There's something special about Amanda Frye's book collection. I don't know what it is because I haven't examined all the books, but there must be a reason Kenneth tried so hard to stop them from being given to the person named in his mother's will."

"Andrews, we'll need a statement from Ms. Pennington. I also want you to find out who interacted with Frye last night. We can finish up here. Ma'am." The sheriff dipped his chin at Nora before heading over to where the paramedics were standing around Frye's body.

When McCabe was out of earshot, Nora whispered, "Did Frye fall or was he pushed?"

Andrews didn't respond, but Nora saw the muscle in his jaw tense. Whatever the evidence, he believed Kenneth Frye had been pushed. To Andrews, this was a murder scene.

"Could someone get so drunk that they'd fall off a balcony?" she asked, looking up at the cabin.

Wishing she could pull the words back into her mouth, she felt a knot of shame form in her throat. How could she, who had such an intimate knowledge of the harmful power of alcohol, voice such a question?

"Are you okay?" Andrews was studying her with concern.

She looked into his kind eyes and nodded. "I'm not trying to gather juicy details to spread around town. I'm genuinely worried. It's been an unsettling week with two deaths combined with newcomers to town. It feels like life is unbalanced—like it was earlier this summer."

Andrews cocked his head. "Newcomers? Don't tell me that you think there's a connection between the Virtual Genie folks and *this*?" He waved his hand at the crime scene.

The newcomer I was thinking of was Abilene, Nora thought.

She didn't share this with Andrews, as she planned to hunt for Abilene online as soon as she got to the bookstore. If she couldn't find any hits, Nora would mention the dress to Andrews. She had no choice. If Abilene was somehow involved in the events leading to Kenneth Frye's death, Nora couldn't stay quiet any longer.

Andrews was discussing where and when he'd obtain her statement, but she wasn't listening. She was staring up at the balcony, trying to envision someone pushing Frye from behind.

Frye was a bear of a man. Even inebriated, it wouldn't be easy to get him to go over the rail without a forceful shove. Did Abilene possess that kind of strength? Nora didn't think so.

If not her, then who?

"Does that work for you?" Andrews asked.

Since Nora hadn't been listening, she simply said, "I have to go. I'm already running late."

She walked away from the flashing lights, the men and women in uniform, and Kenneth Frye's corpse. Questions swarmed her, filling her mind with an incessant buzz. And no matter how fast she moved, Nora couldn't escape the noise.

Though she didn't have as much time to shop at the flea market as she would have liked, Nora rode her bike to the renovated barn where it was held anyway. She needed the flea market this morning. She needed the din of the crowd and the aroma of popcorn and candied nuts wafting out of the snack bar. Most of all, she needed the vintage treasures to distract her from the deaths of Amanda and Kenneth Frye.

Nora had her favorite vendors at the flea market. They were men and women who'd grown accustomed to her scars and no longer noticed them. When they spoke to Nora, they looked her in the eye and bartered with her with polite fierceness.

Because she couldn't afford to listen to the history of each item today, Nora informed the vendors that she was running late and got right down to haggling. When she was done, she pedaled away with both her bike basket and a backpack filled with new treasures to display at Miracle Books.

She loved cleaning, pricing, and arranging new shelf enhancers. The moment she entered the bookstore, she switched
on the lights and the radio, and unwrapped her finds. She carefully removed price stickers from a scrimshaw tooth, a Limoges
vase decorated with daffodils, a porcelain tobacco jar in the
shape of a sea captain, a carved stone snuff bottle, coasters
rimmed in silver, and a Japanese rosewood box.

After brewing coffee and unlocking the front door, Nora
was ready to rearrange all the shelf décor. This was a customary
Saturday morning activity, but one she had to postpone today
because a familiar family entered the shop. It was the young
mother with her three children. It hadn't been long since Nora
gave the *Time Warp Trio* book to the oldest child, the boy.
Hoping he'd talk to her about the book, she sat behind the
checkout counter and started cleaning the stone snuff bottle.

The boy waited for his mother and siblings to head to the
children's section before shyly approaching Nora.

"Hi," he said.

"Hi," Nora replied and smiled warmly at him.

The boy shoved his hands deep into his shorts pockets. "I really
liked the book you gave me. I was wondering if you had any
more."

"Yes, I think I do. And I'm glad you liked the first one." She
laced her hands together and asked, "Were the gross parts funny?"

"They were *so* funny!" the boy exclaimed. "I read it in two
days, but we couldn't come back until today."

Nora led her young reader to Scieszka's books. "If I'm missing the next book in the series, I can order it—"

"You're not! It's right here!" His face shining with joy, the
boy reached for *The Not-So-Jolly Roger*. He also pulled out
The Good, the Bad, and the Goofy.

"You can't have two!" his sister immediately protested from
the next bookcase over.

"I'm using my own money," the boy said. He proudly pulled

a few bills from his pocket and showed them to his sister. "I worked in Mrs. Pope's yard."

Her eyes went round. "Not fair!" She turned to her mother, who was in the middle of reading *Make Way for Ducklings* to her youngest child, and said, "Harry has his *own* money! Why can't *I* work for Mrs. Pope?"

"Because you're afraid of worms, Delilah, and Mrs. Pope's garden has lots of them."

At the mention of worms, Delilah grimaced.

"You can have two picks in a row," Harry said magnanimously. "It's my turn, but you can have it."

Delilah threw her arms around her brother before hurriedly letting go. Harry blushed, embarrassed by his sister's gratitude.

Later, as Nora totaled the family's purchases, she noticed that Delilah had chosen *Aliens Don't Wear Braces* as her pick. This was the very book her brother had wanted the last time they'd been in the shop, but it hadn't been his turn to choose.

"Your children have good hearts," Nora said to their mother. "I wish I had lollipops or something. I'd like to reward them."

The woman smiled at Nora. "What you give them is better than candy," she said. "This bookstore is their magic carpet ride. The stories can take them anywhere they want to go, and every journey makes them better people. This bookstore is a circus, magic show, candy store, and amusement park rolled into one. I should be giving *you* a lollipop each time we come." With a laugh, she ushered her children toward the exit.

The family's visit reminded Nora of all that was good in life. It also woke the hibernating ache in her heart where she'd tucked away a long-dead dream of being a mother like the woman who'd just left. Nora was surprised by the ache. It was like someone throwing a rock into a well that was supposed to be dry, only to hear a splash of water from the lightless depths below.

Eager to turn her thoughts elsewhere, Nora poured a cup of coffee and carried her laptop and mug back to the checkout counter. She took a sip of coffee and began an online search for a woman named Abilene Tyler.

She'd been working for about forty minutes when one of Nora's regular customers approached the counter.

"Do you have any book pastries left?" the woman asked. "I'm having friends over for afternoon tea, and I'd love to serve those darling treats, but I didn't see any on display."

"I haven't gotten my delivery from the Gingerbread House yet," Nora said. "Do you mind browsing while I call over there and find out what's going on?"

"It would be my pleasure," the woman said and wandered off.

After many rings, Hester finally answered the phone. Nora hoped she wasn't interrupting Hester during a midmorning rush. Saturdays were her busiest days.

"I'm sorry to bother you." Nora was contrite from the get-go. She didn't want Hester to hang up the moment she recognized Nora's voice. "I have a customer looking to buy a bunch of book pockets. What should I tell her?"

"If she's willing to wait a few minutes, Abilene can bring you a box. There's only apple this morning because that's all she had time to make. We're slammed."

"Thanks, Hester."

Nora could hear people talking in the background and imagined the line in front of Hester's display cases growing longer and longer by the second.

"Just be nice to her when she shows up," Hester said.

Sensing Hester was about to end the call, Nora said, "Hester! I'll be nice. I will. And I know you need to go, but I want to ask you one thing. Have you made her a comfort scone?"

"Not yet," Hester said tersely.

"Will you? Will you make her one today if you can?"

Hester didn't reply and, after a few seconds, the line went dead.

Nora wanted Hester to bake one of her customized scones

because it might allow her to view Abilene in a different light. She might be able to see beyond the young woman in need of shelter and protection. Nora wanted Hester to work the magic only she could work. Hester had a way of teasing memories from people through her comfort scones. The ingredients Hester chose transported each person back in time to a powerful memory. The scent of oranges, cinnamon, peppermint, hazelnut, blackberries, lemon, coffee, chocolate, and whatever else she added to one of these scones became a means of time travel.

Nora found it telling that Hester hadn't made a comfort scone for Abilene. After all, wasn't comfort the very thing Hester wanted most for her new employee? Even before safety or a means to make a living, Hester longed to give this mysterious girl comfort.

Nora was placing the snuff bottle on a shelf when Abilene came in through the bookstore's back entrance. Nora took the large box of pastries from her and thanked her for coming.

"My customers love these," she added. "They also love your window display. Do you think you could come up with a theme for autumn? Something really colorful and imaginative?"

Abilene, who'd been avoiding Nora's gaze, looked toward the front of the store. "Sure," she said. Her voice was guarded.

"If you let me know what materials you need, I'll buy them. Construction paper or poster board or whatever."

Though Abilene nodded, she was already walking away.

Nora let her go and returned to her laptop. After another forty minutes of scanning social media profiles, obituaries, and small-town newspaper articles, she grew frustrated.

She was about to abandon the search when a random result caught her eye. It was a map showing the distance between two Texas cities. Tyler and Abilene. Nora felt a slight tingle in the space above her pinkie knuckle.

Clicking the link, Nora opened the map image. Interstate 20 ran through both cities.

She stared at the map and considered different theories and possibilities. Even when the sleigh bells banged against the door, she didn't look away from her screen.

She kept thinking that Amanda Frye had left her book collection to a former neighbor.

Nora had assumed that this person was from Miracle Springs, but with the map looming in front of her, she realized how silly this assumption was. Maybe it wasn't the neighbor who'd moved away, but Amanda.

Nora had been a librarian long enough to know that it was difficult to hide either current or previous addresses, and it took her less than a minute to find a short list of places Amanda had lived.

The air above Nora's knuckle tingled again and she grabbed her right hand with her left. The sensation stopped, but adrenaline surged through her as she stared at the address where Amanda had lived for fifteen years. The residence was on Bluebird Lane in Lubbock, Texas.

Switching to the map of Texas again, Nora searched for Lubbock. She saw that it was a straight shot down Route 84 to Interstate 20.

Though Nora couldn't draw an immediate conclusion from this information, she wondered if Abilene had fled from Lubbock.

Is Abilene Tyler a fictitious name taken from two Texan cities? she thought. *Is there a chance she and Amanda Frye knew each other?*

Nora copied Amanda's Lubbock address and pasted it into Google's search box, hoping for hits from real estate sites. She found multiple results that included images.

The house, a one-story ranch, had been built in the early sixties. An enormous tree dominated the front lawn and the shrubbery beneath the windows was lush and looked freshly trimmed. An American flag flew from the pole mounted to the stucco next to the garage, and flower pots flanked the stairs leading to the door. It was a pretty house—far nicer than the Miracle Springs house where Amanda had spent the rest of her too-short life.

Nora wanted to see what the neighboring houses on Blue-bird Lane looked like, so she plugged the address into Google Maps and was immediately drawn to the house on the left. It was impossible not to be drawn to it because its image had been entirely blurred. It looked like someone had taken an eraser to the photo but failed to obliterate the whole image.

Nora had heard that people could request a blurring of their residence, especially if the photo threatened their privacy. If a child, a person's license plate, or anything else that threatened a person's privacy appeared in the photo, a request to blur was usually granted.

Nora didn't believe a child lived in the house. She didn't be-lieve a car was parked in the driveway. She believed there was another reason for the owner to request a blurring of their house.

She believed they were hiding.

Chapter 11

Books are good company, in sad times and happy times, for books are people—people who have managed to stay alive by hiding between the covers of a book.

—E. B. White

"I don't want to hear about towns in Texas," Estella said, taking a seat in her favorite Miracle Books chair. "I want to hear about your date with Jed. And don't be shy. I'm on a dry spell on the man front, so I need to live vicariously through you."

Nora shot her a dirty look. "It's not like you've been abstaining for months. It's been a few weeks at most."

Estella fanned herself with her clutch purse. "Don't remind me!"

At that moment, June entered the circle of chairs, and Nora was relieved to see Hester trailing behind her. Hester sat down and immediately began to pick at the piece of duct tape covering a tear in the cushion.

"Thanks for coming," Nora said. Though she was including all three of her friends in this remark, she directed it at Hester. "I know things have been a bit strained in our little society. That's my fault. I'm sorry for being hurtful or insensitive. Especially to you, Hester."

Nora waited for Hester to meet her gaze. When she didn't, Nora went on. "I feel protective of you in the same way you feel protective of Abilene. I feel like your older sister. I'm not smarter or better than you. Just older. I worry about you, Hester. I worry about June and Estella too." She shrugged. "That's what happens when you care. Caring and worrying go hand in hand."

When Hester still didn't look at her, Nora glanced between June and Hester, silently asking for help.

Estella sighed. "I guess you're not going to give us the dirt on your date. Other than that, you have nothing to be sorry for. I feel the same way you do. And Hester?"

Hester finally looked up to meet Estella's eyes.

"We don't feel as strongly as you about Abilene," Estella finished. "How could we? We don't know her. My question is, do you?"

Hester's brow furrowed in anger. "I know she's a good person. Bad people can't bake the way Abilene does. She and I don't just pump out loaves of bread or batches of cookies at the Gingerbread House. We put *ourselves* into everything we bake. Our food would never taste as sweet and light if there was evil in us."

"Evil?" June was nonplussed. "No one thinks of her like that, honey. But Estella is asking a bona fide question. Do you know Abilene any better than you did the night she showed up in this bookstore?"

Hester bolted to her feet. "Is this your agenda? Is it gang-up-on-Hester night? Because I'd rather be at home, watching TV, than here, playing this game."

June rose to her feet too. Very gently, she said, "We're looking out for you. It might not feel that way, but we are." She took hold of Hester's hand. "Sweetheart, has all of this made you wonder about your daughter? Has she been on your mind a whole lot more since Abilene arrived?"

Hester crumpled. She dropped into her chair like a stone, hid her face in her hands, and began to sob.

Nora stared at June in astonishment. How had she known? She was adept at reading people, it was true, but how had she known that Hester had been thinking about the baby she'd given up for adoption nearly two decades ago?

And then, it hit her.

Abilene was about the same age as Hester's daughter. When Hester met Abilene, she saw a lost girl. Maybe she'd seen her lost daughter in Abilene.

"We can help you find her if you want," Nora said, kneeling at Hester's side.

"I don't know what I want!" Hester shouted. The pain in her voice swept over the circle of chairs like a storm surge. Nora could almost imagine the liquid in her coffee mug forming whitecaps and Estella's red hair whipping around her head like a fiery funnel cloud.

"That's okay," June soothed. "Listen to me, honey. You don't have to deal with these feelings all by yourself. They're too big. They're mountain-sized. You don't have to deal with this on your own. We're right here. Talk to us."

Nora didn't think Hester would respond to June's cajoling, but she did. After accepting a wad of tissues from Estella, she wiped her face and took several deep breaths.

"I should be the one apologizing," she said to Nora. "I didn't even know what was going on with me until June put it into words. I mean, I think about my baby all the time. Even when I try not to. By this point, she's already lived her whole life without me. Why turn her world upside down? It seems selfish. But ever since my daughter was taken away, there's been a giant hole inside me. I think I've been mothering Abilene to try to fill the hole."

The other members of the Secret, Book, and Scone Society

understood exactly what Hester meant. A traumatizing experience could do more than cause a scar. It could create a deep and permanent pit in one's soul. The passage of time couldn't fill such an abyss. Only love could.

Friendship was a powerful kind of love. It's what Nora wanted to offer to these women. The kind of friendship that never faded. The kind that weathered the hard times and highlighted the good times.

She was about to voice this feeling, but when she searched for the right words, they evaded her, flitting away like moths after the porch lights have gone dark.

"I don't know Abilene," Hester said. "She doesn't want me to get close. It hurts to admit that, but there it is. All I can tell you is that she's an incredible baker."

"And she can evaluate jewelry and clocks," Nora said. "She's also very well-read."

Estella gestured toward the front of the store. "And artistic. Don't forget about the window display she created."

June touched Nora's laptop. "She's baffled by technology, is afraid to trust people, and she won't let her guard down. But what is she on guard against?"

"Or whom." Nora opened her laptop and showed her friends Amanda Frye's former house. Next, she showed them the blurred image of the neighbor's house. "The owner of the fuzzy house is a man named Ezekiel Crane," Nora explained. "He runs a small business in downtown Lubbock."

Estella leaned forward to get a closer look. "Let me guess. He owns an antique store."

"Close," Nora said, shooting her an admiring glance. "A clock and watch store. He sells and repairs old timepieces. His shop is called Master Humphrey's."

June grunted in disapproval. "I bet all the black folks in Lubbock love a store with *master* in the name."

"It's actually a literary reference, though I doubt many people realize that. I didn't. I had to look it up," Nora said. "Charles Dickens wrote a weekly serial called *Master Humphrey's Clock*. Master Humphrey was lonely, so he started a club for aspiring writers in order to have companions. Humphrey kept his manuscript inside a clock."

Hester stared at Nora. "Maybe Abilene knew the store owner. This Ezekiel Crane guy. Maybe he's the one who taught her so much about literature, appraising antique watches, and . . ." She trailed off.

"Cooking?" June finished for her. "Maybe. Maybe he's also the person she's afraid of. There's something sketchy about his blurry house."

Nora was relieved that her friends were willing to bat around theories about Ezekiel. "Crane doesn't seem fond of technology either. He doesn't have a website or an email address for his business. Only a landline. No one else was listed as a resident of the blurred house other than Ezekiel Crane. However, I did find a different real estate site showing a street view of his house. Look."

Her friends crowded around the laptop, taking in the image on the screen. They studied the massive trees on the front lawn, the overgrown bushes partially obscuring the windows, the drawn blinds, and the high privacy fence enclosing the side- and backyards.

"I bet there's no welcome mat on that stoop," June said.

Estella grimaced. "It wouldn't help. I didn't know it was possible for a ranch house in Texas to look haunted, but this one does. Talk about your lack of curb appeal. The bricks are stained with mold, the landscaping is overgrown, and those blinds!" She turned to Nora. "Any interior shots?"

"No," said Nora. "Just data about the house, like the year it was built and that it's still occupied by the original owner. It's also the only house on the street with a basement."

A heavy, contemplative silence fell among the women.

Watching her friends, Nora believed they were arriving at the same disturbing conclusion she'd already drawn. They were thinking about the basement, of Abilene's pallor and thinness. And her hospital bracelet. They were asking themselves if the young woman living in the tiny studio apartment above Virtual Genie had once been imprisoned by the man who used to live next door to Amanda Frye.

"Does Ezekiel Crane have a criminal record?" Hester asked.

"I'd have to pay for a background check to learn that," Nora said. "Unless we could convince a certain deputy to check for us."

Hester shook her head. "He'll want to know why, and we can't go there yet." She looked at Nora. "We need to talk to Abilene first."

Though this was the result Nora had been hoping for, she didn't feel the slightest bit triumphant. She was still concerned about Hester and had no idea how to offer her comfort. She'd never been a big hugger. After her accident, she avoided physical contact more than before. Unless that contact came from Jed.

"I'm going to bring her here," Hester said, slowly getting to her feet. "Tomorrow night. Does that work for everyone?"

Nora and June nodded, but Estella asked, "Why not now?"

"Because there's something I need to do first. I need to make Abilene a comfort scone."

June's eyes widened. "You have a feeling?"

"I knew what I'd make her the night we met," Hester said softly. "I just haven't gone through with it because I think the scone is going to hurt her." Hester spread her hands in a helpless gesture. "You know that my scones don't always carry people back to a pleasant memory. Sometimes, the scents and tastes conjure things my customers would rather forget. I try to put positive energy and hope into all my comfort scones, but it's not a science."

"That's because it's magic. Culinary magic." June smiled at Hester. "You're a beautiful person, Hester Winthrop, and there's beauty in every crumb of food you make. If one of your scones turns sour in somebody's mouth, it's because that person's darkness is bigger than your brightness. That's on them, not you."

Hester returned June's smile, but she couldn't hold on to it and it changed into a grimace. "If Abilene was involved in Amanda's death, we'll know. We'll know the moment she bites into her comfort scone. If she did something bad, the darkness inside her is going to come out. Here, where we don't hide things from each other."

Estella stood up and put her hands on her hips. "We're the Night Angels, remember? We *own* the dark!"

The members of the Secret, Book, and Scone Society broke into laughter. The high, bubbly sounds floated up and outward, eventually roosting in the nooks and crevices in the bookshelves.

Even after the other women left, Nora could still sense it. Not just the laughter, but the connection between the four of them. It moved through her like a cup of hot, honeyed tea on a cold day.

She walked around her beloved bookstore, preparing to turn off overhead lights and reading lamps when she was suddenly overcome with gratitude. This place was hers. This wonderful, enchanting, book-filled haven. As was her tiny house. Her perfectly sized parcel of coziness. And now, so unexpectedly, she had these incredible friends. Three strong, smart, scarred women who accepted her exactly as she was.

She turned off every light but one, and the shop was hushed and dark. It was a comfortable darkness, for Nora could feel the presence of the books. In the company of a thousand stories, of a thousand voices, she felt at peace.

Nora carried that feeling home where, for the first time in a long time, she fell into a deep and dreamless sleep.

*   *   *

The local paper didn't have much to say about Kenneth Frye's lethal fall. The sheriff's department issued a vague "open investigation" statement, and the manager of the Tree House Cabins was questioned, but neither he nor his staff members had much to add. No one had seen Kenneth enter his cabin and they couldn't say if he'd entertained visitors.

"I'd have noticed his car if he passed the office. Even at night, you can't miss that shade of yellow," the manager told the reporter. "He must have come back on the late side."

The manager went on to explain that he stopped manning the front office desk at nine, preferring to be on call from home. Both the office and his residence were in a small cabin built on terra firma, and the living room where the manager spent an hour or two watching television before bed was located at the rear, safely protected from the headlights of approaching cars.

Nora didn't expect to learn much from the paper, but she'd hoped for a few kernels of useful information. Hadn't anyone else seen Kenneth at the festival? He'd been in Miracle Springs long enough for the locals to recognize his massive figure and hostile personality.

The ladies of the gossip chain will eat this up, Nora thought, staring at the headline.

She could picture them streaming out of church sanctuaries into fellowship halls to dissect the news over cups of watery coffee and Lorna Doone cookies. The rest of the chatterboxes would be at the festival, gathering around craft stalls to whisper in mock horror over the death of Amanda Frye's son.

Though Nora had the day off, she wasn't interested in church services or festivals. She didn't want company. Not even Jed's. He'd texted several times. She'd sent short replies, but she was too preoccupied by Kenneth's death and the upcoming meeting with Abilene to have a real conversation with him.

Because it was her day off, Nora could take advantage of the cool morning and hike to her favorite scenic outlook. This one featured a grassy clearing lined by big, flat-topped boulders. If it was a clear day, a lucky hiker could gaze to the west and see three states meeting in the distance. North Carolina, Tennessee, and Virginia came together in a group of blue-smudged mountain peaks. Standing on the lookout, the invisible borders created by man meant nothing. What map lines divided, mountains united. They stood, ancient and silent, offering solace and renewal to anyone willing to climb them.

On this September morning, a long hike was just what Nora needed. She brought along her current read, Sharon Kay Penman's *The Land Beyond the Sea*, and quickly became lost in the story.

It was almost noon when Nora applied a fresh coat of sunscreen before turning back toward home.

She'd just started a load of laundry when Nora heard the text message alert on her phone. It was June, inviting her to bathe in the thermal pools.

"Estella and Hester are coming," she'd written, as if Nora wouldn't show up without them.

Nora called June.

"Are you coming to relax with us?" June asked.

"No," said Nora. "This is my only day to catch up on cleaning, laundry, and grocery shopping." She hadn't wanted to admit to June that she had an aversion to hot springs and thermal pools, but she decided it was time to be honest. "Don't take this personally, but I'll never want to go in the pools. Soaking in hot water is uncomfortable for me. Have you ever seen someone with burn scars bathing there?"

June admitted that she hadn't. "I'm sorry, hon. It's just such an effective stress reliever, and I thought you could use some before tonight's meeting."

"I appreciate the invitation," Nora said. And she did. Which is why she felt she owed June further explanation. "When I was in the burn center, my doctors asked if I wanted hydrotherapy. It's a controversial therapy in the field of burn treatment. Some physicians believe the sulfurinated hot water decreases scarring, redness, and itching. Others see it as detrimental because of the possibility of bacterial infection. I agreed to the treatment because I didn't care what they did to me." Nora paused before continuing. She could remember each session as if they'd happened yesterday.

"What was it like? The hydrotherapy?" June asked.

"Painful. Really painful," Nora said quietly. "During the daily sessions, my dressing was changed and my wounds were cleaned. I was given medicine, but there's no medicine in the world that could block out the pain entirely. Not with my being awake. I longed to sleep, June. Forever. But they wouldn't let me."

"Well, I can see why you aren't thrilled by the thought of visiting me at work," June said. "I'll make you a special pair of socks instead. The right scent might help you to de-stress."

Nora thanked her and got back to her chores.

The thunderstorm predicted by the local news rolled in late that afternoon and settled in for a long visit. Dark clouds blanketed Miracle Springs, releasing sheets of rain, cracks of thunder, and strobe-light flashes of lightning. The storm put a swift end to the outdoor events at the Fruits of Labor Festival, including the fireworks display.

Nora loved a summer storm, and it seemed fitting that this year's summer was ending in a downpour. It had been such a tumultuous season for so many locals, and Nora knew she wasn't the only one looking forward to autumn—to a new season filled with crisp mornings, golden hues, and invigorating air.

Influenced by the storm, Nora placed pillar candles on the bookshelves surrounding the circle of chairs where she and her friends always met. She didn't turn on any lamps, preferring to let the soft candlelight dance over the book spines.

The members of the Secret, Book, and Scone Society poured in through the back door. Water dripped from their jackets and from the hair escaping from under their hoods.

Abilene, who trailed after Hester, wasn't wearing a jacket. Her gray sweatshirt was so wet that it had gone from a pale pewter to a dark charcoal.

Nora hurried to fetch her throw blanket from under the register. She kept one for those chilly winter days when she was alone in the store and wanted to grab a few minutes to get cozy with a good book. The throw blanket was soft and warm. Nora draped it around Abilene's bony shoulders and wondered what else she could do to make Abilene more comfortable.

"Thanks," Abilene said before Hester steered her to a chair.

June, Estella, and Hester had previously agreed that Hester should present Abilene with her scone right away. To make the gift seem less obvious, she'd also made desserts for her friends. While Nora served decaf coffee or tea, Hester removed the plastic wrap from a small platter and set it on the coffee table. "Maple butter blondies."

"Lord, I am *so* glad that we're only a few weeks away from busting out our baggy sweaters and jeans," June said. "With the way I eat around you gals, I'm going to need elastic waist *everything*."

Hester flashed her a wicked smile. "I added white chocolate chips to those blondies and the maple sauce is made of pure maple syrup, butter, sugar, vanilla, and cream cheese." She then turned to Abilene. "I have something else for you. A custom treat."

Abilene stared at the bakery box Hester offered, but didn't move to take it.

"It's a comfort scone," Hester said. "You've seen me bake these at the Gingerbread House."

With obvious reluctance, Abilene took the box.

Estella, sensing that this was a good time to call attention to herself, picked up a maple butter blondie and took a large bite out of it. She chewed. She moaned. She glared at Hester.

"If I keep eating like this, I'm going to turn into a sweet person. Being sweet is *not* one of my life goals."

"You gals do plenty of complaining about my food, but I never seem to take home any leftovers," Hester said. She served blondies to June and Nora and waved at Abilene to eat her scone.

Though Nora and her friends were doing their best to act natural, Abilene's expression remained guarded. In the face of Hester's prompting, however, she had little choice but to raise the lid of the bakery box. Almost against her will, she lowered her face closer to the box. The aroma of the scone wafted over her and she immediately closed her eyes.

When she opened them again, they were glistening with tears.

Estella was prattling on about one of her clients to keep the focus off Abilene, but she needn't have bothered. Abilene appeared to be lost in another time and place. She broke off a piece of scone and absently put it into her mouth.

An expectant silence swept over the members of the Secret, Book, and Scone Society. No one could speak. They were all hypnotized by the emotions passing over Abilene's face.

One emotion came to the forefront, however. Nora recognized it at once.

It was pain.

The memory Hester's scone had coaxed from Abilene wasn't at all pleasant. Her eyes filled with hurt and her lips quivered.

"I'm sorry," Hester said, reaching for Abilene's hand. "It was supposed to bring you comfort."

Ignoring Hester's hand, Abilene signaled "hold on" with her index finger, and surprisingly, took a second bite.

A few seconds later, she said, "My mom used to make cookies with chopped dates. This scone made me remember those cookies. And my mom."

The women waited for her to continue, but she didn't. She just sat in her chair, cradling the white box as if it were a baby.

"Where's your mama now?" June asked.

Abilene looked at her. "Dead. My daddy too. I was really little when it happened. They were in Africa. On a church mission trip. I wasn't with them."

"But they're with you," June said. Nora would have gone on to ask more questions about Abilene's upbringing, but June was wiser. "I bet your mama watches you every day. I bet she wishes she could make those cookies for you. What did they taste like?"

A tear slipped down Abilene's cheek. "They were sweetened with honey. And there was another flavor . . ."

"Was it ginger? Because I added that to your scone," Hester said. "Just a sprinkle."

"I think that was it, yes. Those cookies were warm and light and sweet. Just like my mom." A second tear followed the first as she turned to Hester. "Can you miss someone you barely remember?"

Hester's eyes now grew moist. "Yes. You can miss them with your whole being."

Estella gave both women a moment to gather themselves before saying, "I have a feeling that the person who raised you was nothing like your mom." She waited for Abilene to shake her head before adding, "It was a man, wasn't it?"

Abilene went very still.

"Darling, I know what it's like to be mistreated by men." Estella spoke without a trace of emotion. "I know what that kind of life does to a girl. How it molds her. She can never relax. She is always afraid. It's taken me years to stop glancing over my shoulder to see if someone's creeping up behind me. It's taken me decades to remember that I don't have to worry about being too loud, too quiet, too present, or too absent. Is that how he made you feel?"

Abilene managed another nod.

"I've been there too." Estella cupped her mug of hot tea with both hands and Nora pictured the frightened girl Estella must have been. A girl who'd been abandoned by her biological father and beaten by her stepfather.

Why does life have to be so hard? Nora thought, her gaze leaving the circle of women to land on the nearest bookshelf.

She knew there was no logical answer. Life was hard. But it was also surprisingly beautiful. Nora felt the beauty as she looked back at the other women in the room. At her fellow survivors.

"I grew up in a basement," Abilene said. She pressed the bakery box against her chest as if she could somehow drink in the scent of the honey-date scone. For her, this was her mother's perfume.

No one moved or spoke. They knew Abilene was trying to let her secret out. She was trying to wrench it free from the dark, tangled place where it had been locked. But like all secrets, it wanted to stay hidden.

"I could only come out to do chores. I cooked, I cleaned my uncle's house, and I washed clothes. I left the basement for three hours every night. When he was at work, I was allowed to read. My uncle chose the books. While we ate supper, I'd have to tell him what I'd learned."

She sank back in her chair. Her face was pale and she seemed shrunken. Diminished.

Nora hated seeing another woman look this way. She hated hearing what Abilene had endured. "Did you ever try to escape?" she asked. "I mean, before this time. Before you succeeded."

"I haven't." The words were a whisper. They hovered around

the circle of chairs for a long moment before being swallowed by shadow.

"You haven't succeeded?" Nora asked, half afraid of the answer. "Do you think your uncle's looking for you?"

Abilene shot a fearful glance toward the front of the store, as if someone was staring at them through the window. "I know he is. And when he finds me, he'll kill me."

Chapter 12

The caged bird sings with a fearful trill of things un-known but longed for still

—Maya Angelou

In the silence following Abilene's statement, the tempo of the rain increased. It fell harder and faster, hammering the book-store's roof. A second later, thunder rumbled like an empty stomach.

Nora felt chilled, and she hadn't been caught in the storm with-out a jacket like Abilene had. Without asking, Nora gave Abilene a fresh cup of coffee. She wished she had a cozy sweater for her, but a throw blanket was the best she could do.

June was clearly thinking similar thoughts, for she started fussing over the condition of Abilene's wet shoes.

"Your sneakers are paper thin. And where are your socks?" June clucked like a hen and began digging around in her purse. She told Abilene to kick off her shoes and when she complied, Nora could see angry red welts on the back of Abilene's heels. She guessed that Abilene had bought the cheapest sneakers she could find. They obviously weren't a good fit.

"I made these for Nora, but I'll knit her another pair." June handed Abilene some of her handmade socks. "Put these on be-fore you catch a cold. I don't care if modern science says that being soaked to the bone doesn't make you sick. *I* don't believe their mumbo jumbo for a second."

"Hey, those are different," Estella said, pointing at the socks in Abilene's hands. "You can make animal designs now?"

June smiled. "Just a few. I added foxes to Nora's socks because they remind me of the fox on her walking stick." She gestured for Abilene to hurry up and don the sock. "Go on, honey. We want you to be as dry and comfy as possible. We're going to make you feel better, starting with those feet of yours."

Abilene did as she was told. Once she had June's socks on, she reached for her coffee. She cradled the warm mug between her palms while gazing at the bookshelves opposite her.

"Are you up to telling us more?" Hester asked.

Reluctantly, Abilene turned away from the books. "I thought about killing him," she said in a thin voice. "For a long time, it was what I thought about the most. I did all the cooking, so I thought about poisoning his food, but he had me taste everything first. He never turned his back to me. Also, there were cameras mounted all over the house so he could watch me while he was at work or went out to do an errand. The phone and TV were locked in his bedroom. If I broke a rule, I'd have to stay in the basement for days."

"What a sick bastard," Estella said angrily.

"When I was older, he brought work home from his shop for me to do. I had to meet his deadlines or I was punished." She paused for a long moment. "The worst punishment was losing my books. It was worse than going without food. My books were everything to me. My friends lived in books. My dreams lived there too. Anything that's good about me came from reading books."

Glancing around her shop, Nora thought of how she'd always drawn solace from books. The needs she'd been trying to meet were different from Abilene's. For Abilene, a girl held hostage for her entire childhood, there was nothing beautiful, magical, or positive in her world unless it came from a book. Books were her only means of escape from her prison. She had no phone, no television, no friends, no schoolmates, and no family. She was a living ghost.

"Were you able to go outside?" Nora asked.

"Sometimes," Abilene said. "The backyard had a really high privacy fence, and I was allowed to work in the garden after supper. My uncle always watched me. If the neighbors were outside, then I couldn't go out."

June shook her head in disbelief. "What about folks coming to the front door? People delivering packages? Soliciting? Was there ever a chance for you to yell for help?"

Abilene released a sigh. It was so heavy, so weighed down with sorrow that it felt like an anchor dropping into the dark depths of the ocean.

Nora looked at Abilene and realized that she possessed an inner strength that defied belief. This girl had grown up without love or companionship. She'd probably experienced little or no joy. She'd never had a birthday party, a restaurant meal, or bought something from a shopping mall. She'd never received a personal letter or a phone call. She'd traveled nowhere and spoken to no one save the man who'd locked her, this friendless orphan, in a basement.

"Why did he treat you that way?" Hester asked. "Why did he feel compelled to control you?"

"He hated children," Abilene said without hesitation. "He was furious with my parents for dumping me on him. For ruining his life. Those are his exact words. I heard them a million times."

Estella curled her fists into tight balls. "I don't know how you survived. I would have killed the bastard. Somehow, I would have found a way."

Abilene gave Estella a look of resignation. "In the end, I decided not to try. Because if I succeeded, I'd be a monster, just like him. I didn't want to be like him." She gestured at the bookshelves. "I wanted to be Jo March, Lizzie Bennet, Hermione Granger, Anne Shirley, Nancy Drew, Meg Murry, and Laura Ingalls."

June followed her gaze. "Meg Murry?"

"She's the heroine from *A Wrinkle in Time*." Nora smiled at Abilene. "I love that book."

Abilene smiled back at her. It was a real smile with no timidity. Abilene became something else when she talked about books. Something bigger than her past. "Me too. Did you know that L'Engle described books as stars? As 'explosive material, capable of stirring up fresh life endlessly.' That's how I felt. Every book I was lucky enough to read was a star. It was filled with light. I never grew tired of the stories. Every time I reread a favorite book, I'd find something new in it. Not because the story changed, but because I did."

The other women in the room nodded in agreement.

"How did you finally get away?" June asked.

Abilene didn't answer. Instead, she sipped from her coffee cup and kept her gaze lowered.

"It's okay. You don't have to talk about that if you don't want to," Hester said.

When it was obvious that Abilene wasn't going to respond, Nora said, "There are other things we have to talk about. And the last thing I want to do is pressure you, but you have to tell us about Amanda."

There was no movement from Abilene. She was like a rabbit, frozen in fright, and Nora had no idea how to coax the truth from her. Bullying or threatening wouldn't work. Cajoling probably wouldn't help either. Even if Abilene wanted to speak, something was holding her back. Something powerful. Something like fear.

Nora stood up and wandered over to a bookshelf. "You and

Amanda Frye had something in common. Her books were her pride and joy. Stories were her portal to a different life. Her escape hatch. She didn't have money or a career. She didn't have close friends or family. She was alone and isolated. She also didn't have your strength, Abilene, or your determination to believe in a better future."

Abilene shifted in her seat and though Nora waited for her to respond, she said nothing.

"I guess time and disappointment beat the hope out of Amanda, which is why she swallowed a bottle of pain killers and stumbled into her pond to drown." Nora touched the nearest book. Its title winked, as if the gilt letters were encouraging her to continue. "The four of us found her floating in that gross pond. Do you know why? Because her books couldn't save her. In the end, the books failed."

"No, they didn't," Abilene said, leaping to the defense of her favorite things. "She died because of me."

Hester jumped out of her seat like a spooked cat. Standing by an endcap of books with autumnal covers, she said, "What are you talking about? Amanda committed suicide. According to the paper and to Jasper, that's the official ruling. Once the labs came back confirming the presence of the drugs . . ." She trailed off and turned to the books on display. It was as if she sought an explanation from *Red Leaf, Yellow Leaf, The Cider House Rules*, and *The Witches of Eastwick*.

"Anything else you'd like to share with us?" Estella asked Hester. "Something your man might have let slip in a moment of passion, perhaps?" When Hester shook her head, Estella turned to Abilene. "Can you explain what you mean? You've been through hell. Lifetimes of it. But you're no killer. If you had that in you, your uncle would already be dead. And he's not dead, is he?"

Abilene whispered a barely audible no.

"So how could someone who refused to be infected by hate

and hurt have caused Amanda's death?" Estella wanted to know.

"I led him to her. My uncle." Abilene spoke so softly that the rainfall almost washed her words away. "After the hospital, I had nowhere to go." She shook her head and started again. "When I was growing up, the only person my uncle invited over was our next-door neighbor. She was a reader. My uncle was a reader. They talked about books in the backyard. She never came inside because of all the cameras."

Estella cursed under her breath.

Abilene cast her a surprised glance before continuing. "She'd bake him cookies. He'd make her margaritas. When she moved away, he was even angrier than before."

June whistled. "Your perv of an uncle was having a suburban love affair."

"No," Abilene said firmly. "He wouldn't have touched her. He was repulsed by sex and anything to do with it. To him, nudity was disgusting and physical relationships were for base people. Animals, he called them. The books he read—the books I was allowed to read—couldn't focus on those subjects or he'd call them filth and destroy them."

Estella, who'd been sitting on the edge of her chair, visibly relaxed. "So he never touched you?"

"No!" Red patches bloomed on Abilene's cheeks. "When he was very angry, he'd twist my arm or squeeze my neck. Afterward, he'd scrub his hands while reciting the Pledge of Allegiance. He wasn't a germophobe, he just hated touching people."

Nora studied Estella. Abilene's story was undoubtedly calling forth memories that Estella had rather stay buried. A stepfather's physical and verbal abuse. A mother's negligence. A father's abandonment.

"He'll never touch you again," Estella said, her eyes shining with cold fury. "If your asshole uncle followed you to Miracle Springs, he'll regret it. I promise."

Hester passed her hands over her face while June picked up her mug, gave it a dismissive glance, and put it back down on the coffee table.

"I wish there was something stronger in my mug than roasted beans," June said. "I'd kill for a real drink right now."

"Me too," said Estella. "But no one needs it more than Abilene, and she's probably never had liquor before. Am I right?"

Abilene looked embarrassed. "My uncle made me sip his wine before serving it to him. I didn't like it. It tasted like balsamic vinegar."

"You're probably more a chocolate martini girl," Estella said. "But we can hardly move to the Oasis Bar until we're done here. Finish telling us about Amanda."

The talking had taken its toll on Abilene. She'd kept all of these words and feelings locked inside for so long, that it had obviously taxed her to let them all out.

Still, she went on. "I knew where Mrs. Frye lived because she sent letters to my uncle and I memorized her address. My uncle never wrote back. After she was gone, he became even meaner. I knew I had to escape or he'd take all of the anger out on me. I decided to run to Amanda. It was stupid, but I figured that she must be a decent person because she loved to read. I did crazy things to get here." She paused. "When I showed up at Amanda's house, she didn't know me."

"She'd never seen you," Nora said, trying to imagine Abilene's desperate journey from Texas to North Carolina.

"I was wearing hospital scrubs and paper booties," Abilene said. "Mrs. Frye wouldn't let me in at first, but I told her enough things about my uncle that she finally believed my story."

June grunted. "It's a wonder she didn't call your uncle."

Fear flitted through Abilene's pale blue eyes. "I think she did. I was so tired and hungry that I fell onto the bed in her spare room and slept for ten hours. Then, Mrs. Frye gave me something to eat, and we talked a little more. She seemed nervous. Every sound made her jump and she kept looking out the window. It was scaring me, so I told her I couldn't stay."

"How did she react?" Hester asked.

"She was relieved. She wanted to give me something to wear, so she took me outside and pulled a clean dress off her clothesline. She'd just handed it to me, along with a pair of flip-flops, when the neighbor's dogs started barking. All the blood rushed out of Mrs. Frye's face. She gave me a shove and whispered a single word."

Nora felt like she was there, standing with Abilene and Amanda. She saw the sun on their shoulders and the breeze rippling the dresses on the line. She smelled the faint scent of laundry detergent and heard the frenzied baying of the dogs. For some reason, the hair on her forearms stood on end. "What was the word?"

Abilene's voice trembled when she said, "Run."

Nora knew what had happened next. Abilene had seen terror in Amanda's eyes and she'd reacted like any true survivor would. She'd run.

She ran all the way to town, Nora thought. *She ran to the building with books in the window. In the books, she saw sanctuary. She hid among them, taking refuge in the only companions she'd ever known.*

"You'll never have to run again," Nora said. "You're never going back to that basement, that man, or that life. You have a new home now. You have a new family. And you have four big sisters who will protect you."

Nora embraced Abilene. Abilene didn't return the gesture, but just as Nora was about to pull away, a pair of thin arms encircled her back. Abilene expelled a honey-scented sigh into Nora's shoulder.

"Let's get that drink now," Estella said, reaching for her raincoat.

The women piled into June's car and drove to the Miracle Springs Lodge, a sprawling brick structure perched atop a hill. With over two hundred guest rooms, multiple gardens, several eateries and cocktail lounges, gazebos for small group meetings and private meditation sessions, and the thermal pools, it was the biggest property in the area.

Estella had spent many an evening in the Oasis Bar, but tonight, she suggested the Bamboo Bistro instead of her regular haunt.

The women chose a secluded table near the entrance to the Japanese Zen garden and left the ordering to Estella. She sauntered up to the bar and a few minutes later, a waiter served them drinks in tall glasses garnished with translucent apple slices.

"Your Indian Summers," he said as he set their drinks down on cocktail napkins embossed with a green bamboo stalk. "Enjoy."

"This is basically cider spiked with vodka and elderflower liqueur," Estella explained to Abilene. "It's the perfect refreshment for this between-season time."

"To a new season." Hester held her glass out for a toast.

Everyone else touched rims with her except for Abilene, who clearly didn't understand the ritual. She raised her glass to her mouth and took a tentative sip.

Nora's sip was tentative as well. She was a little worried by how much she was anticipating this drink, and how eager she was to soften the sharp edges of the past two weeks.

Darkness had settled around the hills. The five women were seated under a wide arc of stars. The candle in the center of their table softly flickered. The din of the bistro diners was as gentle as the lull of a moving stream.

Hester asked Abilene about the education she'd received in her uncle's house and Abilene explained that everything she'd learned came from books. When she was old enough, her uncle had taught her to repair clocks and watches. He brought home repairs and had her help with appraisals. Because she needed computer access to determine current market values, he showed her how to navigate the Internet. She could use the computer only under her uncle's supervision.

"I liked the work, but I loved being in the kitchen. I could make magic there." Abilene looked at Hester. "The things I created were *mine*. Cooking was my freedom."

Hester's experience had been eerily similar. She'd lived with a domineering aunt who was willing to let Hester borrow books from her extraordinary library in exchange for home-made baked goods. So Hester had learned to bake.

Abilene finished her drink and Estella immediately hailed the waiter.

After draining the last drops of her cocktail, Nora decided to ask a more crucial question than how Abilene had acquired an education. "Do you think your uncle wanted to hurt Amanda because she sheltered you?"

"All I can say is that she'd still be alive if it weren't for me." Abilene looked at Nora, her eyes plaintive and sad. "I don't want him to hurt anyone else. You've all been so—"

"Hold that thought, love," Estella interrupted. She'd been watching the waiter and he was now approaching their table.

"Ladies?" He directed his smile at Estella. "Another round?"

"We'll switch to Winter Is Coming. We like our literary references," Estella said. The waiter cleared away their highball glasses and returned to the bar. When he was out of earshot, Estella leaned forward. "Listen to me, Abilene. The only way everyone in this circle will be safe is for us to know what we're dealing with. Your uncle is a special kind of crazy bastard. He breaks the mold. But he's just a man. One man."

June bobbed her head in agreement. "He'll have to face five of us. Five badass women."

"We could tell Jasper too, "Hester said. "He can track down your uncle and toss him in a cell. Hopefully, the tossing part will be especially rough."

They all went quiet and Nora assumed her friends were

wondering the same thing as her. Could the sheriff's department really help?

"Can you prove that your uncle killed Amanda?" Nora asked Abilene.

She glanced around the garden as if the man might be hiding behind a potted tree or the row of bushes lining the gravel path. "No," she whispered. "Probably not."

The waiter reappeared carrying a tray of martini glasses.

"What's this?" June asked Estella. "Milk and cookie time?"

"This is our most popular dessert cocktail," the waiter answered. "Godiva white chocolate liqueur, vanilla vodka, white crème de cacao, half-and-half, and white sanding sugar. Rich and sweet."

Estella reached for her glass. "Just how I like my men."

The waiter didn't know how to respond to this, so he smiled awkwardly and went to check on another table.

There was something ethereal about the white liquid and the sanding sugar sparkling from the rims of the martini glasses. The drinks looked like they were meant for a fairy queen, not for the odd assemblage that was the Secret, Book, and Scone Society and their young guest.

Nora looked at the stars and thought of how Abilene had ended up in a bookstore called Miracle Books.

She needs a miracle, Nora thought. *She needs to be released from the prison she carries around with her.*

When she lowered her gaze, her eyes met Abilene's. "Do you want to tell us your real name?"

"It's Hannah. Hannah Tupper."

Nora stared at her. "Were you named after a book character?"

"Yes." Abilene was clearly unhappy to admit this.

Nora couldn't understand why Abilene was so wretched. "She's a wonderful character. She's smart and kind, a fan of kittens and blueberry cake, and—"

"A witch," Abilene said.

Estella put her drink down and waved her hands. "Wait. What book are you talking about?"

"*The Witch of Blackbird Pond*," Nora said. "And Hannah *isn't* a witch. She's different from the other villagers because she's a Quaker. She's also the scapegoat for any and all negative occurrences. She befriends a young girl, Kit, and teaches her that the true meaning of home is the love and friendship found within its walls."

"I need to read that book," June said. "I've been called a witch a time or two because of my cat parades." She blew out an exasperated sigh. "It's not like I've tried to charm those whiskered catnip addicts."

Estella snorted. "Other women don't call *me* a witch because of cats. But I don't care. I've been called worse."

"People use the word *witch* when they feel threatened by a woman who is strong, confident, and independent. A woman who's comfortable in her own skin," June said. "But would you prefer us to call you Abilene?"

"My parents picked Hannah," she said. "They named me, but they didn't raise me. They left me with a couple from their church and headed off to Africa so they could work at an orphanage. They made *me* an orphan. My church-loving parents left me with the Devil. I don't want their name."

Nora smiled. "It's good to have a new name to complement your new life."

Abilene glanced up at the star-speckled sky. "Can I do that? Can I get rid of Hannah? Like a snake shedding its skin?"

Hester touched her on the shoulder. "More like a butterfly shedding its cocoon. You've never been able to spread your wings. You weren't even allowed to try. I think it's time for that part of your life to be over. It's time for you to fly."

Her eyes locked on the glittering canopy overhead, Abilene

took Hester's hand and whispered a verse from an Emily Dickinson poem:

> " '*A power of Butterfly must be—*
> *The Aptitude to fly*
> *Meadows of Majesty concedes*
> *And easy Sweeps of Sky—*' "

And then she picked up her glass and drank her entire cocktail without pausing for breath.

Chapter 13

*My doctor told me to stop having intimate dinners
for four. Unless there are three other people.*
                                                —Orson Welles

Abilene refused to speak with Deputy Andrews or anyone
else from the sheriff's department. Exhausted after so much
talking, she asked to be driven straight back to her apartment.

Hester walked Abilene into her building. When she returned
to the car, her face was tight with concern.

"We have to do something about that apartment," she said.
"Abilene didn't want me to come in and I can see why. She has
one towel, two dishes, and a few sets of plastic cutlery, no
doubt taken from the salad bar at the grocery store. She still has
nothing to wear. I've given her a couple of things, but they're
too big on her."

Estella immediately came up with a plan. She'd invite Abilene to the Magnolia Spa for a complimentary shampoo, cut,
and style. In the meantime, the other Secret, Book, and Scone
Society members could scour the thrift shops for household
items. Though none of them had much in the way of extra cash
to spare, they all wanted to contribute.

"I'll check my calendar," said Estella as she alighted from
June's Bronco. "But I think I can fit Abilene in late Thursday.
After five."

Knowing Nora would be working until at least six, June and Hester suggested they go shopping without her. Otherwise, the thrift store would close before they could buy anything.

Nora was fine with this decision. She gave June some money and waved good-bye to her friends. She wasn't thinking about pots and pans or bath towels. Her mind was completely focused on Ezekiel Crane.

She continued to think about him the next day, despite how busy Miracle Books was that morning. Crane cast a pall over everything and Nora couldn't stop wondering if he was in Miracle Springs right now. And had he killed Amanda Frye? What about Kenneth?

Just before lunch, with all her customers contentedly browsing, Nora called Ezekiel Crane's clock and jewelry shop in Lubbock. She used her cell phone instead of the shop's landline and blocked her number before placing the call.

Nora had no idea what she'd say if Crane picked up. She could pretend that she'd dialed the wrong number and hang up. If he did answer, she'd breathe much easier knowing that he was in Lubbock, which was a long way from Miracle Springs.

However, Crane didn't pick up. After six unanswered rings, the voicemail message kicked in and a gravelly male voice announced that Master Humphrey's was temporarily closed. The voice went on to say that customers with incomplete repairs would be contacted soon with a new pickup date.

Nora disconnected the call.

Without waiting to consult her friends, she dialed the sheriff's department non-emergency number. After asking to speak with Sheriff McCabe, she was placed on a brief hold. When the sheriff picked up, he surprised Nora by saying, "Ms. Pennington. You got to me before I could get to you."

Nora was confused. "Sorry?"

"We still need your statement on Mr. Frye," the sheriff said.

Encouraged by his lack of criticism for her failure to provide a statement, Nora made the bold suggestion that he stop by Miracle Books after closing. When he didn't reply, she hurriedly continued. "I need to speak with you privately. It might be related to your ongoing investigations, but I can't go into details now and I can't close my business to come to the station. I don't have employees. It's just me, and I need to stay open."

The sheriff fell into a contemplative silence. After a moment, he said, "All right, Ms. Pennington. I'll drop by this evening, though I don't think your shop is exactly private. The second I park in your lot, people will wonder why I'm visiting after hours. Wouldn't it be better if I picked you up and we drove a train stop or two away? We could grab a bite to eat while we talk. If that works for you."

Unable to tell if McCabe had an ulterior motive for inviting her to dinner, Nora agreed to his plan.

Minutes later, the sleigh bells banged against the back of the door and she glanced up, ready to greet her next customer. There were actually two customers—a man and a woman who'd clearly been in the middle of an argument and weren't prepared to stop just because they'd moved from street to store. They continued to exchange a flurry of angry whispers by the bookmark spinner until the woman abruptly turned to leave.

Nora heard her hiss, "Don't buy *anything* unless you can ingest it. I'm serious, Monroe."

Looking chastised, the man named Monroe nodded and the woman exited the store. Monroe watched the bells bang against the door in her wake and then ambled past the checkout counter. As he walked by, he gave Nora a shy smile and a soft hello.

She told him to make himself at home and that he could come find her if he needed any help.

"I wish you could help," he said, sounding miserable. "But I think I'm beyond saving at this point."

"No one is that far gone," Nora said and beckoned him to follow her to the ticket agent's window. Pointing at the menu, she suggested he order something and, after she'd prepared his drink, he could share his troubles with her.

Brightening a little, Monroe chose a Jack London and a chocolate book pocket.

When his order was ready, Nora didn't place it on the sill. Instead, she served it to him where the Secret, Book, and Scone Society met. She then settled in a chair beside him.

"The woman you came in with. Is she . . . ?" Nora trailed off, waiting for Monroe to answer.

"My wife," he said. "I love her to pieces, but no matter how hard I try, I keep disappointing her." He took a sip of his drink and added, "I have an issue with stuff."

Nora studied him. He wore jeans in a dark wash, red Converse sneakers, and a Cubs baseball shirt. He was clean shaven with an approachable face and a shy smile. A pair of glasses framed his sad eyes. Nora guessed that he was in his early thirties.

"What type of stuff?" she asked.

"You name it, I have it. Books of every kind, old magazines, baseball cards, action figures, record albums, trophies, and papers from work, school, and a million other sources. I have bills that I've paid but haven't thrown away. I have coupons that expired years ago. That's my issue. I don't get rid of stuff. I just can't. I just put them in piles and the piles multiply. My spaces in our house are a mess. My wife, Laurie, is a neat freak. She now has a room I'm not allowed to enter. She calls it her safe place."

Nora made a sympathetic noise. "I can see how your different lifestyles might generate conflict."

"That's an understatement," Monroe scoffed. "I've tried lots of different tactics to deal with my hoarding—God, I hate that

word—and my stuff will be manageable for a while after I im-
plement some new program. But then, I'll get stressed about
something and I'll start collecting crap all over again. That crap
makes me feel secure. My stuff is like a wall of comfort, even
though I don't really care about any of it. Even when I'm not
stressed, I get stressed thinking about letting go of my stuff.
My house isn't a mess. I am."

"What strategies have you tried?" Nora asked.

Monroe seemed reluctant to answer, but eventually, he did.
"I saw a specialist for months. He recommended antianxiety
meds. Medication might be an option for other people, but it
isn't for me. Let's just say that when I was in my early twenties,
I got hooked on an addictive product and I never want to go
down that road again."

"I understand."

Nora sat back in her chair and allowed the comforting quiet
of the bookstore to envelop them. Monroe sipped his coffee,
looking more than a little self-conscious, while titles popped up
in Nora's mind. However, she remembered Laurie's warning.
Monroe was not supposed to buy anything he couldn't ingest.

If Nora really wanted to help this couple, she'd have to be a
little pushy. "May I ask you something personal? Bordering on
rude?" she asked Monroe.

He responded with a nervous nod.

"During your time as an addict, did you have to live without
some or all of your possessions?"

Monroe stared at Nora as if she knew his secret history in its
entirety. "I don't know how you guessed that, but I actually
lived on the streets for a year or so. All my money went into
pills. Booze too. I lost everything."

Nora smiled at him. "Until you found your wife?"

He smiled back, his love for his wife making his face glow
like a star. He suddenly looked years younger. And far more
carefree. "Until I found Laurie," he said. His smile faded. "I

don't want to keep screwing up with her. I'd trade everything I own to make her happy. I'd toss every scrap of stuff into the trash. But I don't. I can't let it go."

"I believe you and Laurie can get through this together," Nora said. "And I have a few books that may help. I'll pull them from the shelves and put them at the checkout counter. When you're ready, you can ask your wife to look at them. The key here is to tackle this issue as a team. The Monroe-and-Laurie team."

Monroe thanked her and turned his attention to his book pocket. He wolfed the pastry down in four bites and licked dollops of chocolate off his fingers.

"Man, that was *so* good," he said. "I need to get one for Laurie."

His boyish enthusiasm was a delight to behold and Nora was glad that he'd found his way to Miracle Books.

"Tell you what," she said. "You find your wife and I'll pull titles and heat up another book pocket. By the time you come back, I'll have everything ready."

When the couple returned, Monroe led Laurie directly to the ticket agent's window. Nora noticed that they were holding hands. This was a good sign.

Nora asked Laurie if she'd care for anything to drink. She ordered a Louisa May Alcott.

Nora had chosen Laurie's mug with great care, and as she placed it on the counter, she watched the other woman read the message printed on the light blue ceramic.

The hush in the bookstore was abruptly broken by a bark of laughter.

"What it is?" Monroe asked, smiling in anticipation of sharing in the joke.

Showing the mug to her husband, Laurie said, "See where it says, PATIENCE. SUCH A WASTE OF TIME? I need this printed on a T-shirt."

Monroe chuckled and Nora knew that she'd successfully

broken the ice with Laurie. To make her even more amenable, she served her a chocolate book pocket.

"This is amazing!" Laurie exclaimed after one bite, and glanced at Monroe. "You're right. This place *is* special." She then turned to Nora. "My husband said that he talked to you about our situation. I don't mean to sound doubtful, but we've tried books before and they didn't work."

When Nora asked her which books they'd tried, Laurie said that most of the titles had been suggested by therapists and dealt with anxiety.

"In other words, the focus was solely on your husband?"

Laurie considered this. "Yeah, I guess so. I never thought about it that way, but the books were meant to help him change his behavior."

"What if you worked on this together? Saw it as a couple's challenge instead of Monroe's issue?" Nora asked. "People are usually more successful in making changes when they have the support of a loving partner. In this case, you could support each other. Together, you could build the life you want."

Monroe reached for Laurie's free hand and she slid hers into his. To Nora, she said, "I'd do anything to support my husband. That's why we came to Miracle Springs. We've done lots of talking, but we've talked about this for years. I'm ready for action."

"Patience," Nora teased, and both Laurie and Monroe laughed. "I recommend reading these together." She touched the top book on the short stack she'd placed on the coffee table. "Make the decisions together. Heal together. Change together. And know that nothing can happen overnight. Nor will it be easy. Take a look at these and let me know if you need anything else. I'll be up front."

Nora left them to examine *Spark Joy: An Illustrated Master Class on the Art of Organizing and Tidying Up* by Marie Kondo; Lisa Jewell's *The House We Grew Up In*; *The Little Book of*

Hygge: Danish Secrets to Happy Living by Meik Wiking; and *Coming Clean* by Kimberly Rae Miller. The list was a mixture of hardship and hope. Pain and renewal. It would serve as a recurring reminder that, though the past colors our present, it doesn't have to dictate the future. Love and faith can change one's course forever. And that's what Nora wished for Monroe and Laurie.

The couple bought all the books and promised to send Nora a postcard a few months down the road informing her of their progress.

Nora told them that she'd like that very much.

The couple left, holding the door for another customer on their way out.

From then on, a steady flow of customers kept Nora occupied until closing time.

When she finally locked up, she was glad that Sheriff McCabe had suggested they grab a bite to eat. Nora's lunch, a turkey sandwich and Honeycrisp apple, felt like a distant memory.

"Hungry?" the sheriff asked as he opened his passenger door for Nora.

"Famished," she said.

McCabe nodded in approval. "Good. I'd feel like a prize pig destroying a big platter of baby back ribs if you just ordered a side salad."

"Are we going to a barbecue place?" Nora tried to hide her disappointment. She'd never been a fan of North Carolina barbecue, but was wise enough not to voice her opinion aloud. Disliking barbecue was a sin in these parts.

"Not exactly. The place I have in mind is famous for their chicken and waffles," the sheriff said. "I've had a hankering for them lately. I even asked Jack to add them to the Pink Lady's menu, but he said he doesn't believe breakfast and supper foods should mix. You ever tried chicken and waffles?"

Nora said that she hadn't.

"You're in for a treat. And since we'll be in the car for a bit, do you want to clue me in on what it is you think might be relevant to my cases?"

This was not a suggestion but a polite command, and Nora realized she hadn't given McCabe enough credit. He was shrewd and intuitive. Deputy Andrews had undoubtedly told his boss everything Nora had previously shared, which was to be expected, and now he wanted to hear what she hadn't shared. Nora suddenly felt guilty for having waited so long to speak directly to the sheriff.

"I didn't know much until last night," she said they drove out of town. "Which is when I learned that a young woman, a newcomer to Miracle Springs, was probably the last person to see Amanda Frye alive."

If this news shocked the sheriff, he didn't show it. He kept his hands at two and ten and his eyes on the road. "Are you referring to Ms. Abilene Tyler? The young woman working at the Gingerbread House?"

Nora was impressed. McCabe certainly kept his ear to the ground. "Yes, but Abilene Tyler isn't her real name. It's not for me to spill all the secrets Abilene shared. I'm only going to tell you information relating to Amanda's death."

McCabe's brow creased and he seemed to be weighing how much leeway to give Nora. In the end, he simply said, "Go on."

"Would you answer one question first? Did Amanda Frye leave her book collection to a man called Ezekiel Crane?"

McCabe failed to mask his astonishment. "How did you know that? Only certain members of my department and two lawyers were given his name."

Nora spent the rest of the drive telling McCabe an abbreviated version of Abilene's tragic history.

"It was really hard for her to talk about these things," Nora said when she was done. "She was with a group of four women who've been trying to help since she got to town. I'm not trying to tell you how to do your job, but if you interview her now, she'll shut down. She's terrified, Sheriff."

McCabe pulled in to a ramshackle building that looked more like an abandoned auto garage than a restaurant. The sign above the door read, PEARL'S.

There were no posted hours, no sign indicating that the eatery was open or closed, and no outdoor décor whatsoever—not even a potted plant or a bench.

Nora was tempted to ask the sheriff if he'd made a wrong turn, but he turned off the engine and asked, "Is Ms. Tyler in a safe place?"

"I don't know." Nora described Abilene's apartment. She liked that McCabe focused on Abilene's welfare first and the case, second. After all, he was a man under pressure. He was an interim sheriff filling a pair of shoes left open by a corrupt predecessor. Almost immediately after taking the job, McCabe had had to deal with Amanda Frye's sudden death. Days later, he was faced with her son's fatal fall. Two suspicious deaths were a heavy weight for any small-town sheriff to shoulder, let alone one who'd barely had time to learn street names.

McCabe gestured at the building in front of them. "Let's go in. We can keep talking over a basket of homemade sweet potato chips."

Nora's stomach issued an audible rumble and the sheriff smiled.

When he opened the restaurant door, the boisterous strains of a jazz saxophone and a cloud of fried-chicken-scented air floated out from inside to greet them.

"How'd you hear about this place?" Nora asked. "I've lived two towns over for years and never knew it existed."

"I stopped here on my way to my new job," McCabe said. "I come back every chance I get. Pearl is the sweetest lady on earth. And her husband? The guy's always laughing. He's the happiest man I've ever seen. If I've had a bad day, he can make me forget about it."

From the inside, it was clear that the building had once been a garage. The lifts were gone, the floor was smooth gray concrete, and the garage bays were filled with round tables instead of cars. String lights with old-timey bare bulbs were strung across the high ceiling. The bar area was actually a VW bus without a roof or windows. Nora thought it was one of the coolest things she'd ever seen.

The sheriff pointed at the bartender, who had the physique of a linebacker and skin the color of dark roast coffee.

"That's Samuel, Pearl's husband," McCabe said.

Samuel spotted the sheriff and waved. As he waved, a smile lit his entire face. In fact, the man seemed to shine in the dim light, as if his smile electrified the space around him.

"You just can't get enough soul food, can you, Sheriff?" the woman behind the podium teased McCabe as she showed them to a table.

"No, ma'am. I dream about Pearl's chicken and waffles," McCabe said.

"I'll tell her to get started on your sweet potato chips. This your first time, sugar?" the hostess asked Nora. Without giving Nora a chance to reply, she said, "I'll have Pearl whip up some buttermilk hush puppies for you. You've never had a hush puppy 'til you've had Pearl's."

Nora and the sheriff made quick work of the sweet potato chips and hush puppies. They placed their entrée orders—chicken and waffles for the sheriff and shrimp and grits for Nora—and Pearl delivered the food in person. She served their entrées, as well as side dishes of collard greens and black-eyed peas. Before leaving them to their meals, she warned them to eat their vegetables or she'd call their mamas and snitch on them.

Pearl was as small as her husband was large. She wore fake

eyelashes, feather earrings that brushed her shoulders, and glittery pink eyeshadow. Her food was like her husband—full of merriment. Every bite was as uplifting as spring sunshine after a long and bitter winter.

McCabe, who'd decided to curtail talk of the investigation until after they'd sampled their meals, dug into his food with gusto.

"You sure I can't coerce you into trying this?" he asked Nora. When she demurred, he said, "Most people think this is a Southern dish, but it actually had its start north of the Mason-Dixon Line. Unlike their Southern brethren, African Americans living in the North could afford chicken. Waffles, on the other hand, were a real treat. Flapjacks were much more common, so what I'm eating was once a delicacy. To me, it still tastes like one."

Nora was intrigued by McCabe's culinary knowledge. "Do you know the origin of my meal?"

The sheriff laughed and Nora realized that Grant McCabe was a good-looking man. He was older than Jed by a decade and didn't exude raw sex appeal as Jed did, but McCabe's intelligent, walnut-brown eyes and rugged face held plenty of allure. Nora hadn't seen him in this light because she'd viewed him strictly as a man in uniform. As the guy in charge. But right now, he wasn't a lawman. He was just a man sitting across the table from a woman.

"My guess is that grits were originally a Native American food. But putting them with shrimp? I have no idea who came up with that. If shrimp and grits is your thing, you should try them Cajun style. That's how they're served in Nawlins." He pronounced the city with an exaggerated Louisiana drawl.

Nora didn't know whether it was the beer, the food, or the setting that had put McCabe in a playful mood, but she liked it.

They finished their meals and the server asked if they'd saved room for dessert. Despite their claims that they hadn't, Pearl insisted on making an order of her homemade peach pie to split.

While they waited on the pie, McCabe said, "Much as I'd rather not drag work into this setting, we should circle back to what we were talking about in the car. I'm going to look into Ezekiel Crane. I don't like the thought of him sneaking up on Ms. Tyler." He cocked his head. "Was she hospitalized because of him?"

"She didn't get into that with us, but it's a logical assumption," Nora said. She pointed at her chest. "My turn to ask a question."

The sheriff spread his hands. "Fire away."

"Was Kenneth Frye pushed or did he fall?"

"We don't have enough information to make that ruling yet," McCabe answered. His expression, like his voice, betrayed nothing.

"Was he drunk?" Nora persisted.

McCabe nodded.

"A mother overdosing on painkillers and a son falling from a tree house cabin." Nora shook her head. "Two deaths in such proximity? They can't be accidental."

At that inopportune moment, Pearl arrived with a large wedge of peach pie topped with a scoop of vanilla ice cream. She placed two forks and a pile of napkins on the table. "This will light you up like Christmas," she said before returning to the kitchen.

Pearl wasn't exaggerating. The piecrust was flaky and crisp, and the filling tasted of summer. The pie warmed Nora to the core. Though she could manage only a few bites, they were enough to convince her that Pearl possessed the same magical cooking ability as Hester. Both women knew how to transform food into something transcendent. Their creations provided not only nourishment to the body, but to the hungry parts of the soul as well.

"That's why they call it soul food," McCabe said as if Nora had spoken aloud. He finished his glass of water and signaled for the check. "Andrews tells me that you believe there's a connection between the two deaths and Amanda Frye's book collection. Why?"

"I can't say for certain because I haven't seen the entire collection," Nora said. "But those books are the only things that might provide a motive. There must be *something* about one of the books, or something tucked inside one of them, wanted by the person Kenneth shouted at during the festival. That person may have killed Kenneth to keep him from finding it."

The bill came and the sheriff insisted on paying. When Nora started to protest, he said, "It's not often that I get the chance to share a meal with such an extraordinary woman. Allow me to treat you."

Surprised by the compliment, Nora thanked him for introducing her to Pearl's. "I'll have to call you if I want to come back," she joked. "It would take me all day to ride my bike here."

"Well, that gives me something to look forward to," McCabe said. He paid the server with cash and picked up his hat. He didn't put it on, but held it in his hands while studying Nora. She had the feeling he was coming to an important decision.

"Ms. Pennington." He'd switched back to his lawman voice. "Would you examine Mrs. Frye's book collection? Your expertise might just prove invaluable."

Nora felt excitement surge through her body. It was the same rush she experienced when finding a valuable book at a yard sale or completing a successful bibliotherapy session. She was already on a high from Pearl's excellent food. Now, to cap it all off, she was being asked to examine Amanda's books.

"I can do it first thing in the morning," she said, trying to suppress a grin. "On one condition."

The sheriff arched his brows. "Which is?"

"You call me Nora from now on. At least, when it's just the two of us. Seeing as we shared a pie, I think it's fitting."

McCabe smiled. "All right, then. Are you ready to go? Nora?"

Chapter 14

The greater part of the truth is always hidden . . .
—J. R. R. Tolkien

Nora approached Amanda Frye's book collection with a mixture of anxiety and reverence. If a clue wasn't hidden among the books, Nora might never know what they had to do with the unexpected deaths of a mother and son.

She stared at the plastic-wrapped spines in their crate displays. To her, it seemed impossible for such beloved books to be connected to such dark deeds. But she knew better. Anything was possible.

Nora readjusted the gloves Sheriff McCabe had given her right before he'd unlocked Amanda's house.

She didn't like gloves.

Many people were surprised by this fact. After all, she could easily conceal her disfigured right hand by slipping on a glove, which is precisely why she didn't. Gloves reminded her of the times she'd tried to hide her scars. Once, she'd worn only long-sleeved shirts paired with light scarves and wide-brimmed hats. And gloves. She'd had cotton, lace, and leather gloves. They all made her hands sweat. Which made her skin itch. She also hadn't liked how the top half of the pinkie finger would droop with certain gloves. This wet noodle effect made her feel even more freakish.

After a year of hiding, she decided to let everyone see her as she was. She donated her gloves to a charity thrift store.

McCabe waited until the gloves he'd given her were snugly in place. He then asked Nora if she'd catalogue each book after examining it.

"I'd like an estimate of the entire collection's worth," he told her. "It doesn't have to be a formal appraisal. I just want to know if these books could be a motive for murder."

Nora and McCabe were standing in front of Amanda's makeshift bookcases. The house smelled of rot. Mold, damp wood, and stale air had infested every niche and corner. The sheriff left Nora to her work and walked through the house, opening windows. Nora was grateful for the influx of a grass-scented breeze.

She took out a notebook and began to search for and catalog the Catherine Cookson novels. In addition to taking down copyright information, Nora added brief notes on the condition of each book. She also carefully fanned the book pages, hoping to discover a letter or photograph that would answer all the questions Amanda's death had raised.

She'd just started on Cornelia Funke's Inkheart series when the sheriff received a phone call. Excusing himself, he moved into the kitchen to take the call. Nora heard phrases like "we should expand our hotel search" and "be sure to check with rental car companies" and knew McCabe was referring to Ezekiel Crane. From the sound of it, the sheriff's department had yet to locate him.

When McCabe suggested that they also speak with the businesses neighboring Crane's shop, Nora's suspicion was confirmed.

The sheriff returned to the living room to find Nora gazing into the middle distance.

"Are the books bringing back memories?" he asked.

She gave him a self-conscious smile. "They usually do, but not this time. After listening to Abilene's story, it seems unlikely that Crane could have come to Miracle Springs and left her in peace for this long. I mean, he must be furious with her. He had to close his business to hunt for her. His anger must have grown with every day she was gone."

"He has to be careful though," the sheriff said. "He can't be seen approaching her. Especially not in a public place."

"Because her freedom means the end of his freedom. If she were to tell anyone—a member of law enforcement, a health care practitioner, a social worker—what that man did to her, he'd be ruined."

Sensing that Nora hadn't completed her train of thought, Sheriff McCabe didn't reply. He quietly waited for her to go on.

"After listening to Abilene, it's clear that impulse control isn't one of Ezekiel Crane's strong points. Which makes me wonder about his lack of action. Why hasn't he gone after Abilene when she's alone? Because of these?" Nora gestured at the books. "The collection would be his, in due time. Kenneth might have delayed the gift by contesting his mother's will, but no judge would rule that Amanda wasn't of sound mind and body when she had it made. Unless she altered it prior to her supposed suicide, that is."

"Mrs. Frye's will hasn't been altered for decades," McCabe said. "She and her husband wrote their wills together when their son was still a boy. They both left everything to him, with the exception of Mrs. Frye's book collection. She left that to Ezekiel Crane."

"Amanda must have done that because she still cared about him on some level" Nora said. "She left her books to the only person she knew who'd appreciate their true worth."

Nora turned back to the books. They had to hold the answers.

Reaching for Dean Koontz's *Odd Thomas*, Nora wondered if her viewpoint was colored because of her unwavering love of books.

To her, books held the answer to every question, every problem. Books had the power to make difficult things better. Books were a magical medicine. They were a soft blanket, a cup of hot tea, and a strong hug bound between sturdy covers. Why wouldn't they have the answers to this riddle?

Yet doubts wormed their way into Nora's mind. These doubts increased as the sheriff fielded phone call after phone call. Though he never said anything directly to her, she could sense his growing restlessness.

She took *Harry Potter and the Philosopher's Stone* down from the shelf and paused before opening the cover. J. K. Rowling's series didn't fit with the rest of Amanda's collection because it wasn't a trilogy. Even in the cases of the Inkheart or Philip Pullman novels, which now included additional installments in the series, Amanda had acquired only the original three titles. She hadn't added Funke's *Dragon Rider* or Pullman's *Once Upon a Time in the North* to her collection.

However, the Harry Potter series couldn't qualify as a trilogy in any sense of the word. It was common knowledge that the series would extend beyond three books, which meant either Amanda simply loved the first three books or she had another reason for putting them on her shelf.

Nora examined the spine of the J. K. Rowling book again and frowned. Had Amanda gotten her hands on the limited print run of *Harry Potter and the Philosopher's Stone*? The one that credited Ms. Rowling as Joanne instead of J. K. on the copyright page? Because *that* book would definitely be worth keeping.

"Find something good?" McCabe asked.

Nora gently turned to the copyright page and said, "Yes. In America, this book was published as *Harry Potter and the Sor-*

cerer's Stone. Amanda has the UK version. It's an unusual copy. I'll have to look up the current value on my computer. I have no idea what it sells for." She glanced at the sheriff. "Do you read?"

"I mostly listen to audiobooks," he said. "Whenever I exercise, drive, or work on a project around the house, I'm plugged in." He tapped his ear.

"Do you have a favorite genre?" she asked.

He shrugged. "I bounce around. One week, I might listen to a medical thriller and the next, an informative book on economics. It all depends on my mood, but I like books that teach me something. I like to finish a book and feel like I'm a little bit smarter than I was before I read it."

McCabe's phone rang again and he returned to the kitchen to answer it.

Alone again, Nora pulled *Harry Potter and the Chamber of Secrets* down from the shelf. The book felt wrong. It was way too light.

As soon as she opened the cover, she understood why.

The book had been hollowed out.

The pages were still intact, but someone had cut a hole in the center of the book. Inside the hole was a gold pocket watch.

Slightly dazed by her discovery, Nora stood up and carried the book into the kitchen.

McCabe was looking out the window and had his phone pressed to his ear, but he heard Nora's approach and turned to face her.

She held out the book, cradling it in her palms, and waited for the sheriff to react.

"I need to call you back," he said and lowered his phone, his thumb hitting the END button as his arm dropped. His gaze flitted from the book, to Nora's face, and back to the book again.

"I haven't touched the watch," Nora whispered. She wasn't sure why she was whispering, but the significance of the moment seemed to call for it.

McCabe quickly put on a pair of gloves and took the book from Nora. "I'll be damned." The sunlight streaming in through the kitchen window glinted off the watch's gold surface, casting yellow speckles onto the sheriff's face. "Show me where you found this."

Nora preceded him into the living room and pointed at the space where the book had been shelved.

After taking a few photos of the crate, McCabe carefully slid the book into a paper evidence bag.

Nora examined the remaining books, but none were as remarkable as the hollowed-out *Harry Potter*.

"When can you come up with an estimate for the whole collection?" McCabe asked on the way back to town.

"I'll start working on it right away," Nora said. "What about the watch? Will you take it to Virtual Genie?"

"I hadn't planned to, but I might get answers more quickly that way." The sheriff frowned. "I have a gut feeling that we're short on time."

Nora shared his feeling. With two consecutive deaths combined with Ezekiel Crane's leave of absence from work, the sense of urgency was a shadowy presence looming over them all. McCabe had to close these investigations to protect his career while Nora and her friends had to keep Abilene safe.

At the railroad tracks, the sheriff stopped for a passing freight train. Drumming the steering wheel in frustration, he repeatedly glanced at his watch as the train chugged by.

Nora touched his forearm. "Ezekiel Crane's business is timepieces and jewelry. Do you think he knows about the pocket watch?"

"It's possible," the sheriff said and ceased his fidgeting.

"Can I tag along when you go to Virtual Genie?" she asked. "I can walk back to Miracle Books from there."

McCabe screwed up his lips. "Why do you want to go?"

Nora watched the cars clatter past. For a long time, she didn't answer.

"Because I let Amanda down," she finally said. "I could have been kinder to her, but I wasn't. I didn't like her, so I didn't try to get to know her. I put more effort into the well-being of complete strangers than I did with Amanda. And she needed help as much as anyone who travels to Miracle Springs in search of healing."

"I get that. And while I think you're being too hard on yourself, I have to ask why your history with Amanda is connected to a mysterious pocket watch?"

Nora threw up her hands in exasperation. It was hard to explain her investment in this case and her need to seek justice for Amanda. Taking a fortifying breath, she tried to find the right words. "I found Amanda, a woman I'd ignored, floating in her pond. I saw her book, with its broken spine, splayed on her kitchen counter. I *knew* she'd never leave a book like that. Not after seeing her collection. *If* she'd voluntarily taken those pain pills, she wouldn't stand in the kitchen and read one of her first editions while waiting for the drugs to kick in. She wouldn't have gone outside either. She would have sat in the living room, needing to be close to the only things in the world that brought her comfort. Her books."

The sheriff nodded to show that he was listening.

"I think someone killed her," Nora went on. "After Kenneth asked Griffin Kingsley and then me about his mother's books, I started thinking that the motive lay with them. But only one book really matters. The book turned into a safe. The book hiding a pocket watch. And if someone at Virtual Genie can say what's so special about this watch, then I want to hear what it is. I want to represent Amanda's interests in a way I never did when she was alive."

The end of the train lumbered past the crossing. Nora was sad to see that there was no caboose. There was just another engine, facing backward. It was a story without an ending.

"It's like a snake with two heads," McCabe said, his gaze following the receding locomotive. Though the red crossing-signal lights were still flashing, the gates were slowly rising. The sheriff turned to Nora. "Okay. You can come along."

McCabe nabbed a parking spot right in front of Virtual Genie. The moment they entered the lush main room, Nora spotted Jed. He was shaking hands with Tamara and clasping a white envelope in his free hand.

Nora hung back a few feet, allowing the sheriff to approach Griffin Kingsley's desk unaccompanied.

Jed turned to leave. He immediately caught sight of Nora and his face broke into a wide grin.

"That's twice you've followed me in here," he said after closing the distance between them. He leaned over to kiss her. It was just a brief peck on the mouth, but Nora was too stunned to react. If Jed noticed her stiffness, he didn't let it show. "You're getting pretty bold for a stalker. Coming in while the sheriff's here."

"We came in together, actually," Nora said. "He asked me to do a rough appraisal of Amanda Frye's book collection."

Jed glanced back at McCabe. "Do you have a thing for men in uniform? Tell me now, because I need to know if I have to worry about the firemen. I'd really like to catch a break from having to compete with those guys!"

Nora couldn't properly respond to Jed's teasing style of flirtation. She was too eager to hear what the sheriff and Griffin were saying. "I'm sorry, Jed. I have to go. Call you later?"

He was hurt, but he tried to hide it. "Yeah. Sure. I need to deposit this before my shift starts anyway." He waved the envelope. "Tamara got a great price for my old bank."

Stuffing the envelope into his pocket, Jed exited Virtual Genie.

Nora stared after him for a moment. She could have handled that encounter better, but she hadn't expected him to kiss her. Not in the middle of the day. Not in front of others. It had been too public for Nora's tastes, and possibly too possessive as well.

"Ms. Pennington?" Sheriff McCabe called. "Would you like to join us?"

As Nora hurried to the sheriff's side, she noticed Griffin's puzzled expression. Instead of explaining Nora's presence, the sheriff said, "I'd like to show you in private."

Griffin led them to the back room. After switching on the high-powered lamp in the center of a worktable, he stepped away to allow McCabe room.

The sheriff, who'd donned a fresh pair of examination gloves, removed the book from the evidence bag. He placed it on the table and opened the cover. "As I mentioned, this book and its contents are evidence in an ongoing investigation, so I'll ask you to keep to yourself what you see. I'd also appreciate your expertise in identifying this pocket watch."

Griffin's eyes immediately lit with a zealous gleam. The pocket watch was clearly valuable.

The naked longing in his face lasted only a second or two. By the time Griffin pulled on his own gloves, he'd mastered his emotions. "Happy to help," he said with his usual courtesy.

His hands betrayed his eagerness. There was yearning in Griffin's fingers as they pried the pocket watch from its snug nest of book pages. After selecting a magnifying glass from the table's desk caddy, Griffin turned the watch over. He examined the back and said, "Definitely gold, but lighter than fourteen karats. Maybe nine karats?" He flipped the watch over again.

"Lovely filigree engraving. Looks like a ram's head in the central medallion. I haven't come across that before."

Nora held her breath as Griffin pushed the latch release. The watch cover popped open to reveal a white face with roman numerals. "Here's our maker." Griffin pointed at the script running across the lower half of the face. "Monnier and Musard. A Swiss timepiece. I believe it's quite old."

"Can you tell me what it's worth?" the sheriff asked.

"I'll have to search around online," Griffin said. "I could give you an estimate, but it would be inaccurate because I don't know if the watch works. Many antique pocket watches require a key for winding. Some watches require two keys. This watch is very unusual in that it requires three keys. Like the ram's head, I've never encountered that before."

McCabe frowned. He wasn't getting what he was looking for from Griffin. "Is there anything else you can add?"

Griffin managed to tear his gaze from the watch. "I have a collection of spare pocket watch keys," he told the sheriff. "I could try them to see if they'll open this face. It might take some time because there's another unusual element to this watch. Judging from the shape of the pins in the face, each key is unique. In other words, this watch requires three unique keys to function. I could force it open, but that would probably damage the case."

"No, no," McCabe was quick to say. "Let's give your keys a try."

As much as Nora wanted to observe Griffin fit keys into the watch face, she couldn't. She needed to open the bookstore.

"I have to get to work. Thank you for including me," she said to the sheriff. He responded with a brief nod, his focus clearly on the watch, so Nora passed through the curtain and reentered the main room.

Tamara grinned at Nora as she walked by her desk. "What's

going on back there? Did you find a priceless heirloom or an incriminating document tucked inside a book?"

Nora knew better than to breathe a word about the watch. "Something like that," she said and left.

Out on the sidewalk, she ran into Jack Nakamura.

"Hello, Ms. Nora. Are you selling something too?" he asked, gesturing at the Virtual Genie sign.

She glanced up at the brass lamp with its sparkling plume of smoke. "I don't have anything to sell. I use everything I own."

Jack placed his hands together in front of his chest and bowed in respect. "If you have nothing extra, then nothing can weigh you down. You know a secret many people will never learn. You know that the real treasures in life are the connections we make with other people. Things rust, break, or lose their worth. Love only increases in value. To be sure it does, we must repair any little breaks or cracks using *kintsugi.*"

"*Kintsugi?*" Nora tried to mimic Jack's pronunciation.

"It's the ancient Japanese practice of repairing broken pottery using lacquer mixed with gold dust. After the repair, the pot has golden seams and is more beautiful than it was before." Jack smiled. "It's how we should repair broken hearts. A heart repaired with love will be scarred, but will also be more beautiful than it was before."

Nora didn't know how to respond to Jack's sidewalk philosophy or why he'd decided to bring up the subject of broken hearts, so she asked if his antique box had already sold.

"That's why I'm here." A shadow darkened his cheerful face. "I can't find the auction listing. Either I'm searching the wrong site or Mr. Kingsley forgot to post the listing."

"I'm sure there's an explanation," Nora assured Jack and hurried on to Miracle Books.

It took her most of the day to assign a value to Amanda's collection. While she was online looking up prices, she also researched Monnier and Musard pocket watches. She found an auction site that had sold a watch closely resembling the one hidden inside the Harry Potter book. The watch sold at auction didn't have a ram's head and required only two keys, but it was in very fine condition and functioned perfectly. It had sold for a whopping sixteen thousand dollars. And that was two years ago.

By day's end, Nora knew that the watch was worth twice as much as Amanda's entire book collection.

Nora called Sheriff McCabe to tell him what she'd found.

"Interesting," he said. "Mr. Kingsley told me that the watch from Amanda Frye's house was probably worth a few thousand. Sixteen thousand is more than a few."

Though Nora wondered why Griffin had assigned the pocket watch such a low value, she assumed that he placed a great deal of importance on the watch's functionality. "Whatever the monetary value, I'd question whether a person would commit two murders to get their hands on that watch. But people kill each other over less. We live in that kind of world now, don't we?"

"We also live in a world where people help each other," McCabe said. "And I want to thank you for your help . . . Nora."

The sheriff ended the call seconds before a whistle announced the arrival of the afternoon train. This meant an influx of new guests to Miracle Springs and the departure of those whose time in the town had come to an end.

It struck Nora that Ezekiel wouldn't need a car if he traveled to Miracle Springs from a town on the same train line. She also realized that she had no idea what he looked like. Though she'd searched for images of him online, she hadn't found any.

Another ghost, Nora thought. *Like Abilene. She was never allowed to exist outside Crane's house. She haunted a few rooms and a twilight garden.*

In a sense, Nora was a ghost too. She'd completely disappeared from her previous life. To those who once knew her, she was as good as dead.

While she was closing the bookstore, Nora decided to surprise Abilene with an offer of dinner at the Pink Lady. Either that or Nora would order takeout and they could eat together at Caboose Cottage. Though it was a little chilly to sit out on the deck, Nora could lend Abilene a sweater. They could eat something warm and comforting like a chicken pot pie while watching the stars wink into life.

Nora was halfway to Abilene's studio apartment when June called. She and Hester were heading to Abilene's to deliver the goodies they'd purchased that afternoon.

"I feel like Santa," June said. "I'm not quite as round in the belly yet, but I'm working on it. I do grow the odd white chin-hair now and then, so I guess I'm working on the beard too."

She laughed and Nora heard Hester chuckling in the background.

"I'm actually walking to Abilene's place right now," Nora said and shared her idea for taking Abilene to the Pink Lady.

"We should eat at her place," June said. "Hester and I bought her dishes, flatware, and glasses. We might have to sit on the floor, but it'll be like an indoor picnic. Hester, call Estella and tell her to get her flat butt over to Abilene's. We're having an impromptu girls' night."

Nora quickened her pace because she wanted to see the look on Abilene's face when June and Hester showed up with her gifts. More than that, Nora needed to be reassured that Abilene was okay. Since Ezekiel hadn't been located, he could be anywhere. And anywhere included Abilene's apartment.

When she arrived, Nora didn't wait for her friends. She opened the outer door and stepped into the foyer.

As the door creaked shut behind her, the space above her missing pinkie finger began to tingle. Nora was enveloped by shadows. The lights were all off. There was only the angry red glow cast by the exit sign above the door.

She caught a waft of sour, rust-tinged air.

The tingling above Nora's pinkie intensified.

She grabbed her right hand with her left, hoping to make the sensation go away, but it didn't stop.

Nora mounted the stairs. She'd ascended three steps when the odor assaulted her again.

She realized that what she smelled wasn't rust. It was another metallic scent.

The scent of blood.

Chapter 15

Out of a gap
A million soldiers run,
Redcoats, every one.
—Sylvia Plath

"Abilene!" Nora shouted, taking the steps two at a time.
"*Abilene!*"

The name soared up the stairwell and bounced off the high ceiling. The echo that came back sounded like the scuffling of bats.

Nora looked up the stairs and saw blood.

Thin rivulets ran down the steps above her and a glossy red puddle was pooling on the fifth stair from the top.

What will I do if Ezekiel Crane is on the landing, waiting for me? Nora thought, hesitating.

She was unarmed and had no way of defending herself.

But when Nora thought of Abilene, her own vulnerability no longer seemed important. Taking out her phone, she hit the emergency button and continued to ascend the steps.

The source of the ruddy rivulets was on the landing.

Nora was too shocked to reply to the 911operator's questions. The woman asked what kind of assistance she needed, but Nora couldn't even hold the phone to her ear. Her arm dropped to her side and her lips parted, but she couldn't speak. She could only expel the extra air in her lungs in a slow, silent sigh.

There were two people on the landing. One was alive. The other was dead.

The dead person was a man.

He was sprawled on the floor, his face turned in profile. Nora tried to process a blur of details. The temple of the man's black glasses against his silver hair. The neatly trimmed beard and mustache framing his open mouth. Teeth slightly yellowed by age. A blue dress shirt. Khakis. Brown loafers. A gold wristwatch. A glassy blue eye.

Nora's gaze fixed on the wound in the man's side. The shirt was cut near the lower ribs, revealing a red-rimmed gash in the pale flesh. This was where his life had leaked out.

Not leaked, Nora thought in horror. *Streamed.*

Tearing her eyes away from the dead man, Nora looked at the living person.

Abilene stood directly across from Nora. They were separated by the body—an isthmus of flesh on a sea of dirty tile.

Abilene looked more marble sculpture than human. She was fish-belly white and completely still. Her back was pressed against the wall and her face was a contorted mask of fear. She held a knife in both hands and stared unblinking at the dead man.

"Abilene," Nora whispered.

There was no response from Abilene, but Nora heard another voice.

Suddenly remembering the phone in her hand, Nora lifted it to her ear.

"Ma'am?" the operator said with saintly patience. "Ma'am? Are you there?"

"I need an ambulance," Nora said.

This wasn't good enough for the operator. She wanted clarification. "What's the nature of your emergency?"

"Just send an ambulance." Even more softly, Nora added, "And the sheriff." She rattled off the address and hung up.

Abilene still hadn't moved and Nora knew she had to get to her.

Nora shuddered as she stepped over the dead man's legs. It was jarring to walk over him like he was a piece of roadkill. It was even harder to avoid putting her foot down in the blood seeping from his body.

When she was close enough to touch Abilene, Nora whispered, "It's over. It's over now."

Nora didn't know what to do with her hands. She didn't dare touch Abilene—not with her death-grip on the bloody knife. In the gloom, it looked like the horn of some dangerous, mythological animal.

After a very long, very tense moment, Abilene's gaze slid away from the dead man and came to rest on Nora's face. She blinked in recognition.

"There you are." Nora managed a smile. "It's okay, Abilene. Come away now. Come with me. We'll just go into your apartment. Okay?"

Abilene's head moved up and down in a mechanical nod, as if her brain was disconnected from her body. She stood there, bobbing her head up and down. Up and down. She didn't move any other parts of her body.

"Will you let go of the knife?" Nora asked. "Please?"

Looking at her hands, Abilene gave a little jump of fright and released the knife. It clattered to the floor.

Abilene immediately scooped it up again. "I have to hide it."

She pushed past Nora, rushed into her apartment, and frantically paced in front of her kitchen cabinets. Then she yanked the oven door open and was about to toss the knife inside when Nora grabbed her by the wrist.

"Just put it in the sink," she said. "We can't hide it."

Abilene's mouth quivered. "I have to. If I don't, Hester . . ."

Nora didn't understand. "What about Hester?"

The hand gripping the knife violently trembled. "She'll get in trouble."

At that moment, the terrible reality of what had happened struck Abilene like a high-speed train. She pulled in a shallow breath and when she released it, a cry rushed out. It was a primal sound. An animalistic keen that came from the deepest crevice in Abilene's soul. It was the sound of pain. Years and years of it.

Guiding Abilene's hand toward the sink, Nora told her to let go.

Abilene dropped the knife and sagged against Nora.

Nora put her arms around the young woman, who felt as hollowed out as the book in Amanda's house. Abilene sobbed into Nora's shirt. Her tears dampened the skin of Nora's neck. Nora stroked her hair and murmured that it was all over now.

After a time, Abilene grew calmer.

"What will happen?" she asked.

Nora heard the ambulance sirens. They were close. Very close.

June and Hester were probably seconds away as well.

"Is that your uncle?" Nora pointed toward the landing. She didn't want to speak his name. If that horrible man was dead, then Nora wanted every part of him to be dead. She didn't want to grant him an ounce of power by letting his name enter Abilene's apartment. This was the first and only place she could call her own and Nora wanted to preserve its sanctity for a little longer.

Abilene made a noise that Nora interpreted as a confirmation.

"I'm going to take care of everything," Nora said. "Starting with you."

At that moment, she would have given anything for a blanket and a black coffee laced with Irish cream. Abilene was nothing but skin, bone, and shivers. She'd stopped crying, but seemed too weak to stand.

Nora led her to the futon and had just coaxed her into sitting when she heard a shriek reverberate in the stairwell.

"Jesus!" Nora crossed the room and whipped open the door. "Don't come up here!" she shouted down to her friends. Her words ricocheted off the ceiling and walls like gunfire.

"Where's that blood coming from?" June yelled back. "What's going on?"

Keeping her distance from Crane's head, Nora leaned over the landing railing. She could see her friends standing in the hallway below.

Hester had her arm looped through June's and was staring upward with big, frightened eyes. "Is it Abilene?"

"No, no." Nora waved her arms back and forth to dispel the idea. "It's her uncle."

Further conversation was curtailed by the arrival of two paramedics, one of whom was Jed.

He saw Nora on the landing and bounded up the stairs. Nora didn't need to warn him about the blood. He came to an abrupt halt before reaching the slick pool on the fifth step.

"Are you hurt?" he asked Nora.

She pointed down at the dead man. "No, and he's already gone. Abilene's inside. I think she's on the brink of passing out. She needs a blanket."

When Jed pivoted to speak with his partner, Nora returned to Abilene's side.

"Help is here." She placed her hand over Abilene's. Her skin was cold to the touch.

There were noises outside the apartment door. Voices and footfalls on the stairs. Nora's time alone with Abilene was almost up.

"People are going to ask you questions," she said, giving Abilene's hand a shake to get her to listen. "Lots of questions. But you don't have to answer them. You don't have to talk until you're ready."

Abilene didn't seem to hear her. "When they find the knife, they'll take Hester away. It's my fault."

Nora didn't understand this until it dawned on her that Abilene couldn't afford such a fine culinary tool. "It's Hester's knife?"

"Yes."

"And you took it from the bakery?"

"No!" Abilene's eyes flew open wide. "I'd never take anything from Hester!"

Nora was really confused now. "Are you saying that you didn't use Hester's knife . . . on your uncle?"

Abilene shook her head so violently that her hair stuck to her tear tracks.

"Are you telling me that you didn't kill him?" Nora stared at her intently.

"*No!*" Abilene's shout came out as a hoarse whisper.

Nora didn't think anyone would believe this. She wasn't sure if she did. When she'd come upon Ezekiel Crane, his body was probably still warm. His life was still leaking out, still dripping down the stairs. How could someone else have killed him?

There was a forceful knocking on the door and a man's gruff voice. "Sheriff's department."

Nora turned to see a deputy she didn't recognize.

"Ma'am, please take a seat next to the other lady." Catching sight of the bloodstains on Abilene's gray sweatshirt, the deputy asked, "Are you hurt?"

Abilene gazed at her clasped hands and didn't answer.

"She's in shock," Nora said. "She needs a blanket. Could Jedediah—he's one of the paramedics—take care of her? Now?"

A crackle of static burst from the lawman's radio followed by Sheriff McCabe's voice. "Is the room secure, Fuentes?"

Fuentes nodded. "Yes, sir."

"I'm coming up," the sheriff said, and the deputy's radio fell silent.

Two minutes later, McCabe entered the apartment. He scanned the scene before gesturing to his deputy, and the two men conferred by the door. Nora couldn't hear their exchange, but she saw Deputy Fuentes point at the sink.

The sheriff walked into the kitchen area, peered into the sink, and passed a hand over his mouth. He then approached the futon.

"What happened?" he asked Nora.

"I'm not sure," she said. "The man on the landing is her uncle. She says she didn't kill him and I don't think she can talk right now. She needs medical attention."

McCabe walked to the doorway and crooked his finger at whoever was waiting outside.

Jed strode into the apartment and made a beeline for Abilene. He had his kit in one hand and a blanket in the other. Setting his kit down, he draped the blanket over Abilene's shoulders. Next, he removed a blood pressure cuff and a package of smelling salts from his kit. He told Abilene where he was going to touch her and why, assuring her that he was there to see to her medical needs and that was all. He asked if she felt any pain. She didn't respond.

Nora felt a hand on her shoulder.

When she turned, Sheriff McCabe gestured at the kitchen area. "Can we talk over there?"

Deputy Fuentes was already standing in front of the sink, taking photos of the knife. The flash blinked like a strobe light and Nora put her back to the scene.

McCabe acted like no one else was in the room. He kept his sharp gaze on Nora's face. "Walk me through what you saw."

She told him everything, quickly and quietly. When she was done, she said, "I don't think you'll get anything out of her. She's in a deep state of shock. That man was her jailor for her entire life. And now . . ."

"He's dead. Stabbed. He's outside her door and there's a bloody knife in her sink." McCabe spread his hands. "I have to take her in."

"She said the knife belongs to Hester," Nora said. "She also says that she didn't take it from the bakery."

When McCabe's brows rose, she couldn't blame him for his disbelief. If Abilene hadn't stolen the knife and used it to kill her uncle, then who had?

At that point, Jed came over to update the sheriff on Abilene's condition.

"Physically, she's okay," Jed said. He tapped his temple. "But up here? She's checked out. I'm not sure if she can answer questions, let alone understand them."

The sheriff glanced at Abilene. His eyes were hard, unyielding. "She'll have to. Did you use the smelling salts?"

"No need. She's conscious and alert. But she's in shock. She may need a thermal blanket. She's shivering pretty badly."

"Give her the blanket and we'll warm her up more at the station." McCabe waited for Jed to move before saying to Nora, "You and Ms. Winthrop need to come too."

"You couldn't keep us away," Nora said tersely, and hurried over to make promises to Abilene. "You might not see us, but we'll be there. We won't leave you."

Abilene didn't react. She just stared at her trembling hands. The blanket hung over her shoulders like a dead animal and Nora readjusted it so that it covered more of her thin torso.

On the landing, two deputies had begun processing the scene. The strobe sensation of camera flashes was even more disconcerting in the gloom. Nora tried to put her feet exactly where the deputy wanted her to, but she felt detached from her body, like she was floating above the stairwell, completely disconnected from the madness.

"You're doing fine," the deputy said kindly and put his hand under her elbow.

The touch brought Nora back to herself and she completed her descent.

Hester, June, and Estella were waiting outside. As soon as they saw Nora, they fired questions at her with the ruthlessness of an invading army.

Nora threw up her hands as if she could shield herself from the assault. "Slow down! I know you're all freaking out, but so am I! Get in June's car. I'll tell you everything on the way."

"The way where?" Hester asked.

Nora looked at her friend. "To the station. The sheriff is going to interview Abilene about the murder of her uncle. We need to be there for her, but we have to make a stop first."

Minutes later, the members of the Secret, Book, and Scone Society stood in front of the wooden knife block on the bakery's biggest worktable. Hester had turned on every light inside the Gingerbread House, as if illuminating the space would reveal all the answers to her questions. She now stood, arms crossed over her chest, glancing from the knife block to Nora.

"Do I need a lawyer?" she asked. More questions immediately followed. "Does Abilene? Did you see the knife? Did it have the same black handle as the others? Did you see my initials on the blade? Did you see the *HW*?"

Nora hadn't, but she didn't want to tell Hester that most of the blade had been covered with blood. The handles matched. Nora was sure of this because the knife-maker's emblem, two white figures enclosed in a red box, were on the end of every handle. There was no doubt in her mind that the knife used to kill Ezekiel Crane had come from the set in Hester's kitchen.

The four women stared at the empty slot in the knife block. The black gash in the wood spelled serious trouble for Abilene, Hester, or both.

"I'm glad that asshole's dead," Estella said, tracing the rounded end of a knife handle with her fingertip. "No matter what, he'll never hurt anyone again."

"No matter what?" Hester cried. "The *what* in this case is prison. For *murder*."

Estella looked at her blandly. "Sometimes you have to put a monster down. Abilene's uncle was just like my stepdaddy. Abuse is abuse. I couldn't fight back. I couldn't run. Neither could Abilene. Monsters never leave you. They keep coming."

"But we don't want her trading one prison for another," June said to Estella before turning to Hester. "Could she have taken the knife?"

Hope flashed in Hester's eyes. "No! She couldn't have! I used it after she'd already left for the day."

Confounded, the women glanced around Hester's kitchen as if the spice jars or saucepans could unravel the riddle of the stolen knife.

"Could someone have acted like they were heading back to the restroom, but ducked into the kitchen instead? It's only a door away," Nora said. "Would you have noticed?"

Hester took a second to consider this. "Not in the middle of a rush, like when the afternoon train or the lodge trolley arrives. Bigfoot could be in the kitchen and I'd be totally clueless."

"That's got to be it." June steered Hester toward the empty display cases and positioned her in front of the cash register. "Try to think back to that busy time. Which local folks came in?"

Flustered, Hester, said, "I don't know. A few lodge employees. Nick from the hardware store, Lucy from the vet's office, some lawyers from the courthouse." She plunged her hands into her hair, grasping at clumps of honey-colored curls. "I'm sure there were more, but their faces blend together. Day after day, it's sometimes just a blur. I don't have time to chat during a rush. I just serve and take their money. And repeat."

Nora understood. Unless she'd spent a minute or two talking with a particular customer, she couldn't recite a list of everyone who'd visited Miracle Books on a given day.

"I wonder if Ezekiel Crane came here looking for Abilene," she said to her friends. "Maybe he took the knife to use on her. If you were framed for her murder, Hester, he might feel justified. He'd be punishing his ungrateful niece and the woman who helped her at the same time."

"If he came in here, I wouldn't have known it," Hester said. "I have no idea what he looks like. At Abilene's, you told us not to come up the stairs, so we didn't."

Nora shared what she'd noticed about Crane's appearance.

"I probably had a dozen customers who fit that description," Hester said. "Maybe the sheriff will find another set of fingerprints on the knife besides mine. And Abilene's."

With no answers to be found at the Gingerbread House, the four women headed to the station.

Nora gave their names to the desk clerk. Within minutes, a deputy came to collect Hester, explaining that he needed both her statement and her fingerprints. She looked frightened, but squared her shoulders and followed him. The pair disappeared into the building's inner sanctum.

"I bet she wishes Jasper was taking her prints," Estella whispered. "He'd tell her not to worry. Make her feel safe."

June snorted. "He's not going to compromise his job just so Hester thinks he's the world's best boyfriend. He and the rest of these folks have three deaths on their hands. The media's going to catch wind of this soon. It's only a matter of time before the news vans start chugging down the mountain road."

Nora was remembering how relieved everyone had felt after the last plague of journalists had departed Miracle Springs, when Deputy Andrews appeared in the waiting area.

"Ms. Pennington, please come with me."

"We'll be right here," said June, giving Nora's hand a quick squeeze. "Like two rocks of Gibraltar. No one can move us."

Andrews escorted Nora directly to the sheriff's office and asked her to take a seat in the chair facing his desk.

Nora was studying the framed war bond posters from World War I when McCabe entered the room.

"How is she?" Nora asked.

"Not talking," said McCabe, dropping into his chair as if the burdens he carried weighed too heavily on his shoulders. "She didn't even react when I called her Hannah."

Nora winced. "That probably made her retreat even more. I think she was telling me the truth when she said that she didn't kill her uncle. Hester was using the knife—the murder weapon—at the Gingerbread Bread House *after* Abilene left to work her shift at Virtual Genie."

"She could have easily slipped back into the bakery," the sheriff said. "I'll have to ask Mr. Kingsley or Ms. Beacham if they saw her leave." He rubbed his chin, staring pensively at his computer screen. "Since Abilene Tyler is an alias, how is she being paid?"

Nora didn't understand why this was relevant at the moment. "She works for Griffin in exchange for that crappy apartment. As for her part-time gig at the bakery, I can only assume that Hester pays Abilene in cash. Does it really matter that she's not giving a share of her paltry wages to Uncle Sam?"

Too late, she realized that she hadn't chosen her words wisely. The war bond closest to her chair featured a gun-toting Uncle Sam standing in front of the American flag. The sky above him was filled with bombers and below him, an army charged toward an unseen enemy. McCabe was a lawman. The epitome of an upstanding citizen. A crime was a crime, no matter who'd committed it or why.

However, he answered Nora's question without any rancor. "It matters because I wanted to know how she convinced the Virtual Genie owners to forgo a lease. Considering their business depends on having a sterling reputation, this arrangement strikes me as odd."

"Abilene had a special skill set to offer. She could repair and appraise—" Nora stopped. "Can I talk to her? I'm not asking for privacy, but can I see her? I could try to ask her something important."

"What thought just ran through your mind?" McCabe put his forearms on his desk and leaned forward. His body language and keen gaze belied his mild tone of voice.

"I was wondering if Abilene had seen the pocket watch from inside Amanda's book before. Her uncle ran a clock and jewelry shop. Every day, he brought work home for her to do. She might recognize the watch. She might know its story."

McCabe got to his feet. "Let's find out."

To Nora's immense relief, Abilene wasn't in a holding cell.

She was sitting in one of the interview rooms, a bottle of water and a cup of coffee on the table in front of her. Both beverages appeared to be untouched.

A female deputy stood in the corner of the room, and when the sheriff's brows rose in a silent question, the deputy responded with a regretful shake of the head.

Abilene still hadn't said a word.

Nora asked the sheriff for a piece of paper and a pen. He signaled to his deputy and she hurried out of the room, returning a minute later with a sheet of printer paper and a black pen.

Nora sat next to Abilene and began to draw a crude imitation of the pocket watch case. As she worked, she spoke to the girl beside her. She didn't mention Hester's knife or ask Abilene if she'd left her job at Virtual Genie for even a few minutes that afternoon. She said nothing about the dead man on the landing. Instead, she talked about the pocket watches she'd come across in books.

"There's the White Rabbit in *Alice's Adventures in Wonderland*. His anxiety was contagious. He was always checking his watch and fretting over being late. And who can forget Agatha Christie's fussy, fastidious, pocket-watch toting detective, Hercule Poirot? He's my favorite Christie sleuth. And in the wizarding world of Harry Potter, Albus Dumbledore's watch has twelve hands and planets instead of numbers."

Having completed a rough sketch of a watch cover with a ram's head in the center, Nora sketched a face with three keyholes. Taking Abilene's hand, she gently laid it on top of the paper. "I bet you've seen lots of pocket watches, but have you ever seen one with a ram's head on the case. Like this?"

Nora placed Abilene's index finger on the head.

When Abilene didn't look up from her lap, Nora moved the other woman's finger to the sketch she'd made of the face. "What about a watch with three keyholes? One." She moved Abilene's finger over each shaded dot representing a keyhole. "Two. Three."

Abilene jerked her hand away as if she'd been burned, and Nora sighed inwardly. Once again, she'd failed to get through to her.

Just as Nora was about to stand up, Abilene leaned over and whispered, "The keys came when I turned eighteen. In the mail. He wore them around his neck. He never took them off."

"Your uncle?"

Abilene released a soft puff of air. "Yes."

Nora put her arm around Abilene in a half hug. She held her that way and glanced at McCabe. He'd heard their whispered conversation, and when he looked away as if to hide his disappointment, Nora had the answer to the question she was just about to ask.

The keys hadn't been found on Crane's body.

The keys were gone.

Chapter 16

God hath given you one face, and you make your-
selves another.

                                        —William Shakespeare

The members of the Secret, Book, and Scone Society settled in
for a long wait at the sheriff's department. As the time dragged,
the women bought coffee from the lobby vending machine. It
wasn't very good, but it was hot.

"You don't have to stay," Deputy Andrews had told Nora
after she'd signed her statement.

"I'm not leaving Abilene," she'd said. "I told her that she
wouldn't be alone."

Apparently, no one else planned to leave either. This became
clear when June took her knitting needles out of her handbag.

"Guess I'll get to work on your fox socks," June said.

Estella watched her work, fascinated. "I've always pictured
knitters as old ladies in rocking chairs, shooing cats away from
their yarn with an orthopedic shoe. You've got the cats. You
just need a rocking chair and the shoes."

June threatened to give Estella a body piercing if she ever
dared to stereotype a knitter again. She then turned to Nora. "I
should knit you and Jed one of those chastity cocoons. "What
was it called—that practice of sewing folks in their own cloth
sacks so they couldn't touch each other?"

"Bundling," Estella said. "I read too, you know, and at least a dozen of the historical romances I've read have mentioned bundling. Even if I hadn't come across that in books, I'd remember it from my history classes in school. They were my favorite." A secretive smile tugged at her lips. "I really enjoyed talking to Jack about Japanese history the other day. He thinks I'm the smartest woman in town."

Hester, who'd been very quiet until now, gaped at Estella. "Jack? As in the Pink Lady? Don't tell me you're going to break his heart next."

Estella frowned. "It's not like that. We're friends. I've never had a guy friend before, but it's really nice."

Nora thought of her recent run-in with Jack.

"Has he mentioned the antique box Virtual Genie is selling for him?" she asked Estella.

"No," she said. "I'm supposed to drop by the diner tomorrow at three. Jack wants to serve me a traditional Japanese tea. I can ask about the box then."

Happy to find a subject to distract them from their current circumstance, Nora's friends chatted about tea traditions across the globe. Instead of participating, she tuned them out. Something about Jack and his box struck her as unusual. Griffin Kingsley didn't seem like the type of person who'd forget to post an auction. He was the type to pay close attention to every detail.

Estella got up and tossed her coffee cup in the trash. When she sat back down, she took the chair next to Nora's.

"What's going on in that head of yours?" she asked.

"I was thinking about Virtual Genie," Nora said. "Of that gorgeous main room. Of the Belgian chocolate, the iced chai, and the quotes from *The Arabian Nights*."

Estella dug around in her bag for a compact. "That reminds me to reapply my powder." She opened the compact and showed it to Nora. "Sand Dune Shimmer."

Nora watched Estella dab powder on her smooth skin. Next, she refreshed her lipstick. It was the same shade of red as the fabric covering the walls of Virtual Genie.

An illusion, Nora thought. *Their décor is like the photoshopped image of a fashion model. It's all smoke and mirrors. The appearance of luxury. Ali Baba's exotic cave. Griffin said that they didn't stay anywhere for long. He admitted that he and Tamara are travelers. Magic carpet riders.*

"Now what are you thinking?" Estella asked. "I can hear your gears turning."

"I was thinking about magicians and their use of misdirection." Nora touched her friend's bag. "Will you call Jack and ask him what happened with his box?"

Estella wanted to know why, but Nora waved off her query. She couldn't organize her thoughts into anything cohesive. She felt, without having concrete evidence for feeling the way she did, that Virtual Genie had played a part in recent events.

The conversation between Estella and Jack was brief. When it was over, Estella wore a befuddled expression.

"Tamara decided to delay his listing for a few days," Estella said. "Apparently, other boxes similar to Jack's were posted to sell and she didn't want to saturate the market."

Nora was disappointed. She thought she'd been on the right track with Jack's box, which was both valuable and portable. An easy thing to throw into one's suitcase before hitting the road.

"That makes sense," she said.

"Jack doesn't agree. He checked out the auction sites she mentioned and none of the other boxes could hold a candle to his. If anything, they'd only make his look better. He called Tamara to complain and she promised to list it on Monday. She said that weekend listings don't perform as well as weekday listings."

This sounded sketchy to Nora.

"What's he going to do?"

Estella shrugged. "If the box isn't listed first thing in the morning, then Jack's going to march over to Virtual Genie, take back the box, and sell it himself. How hard can it be?"

Nora thought this was a crucial question. Not all of Virtual Genie's customers were inept with computers. Why didn't they sell their items directly?

"It's the perception they've created," Nora said, answering her own question aloud. "The whole purpose of their décor is to convey the message that they're connoisseurs of luxury and wealth. People are influenced by Virtual Genie's atmosphere the moment they step inside. They *want* to entrust their valuables to Griffin and Tamara. And if that's true, why doesn't Virtual Genie ever put down roots? Why do they keep moving?"

"Where are you going?" Estella asked, for Nora had risen to her feet during her short monologue.

"To ask the sheriff if Virtual Genie ever hung their shingle in Lubbock, Texas."

McCabe looked as tired as Nora felt.

"It's not enough to distrust people," he said after listening to Nora's question. "We need evidence. I visited Virtual Genie. I reviewed their paperwork. They're legit."

Nora couldn't stop playing devil's advocate. "Based on what? Their consignor contracts? What if the gleam in Griffin's eyes when he saw that pocket watch was more than professional interest? Maybe he recognized it. Maybe he and Crane worked together in the past. Griffin could have stolen the three watch keys from Crane."

McCabe waved this suggestion off. "What good would the keys do him when we have the watch?"

Nora was suddenly ashamed of herself. Was she trying to deflect blame from Abilene by placing it on other people? People whose focus had been helping townsfolk from the moment they'd opened for business.

"You need to go home," the sheriff said, curbing his annoyance. "Get some sleep. All of you. Ms. Tyler will be spending the night with us. There's no way around that. She was found with the murder weapon and she knew the victim intimately."

"Intimately?" Nora's anger flared. "Way to put a positive spin on Abilene's imprisonment. A childhood marked with emotional and physical abuse! Is that how you define intimate? Until she came to Miracle Springs, that girl lived in Hell. And her only miracle is *us*. The four of *us!*" Nora pointed in the direction where her friends waited. "If we leave her alone now, she might never recover. She's already fractured. She's like a cracked egg. If someone doesn't hold her together, she's going to fall apart."

The sheriff held out his hands. "What do you want me to do? Put all of you in the cell with her?"

Nora looked him in the eye and said, "Yes."

"This isn't a hotel." McCabe made it plain that he was losing patience.

"Okay. I'll commit a crime. That way, it'll just be me. No need to book us a suite. How about assaulting an officer? Will that get me thrown in Abilene's cell?"

McCabe's mouth twitched. "I would *not* advise that course of action. It's been a long night and—"

Nora slapped his cheek before he could finish.

She immediately drew back, stunned by what she'd done.

"I'm sorry," she whispered. She meant it. She liked Grant McCabe. He wasn't the enemy. All her fear and anger had surged through her. It had taken over, just for a few seconds. But they'd been explosive seconds.

With incredible self-control, the sheriff got to his feet and took hold of Nora's arm. "All right. Have it your way."

As he marched her out of his office, Nora boldly suggested

that someone in the department check to see if Virtual Genie had ever operated in or around Lubbock.

McCabe didn't reply. Nora could feel exasperation rolling off him in heated waves.

He escorted her down a flight of stairs to the holding cells and left her standing in the hallway as he stepped into a small office and spoke with a stocky bald man in his late fifties. The office was crammed with papers, buttons, and screens displaying security-camera feeds. It was a jailor's office.

Nora felt a stab of panic. *What the hell did I do?*

She had no time to reflect on her rash behavior, for the bald man exited his office, said good night to the sheriff, and grabbed Nora's arm. Seeing the burn scars on the back of her hand, he immediately loosened his grip.

"Did I hurt you?" he asked, casting a worried look at her forearm.

Nora was touched by his solicitousness. "No. They don't hurt anymore."

Satisfied, the man walked her to a cell containing two sets of metal bunk beds. Abilene was curled up on the lower bunk. The rest of the beds were unoccupied.

"These are our group accommodations," the man said. "Blankets are folded at the end of the bed. Ms. Tyler was seen by our nurse before being turned over to me. I'm Sergeant Whitfield. I'll be looking in on you."

The sergeant signaled for Nora to enter the cell. "Your personal items will be returned in the morning. The sheriff said you're going home first thing tomorrow. For now, try to get some sleep."

"What about her?" Nora pointed at Abilene, who was curled in the fetal position with her face turned to the wall.

The sergeant made it clear he wasn't going to answer any questions, so Nora entered the cell and knelt beside the bony form on the lower bunk.

"I'm here," she whispered, and laid a hand on Abilene's shoulder.

Abilene flinched and rolled over.

Nora pushed a strand of hair out of Abilene's eyes. "I promised you wouldn't be alone."

Without warning, Abilene grabbed Nora's hand and pressed it flat against her chest, directly over her heart. It fluttered like a bird in a trap. Nora covered Abilene's hands with her own and vowed to go to any length to comfort her young friend.

"When I was little, my mom used to say that even the worst things look a little less horrible in the morning. The dark night is always followed by sunrise."

"Where is she?" Abilene whispered. "Your mom."

Nora reached for a blanket. After spreading it over Abilene, she grabbed the second blanket from the top bunk. "My guess is that she's still where she was five years ago, but I couldn't say for sure."

"You should find her," Abilene said.

Nora would never search for her parents or anyone else from her former life, but she couldn't explain why the person she used to be was now gone. Abilene didn't need to hear about more loss. She needed something to hold on to. Something to get her through the night. To get her to the next sunrise.

"Want to know a secret?" Nora asked as she squeezed in next to Abilene.

Abilene took Nora's hand again. "Yes."

"Nora isn't my real name. I didn't like my old one, so I changed it. Just like you."

"Really?" Abilene perked up for the first time since Nora had discovered her on the landing, clutching the bloody knife. A tiny spark ignited in her pupils.

"Really. Your parents named you after a book character. I picked a book character too. I chose Nora after the heroine in Ibsen's *A Doll's House.*

The spark in Abilene's eyes grew brighter. "Nora Helmer," she said. "Why her?"

"Because she throws away her old self to become something more. I believe you can do that too."

Abilene stared at the underside of the upper bunk, as if wondering what was possible for her. "Before you were Nora, who were you?"

"If you tell me some things, then I'll tell you some things."

When Sergeant Whitfield opened the cell door the next morning, Nora was curled up next to Abilene, her arm draped protectively around the younger woman's waist.

Nora heard him coming, but she hadn't wanted to move. She'd been surfacing from sleep when the sound of his footfalls had pulled her the rest of the way out. Though tempted to close her eyes and keep reality at bay for a few more minutes, she sat up. Her mouth was filled with sand, her eyes were dry, and she ached everywhere.

"Time to go, Ms. Pennington." The sergeant didn't bother whispering.

Nora shook her head. "What can I do to stay? I'd rather not slap you, so is there a coworker you dislike?"

A ghost of a smile appeared on the sergeant's face. "I don't recommend that, ma'am. The sheriff's going to drive you home and he's had a *very* long night. The way I see it, you can help your friend better from the outside."

Abilene stirred and sat up. "It's okay," she said, her voice still thick with sleep. "You'll come back for me."

Her throat tightening with emotion, Nora promised that she would. She then followed the sergeant out of the cell.

The sergeant turned her over to McCabe, who was leaning against his car. He looked terrible. His eyes were bloodshot, his hair was wild, and the bags under his eyes had a gray-blue cast.

"I'm sorry," Nora said.

"No, you're not. But I appreciate the sentiment." He opened his passenger door. The action reminded Nora of the night they'd had dinner together at Pearl's. She doubted McCabe would ever want to share a meal with her again.

McCabe had left her purse on the seat and Nora was tempted to check her phone for messages from the Secret, Book, and Scone Society members, but she decided to wait until she was home to connect with her friends.

The sheriff slid into the driver's seat and sat quietly for a long moment. Finally, he said, "Virtual Genie never operated out of Lubbock or anywhere else in Texas."

"Oh." Nora's voice was small. "I—"

"I'm not finished." McCabe turned to face her. "I was unable to find *any* previous locations for a business by that name. The only record I found on Griffin Kingsley was a New York State obituary. *That* Mr. Kingsley died last year. As for Ms. Beacham, I located numerous records. Too many to dig through last night. One struck me as significant because it was another obituary. From Florida. I can't help wondering if the partners are using stolen identities."

Despite her fatigue and a powerful yearning to shower and drink a giant mug of coffee, Nora's mind began running through possibilities. "I think the watch is the key to your cases. The books were only relevant because the watch was hidden inside a book. Amanda was killed by either Ezekiel Crane or Griffin Kingsley when she refused to turn over the hollowed book. The same man killed Kenneth. The same man was the target of Kenneth's anger at the Fruits of Labor Festival. Considering Ezekiel was just murdered, Griffin gets my vote. I saw his face when you showed him that watch."

McCabe put the car in DRIVE and exited the parking lot. "After I drop you off, I'm going to call the owner of the building Virtual Genie is leasing. I want to know every detail about that lease. But don't get your hopes up. Even if Mr. Kingsley and Ms. Beacham have been operating under false pretenses, I can't link them to the murders at this juncture. There's no evidence."

After contemplating in silence for several minutes, Nora said, "Last night, Abilene and I talked. She told me what she could about Ezekiel's death. She'd just taken a shower and was heading into the kitchen to make supper when she heard footsteps on the other side of her door. Next, she heard a grunt followed by a thud. Something heavy had fallen. She heard more footsteps going down the stairs. Abilene was scared by the strange sounds, so she hid in the bathroom. When everything had been quiet for several minutes, she dared to peek out her door. She recognized her uncle immediately. She saw the knife sticking out of his back, close to his left side. She wasn't sure if he was dead or not."

"Maybe she didn't know what dead looked like," McCabe said.

Nora realized this was probably true. Most children experience death through the loss of a pet or an elderly family member. This was a difficult milestone. If a child was lucky, he or she received support from parents, teachers, or a mentor.

Not Abilene. She had no parents, teachers, or mentors. She had only her uncle. Like most things, she'd undoubtedly learned about death from books. But she'd never seen it up close.

"Abilene's desire to protect Hester was so powerful that she was able to muster the courage to pull the knife out of her uncle," Nora said, continuing her narrative. "This caused a fresh flow of blood. Abilene had never seen anything like that. It paralyzed her."

McCabe shot her a glance. "Anything else?"

"If Abilene's story is true, then someone else killed Ezekiel. Someone determined to get that pocket watch."

"Which is in our custody," the sheriff said. "It doesn't add up, Nora. The killer would have no hope of obtaining the watch."

McCabe stopped the car in the Miracle Books parking lot and kept the engine running. Nora got out, but immediately turned back to face the sheriff. "What if you gave him hope?"

Though McCabe was practically buzzing with impatience, his curiosity convinced him to tarry a few seconds longer. "You have an idea on how that could be accomplished, I take it."

Nora managed a tired smile. "I do."

Nora's plan required the help of several people. After a shower and a cup of coffee, she was able to put her thoughts down on paper. From that point, she began making phone calls.

Every time she enlisted another person, she was assailed by doubt. Not only was she gambling with Abilene's freedom, but she was quite possibly endangering her friends as well.

There's no other choice, Nora told herself en route to Virtual Genie. *If I don't do something now, Abilene will be a prisoner forever. She'll hide so deep inside herself that no one will ever find her again.*

As Nora walked, she noticed the beauty surrounding her. The morning sun bathed the park, and the maple trees held the golden light captive. Dried leaves skipped over the sidewalks like children heading home from school. The hills encircling the town were a kaleidoscope of squash yellow, pumpkin orange, and apple red. The postcard setting seemed surreal following yesterday's traumatic events, but Nora gathered strength from the colors and the scents of wood fires and dried hay. Like many of the faces she passed on the street, the scents were familiar. Comforting. They spoke of home, of the place where she'd found her second chance, and she'd do anything she could to protect it.

This meant confronting a murderer.

Griffin Kingsley was seated at his massive desk. He had a cell phone pressed to his ear and his gaze fixed on his laptop screen. Nora paused near the door to look at the framed quotes from

One Thousand and One Nights, the fabric draping the walls, the glimmering chandelier, and the plush sofas and chairs in the sitting area. She thought of Tamara serving exotic drinks and chocolate, and suppressed a grimace. If this was all just an act, then Griffin and Tamara were masters of deception.

Nora sat down and waited for Griffin to finish his call, but Tamara came out of the back room, caught sight of her, and came over to greet her.

"Ms. Pennington. Hello." Her voice was friendly but strained. Like Sheriff McCabe, Tamara had bags under her eyes. This was hardly surprising, considering the apartment above Virtual Genie was now a murder scene. "Is Abilene—?" She stopped and started again. "Have you seen her?"

"Yes." The word echoed with weariness. "It's been a long night, but I wanted to drop by and tell you that she won't be back anytime soon. I'm not sure what will happen with her."

Tamara shook her head. "She can't have done it. There's no way."

"I think she's innocent too," Nora said. "Not that the sheriff's department cares what I think. There's too much stacked against her. She's a stranger to Miracle Springs, she knew the dead man, and the murder weapon was in her apartment."

Tamara's eyes went round. "*No.*"

Nora stood up. "I'll do what I can. And if you and Griffin think of anything that might help exonerate her, please share it."

"Of course," Tamara said.

"Speaking of helping, I found a sold listing for a pocket watch similar to the one Sheriff McCabe showed Griffin. Yesterday, before all this craziness happened, I was looking up book values on my favorite auction site and I decided to see if I could find anything similar to that watch."

Tamara was confused. "I'm not sure why you're telling me about it. Doesn't the sheriff have the watch?"

"Yes, but he hasn't had time to do any research." Nora made

a show of hesitating. "I was just hoping—which is probably stupid of me—that the watch could shed a little light on this crime. If Griffin could prove to the sheriff how valuable it is, then McCabe might consider other suspects besides Abilene. If the watch was the motive, that is."

"I'm not following you," Tamara said. The whole conversation had her flustered. She glanced over at her partner more than once to see if he'd finished his phone call. "Griffin won't be long. I'm sure he'll be able to help. I'm sorry, but I need to get back to work."

Nora didn't have a chance to reply because a female deputy entered Virtual Genie and strode up to Tamara. "Ms. Beacham? I'm Deputy Wilcox." She introduced herself without offering her hand, making it plain that she was there in an official capacity. "I need to speak with Mr. Kingsley as soon as possible. Can you ask him to wrap up his call?"

Tamara didn't have to do anything, however, because as soon as Griffin spotted the deputy, he put his cell phone down. The deputy headed for Griffin's desk, taking a plastic evidence bag from her uniform blouse pocket as she walked. Tamara followed the deputy with her eyes.

The front door opened again and Estella breezed in. She wore a dark skirt suit with a white blouse and a string of pearls. Nora thought she looked like the CEO of a Fortune 500 company.

Tamara shifted her gaze from the deputy to Estella. She went stiff all over, as if preparing for a fight. Nora knew then that Jack's antique cloisonné box had yet to be listed and that Tamara assumed Jack and Estella were romantically involved.

"Good morning, Ms. Sadler." Tamara produced a cool smile. "I was just going to ask Ms. Pennington if she'd like anything to drink. I can ask you both now."

"It's early, but I wouldn't mind some of your special Belgian chocolates," Estella said in a silky voice.

Tamara's forced smile stretched a bit thinner. "Of course. Ms. Pennington?"

"Nothing for me, thank you."

Tamara hurried off to retrieve the chocolates. She'd barely set a silver tray bearing a gold box of chocolates down on the coffee table when Jack walked through the door. He glanced at Tamara before his gaze landed on Estella. His eyes narrowed in indignation.

"I thought you came here to find out about my box," Jack said to Estella. "Looks like you're more interested in that *box* of Belgian chocolate."

"Belgian?" Estella spluttered. "This chocolate is *not* imported. It's drug-store chocolate, the kind you give as a last-minute gift when you've forgotten someone's birthday. See? I have proof."

Reaching into her voluminous handbag, Estella pulled out a yellow box with green script. "This *sampler* has the same chocolates as the *Belgian* box." Estella selected an oval-shaped chocolate from the drug-store box and an identical chocolate from the gold box Tamara had given her. She broke each piece in half and showed Jack and Nora the nougat innards. "Looks the same." She took a nibble from each candy while glaring at Tamara. "Tastes the same."

Tamara was nonplussed by the demonstration. "We ran out. The order from our usual vendor was delayed and we didn't want our customers to be disappointed."

"You ran out?" Estella held up the yellow box. "Because Virgil's wife is a client of mine—Virgil collects your trash, by the way—and his wife told me that you've thrown out a bunch of these drugstore chocolate boxes."

Ignoring Estella, Tamara turned to Jack. "I'm sorry about the slip up with your listing. Your item is ready to go live at noon today. I know I originally said it would be ready at nine, but we've had a tragedy." She gestured at Estella. "There's no need for this."

Completely affronted, Estella bolted her feet. "This place is a sham. From your chocolate to your rented furniture to your promises about listings. It's a total sham!"

Tamara glanced in the direction of Griffin's desk, clearly seeking help, but he was leading Deputy Wilcox to the back room. He moved with urgency. Nora could see sweat beading his forehead.

"Excuse me," she said, leaving Tamara to Estella's mercy. She hurried through the opening in the fabric and appeared in the back room just as Griffin was sliding the pocket watch out of the evidence bag onto his gloved palm.

Deputy Wilcox stood close to the worktable while still allowing Griffin space to maneuver. When she looked up to see who'd entered the cool, shadowy space, Griffin transferred the pocket watch to his left hand, leaving his right hand free to dart into his jacket pocket. Though Nora believed she knew what he had in his closed fist, she couldn't let her gaze linger.

"Sorry to interrupt. I just wanted to give Griffin this print-out"—Nora removed a folded sheet of paper from her purse—"and I'll be on my way."

Deputy Wilcox passed the paper to Griffin. Instead of unfolding it, he gave Nora an inquisitive look.

"I did a little research on that." Nora pointed at the pocket watch nestled in the palm of Griffin's hand. "I thought we could combine forces. For Abilene's sake."

"I'll do everything in my power to help her. She's a sweet and hardworking young lady," Griffin said with such sincerity that Nora almost believed him.

He unfurled the fingers of his right hand and deposited several tiny watch keys onto the worktable. Nora stared at them, a cold dread blossoming in the center of her chest. Had she been wrong? Was she attempting to entrap an innocent man?

Griffin selected one of the keys. He didn't try to fit it in a keyhole, however, and Nora realized that he was waiting for her to leave.

At that moment, Estella burst into the back room. Hands on hips, she glowered at the shelving, the photography area, and finally, at Griffin.

"Can a person press charges if the owners of a business don't live up to the terms of their contract?" she asked Deputy Wilcox.

"Ma'am, you should take this up with the consumer protection office. I need Mr. Kingsley's time and attention."

Tamara was waiting to show Estella out through the back door. Estella hesitated, but when Deputy Wilcox gave her a stern look, Estella settled for hissing, "This isn't over," before following Tamara to the exit.

"She's just upset about Abilene," Nora said to Griffin by way of explanation. "My friends and I have grown close to her. What happened last night has us all turned inside out."

Tamara, who'd already returned from showing Estella the door, gestured to Nora. "I have a key to the apartment. If it's okay with Deputy Wilcox, I could let you in to get clothes or toiletries for Abilene."

Deputy Wilcox inclined her head before turning back to Griffin. "Any luck?"

"Not yet," he said.

If Nora's theory was correct, Griffin would make a big show of trying a dozen different keys. In truth, he had no intention of opening the watch for Deputy Wilcox or anyone else from the sheriff's department. Nora didn't know what secrets were hidden inside the watch, if any, but she was certain that Griffin wanted them to remain hidden.

Tamara ascended the stairs leading to Abilene's studio apartment without speaking. Nora was grateful for the silence for she was struggling to face the staircase again. She hated this space. Hated the crime scene tape, the stained stairs, the cloying chemical aroma, and the gloom. Averting her eyes from the outline that had been drawn around Ezekiel Crane's body, Nora willed Tamara to hurry up and unlock the door.

As soon as she was inside Abilene's pathetic home, Nora regretted her impatience.

Tamara closed the door and leaned her back against it. Her face was taut with anger and she held a gun in her hand. It was a small pistol. A dainty, shiny weapon perfectly capable of delivering death.

Tamara was pointing the barrel at Nora's chest.

Right at her heart.

Chapter 17

The Bible tells us to love our neighbors, and also to love our enemies; probably because generally they are the same people.

—G. K. Chesterton

"You should have kept your nose in your books." Tamara sneered. "You three put on a good show downstairs. You, Diner Boy, and that Magnolia Spa bitch. I won't enjoy killing you, but I'd love to take a shot at her."

Nora stared at the gun barrel. She wasn't taking in the fact that its dark maw meant the end of her life because she was too busy thinking of all the mistakes she'd made. Why had she zeroed in on Griffin as the killer and not Tamara? Then she remembered why she'd drawn such an erroneous conclusion—why she'd made a mistake that could cost her everything.

"I thought Griffin was the killer," she said.

"Obviously." Tamara rolled her eyes. "You wouldn't have come up here otherwise. I guess you're one of those people with book smarts, but not street smarts. You thought I was Griffin's sidekick. His assistant. His business partner with benefits. But I'm none of those things. Griffin is *my* partner. I brought *him* in on . . ." She trailed off, gave a shake of her head, and continued. "I'm disappointed in you, Nora. You run a business. You know that it takes grit for a woman to succeed in a male-dominated world. You should have recognized me as one of your own."

Nora gave a helpless shrug. "You played the assistant. You served tea and chocolates to your clients. Griffin would offer, but you did the waitressing part. He never served anyone."

"That was deliberate." Tamara looked pleased by Nora's observation. "People in small towns are more comfortable with traditional gender roles, especially when they're entrusting their treasures to strangers. I hated making that stupid tea. I hated those silver trays. I hated having to let Griffin take the lead. Wouldn't you?"

Tamara's indignation almost made Nora feel ashamed. Almost. But there were millions of women across the globe who'd been overlooked or undervalued at some point in their lives, and they didn't use this as an excuse to commit murder. It seemed unwise to make this argument to Tara, however.

"You're right. I should have seen you as an equal," Nora said. "To be completely honest, I assumed Griffin was behind the murders because I didn't think a woman would be strong enough to push Kenneth Frye off the balcony of that treehouse cabin. I mean, the man was a monster."

"A monster-sized bastard." Tamara's mouth twisted in anger. The gun dipped a little. The barrel was now pointed at Nora's belly. "He threatened me at the festival. He thought I was scared of him—that I was working for him and not the other way around. Stupid ass. He was a bully with mommy issues. The world is a better place without him."

Though Nora couldn't argue with that, she wanted to keep Tamara talking. The longer Nora could stall her, the greater the chance someone would notice their absence. And it seemed like Tamara wanted to share her story.

"I have no problem with the late-night flight you sent him on. I just don't get how you did it. The strength it would have taken to move that mountain of a man . . ." She trailed off and splayed her hands as if begging for an explanation.

Laughter bubbled out of Tamara's throat. She was enjoying this. "You don't need strength when you have booze. Frye was totally wrecked by the time he stepped out on that balcony. He'd spent hours downing every type of booze the festival had to offer. Can you imagine the combo of beer and 'shine swirling around in your stomach?" She shuddered. "I went out to the balcony first, claiming I needed fresh air. Then, I tricked him into leaning over the railing by telling him there was a bear down below. The man was a dumb ass. He actually thought I came to his cabin to show him what had been hidden in his mother's book."

"Is that why he had two hotel rooms? The tree-house cabin was reserved for meetings with you?"

"There was only one meeting," Tamara said. "And he was never going to survive it. If he hadn't gotten sloshed at the festival, I would have spiked a bottle of vodka with sedatives. No matter what, Frye was going to be a Humpty Dumpty. He was going to fall, he was going to break, and no one was going to put him back together again."

Despite the precariousness of her situation, Nora felt a small surge of excitement. She could finally learn the secret of the pocket watch.

"Kenneth stood between you and the watch. You wanted that watch. Who was the original owner? Ezekiel Crane?"

At the sound of his name, Tamara went rigid. "That bastard got what he deserved too. That man cheated me over and over again. Back when I was new to the business, I was naïve and trusting. I took jewelry, watches, and clocks to Crane in exchange for a commission. He underpaid me from the get-go."

"Were they stolen?" Nora asked. Bluntness was a risk, but she sensed that Tamara respected people who spoke their minds.

Tamara's eyes narrowed. "Just trinkets from estates. Stuff that old people loved but their kids didn't know or care about. Most of the time, the family would take what they wanted and leave the rest for me to sell. It was hard work. Dirty work. Have you ever cleaned out a house where a ninety-year-old and her ten cats lived for decades? Or dealt with an apartment where an eighty-year-old bachelor had amassed a huge collection of butterflies and bugs? I deserved more than what I was paid, so I always kept a few things for myself. I took the things to Crane and we split the profits. I just didn't know how uneven our split was."

"Maybe you should have charged your customers more," Nora suggested flatly.

Taking this remark in stride, Tamara shrugged. "Maybe. But I was a woman in a man's line of work. In Texas. So I charged less to attract clients. Everything was peachy until Crane ruined me. He started a rumor that I was a crook."

"Because you accused him of keeping more than his share of the profits?" Nora guessed.

"Bingo!" Tamara exclaimed. She gazed off into the middle distance and pressed her lips into a hard, thin line. She'd gone back to that time in her life when things had turned sour. She'd been forced to run, moving from town to town, constantly changing identities.

Nora thought of the framed prints lining the walls of Virtual Genie. Maybe she could appeal to a softer side of Tamara by talking to her about books. "Are you the *Arabian Nights* fan?"

Tamara pointed at her chest with her free hand. "Me? I can't sit still long enough to read a book."

"You've been on the run. Just like Abilene," Nora said, seizing on the comparison. "She didn't hurt you, Tamara. She was mistreated by Crane far worse than you were. You're going to let her rot away in prison after she spent her entire childhood locked up in that sicko's basement? He was more of a monster than Kenneth Frye. If you truly believe in equality for women, then you won't let the injustice continue."

Tamara gaped in astonishment. "What are you talking about? Abilene and Crane? How are they connected?"

"He was her uncle," Nora said. "That's why she's so good at watch and clock appraisals. She's been doing it for years. In her uncle's basement. Where she was locked up every single day."

Tamara looked like she might be sick. She lowered the gun to her side and stared at Nora. "I didn't know. She just showed up, asking about the apartment. She said she could pay partially in cash and partially in labor. She knew her stuff and the deal suited us because we didn't want to draw up a lease agreement."

"Because none of you are using your real names. Abilene included."

"Son of a bitch," Tamara muttered.

She seemed unaware of her gun and, for a second, Nora considered lunging for it. She studied the space between her and Tamara and knew she wouldn't make it. There were no other weapons within reach. Nothing she could use to gain her freedom.

"Don't bother trying to get out of this," Tamara said, raising her gun. "I'm sorry about Abilene, but I can't help her. I have a train to catch. Your journey ends here, in that nasty bathtub. I'm sorry, but this is your own fault. You inserted yourself into this story. And it ends here."

Tamara waved Nora toward the bathroom, but Nora didn't budge. If she walked into that bathroom, it would be the last place she'd ever see. Tamara would have her lie down in the tub so she could shoot her, close the door, and leave. She'd go downstairs, grab the watch, her laptop, and the valuables she planned to steal from the people of Miracle Springs, and skip town.

"Deputy Wilcox will hear the shot. You'll be caught," Nora said, feeling desperate now.

Tamara scooped a pillow off the futon. "No, I won't," she said with chilling assurance.

Nora raised her hands in surrender. "I'll go, but would you please answer one more question? I need to know why the pocket watch is so important. I looked up the market value. Fifteen grand isn't chump change, but it doesn't seem worth the risk of committing three murders. I say three because I'm guessing you were responsible for Amanda Frye's involuntary swim in the pond."

"She could have avoided that fate if she'd just told me where the watch was hidden. Dumb cow!" Tamara snapped, her anger flaring with fresh intensity. "Her death is on Ezekiel. I told him not to show himself to Amanda before I had a second go at getting her to trust me, but he didn't listen. Of course he didn't. He was going to screw me over. Again! He was going to find the watch himself. By the time I got to her place, she was already spooked because she'd seen Ezekiel."

Nora furrowed her brow in confusion. "They used to be lovers. Why should she be afraid? Did she steal his watch?"

Tamara smiled. "Not on purpose! She wanted something that belonged to him—something to remember him by after she moved away. Her Romeo next door. I mean, the two of them didn't even kiss. Not once! Theirs was a love affair of *words*," Tamara said with contempt. "She told me that she grabbed one of his books as a keepsake. He'd left it in the garden and she swiped it. By the time he realized it was gone, she was headed for her new life in Miracle Springs. I have no idea why he didn't try to get it back before now."

Nora could picture Amanda hiding in the bathroom of her house in Miracle Springs. In that space, she could take out Ezekiel's book and reminisce. How stunned she must have been to open the cover and discover the watch. How long had it taken her to tell Ezekiel about it? Had he asked her to mail it back? Demanded its return? Had his letters turned cold and harsh, shattering the lovely fantasy that had once defined their relationship?

"Crane couldn't travel to Miracle Springs to reclaim the watch," Nora told Tamara. "Because of Abilene. He lived in fear of her escaping and telling the world how he'd kept her prisoner."

Tamara took this in. "It seems like a helluva long time to wait."

Nora was irritated that she'd given up information without getting the answer she wanted, but she tried to stay calm. She really did need to know why the watch was so special. Why was it more valuable than three human lives, regardless of how flawed those lives were?

"Amanda didn't return it and she didn't sell it. Even though she was nearly penniless when she died, she still had that pocket watch." Nora imagined Amanda in her backyard, the dresses on the clothesline riffling in the summer breeze. "When she saw Ezekiel on her property, she knew he'd come for the watch. Anything they'd once shared was gone and she knew he was to be feared. She was outside with Abilene when she saw him. That must be how things played out because she gave Abilene one of her dresses and whispered a single word."

"Which was?" Tamara asked. She'd lowered her pistol again, utterly entranced by the picture Nora was painting.

Nora cupped her hands around her mouth. Injecting urgency into her voice, she used a stage whisper to heighten the drama and said, "Run."

As if compelled by an instinct more powerful than logic, Tamara did exactly as Amanda must have done. She glanced back over her shoulder, looking for the threat.

In Tamara's case, the threat wasn't behind her. It was in front of her.

Nora reacted without hesitation. She sprang at Tamara and kicked her gun hand with all the force she could muster.

Tamara's head whipped around and she cried out in pain and surprise.

But she didn't drop the gun.

She was raising her right hand to take aim when Nora crashed into her.

Tamara fell backward and struck the floor. The gun skittered several feet away. Tamara twisted violently to the side, reaching for the weapon, but Nora drove her fist into her face. There was a crunching noise as Nora's knuckles met Tamara's nose.

Tamara shrieked with rage and brought her hands up to Nora's face. Her fingernails bit into the burn scars on Nora's cheek and her shriek became a growl as she raked her nails through Nora's skin.

The pain ripped through Nora. It felt like dozens of white-hot needles had pierced her cheek. For several seconds she couldn't breathe, and she desperately tried to shove Tamara away.

Nora couldn't escape the pain, so she used it to channel her anger. Anger gave her strength.

She struck out with her fist again. Her vision was clouded by unshed tears, so she didn't know where the blow landed, but Tamara grunted in surprise. She then plunged her nails into Nora's damaged cheek for a second time.

The agony nearly blinded Nora.

She sensed Tamara scrambling for the gun. She heard furious cursing and felt Tamara squirming out from under her. If Nora didn't stop her, it would be all over.

Fight! an internal voice screamed at Nora. *Get the gun!*

For the second time, she hurled herself at Tamara. On the floor, the two women kicked and punched and clawed at each other until, as if from some great distance, Nora heard shouting from the stairwell.

Time seemed to stop. There was an unreal stillness surrounding them. The room became charged, like the breathless moment preceding a lightning strike.

The feeling of being outside of time didn't last. There was a loud crack and a splintering of wood. The door to the landing burst open. Nora could feel a whisper of cool air waft over her.

"Freeze!" a voice boomed.

Sheriff McCabe's voice.

Nora blinked hard, squeezing the water out of her eyes until she could focus on a black boot.

The boot kicked Tamara's pistol to the other end of the kitchen.

"Stay on the ground!" McCabe commanded. "Don't move!"

Nora scooted away from Tamara and slowly, gingerly, sat back on her heels.

Uniformed men and women flowed into the room. Nora watched them crowd around Tamara, too dazed to react.

Something tickled her chin and Nora wiped away a droplet of blood. Foolishly, she then touched her cheek with her fingertips. Nausea immediately roiled in her belly and she lowered her head and pulled in a deep breath of oxygen to stop herself from being sick.

McCabe was suddenly kneeling at her side, his hand under her elbow. "Steady. Steady now."

He barked at someone to get the paramedics. This was followed by other orders, but Nora couldn't process them.

When the twisting in her gut had ceased, she sat up again.

Tamara was being hauled to her feet. She hissed and spit like a cornered cat. Before Deputies Wilcox and Fuentes could remove her from the apartment, she turned to Nora and said, "Of all the towns and all the people, I can't believe you took me down. But better you than an Ezekiel. Or a Kenneth Frye." She tilted her head so that her cheek touched her shoulder. "Your face is pretty bad. Looks like I gave you something to remember me by. It's no pocket watch, but that didn't work out too well for Amanda, did it?"

Deputy Wilcox had heard enough. She put a hand on Tamara's back and pushed her toward the doorway.

"Wait!" Nora called. Shouting sent a bolt of pain through her cheek, but she tried to push the feeling aside. "Who are you, really?" she asked Tamara.

"Tara Liebold." She seemed pleased by the question. "I've also been Mary, Mare, Moira, Aria, and Tamara. I have no idea who I really am anymore. Does anyone?"

With that, the woman who'd committed three murders was taken away.

When the paramedics entered, Nora was both disappointed and relieved that Jed wasn't one of them. She was disappointed because he'd make her feel better with a word or a smile. She was relieved because she disliked being a damsel in distress. Besides, how could she explain that her pride smarted as much her cheek? She'd been so shortsighted.

"You'll need stitches," the male paramedic said as he gently pressed a bandage over Nora's cheek. "From a skilled hand."

He went on to say that he could recommend a plastic surgeon, but Nora wasn't listening.

When the paramedic was finished, Sheriff McCabe helped Nora to her feet.

"Deputy Andrews will drive you to the hospital," he said and insisted on holding her arm down the stairs and through the back exit. "On the way, you can tell him what happened. If you're up for it, just give him a sketch. I'm sure it hurts to talk. And if it hurts too much, tell him later."

"The watch?" Nora asked and winced. Talking hurt like hell. "Did Griffin have the keys?"

McCabe shook his head. "Let's hope his partner does."

After giving her arm a slight squeeze, the sheriff handed her over to Deputy Andrews. "Don't leave her side," he told his deputy. "Make sure she's given the very best care. Understood?"

Andrews stood a little taller. "I will, sir," he promised.

Nora watched Sheriff McCabe walk away.

Miracle Springs hit the jackpot with him, she thought. *It might be the only thing that's gone right for this town lately.*

"I have bottled water," Andrews said after pulling out of the lot. "Do you need anything else? Food? Coffee?"

"No. I just want to get the hospital bit over with."

As Andrews drove past Miracle Books, Nora glanced at the bold letters of the CLOSED sign. Normally, she'd be upset over losing a day's worth of sales, but not today. She was thinking of another sign—the HELP WANTED sign she'd recently taped to the window. If Abilene had never seen that sign, if she'd never taken it down and pressed it to her chest like a teddy bear, where would she be now?

Nora's phone buzzed inside her handbag. She'd turned the volume off before entering Virtual Genie and saw that she'd missed calls from the members of the Secret, Book, and Scone Society. This call, however, was from Jed.

"I hear you were hurt saving the town. Again." He tried to cover his concern with levity, but Nora heard it all the same. "Clearly, you need a cape and a pair of latex boots. And a cool name. Super Biblio Woman? No, that's too cheesy. I'll keep thinking about it. Seriously, Nora, what's your pain like right now? And don't play tough with me. I want the truth."

"A moderate throb," she said. "Talking makes it worse."

"Okay, don't talk," Jed was quick to say. "I'm going to meet you at the hospital. I called in a favor from a physician I know. He's the best at what he does. Will you let him treat you?"

Nora was touched by Jed's thoughtfulness. "There's no need. My cheek was already scarred."

"Which is exactly why this guy should take care of you. Scar tissue is tricky stuff. This guy owes me one and I'm making a withdrawal from the Favor Bank."

Jed promised that he'd see her soon and hung up.

Andrews shot a glance at Nora. "I talked to Hester while the paramedics were with you. She said she'd close the bakery if you need her to be with you."

Hearing this, Nora's throat tightened with emotion. She shook her head to convey her feelings.

"I thought you'd say that, so I told her that you were okay and that June and Estella should keep working too. I had trouble convincing Estella." Andrews grinned. "She didn't think Mrs. Henderson's root touch-up was important in light of what went down this morning, but Mrs. Henderson threatened to tell all her Red Hat Society friends to find a new stylist if Estella canceled on her."

Nora didn't want her friends wasting the day in a hospital waiting room. None of them could afford to miss work. "Can you tell me about Griffin?"

Andrews was happy to oblige. "Your idea of putting blood on the watch and wiping it off again so that it would show up with Luminol was brilliant. Just like you and the sheriff predicted, Kingsley switched watches. I can't believe he had an identical watch at the ready. Just in case he had the chance to swap them."

"Why? Is there something inside the watch?" Nora asked. She didn't want to talk because it stretched the skin around her mouth and pulled at her wounded cheek, but there were things she had to know.

"Kingsley wouldn't say. He didn't say much. Just a quote from that *Arabian Nights* book."

For some inexplicable reason, Nora was relieved to know that Griffin genuinely liked the collection of Arabian stories. Virtual Genie might have been constructed on a foundation of trickery and deceit, but Nora wanted those framed quotes to have meant something to someone. She hated the idea of literary quotes being used for the sole purpose of adding to Virtual Genie's décor.

"Seeing as you're a book person, I'm guessing you'll want to hear the quote," Andrews said. "'Watch your world burn, light of my heart. Tomorrow we will find another one and burn that too.'"

Nora watched the landscape pass by. The slopes of the mountains were still painted in golden light, but the hues weren't as rich as they'd been earlier that morning. The glow was gone, and while the canvas of autumnal colors was still lovely, it was now a much more muted palette.

The transformation reminded her of Robert Frost's famous poem.

> *So dawn goes down to day.*
> *Nothing gold can stay.*

The line mentioning gold turned Nora's thoughts to the mysterious pocket watch. Was the watch connected to the quote Griffin had spoken? Had Tamara been the light in Griffin's heart? If so, Nora didn't believe the feeling was returned. Tamara didn't seem capable of love. Love required an element of self-lessness, and Tamara was too caught up with the injustices she'd suffered to share her heart with another human being.

Amanda Frye, on the other hand, had fallen in love with her next-door neighbor. Abilene had told the Secret, Book, and Scone Society that Amanda and Ezekiel had started off as friends. That friendship had blossomed until, over time, it became something more.

To Amanda's disappointment, her husband landed a job in another state and she'd been forced to abandon the happiness she'd found with Ezekiel. She made the right choice. The hard one. But she punished her husband and son for that choice. Her misery wore them both down until her husband died and her son became estranged.

As for the man she'd once loved? He ultimately betrayed her. He made it clear that a pocket watch mattered more to him than she ever could.

No wonder she became bitter, Nora thought.

"Tamara must have the keys. She's the killer. She killed Amanda, Kenneth, and Ezekiel. She would have taken me out too." Nora closed her eyes. "She got better at killing as she went along. Her anger grew until she could push one man over a railing and stab another in the back."

That short speech sent spikes of pain through Nora's cheek. Her scarred skin wasn't like healthy skin. It was bubbly, petal-smooth, and as fragile as a seashell.

Despite the pain, she was determined to continue her narrative. She hoped that her words would speed Abilene's release.

Andrews, mindful of Nora's injuries, asked only pertinent questions. He didn't interrupt. He listened attentively. By the time Nora finished, they were at the hospital.

"I don't want to go in there thinking it'll be hours before Abilene is set free." Nora was mumbling now. Not only was her discomfort acute, but the worry, confusion, and shock from the events of the past few days had completely drained her. Like the book she'd discovered in Amanda's house, she felt hollowed out.

Andrews pulled out his phone and showed Nora the screen. Hester had sent him a text saying that she was heading to the station to get Abilene. She planned to take their new friend home and remain with her the rest of the day.

"Guess she closed the Gingerbread House after all," Andrews said. He smiled reassuringly at Nora. "Abilene will be okay. I have to see about you now. You heard the sheriff. He'll have my head if you're not given the best care. And how will I finish the rest of Orson Scott Card's novels without my head?"

Nora opened her door. "Don't make me smile. It hurts."

But she smiled anyway. Just a little.

Jed found Nora in the emergency waiting area. He tenderly kissed her undamaged cheek and helped her with the admission forms. In the privacy of a consultation room, Jed introduced her to his friend, a tall, debonair Indian man named Dr. David Patel. The doctor told Nora that he specialized in facial reconstruction and was known for his correction of burn scars. He went on to explain that skin grafts did not produce the best results and that he preferred facial flaps, skin expanders, and laser technology.

Perhaps sensing that Nora was having a hard time following him, he put a hand on her shoulder and said, "The long and the short of it is this: You need plastic surgery. I'd like to perform that surgery. I can repair today's damage and improve your old scars. You just need to complete another round of forms and we can set this in motion."

Nora filled out more paperwork. She felt disembodied. Weightless. She'd felt that way since entering the hospital. She filled in the information on the form without digesting any of it. And then she was in a hospital gown and Jed was sitting next to her, holding her hand.

"I didn't call David because you need to be fixed," he said. "I think every bit of you is beautiful. Every single centimeter." He rubbed her palm with the tip of his thumb. "I called him because only an artist should be allowed to touch your face. No one else but the best. No one else is good enough for you."

Later, a nurse injected something into Nora's IV line.

The drugs sent a silent invitation to sleep, which she willingly accepted. She couldn't remember the last time she'd been so tired.

As the drugs moved through her veins, the noises in the

room receded and the darkness behind Nora's eyelids deepened to the blackness of outer space.

Seconds before she drifted off, a line written by Hermann Hesse surfaced in her mind.

Some of us think holding on is making us strong; but sometimes it is letting go.

With the warmth of Jed's hand on hers, Nora let go.

Chapter 18

I must stand on my own two feet if I'm to get to know myself and the world outside. That's why I can't stay here with you any longer.

—Henrik Ibsen

Nora left the hospital with a packet of instructions from Dr. Patel and a reminder that he'd be seeing her again for follow-up procedures. When Nora pointed out that she couldn't afford those procedures, he told her that Jed had once saved his son's life. He'd been looking for a chance to repay him ever since.

"Now, I have that opportunity," the surgeon had said.

After Jed dropped Nora at Caboose Cottage so she could shower and change clothes, she opened the bookstore in hopes of earning a few sales before day's end. She wasn't truly concerned about her business, however. Just as she wasn't concerned about her bandaged face. Her only concern was Abilene.

Nora had called Hester and was happy to hear that Abilene had returned to work at the Gingerbread House.

"On the outside, she seems fine," Hester had said. "There's no way she can be fine, but I'm not sure what to do for her."

"She might need more help than we can offer."

To Nora's surprise, Hester had agreed. "I think so too, which is why I asked June to speak with a therapist at the lodge."

The sooner the better, Nora thought, gazing at the display in the front window.

Abilene had created a transparent girl made of transparent packing tape. A girl holding a transparent, bubble-wrap balloon. The only colorful things in the window were the books.

It struck Nora that Abilene had made a self-portrait in the bookstore window. The scene was beautiful and ethereal, but there was another side to it as well. Now that Nora knew Abilene's story, she saw acute loneliness in the invisible girl surrounded by books—her only vehicles of escape.

The sleigh bells banged, startling Nora out of her reverie. She turned to find Sheriff McCabe standing in the shop's threshold.

"I thought I'd drop by for a cup of coffee and a chat," McCabe said. "Is this a good time?"

"I'm closing in ten minutes, so it's perfect."

Nora led the sheriff back to the ticket agent's window. He ordered a Dante Alighieri and asked to defer payment until the end of his visit as he planned on buying a few books.

Having missed too many sales yesterday and today, Nora liked the sound of that. She poured decaf coffee into a heavy mug with the text LAW & ORDER on one side and DUN DUN on the back.

Sheriff McCabe barked out a laugh when he saw the back of the mug. He repeated the famous sound effect and told Nora that he'd seen every episode of the famed crime drama.

He settled into June's chair and touched his cheek. "How is this feeling?"

"Tender," Nora said. She'd made herself an Agatha Chris-TEA, but it was too hot to drink. She set it aside and folded her hands on her lap. "It's easier to talk than it was yesterday."

McCabe smiled. "Good. Let me know if it gets to be too much, all right?" Satisfied by Nora's nod, he went on. "Tamara Beacham—I'm choosing to refer to her by her alias—has confessed to the murders of Amanda Frye, Kenneth Frye, and Ezekiel Crane. It took hours to get her to cave, but she eventually told us everything in hopes of receiving a lighter sentence."

"Good luck with that, sister," Nora murmured darkly.

She could relate to Tamara's anger over having been tricked by a man she trusted. Nora had also been the victim of deceit. Her anger had been so encompassing that she'd nearly killed two people because of it. Nora had acted like a fool in the heat of the moment, but Tamara had made careful and deliberate plans to exact her revenge. She was also motivated by greed. She knew Ezekiel's pocket watch was valuable and she would do anything to possess it.

"Griffin Kingsley has pled guilty to accessory to murder and multiple fraud charges as well," McCabe continued. "Their gypsy life is over. No move traveling from town to town to rob unsuspecting people. Though she was clever in many ways, Ms. Beacham didn't disguise herself well enough to keep Ezekiel Crane from finding her. She was always a swindler and she found another man to partner with. Not a good decision on Mr. Kingsley's part."

"What about the watch?" Nora asked the question plaguing her for days. "Did Tamara have the keys?"

McCabe's smile grew broader. "She did. And yes, we opened it." He placed his phone on the mirror-top coffee table and turned it, giving Nora a clear view of the screen. "I thought you might like to experience this moment for yourself."

Realizing that she was meant to watch a video, Nora picked up her mug of tea and leaned forward.

McCabe pressed the play button and an image of the gold pocket watch with the ram's head filled the screen. A woman's fingers, long and slender with an elegant French manicure, appeared in the frame.

"That's Deputy Wilcox," McCabe explained.

Wilcox pressed the release on the top of the watch and the cover popped open. With the face revealed, the deputy fit a key into the first keyhole, which was located near the Roman numeral three. She inserted another key into the second keyhole, which was near the number nine, and put the final key into a tiny hole in the center of the second-hand dial. She then gently twisted it.

Nothing happened. At least, not that Nora could see.

The deputy must have noticed something, for she used the tips of her fingernails to carefully pry up the watch face. Underneath, embedded in the space where the mechanical elements resided, were small gemstones.

A flashlight beam fell onto the watch, and the gemstones glowed like hot embers.

"Rubies?" Nora asked, utterly entranced.

McCabe pointed at the phone. Nora saw another hand place a shallow tray on the table. Deputy Wilcox turned the pocket watch over, causing the red gemstones to spill out into the tray. She then gestured at the watch and the flashlight beam was directed back into the cavity. Nora saw letters engraved in cursive. Then words. Her mouth moved as she read the message etched inside the watch.

To Hannah,
Our greatest treasure.
Love always, Mom and Dad

Nora wasn't a sentimental person, but tears sprang to her eyes as she read the words written from parents to child. How many years had passed since the message had been engraved inside the watch? How long had it been secreted away, without Abilene's knowledge, until the day Amanda Frye discovered it? What difference would such a message have made to a girl who believed that no one had loved her?

No one.

Not ever.

"We located the law firm that handled Joseph and Caroline Tupper's will and arranged for Hannah's placement with Ezekiel Crane. Joe and Caroline were both only children, so Ezekiel was their closest relative. He was Caroline's second cousin and they weren't close. Like many young parents, the Tuppers didn't believe their child would end up being raised by a stranger. They simply put down Crane's name because he was the logical choice."

"Is that how the pocket watch ended up in Texas? The law firm gave it to Ezekiel?" Nora asked.

McCabe picked up his phone. "The firm mailed it to him. In two parts. The first, the pocket watch, was sent on Hannah's tenth birthday, per her parent's request. Though the package was addressed to Hannah, we assume Crane opened it. The second mailing, delivered on Hannah's eighteenth birthday, contained the watch keys." He paused and seemed to be considering whether he should say more.

"It gets worse?" she guessed.

No trace of a smile lingered on McCabe's face. "For Crane, the watch was his winning lottery ticket. He'd been waiting for those keys for nearly a decade. It's clear from the diary found in Crane's office, and it's clear from his entries following Hannah's last birthday that he was planning to kill her."

Nora wasn't at all shocked by this revelation. "Why did he wait for the keys? He was a jeweler. He could have forced the watch open and taken out the stones years earlier."

"The Lubbock cops have read Crane's diary in its entirety and here's their take. When Hannah first came to live with Crane, it unbalanced him. He wasn't comfortable around most people and barely managed to deal with the public at work. As for children? He was terrified and disgusted by them. He locked her in the basement so he could pretend she wasn't there unless it suited him. As for the pocket watch, he writes about it all the time. He guessed that something precious was inside based on the watch's weight coupled with the Tupper family history of African gem mining. However, he didn't know what kind of gems were inside. He spent years fantasizing about how his life would change after he sold them. He fantasized, but he didn't act. The two people standing in his way were Hannah and, later, Amanda Frye. Insomuch as he was capable of it, Crane cared about Mrs. Frye. Though after he learned of her impending move, his journal entries became embittered. He also began to wonder how he could be rid of Hannah."

Nora shook her head. "It's a wonder she survived as long as she did."

McCabe made a noise of agreement. "Crane was too scared to kill her until she turned eighteen. Once emancipated, people wouldn't look for her—not that they ever had before. Crane never enrolled Hannah in school and only the legal firm knew where she was being raised. Despite this, Crane lived in terror that someone would drop by to check up on Hannah. He hated the sound of the phone or the doorbell. With every passing day, he became more unstable."

"And then, Amanda swiped the book containing the pocket watch."

McCabe sighed. "Yes. Crane could have left Abilene in the basement and gone after the book, but like most bullies, he was a coward. After Mrs. Frye's departure, Crane became more reclusive. He bought pieces only from people he knew and trusted. His business was barely limping along."

Nora sipped her tea. "And that's when the keys came."

"That's when the keys came," McCabe repeated. "Feeling desperate, Ezekiel decided to kill Abilene before traveling to Miracle Springs. He didn't plan on returning."

"The rubies—they'll be returned to Abilene, right? And the watch?"

McCabe's smile reappeared. "Yes. The pocket watch and its contents belong to her. However, the gemstones aren't rubies. Would you like to see another video?"

Puzzled, Nora waved for him to bring out his phone again.

"It will make more of an impression on a bigger screen. Could we use your laptop?"

Nora hurried to get it. She signed in and handed it to McCabe. He wouldn't let her see what he typed into Google's search box, but she could tell that he'd found a video on gemstones.

Nora hit the play button and a woman began to narrate in a silky voice.

"*This is the rarest diamond of them all,*" she said. "*The Fancy Red diamond. There are so few natural red diamonds that they are highly desirable. In 1987, a red diamond shattered the records for price per weight, capturing an astonishing $926,000 per karat.*"

Nora hit the pause button. "Are you telling me—?"

Looking very pleased, McCabe said, "I am. The pocket watch held small red diamonds worth a not-so-small fortune. Joseph Tupper is a descendant of a South African Tupper who had a significant stake in a diamond mine. Joe didn't care for the stones. He felt they were stolen from the people who rightfully owned the land and, therefore, the diamonds. Having received them from his father, he put them away for his daughter."

Too astonished to reply, Nora stared at the computer screen. The frozen image of the red diamond gazed back at her. Once again, Nora was reminded of the glow in the heart of an ember.

"Does Abilene know?"

"Andrews is at the bakery right now. I thought she could use some good news for a change. I thought you could too."

Nora couldn't mimic the sheriff's smile because of her bandaged face, but the joy of this discovery flowed through her with such a powerful warmth that she put down her tea. She didn't need comfort anymore. Abilene was rich. More important, Abilene's parents had reached out from the grave with a message of love. They'd had it engraved in gold. Abilene could read it over and over again for the rest of her days.

OUR GREATEST TREASURE.

Turning her damp eyes away from the sheriff, Nora said, "I think the message from her parents will mean more to her than a mountain's worth of diamonds."

"I believe so too," McCabe said. He carried his coffee cup to the ticket agent's window. This wasn't necessary, but he was clearly giving Nora time to collect herself.

"Andrews has worked tirelessly to find Abilene's hometown. After conversations with her parents' former law firm, he was able to track down their address. He spoke with a dozen neighbors and learned the name of the church the Tuppers attended. Many people remember the family. Two such people were the couple entrusted with Abilene's care while her parents went on their mission trip."

Nora had forgotten about this couple. "Why didn't they check on her afterward? Didn't they care that she'd lost her parents? That her world had crumbled and she'd been sent to live with a stranger?"

"They had their own problems," McCabe said. "The husband was involved in a car accident. He lost the use of his legs and, because of his disability, lost his job as well. Luckily, folks from their church volunteered to help with meals and transportation. According to what Andrews learned, this couple still receives a great deal of support from the church."

"It sounds like a special place," Nora said.

McCabe nodded. "It does. In any case, this couple, the Hubers, are eager to speak with Abilene. They want to tell her how much she was loved by her parents and they have lots of stories to share with her." He gave Nora a quizzical look. "Do you think she'd be up for that?"

"Not at the moment. She needs time to deal with all that's happened to her. She also needs professional help. June is asking around at the lodge, and she'll find the right therapist. Speaking of finding things, which books are you looking for?"

"Abilene suggested I read these." He pulled out a piece of paper and handed it to Nora. "She said they were both classics and not to be missed, so I'm taking her advice."

Nora read the titles Abilene had written. *The Witch of Blackbird Pond* and *A Doll's House.*

Torn between smiling and crying, Nora folded the paper in half and gestured for McCabe to follow her to the Plays section.

"I have a few questions about how Tamara was able to pull off these murders," Nora said as they walked among the books.

"I'll answer if I can," McCabe said.

Nora glanced at a cookbook cover featuring an assortment of artisan cheeses and tools with which to serve them. "Did she steal the knife from the Gingerbread House during business hours?"

"She did. Ms. Beacham entered with a busload of guests and waited until Hester began serving these customers before slipping into the kitchen. She didn't care whether Hester or Abilene took the fall for Crane's murder. She didn't give a damn about either of them."

Nora scowled. "I see her feminist tendencies apply only to herself. When it comes to supporting the rights and interests of other women, Tamara is an abject failure."

"She'd throw either gender under the bus to save her own skin. Let's not forget Kingsley either. After years of being in business with the guy, she didn't bat an eyelash over telling us how they went about duping their customers. Together, they've stolen hundreds of valuables. After amassing a nice pile, the part-ners would pack up and leave. They'd fence the stolen goods and move to a new town featuring residents facing an economic crisis. They were thieves and disaster chasers."

"That's why Tamara never listed Jack's antique box," Nora cried softly. "It was small, portable, and worth several thou-sand dollars. I'm so relieved that he has it back. He's going to help someone with that money."

They reached the section where Nora shelved plays and other drama and theater materials. "I have two copies of *A Doll's House*. Each has a different cover, so I'll let you pick."

"Ask me another question while I choose," McCabe said.

"Okay. If what Tamara told me is true, she went to Amanda's under the guise of having a friendly chat. Mentioning Lubbock probably got her through the door. She was obviously hoping to gain Amanda's trust and learn the location of the pocket watch. If she didn't threaten Amanda, then how did she coerce her into writing a suicide note?"

McCabe chose the Penguin Classics version of Ibsen's play. "I asked the same question and the answer was surprising. The suicide note was actually cut from a letter Mrs. Frye wrote to Crane, but never sent. Over cups of herbal tea, Mrs. Frye told Ms. Beacham about the relationship. She even mentioned this unsent letter, which was in her nightstand. Later, after the spiked tea hit Mrs. Frye and Ms. Beacham pushed her into the pond, she returned to the house and created the suicide scene in the kitchen. And because you'll probably ask this too, she didn't search the house at that time because the neighbor let his dogs out. Ms. Beacham is terrified of dogs. She was bitten when she was very small and their barking sent her into a panic."

Nora stared at the sheriff. "Seriously? Is that why she didn't return to the house later? She could have broken in and searched the place until she found the watch."

"After Mrs. Frye's death, Ms. Beacham was afraid of being seen by the neighbors or a member of law enforcement. She needed Mr. Frye to do the searching for her, but she didn't want him to know about the watch. She was afraid he'd keep it, so she told him to get as many books from his mother's place as he could. Mr. Frye grew angry at the festival because he suspected Ms. Beacham was lying—that there was something more valuable than books in his mother's house. Ms. Beacham promised to tell him everything at his cabin that night. And we know how that story ended."

Moving toward the fiction section, Nora asked, "How did Tamara know about the pocket watch in the first place?"

"She was with Crane when he received it in the mail. He had to sign for the package, which is why the law firm sent it to his shop. He was so worked up after its arrival that she assumed the contents must be very valuable. She didn't know about the gems, but after researching the ram's head, she discovered that it was a Tupper family symbol. When she learned about their connection to a South African diamond mine, she concluded that the watch face must be studded with priceless diamonds."

"She wasn't far off," Nora said. She didn't like Tamara Beacham, but she could still appreciate the woman's sharp mind.

Nora pulled her only copy of *The Witch of Blackbird Pond* from the shelf and handed it to Sheriff McCabe. He carried his selections to the checkout counter, took out his wallet, and paused.

"I'd also like to buy a copy of the book Andrews keeps going on about. What is it again?"

"*Ender's Game*?" Nora guessed.

McCabe snapped his fingers. "That's the one. I hope I find the time to get through these over the next few weeks, but they'll give me something to look forward to at the end of the day."

"I know you prefer audiobooks, so I appreciate your business. I also appreciate the explanations and answers," Nora said. "I love mysteries, but in book form only."

The sheriff paid for the books and collected his bag. "The department owes you, Nora. I guess the rumors are true. Miracle Springs is home to a group of superheroes."

McCabe winked and left the store.

Damn, Nora thought, watching the door close behind him. *We'll never shake that Night Angels nickname now.*

The Secret, Book, and Scone Society gathered at Hester's house to share a hearty meal of lentil chili and cornbread.

Nora loved Hester's Victorian-style cottage because it looked like an iced teacake. The interior was equally charming and Nora had never seen a cozier kitchen. The butter-yellow walls were covered with vintage tins, muffin pans, and advertising memorabilia spotlighting products from Hershey's ice cream to Ritz crackers. A dozen aprons hung from the coatrack by the door. Catching sight of Nora, Hester gestured for her to grab one.

"You're on serving duty," she told Nora. "I'm teaching Abilene how to make cornbread in a cast-iron skillet. I love it this way."

"Do I have the heat on too high?" Abilene asked Hester. She was wearing a blue-and-white checked apron and her hair was pulled into a high ponytail. She looked like a little girl.

Hester repeated her instructions, left Abilene at the stove, and issued commands to the rest of her friends. Estella was asked to set the table while June was to arrange the chili fixings.

The women moved around the kitchen, sharing stories from their day. They deliberately kept the conversation light. They danced around the subject of the recent murders, the arrests of Tamara and Griffin, the pocket watch, and the discovery of the diamonds until the chili was ready. Hester told Nora to ladle chili into bowls and pass them out.

"Add your toppings, grab some cornbread, and have a seat," Hester cheerfully directed.

When it was Abilene's turn to take a bowl of chili from Nora, she accepted the food. Instead of adding toppings, she placed the bowl on the counter. Turning back to Nora, she threw her arms around her and held her tight. She didn't say anything. There was no need for words.

The two women embraced for several seconds before Abilene let go, picked up her bowl, and headed to the table.

June was next in line for chili. She wagged her finger at Nora and said, "Don't you cry in my chili. I don't need extra salt. It's not good for my blood pressure."

Nora laughed. She felt like the tension that had held such a tight grip on her was finally dissipating. Standing in Hester's kitchen, enveloped by the aromas of cayenne, tomato sauce, fresh cornbread, and melted butter, it was impossible not to feel warm through and through.

Once they'd all sampled their chili, June looked at Abilene and said, "Honey, I talked to a friend of mine today. She's a therapist at the lodge and it's her job to help people like you. By that, I mean people who've been through the wringer. Her name is Dr. Lisa. She's very nice and she'd like to meet you. She'll come here and you'll talk. That's how it works. If you're okay with this, she'd like to see you on Monday."

Abilene glanced at Hester. "Do you think I should talk to her?"

"I do," Hester said. "See it as a chance to make a new friend."

Still unconvinced, Abilene turned back to June. "When I was at the hospital, they asked me to fill out a stack of forms. I couldn't, of course. I didn't speak to anyone during my time there, but I heard the nurses whispering about contacting the police about me. Later, they explained that they were required by law to make the call after seeing my bruises and the fractured rib. I only ended up in that hospital because I passed out in a gas station restroom."

"Fractured ribs hurt," said Estella. "I know. I've had them fractured twice and broken once."

Estella's matter-of-fact tone seemed to bring Abilene comfort. In Estella, she saw a fellow survivor.

"I don't know if it was pain and hunger," Abilene said. "The day I got away from my uncle . . . when he came down to the basement, I knew he was going to kill me. I fought back, but I'm not very strong. He hurt me." She spoke quickly, shoving the words out. "When he knocked me to the floor, I thought it was over. Through a haze, I saw a book under my bed. I hit him with it. I hit him again and again until he stopped moving. Then, I went upstairs and took the cash from his wallet. He rode the bus to work, so I walked to the stop and got on the first bus. I took buses east until I ran out of money. You know the rest."

Since none of the women knew how to break the silence following this speech, they focused on their food.

Nora didn't like how the mention of Abilene's uncle had sucked some of the warmth from the room. She didn't want him to have the power to do that anymore.

"After everything settles down, you can legally change your name," Nora said. "If that's what you want."

After a long moment of contemplation, Abilene said, "I don't want the name my uncle called me. I chose Abilene for myself. But I don't want to get rid of the name I shared with my parents, so I'll combine them."

June let out a sigh. "That's perfect, sweetheart."

The women finished their meals and Estella, Nora, and June volunteered to clean up.

When the kitchen was pin-neat again, Hester asked Abilene to take out the trash.

The second she was outside, Hester left the kitchen, running for her bedroom. She returned carrying a cake.

"Abilene never had a birthday party. Or a cake. We're going

to change that tonight," Hester said. "Estella, light the candles. June, get some plates. Nora, grab some forks. Hurry!"

As soon as Abilene reentered the kitchen, Hester turned off the lights. The eighteen candles on Abilene's cake created a soft halo in the center of the table.

"This is for you," Hester said. "It's a birthday cake. The tradition is to make a wish and then blow out all the candles with one breath. Want to give it a try?"

Abilene's eyes shone with wonder. "Do I say the wish out loud?"

June shook her head. "It's better to keep it to yourself."

"Okay, I made my wish." Abilene grinned shyly. "Do I blow out the candles now?"

Estella waved at the cake. "Unless you want us to sing to you. Fair warning. I'm no nightingale."

Hester elbowed her. "We're singing."

The members of the Secret, Book, and Scone Society sang "Happy Birthday" to the girl who'd hidden in a bookstore to be found by four women who would quickly become like sisters to her.

She blew out all of the candles and beamed over the applause that followed.

When Hester cut the cake, there was another round of boisterous clapping. For under the layer of vanilla buttercream were layers of colored sponge cake. An entire rainbow of cake divided by thin ribbons of icing.

"What's your favorite color?" June asked Abilene.

Abilene's gaze turned distant. "It used to blue because I never saw the sky enough, but now, I like a I different color. The book under my bed? The one that helped me get away? It was Mrs. Frye's. She lent it to my uncle, but he never saw it. I took it and hid it."

"What was the name of the book?" Nora asked, though she was fairly certain she already knew the answer.

"*The Color Purple*," Abilene said.

Nora thought of an abused woman escaping captivity using a book about an abused woman as a weapon. The connection between the two women and the empowerment they both craved made Nora smile. "The right book can change your life. The right book, at the right time, can be your miracle." She reached into her purse and pulled out a gift-wrapped package. Handing it to Abilene, she said, "Here's to your new life. And to all the miracles yet to come."

Recalling the day Abilene had quoted Dr. Seuss to her, Nora watched her unwrap *Oh, the Places You'll Go!*

Abilene's face glowed with delight. She opened the cover and began to read to herself.

Nora listened to the whisper of turning pages.

To her, there wasn't a more beautiful sound in the whole world.

Afterword

I am a book of snow, a spacious hand, an open
meadow, a circle that waits . . .
                                        —Pablo Neruda

Nora put the finishing touches on her window display and stood back to admire the book club scene she'd created. The book club members included a plush black bear, a red fox, a barn owl, and a brown rabbit. The animals, who'd gathered around a table set for tea, were each holding a copy of Philip Pullman's *The Golden Compass*. Behind the table was a backdrop of birch trees made of cardboard and white glitter. Nora had attached little ledges to each tree, turning them into book displays that sparkled in the light.

The trees featured winter-themed books like Jan Brett's *The Mitten*, Laura Ingalls Wilder's *The Long Winter*, Elin Hilderbrand's *Winter Storms*, Eowyn Ivey's *The Snow Child*, Gary Paulsen's *Brian's Winter*, Lois Ehlert's *Snowballs*, and Ezra Jack Keats's *The Snowy Day*.

Nora decided to enclose a photo of the window in her next letter to Abilene, who'd been gone for nearly five months now.

Nora was surprised by how often she thought of Abilene. Of how much she missed her.

No one had ever imagined Abilene would leave Miracle Springs so soon, or that her visit to a recovery center in the Poconos would lead to a permanent move.

Abilene and Dr. Lisa had been working together for several weeks when Abilene expressed a desire to visit her childhood home. Dr. Lisa wanted her patient to continue her therapy and to have a support system in place during her time in Pennsylvania, so she made arrangements for Abilene to stay at the recovery center.

Abilene loved the isolation and quiet beauty of the center. She loved waking up each day to the sight of the snow-covered mountains. She wrote the members of the Secret, Book, and Scone Society and told them how her childhood memories were beginning to surface. More and more every day. She remembered her dad pulling her on a sleigh and her mom giving her accessories for her snowman and snow dog. She remembered helping them dig in the soil and dropping seeds into the holes afterward. She remembered pulling carrots and potatoes from the ground. She remembered bedtime hugs and kisses, her parents pushing her on a swing, and a church Christmas pageant.

At the recovery center, she participated in group therapy and found great comfort in the company of people who'd also experienced trauma. When they spoke of their pain, she felt less alone.

When she finally left the center for Lake Harmony, the town where she'd been born, she was filled with a longing to be remembered as the child she once was.

And she was remembered. Especially by the couple who'd cared for her while her parents were in Africa. Karl and Janet Huber were thrilled to see Abilene again. Their initial visit went so smoothly that Abilene returned the next day. And the day after that.

The Hubers convinced her to move from her hotel room to the apartment above their garage. A week later, they asked Abilene if she'd like to live there permanently. To everyone's surprise, Abilene accepted.

She cooked meals and ran errands for the Hubers. Every night, they had supper together. The Hubers were a loving couple who lived a quiet, simple life. With no children of their own, Abilene became the daughter they'd always wanted.

"I feel at home here," Abilene wrote to the Secret, Book, and Scone Society members. "I never understood what that expression meant until now, and I hope my saying this doesn't hurt your feelings. I owe all of you so much. I owe you my life! And I care about you more than I can express, but I belong with Karl and Janet. We belong together."

Having felt at home in Miracle Springs from the moment she'd alighted from the train, Nora knew that Abilene had been granted a small miracle. As Nora folded the letter, she prayed that Abilene would experience many more.

Over time, the Secret, Book, and Scone Society members grew accustomed to Abilene's absence. They missed her. They worried about her. But between letters and phone calls, they knew she was doing fine. Better than fine, actually. She was preparing to take her GED and was even considering registering for a few courses at the local community college.

"She sounds so energetic," Hester had said after showing Nora Abilene's last letter. "I wish I had some of her energy. I really don't know how I'll manage the Gingerbread House without her."

June had given her a sympathetic look and said, "You could put up a HELP WANTED sign."

"After what happened the last time one of us did that? No, thanks," Hester had replied.

The four friends, who'd met to discuss *Eleanor Oliphant Is Completely Fine*, devour slices of cranberry cheesecake, and pack another round of Secret Kindness totes, had fallen silent for a moment to reflect on Hester's comment.

"I'm glad Abilene found us, but I wish all those nut jobs hadn't come along for the ride," Estella had said. "Kenneth, Griffin, Tamara, Ezekiel. What a way to kick off the fall. Most people have Labor Day parties or go apple picking. Not us. We get involved with murder investigations."

June had raised her coffee cup in a toast. "I vote that we take a break from drama and focus our attention on eating and reading."

"I second that motion," Nora had said.

Thinking of the meeting reminded Nora that they'd been so preoccupied with their Night Angels deliveries that they'd failed to pick a new book to read.

Glancing at the books in the front window again, Nora wondered if she should suggest Kristin Hannah's *Winter Garden* or David Guterson's *Snow Falling on Cedars*.

"A few days after we met, I told you that you looked like a fairy queen," said a voice. Nora smiled. Jed had come up behind her on the sidewalk without her realizing it.

"I was picking blackberries," she said, turning to face him.

Jed moved his boot over the snow-dusted ground. "It's hard to imagine a summer day right now, but I remember your green shirt. Standing in front of those bushes, you were almost camouflaged. But like I told you then, you could never blend in with the background. You were meant to stand out." He brushed a snowflake off her cheek. "Today, you look like a snow queen—snow-kissed and beautiful. Are you cold?"

Nora showed him her new mittens. "June made these to match my hat and scarf. At the rate she's going, I'll be able to stay outside all day."

"You'd be too far from your books." Jed gestured at the Miracle Books sign. "Are you ready, or is there something else you need to do inside?"

"I'm ready," Nora said.

In the car, Jed talked about which dishes he wanted to order.

His boyish excitement was contagious, and though Nora was happy to be eating out at a restaurant with him, she felt a little guilty about their going to Pearl's. In her mind, Pearl's belonged to Sheriff McCabe. It was his special place. He and Nora had shared two more dinners there since September. And of all the restaurants in the area, Pearl's was where Jed wanted to go tonight.

Pearl didn't seem the least bit fazed that Nora wasn't with the sheriff.

"Darlin'!" she cried, hurrying over to Nora's table to give her a hug. No one could refuse Pearl's hugs, just as no one dared to refuse to order dessert. Pearl was the living embodiment of Shakespeare's description of Hermia in *A Midsummer Night's Dream*: "Though she be but little, she is fierce."

After Nora waved at Samuel, who stood in his usual position behind the bar, she introduced Pearl to Jed. Pearl flashed him her electric smile and turned back to Nora.

"Baby girl, that doctor did a *wonderful* job. Last time I saw you, you still needed a few procedures. You all done now? Because you look done to me!"

Nora laughed. The movement no longer caused her pain or tugged at her burn scars. There were no more burn scars on her face. Dr. Patel, one of the country's foremost experts in burn scar repair, had worked miracles on Nora's skin. She wasn't without blemishes. There were still thin, surgical scars near her hairline, but they were difficult to see. Her days of being stared at were over.

"I'm done," Nora said. "The doctor was incredible. He even offered to treat my arm and hand, but I wouldn't let him. He fixed my face at no charge. That was more than enough."

Pearl folded her arms. "Sounds like you found a doctor with skill and heart. The good Lord puts the right people in our path just when we need them the most."

"Actually, Jed put him in my path," Nora said.

Pearl rolled her eyes. "And who do you think put *Jed* in your path?" Beaming at Jed, she said, "Okay, you sweet things, tell Pearl what you need to fill up your hungry souls tonight."

After Pearl bustled off to the kitchen with their orders, Jed reached for Nora's scarred hand. "Do you think you'll regret telling Patel no?"

Nora shook her head. "What I told Pearl was a partial truth. I didn't want to take advantage of his kindness, but I also didn't want to erase the evidence of my accident. I *want* a reminder of what I did. I never want to be like that person again. As long as I bear the marks of that night somewhere on my body, I'll remember what matters most."

Jed looked mournful. "You came out of your fire like a phoenix, but I'd erase my mom's scars if I could. I'd erase the past if I could. I'd give anything to see her walk—to toss that damn wheelchair off a cliff."

Jed had told Nora the specifics of the fire that had injured his mother. After working a series of double shifts to cover the void left by a coworker on paternity leave, Jed had come home and decided to have a midnight snack of bacon and eggs. He'd slapped half a rasher of bacon in a frying pan and opened a can of beer. He then went into the living room of the house he shared with his mother and turned on the TV.

"I passed out," he'd explained, his face twisted with remorse. "I was just so tired. But I left the rest of the beer on the counter, right next to the stove. I left the bacon cooking along with a pan of oil I was heating so I could fry up some eggs. Mom was asleep. Henry Higgins was in his crate in the kitchen. He was a puppy and was still being trained."

They'd been in Nora's dark bedroom when Jed had told her the rest of his story. She'd heard the pain in his voice. She'd felt it swell and fill the space around them.

"Mom had been asking me to replace the batteries in the smoke detector for weeks, but I hadn't gotten to it. I just unscrewed it from the ceiling to stop the beeping. Because she slept downstairs, Mom had to go through the kitchen to get out of the house—to escape the fire. She was burned saving Henry Higgins. By the time I woke up, she'd carried Henry Higgins out the back door. Her legs. Her hands. The burns were awful."

Following the fire, Jed's mother received in-home care from a team of therapists who came to the house on a routine basis. Though the cost was staggering, Jed wouldn't consider another alternative. He wanted the best for his mother and he worked as much as he could to get it for her.

Though he never said so, Nora guessed that he'd left his job because he was too ashamed to face his coworkers. Instead, he'd moved to the other end of the state where no one knew his history.

After he'd shared his story, Nora had comforted him with her body. The next morning, she'd made him blueberry pancakes for breakfast and sent him off to work with a tender kiss.

He hadn't mentioned the accident again until tonight.

Luckily, Pearl appeared with a basket of her famous hush puppies and Jed changed the subject by asking after Abilene.

"She started volunteering at her local library," Nora said and went on to describe how much Abilene loved the experience. "She's handling returns, shelving, and other circulation-related tasks. She doesn't have to interact with the public unless she wants to, but according to her letter, she wants to. She loves being around book people. She also likes the hushed atmosphere."

"I can see her as a librarian." Jed plucked another hush puppy from the basket. Smiling coyly at Nora, he said, "I know this really sexy woman who used to be a librarian. I fantasize about her telling me to shush before pulling me behind the reference desk for a—"

Just then, their waitress showed up at their table to top off their water glasses. She asked if she could get either of them something other than water to drink.

"No, thank you," Nora said. When the waitress left, Nora looked at Jed. "For once, I'm going to refuse Pearl when she tries to force dessert on us. Tonight, I want to have dessert at home."

Jed reached for her hand. He kissed her palm, sending a spark of heat all the way up her arm, and said, "Lady, I like the way you think."

The snow continued falling throughout the night and into the next day. As Nora walked the short distance from Caboose Cottage to Miracle Books, she was spellbound by the sight of the white hills rising over town. Miracle Springs was draped in silence. The whole world had become a softer, gentler place.

Rosy-cheeked locals were out and about, bundled up in their heaviest coats and brightest hats and scarfs. Everyone seemed to have succumbed to the snow's spell, smiling or waving amiably as they passed their fellow townsfolk on the sidewalk. Nora watched these exchanges through the bookstore's front window. She recognized most of the people, which meant the tourists were sleeping in or partaking of a late breakfast near a roaring fire.

Just after noon, people began to wander into Miracle Books. Customers entered and were reluctant to leave. Every chair and sofa were soon occupied. Even the fainting couch had been taken by a large man paging through a coffee table book on American songbirds.

Nora hustled from the ticket agent's office, where she made coffee and served book pockets, to the checkout counter, only to return to her barista duties the moment she'd finished bagging books and shelf enhancers.

By five o'clock, she was dead tired.

There were no customers in the shop at the moment, so she dropped into a chair and revisited the idea of hiring part-time help.

"Just two or three days a week to start," she murmured, wishing a cup of tea would magically appear out of thin air. A cup of tea and a throw blanket.

When the sleigh bells clanged, Nora let out a low groan. She didn't want a customer to find her slumped in a chair, looking like she was ready for a long winter's nap, so she dragged herself into the ticket agent's office.

To her delight, the customer turned out to be Hester. She immediately sank into the nearest chair, expelling a weary sigh as she kicked off her shoes.

Nora made tea for both of them and then sat down opposite Hester. "Tough day?"

Hester nodded. "I love what I do, but some days are really hard. Today was one of those days. Every part of me hurts." After sipping her tea, she added, "I'd really like to hire someone for a few hours each morning."

"What's stopping you?" Nora asked.

"What's stopping you?" Hester retorted.

Nora shrugged. "I'm not sure I can trust this place to another person. This store. These books. They're everything to me."

Hester gave her a wan smile. "Exactly. How can we know that we're hiring someone with a level head, a good heart, and the right *soul* for our businesses? Your books. My food. They're the most important things in our lives. Whoever worked with us would have to feel the same way."

"We'd need to find people like us," Nora said. "Which will probably require more effort than a sign in the window. A special ad in the paper, maybe? One that says exactly what we're looking for and ends with the line, *Slackers need not apply*."

Hester laughed.

The two women drank their tea in companionable silence.

When Nora looked at Hester again, her friend was crying.

"What is it?" Nora asked, immediately putting her tea aside to take Hester's hand.

"I was wondering if you'd offer me some bibliotherapy."

Nora was stunned. None of her friends had requested her special gift. "Really?"

"Yes. I need the kind of help you'd give any other woman who . . . gave up a child. Other women who can't find peace because of this." She sniffed. "That's me. It was so long ago, Nora. But it was also yesterday. I'm still that sixteen-year-old who didn't get to hold her baby. I'm still the person who felt her growing inside me. Who didn't get to feed her, or change her, or name her." She smiled through her tears. "I saw her face, though. She was beautiful."

"I'm sure she was. And it's okay to miss her. It's okay to be angry because you weren't given a choice about her future," Nora said softly. "It's also okay if you don't know whether or not you want to search for her. This is complicated stuff, and I can't tell you what to do, but I can find some books to help you find the way to your answer."

Hester squeezed her hand. "Thank you."

"It won't be easy," Nora warned. "No matter what path you choose, there's no guarantee that you'll find peace at the end. And the books will make you hurt. They'll also ease your loneliness. In the end, I hope they bring you clarity. But they'll also bring much closer the feelings you keep at a distance."

"I need to do this, Nora. The only time I feel peace is when I'm baking," Hester said. "As soon as I stop working—stop being a whirlwind of motion—the peaceful feeling vanishes."

Nora stood up. "Take your tea to the chair near the window. Watch the snow fall. Grab my throw blanket if you get cold. I'm going to find you some books."

Usually, Nora could make bibliotherapy selections in twenty

minutes or less, but these books were for her friend. And her friend was hurting. Because of this, Nora took great care picking titles.

The only way out is through, Nora thought, pulling Shilpi Somaya Gowda's *Secret Daughter* down from the shelf. She also retrieved copies of John Irving's *Cider House Rules* and Louisa May Alcott's *Eight Cousins*. She then moved to the children's section and added *Tell Me Again About the Night I Was Born* by Jamie Lee Curtis, and Anne Bradzinsky's *The Mulberry Bird*. She finished with Ann Fessler's *The Girls Who Went Away: The Hidden History of Women Who Surrendered Children for Adoption in the Decades Before Roe v. Wade*.

After leaving the books at the checkout counter, Nora went to tell Hester that she was done making her selections.

Hester was asleep in her chair, the hand holding her empty mug hovering inches off the floor. Nora gently pried the mug loose and carried it back to the ticket agent's office, leaving Hester to doze for a little while longer.

However, it seemed that rest wasn't in either woman's future, for the sleigh bells clanged and the high, bubbly sound of children's laughter floated into Miracle Books.

Delilah's face appeared on the other side of the ticket agent's window.

"Guess what, Ms. Pennington?" The girl's cheeks were pink and her cornflower-blue pompom hat was speckled with snow.

"What?" Nora asked.

The girl bounced on the balls of her feet. She was practically humming with excitement. "Harry made you a present!"

Delilah's mother came up behind her daughter. She put a gloved hand on Delilah's shoulder and said, "Let's give Harry some space, okay?"

At first, it looked like Delilah might argue, but when her little brother raced ahead to the children's section, Delilah smiled and hurried after him. Nora watched them. She loved that a toddler knew exactly where to find his favorite books in her store.

With his brother and sister out of the way, Harry approached the window next.

Over the past few months, Harry had become a regular in Miracle Books. He and his best friend had started a snow removal business and, with a record amount of snowfall in Miracle Springs that winter, the boys were making out like bandits. Not only had success given Harry an extra boost of confidence, but he also earned his own spending money. To his mother's delight, Harry spent half of his earnings on books.

Harry said hello to Nora and proceeded to tell her about his art class. For whatever reason, he found Nora easy to talk to. The feeling was mutual, and Nora looked forward to Harry's visits.

"We're doing a unit on origami," he said, going into more detail about his class. "I'm not very good at art, but I made this last week. It's for you." Harry placed an object bundled in newspaper on the counter.

Nora carefully tore the newspaper, revealing a hardcover copy of *David Copperfield*. The green cover of the discarded library book had been pierced at both ends. Equal lengths of fishing line ran from the cover to a metal ring.

"That's how you can hang it up," Harry explained, pointing at the ring.

Nora hooked her index finger through the ring and raised the book into the air. The fishing line pulled the book apart, and though Nora expected to see a fan of downward-facing pages, a dozen origami birds tumbled out from under the splayed cover instead. Each bird had a unique shape, color, and paper pattern. There was a pink rose flamingo, a white snowflake crane, and a glittering green duck, to name a few. The paper birds, which also hung from fishing line, swayed and twirled as if celebrating their freedom.

"It's a mobile," Harry said. "You could hang it here. If you want to," he hurriedly added.

"Oh, I want to." Nora smiled at him. "Harry, this is the most wonderful gift I've ever received. Thank you so much. I'll hang it at the checkout counter so I can look at it all the time."

Harry was about to turn away when Nora told him to wait. "I have something for you too."

"You do?" Harry's eyes were round with surprise. "A book?"

"Kind of. It has something to do with a famous book character. You and he have the same name. Plus, you remind me of him because he's smart, funny, and kind. Anyway, the newest addition to Miracle Book's menu is named after you both."

Nora asked Harry to wait a moment while she made him something to drink. A few minutes later, she presented him with a steaming cup of hot chocolate topped with a layer of rainbow marshmallows. Floating on this marshmallow island was a cone of whipped cream.

As he took the drink in his hands, Nora showed him the menu board.

"Harry Potter Hot Chocolate with Magical Marshmallows," he read aloud.

"That's right. For you, Harry, this drink will always be free." Nora pointed at the mug he held, which was decorated with a simple pair of round spectacles and a lightning bolt. "Your drink is too hot to try this second, so why don't you get your brother and sister and I'll make some magical hot chocolate for them too?"

Harry went off to fetch the rest of his family and Nora began making two more hot chocolates.

Delilah and her little brother appeared in the ticket agent's window. They waited quietly, though their bright, curious eyes indicated that Harry might have given them a hint of what was to come.

Nora placed the hot chocolate on the ticket agent's window ledge and the children's mother carried the mugs to the coffee table. She covered the surface with napkins and told her kids not to spill a drop or they'd lose their chance to take a new book home. She winked at Nora over the heads of her children, signaling that her words were an empty threat.

Later, after the family had left with their purchases—*Good Night, Gorilla*; *Misty of Chincoteague*; *The Dangerous Book for Boys*; and *The Other Boleyn Girl*, Nora prepared to hang Harry's mobile. She found a little hook in the box of random hardware she kept in the stockroom and hammered the hook above the cash register. She carefully picked up the mobile but didn't hang it right away. Instead, she turned to the beginning of *David Copperfield* and read the first line.

"'Whether I shall turn out to be the hero of my own life, or whether that station will be held by anybody else, these pages must show.'"

Nora didn't read any more. After hanging the mobile, she spent a long time sitting on her stool, watching the paper birds float and spin, pushed along by invisible air currents.

As she sat in her quiet store and watched the flight of the origami birds, she remembered the books and the birds Abilene had created in the display window. Unlike Dickens's character, who didn't know what role he'd play in determining his own future, Nora believed that Abilene would be the hero of her own life. She didn't need anyone else to save her. Like most people, she needed love, support, and understanding. But she didn't need rescuing. She could rescue herself.

On the other side of the window Abilene had once decorated, the snow fell.

Nora sat in her warm and cozy store and watched the paper

birds. Surrounded by her beloved books, she felt a deep sense of contentment.

She will be the hero of her life, Nora thought. *And I'll be the hero of mine.*

Nora Pennington left her stool and went in search of something to read.

Reader's Guide for *The Whispered Word*

1. At the opening of the novel, the Secret, Book, and Scone Society members discover a stranger in Miracle Books. What are some of the stranger's unusual attributes?

2. The members of the Secret, Book, and Scone Society discover Amanda Frye's body while delivering Secret Kindness bags to neighbors facing a tough time. What items would you want to see included in these bags?

3. What was your impression of Amanda's Frye's home? What struck you about the objects on her kitchen counter?

4. Virtual Genie is the newest business in Miracle Springs. Why might such a business thrive in today's world?

5. The subject of absentee parents is raised several times in *The Whispered Word*. Which characters felt abandoned by their parents? In what way?

6. Why does Hester feel so protective of Abilene?

7. Nora prescribes the following books to help heal from heartbreak. Are there others you'd add to her list? *Heart in a Box*, Greg Behrendt's *It's Called a Breakup Because It's Broken*, *Bridget Jones's Diary*, Nora Ephron's *Heartburn*, and *Porn for Women* by Cambridge Women's Pornography Cooperative.

8. How do you feel about the relationship between Nora and Jed? What romantic things does he do for her?

9. Do you feel any sympathy for Kenneth Frye? What is he most motivated by? Have you ever met someone like him?

10. A significant clue is found inside a hollowed book. Have you ever owned a book safe? Do you hide things in usual places other than a safe or a safety deposit box?

11. How does food play a part in the novel?

12. What flavors would be in your custom Comfort Scone?

13. What was your reaction when Abilene finally shared her story with the Secret, Book, and Scone Society?

14. What mistake does Nora make that nearly gets her killed?

15. In the end, the appearance of Nora's face is markedly changed. She opts not to have additional surgeries to correct the burns on her arm. Why does she make this decision?